PASS
B

Three novels from international
bestselling author

PENNY JORDAN

brought to you

With Love

PASSIONATE BRIDES
PENNY JORDAN

All the characters in this book have no existence outside the
imagination of the author, and have no relation whatsoever to anyone
bearing the same name or names. They are not even distantly inspired
by any individual known or unknown to the author, and all the
incidents are pure invention.

M&B™ and M&B™ with the Rose Device
are trademarks of the publisher.
Harlequin Mills & Boon Limited, Eton House,
18-24 Paradise Road, Richmond, Surrey TW9 1SR

PASSIONATE BRIDES © Harlequin Enterprises II B.V./S.à.r.l. 2009

The Italian Duke's Wife, The City-Girl Bride and *The Christmas
Bride* were first published in Great Britain by Harlequin Mills & Boon
Limited in separate, single volumes.

The Italian Duke's Wife © Penny Jordan 2006
The City-Girl Bride © Penny Jordan 2001
The Christmas Bride © Penny Jordan 2006

ISBN: 978 0 263 87533 1

010-1109

Harlequin Mills & Boon policy is to use papers that are
natural, renewable and recyclable products and made from
wood grown in sustainable forests. The logging and
manufacturing processes conform to the legal environmental
regulations of the country of origin.

Printed and bound in Spain
by Litografia Rosés S.A., Barcelona

The Italian Duke's Wife

PENNY JORDAN

A collection of bestselling novels
from some of our favourite writers,
brought to you

With Love

August 2008
BOUGHT BRIDES HELEN BIANCHIN

September 2008
VIRGIN BRIDES LYNNE GRAHAM

October 2008
ROYAL BRIDES LUCY MONROE

November 2008
PASSIONATE BRIDES PENNY JORDAN

Penny Jordan has been writing for more than twenty years and has an outstanding record: over one hunded and seventy novels published, including the phenomenally successful *A Perfect Family, To Love, Honour & Betray, The Perfect Sinner* and *Power Play*, which hit the *Sunday Times* and *New York Times* bestseller lists. Penny Jordan was born in Preston, Lancashire, and now lives in rural Cheshire.

Look out for *The Wealthy Greek's Contract Wife*, coming from Penny Jordan and Modern™ romance in February 2010.

CHAPTER ONE

SHE was *not* going to do the girly thing and burst into tears, Jodie told herself, gritting her teeth. It might be growing dark; she might be feeling sick with that familiar stomach-churning fear that she had made a big mistake—and about more than just the direction she had taken in that last village she had passed through what seemed like for ever ago; tonight might be the night she and John should have been spending at their romantic honeymoon hotel—their first night as husband and wife…but she was not going to cry. Not now, and in fact not ever, ever again over any man. Not ever. Love was out of her life and out of her vocabulary and it was going to stay out.

She winced as her small hire car lurched into a deep rut in the road—a road which was definitely climbing towards the mountains when it should have been dropping down towards the sea.

Her cousin and his wife, her only close family since her parents' death in a car accident when Jodie was nineteen, had tried to dissuade her from coming to Italy.

'But everything's paid for,' she had reminded them. 'And besides…'

Besides, she wanted to be out of the country, and she wanted to stay out of it for the next few weeks during the build-up to John's marriage to his new fiancée, Louise, who had taken Jodie's place in his heart, in his life, and in his future.

5

Not that she'd told her cousin David or Andrea, his wife, about that part of her decision as yet. She knew they would have tried to persuade her to stay at home. But when home was a very small Cotswold market town, where everyone knew you and knew that you had been dumped by your fiancé less than a month before your wedding because he had fallen in love with someone else, it was not somewhere anyone with any pride could possibly want to be. And Jodie had as much pride as the next woman, if not more. So much more that she longed to be able to prove to everyone, but most especially to John and Louise themselves, how little John's treachery mattered to her. Of course the most effective way to do that would be to turn up at their wedding with another man—a man who was better-looking and richer than John, and who adored her. Oh, if only…

In your dreams, she scoffed mentally at herself. There was no way that that scenario was likely to happen.

'Jodie, you can't possibly go to Italy on your own,' David had protested, whilst he and Andrea had exchanged meaningful looks she hadn't been supposed to see. It was probably just as well they were now in Australia on an extended visit to Andrea's parents.

'Why not?' she had demanded with brittle emphasis. 'After all, that's the way I'm going to be spending the rest of my life.'

'Jodie, we both understand how hurt and shocked you are,' Andrea had added gently. 'Don't think that David and I don't feel for you, but behaving like this isn't going to help.'

'It will help *me*,' Jodie had answered stubbornly.

* * *

It had been John's idea that they spend their honeymoon exploring Italy's beautiful Amalfi coast.

Jodie winced as the hire car hit another pothole in the road, which was so badly maintained that it was becoming increasingly uncomfortable to drive.

Her leg was aching badly, and she was beginning to regret not having chosen to spend her first night closer to Naples. Where on earth was she? Nowhere near where she was supposed to be, she suspected. The directions for the small village set back from the coast had been almost impossible to follow, detailing roads she had not been able to find on her tourist map. If John had been here with her none of this would have happened. But John was not with her, and he was never going to be with her again.

She must not think of her now ex-fiancé, or the fact that he had fallen out of love with her and in love with someone else, or that he had been seeing that someone else behind her back, or that virtually everyone in her home village had apparently known about it apart from Jodie herself. Louise, so Jodie's friends had now told her, had made it obvious that she wanted and intended to have John from the moment they had been introduced, following her parents' move to the area. And Jodie, fool that she was, had been oblivious to all of this, simply thinking that Louise, as a newcomer, an outsider, was eager to make friends. Now *she* was the outsider, Jodie reflected bitterly. She should have realised how shallow John was when he had told her that he loved her 'in spite of her leg'. She winced as the pain in it intensified.

She was never going to make the kind of mistake she had made with John again. From now on her heart was going to be impervious to 'love'—yes, even though that meant at twenty-six she would be facing the rest of her life alone. What made it worse was that John had seemed so trustworthy, so honest and so kind. She had let him into her life and, even more humiliatingly painful to acknowledge now, into her fears and her dreams. No way was she going to risk having another man treat her as John had done—one minute swearing eternal love, the next…

And as for John himself, he was welcome to Louise, and they were obviously suited to one another, too, since they were both deceitful cheats and liars. But she, coward that she was, could not face going home until the wedding was over, until all the fuss had died down and until she was not going to be the recipient of pitying looks, the subject of hushed gossip.

'Well, let's look on the bright side,' Andrea had said lightly when she had realised Jodie was not going to be persuaded to abandon her plans. 'You never know—you might meet someone in Italy and fall head over heels in love. Italian men are so gorgeously sexy and passionate.'

Italian men—or any kind of men—were off the life menu for her from now on, Jodie told herself furiously. Men, marriage, love—she no longer wanted anything to do with any of them.

Angrily Jodie depressed the accelerator. She had no idea where this appallingly bumpy road was going to take her, but she wasn't going to turn back. From now on there would be no U-turns in her life, no looking back in misery or despair, no regrets about what might have been. She was going to face firmly forward.

David and Andrea had been wonderfully kind to her, offering her their spare room when she had sold her cottage so that she could put the sale proceeds towards the house she and John were buying—which had not, with hindsight, been the most sensible of things to do—but she couldn't live with her cousin and his wife for ever.

Luckily John had at least given her her money back, but the break-up of their engagement had still cost her her job, since she had worked for his father in the family business. John was due to take over when his father retired.

So now she had neither home nor job, and she was going to be—

She yelped as the offside front wheel hit something hard, the impact causing her to lurch forward painfully against the constraint of her seat belt. How much further was she going to have to drive before she found some form of life? She was booked into a hotel tonight, and according to her calculations she should have reached her destination by now. Where on earth was she? The road was climbing so steeply...

'You, I take it, are responsible for this? It has your manipulative, destructive touch all over it, Caterina,' Lorenzo Niccolo d'Este, Duce di Montesavro, accused his cousin-in-law with savage contempt as he threw his grandmother's will onto the table between them.

'If your grandmother took my feelings into account when she made her will, then that was because—'

'Your feelings!' Lorenzo interrupted her bitingly. 'And what *feelings* exactly would those be? The same feelings that led to you bullying my cousin to his death?' He was making no attempt whatsoever to conceal his contempt for her.

Two ugly red patches of angry colour burned betrayingly on Caterina's immaculately made-up face.

'I did not drive Gino to his death. He had a heart attack.'

'Yes, brought on by your behaviour.'

'You had better be careful what you accuse me of, Lorenzo, otherwise…'

'You dare to threaten me?' Lorenzo demanded. 'You may have managed to deceive my grandmother, but you cannot deceive me.'

He turned his back on her to pace the stone-flagged floor of the Castillo's Great Hall, his pent-up fury rendering him as savagely dangerous as a caged animal of prey.

'Admit it,' he challenged as he swung round again to confront her. 'You came here deliberately intending to manipulate and deceive an elderly dying woman for your own ends.'

'You know that I have no desire to quarrel with you, Lorenzo,' Caterina protested. 'All I want—'

'I already know what you want,' Lorenzo reminded her coldly. 'You want the privilege, the position, and the wealth that becoming my wife would give you—and it is for that reason that you harried a confused elderly woman you knew to be dying into changing her will. If you had any compassion, any—' He broke off in disgust. 'But of course you do not, as I already know.'

His furious contempt had caused the smile to fade from her lips and her body to stiffen into hostility as she abandoned any pretence of innocence.

'You can make as many accusations as you wish,

Lorenzo, but you cannot prove any of them,' she taunted him.

'Perhaps not in a court of law, but that does not alter their veracity. My grandmother's notary has told me that when she summoned him to her bedside in order to alter her will, she confided to him the reason that she was doing so.'

Lorenzo saw the look of unashamed triumph in Caterina's eyes.

'Admit it, Lorenzo. I have bested you. If you want the Castillo—and we both know that you do—then you will have to marry me. You have no other choice.' She laughed, throwing back her head to expose the olive length of her throat, and Lorenzo had a savage impulse to close his hands around it and squeeze the laughter from her it. He did want the Castillo. He wanted it very badly. And he was determined to have it. And he was equally determined that he was not going to be trapped into marrying Caterina.

'You told my grandmother I loved you and wanted to make you my wife. You told her that the fact that you were so newly widowed, and that your husband Gino was my cousin, meant that society would frown upon an immediate marriage between us. And you told her you were afraid my passion would overwhelm me and that I would marry you anyway and thus bring disgrace upon myself, didn't you?' he accused her. 'You knew how naïve my grandmother was, how ignorant of modern mores. You tricked her into believing you were confiding in her out of concern for me. You told her you didn't know what to do or how you could protect me. Then you ''helped'' her to come up with the solution of changing her will, so that instead of inheriting the Castillo from her—as her previous will had stated—I would only inherit it if I was married within six weeks of her death. As you told her, everyone knows how important to me the Castillo is. And then, as though that were not enough, you conceived the added inducement of persuading her to add that if I did not marry within those six weeks, *you* would inherit the Castillo. You led her to believe that in making those changes she was enabling me to marry you, because I could say I was fulfilling the terms of her will rather than following the dictates of my heart.'

'You can't prove any of that.' She shrugged contemptuously.

Lorenzo knew that what she had said was true.

'As I've already told you, Nonna confided her thoughts to her notary,' he continued acidly. 'Unfortunately, by the time he managed to alert me to what was going on, it was too late.'

'Much too late—for you.' Caterina smirked at him.

'So you admit it?'

'So what if I do? You can't prove it,' Caterina repeated. 'And even if you could, what good would it do?'

'Let me make this clear to you, Caterina. No matter what my grandmother has written in her will, you will never become my wife. You are the last woman I would want to give my name to.'

Caterina laughed. 'You have no choice.'

Lorenzo had a reputation for being a formidable and ruthless adversary. He was the kind of man other men both respected and feared—the kind of man women dreamed excitedly of enticing into their beds. He was also a superb male animal, strikingly handsome, with a hormone-unleashing combination of arrogance and a predatory, very dangerous male sexuality—a sexuality that he wore as easily as a panther wore its coat. He was not just a prize, but perhaps the most coveted prize amongst the very best of Italy's most eligible and wealthy men. All through his twenties gossip columns had seethed with excited interest, trying to guess which high-born young woman he would make his duchess. It certainly wasn't from any lack of willing partners to share his wealth and his title, along with enjoying the sexual pleasure of mating with such a vigorously sensual man, that he had escaped into his thirties without making any kind of formal commitment to the women who had pursued him.

Lorenzo looked at his late cousin's wife. He despised and loathed her. But then, he despised most women. From what he had experienced of them they were all willing to give him whatever he wanted because of what he had, what was outside the inner him: wealth, a title, and a handsome male body. What he actually *was* was of no interest to them. His thoughts, his beliefs, all that went to make up the man who was Lorenzo d'Este didn't matter to them anywhere near so much as his money and his social position.

'You have no choice, Lorenzo,' Caterina repeated softly. 'If you want the Castillo you have to marry me.'

Lorenzo permitted his mouth to curl in sardonic disdain.

'I have to marry, yes,' he agreed softly. 'But nowhere does it say that I have to marry *you*. You have obviously not read my grandmother's will thoroughly.'

Her face blanched, her narrowed eyes betraying her confusion and distrust.

'What do you mean? Of course I have read it. I dictated it! I—'

'I repeat, you did not read the will my grandmother signed thoroughly enough,' Lorenzo told her. 'You see, it stipulates only that I must marry within six weeks of her death if I want to inherit the Castillo from her. It does not specify *who* I should marry.'

Caterina stared at him, unable to conceal her anger. It stripped from her the good looks which had in her youth made her a sought-after model, and left in their place the ugliness of her true nature.

'No, that cannot be true. You have altered it, changed it—you and that sneering notary. You have— Where does it say? Let me see!'

She virtually flung herself at him and Lorenzo retrieved the will he had thrown down onto the table earlier. Seizing it, she read it, her face white with rage.

'You have changed it. Somehow you have— She wanted you to marry me!' She was almost hysterical with fury.

'No.' Lorenzo shook his head, his face impassive as he watched her. 'Nonna wanted to give me what she believed I wanted. And that, most assuredly, is not you.'

As Lorenzo stood beneath the flickering light of the old-fashioned flambeaux, the small abrupt movement of his head was reflected and repeated in the shadows from the flames.

The Castillo had been designed as a fortress rather than a home, long before the Montesavro Dukes of the Renaissance had captured it from their foes and then clothed and softened its sheer stone walls with the artistic richness of their age. It still possessed an aura of forbidding and forbidden darkness.

Like Lorenzo himself.

Dark shadows carved hollows beneath the sculptured bone structure he had inherited from the warrior prince who had been the first of their line, and his height and the breadth of his shoulders emphasised the predatory sleekness of his body. His mouth was thin-lipped—'cruel', women liked to call it, as they begged for its hardness against their own and tried to soften it into hunger for them. It was his eyes, though, that were his most arresting feature. Curiously light for an Italian, they were more silver than grey, and piercingly determined to strip away his enemies' defences. His well-groomed hair was thick and dark, his suit hand-made and expensive. But then, he did not need to depend on any inheritance from his late maternal grandmother to make him a wealthy man. He was already that in his own right.

There were those who said, foolishly and theatrically, that for a man to accumulate so much money there had to be some trickery involved—some sleight of hand or hidden use of certain dark powers. But Lorenzo had no time for such stupidity. He had made his money simply by using his intelligence, by making the right investments at the right time, and thus building the respectable sum he had been left by his parents into a fortune that ran into many, many millions.

Unlike his late cousin, Gino, who had allowed his greedy wife to ruin him financially. His greedy *widow* now, Lorenzo reminded himself savagely. Not that

Caterina had ever behaved like a widow, or indeed like a wife.

Poor Gino, who had loved her so much. Lorenzo lifted his hand to his forehead. It felt damp with perspiration. Caused by guilt? It had after all been by claiming friendship with him that Caterina had first brought herself to Gino's attention.

Lorenzo had been eighteen to Caterina's twenty-two when he had first met her, and was easily seduced by her determination. It hadn't taken him long, though, to recognise her for the adventuress that she was. No longer, in fact, than her first hint to him that she expected him to repay her sexual favours with expensive gifts. As a result of that, he had ended his brief fling with her immediately.

He had been at university when she had inveigled herself into his kinder cousin Gino's heart and life, and the next time he had seen her Caterina had been wearing Gino's engagement ring whilst his cousin wore a besotted expression of adoration. He had tried to warn his cousin then, of just what she was, but Gino had been in too deeply ever to listen, and had even accused him of jealousy. For the first time that Lorenzo could remember they had quarrelled, with Gino accusing Lorenzo of wanting Caterina for himself, and she had cleverly played on that to keep them apart until after her and Gino's marriage.

Later, Lorenzo and his cousin had been reconciled, but Gino had never stopped worshipping his wife, even though she had been blatantly unfaithful to him with a string of lovers.

'Where are you going?' Caterina demanded shrilly as Lorenzo turned on his heel and walked away from her.

From the other side of the hall Lorenzo looked back at her.

'I am going,' he told her evenly, 'to find myself a wife—any wife. Just so long as she is not you. You could have seen to it that I was warned that my grandmother was near to death, so that I could have been here with her, but you chose not to. And we both know why.'

'You cannot marry someone else. I will not let you.'

'You cannot stop me.'

She shook her head. 'You will not find another wife, Lorenzo. Or at least not the kind of wife you would be willing to accept—not in such a sort space of time. You are far too proud to marry some little village girl of no social standing, and besides...' She paused, then gave him a taunting look and said softly, 'If necessary I shall tell everyone about the child I was to have had, whom you made me destroy.'

'Your lover's child,' he reminded her. 'Not Gino's child. You told me that yourself.'

'But I shall tell others that it was your child. After all, many people know that Gino believed you loved me.'

'I should have told him that I loathed you.'

'He would not have believed you,' Caterina told him smugly. 'Just as he would not have believed the child was not his. How does it feel to know that you are responsible for the taking of an unborn child's life, Lorenzo?'

He took a step towards her, a look of such blazing fury in his eyes that she ran for the door, pulling it open and sliding through it.

Lorenzo cursed savagely under his breath and then

went back to the table where he had dropped his grandmother's will.

He had been filled with fury and disbelief when his grandmother's notary had finally managed to make contact with him to tell him of his fears, and how he had managed to prevent Caterina from having all her own way by deliberately removing her name from the will so that it merely required Lorenzo to marry in order to inherit, rather than specifically having to marry Caterina.

The notary, almost as elderly as his grandmother had been, had apologised to Lorenzo if he had done the wrong thing, but Lorenzo had quickly reassured him that he had not. Without the notary's interference Caterina would have trapped him very cleverly. She was right about one thing. He did want the Castillo. And he intended to have it.

Right now, though, he had to get away from it before he did something he would regret, he reflected as he strode out into the courtyard and breathed in the clean tang of the evening air, mercifully devoid of Caterina's heavy, smothering perfume.

CHAPTER TWO

SHE was going to have to give in and do that U-turn she had sworn she would not make, Jodie admitted unhappily to herself. She hadn't a clue where she was, and the bright moonlight was illuminating a landscape so barren and hostile that she was actually beginning to feel quite unnerved. To one side of her the ground dropped away with dramatic sharpness, and on the other it was broken by various jagged outcroppings of rock.

Up ahead of her she could see where the narrow track widened out to provide a passing place. Determinedly she headed for it, and started to manoeuvre the vehicle so that she could turn round.

Suddenly there was a loud noise, and the back wheels of the hire car began to spin whilst the car itself lurched horribly to one side. Thoroughly alarmed, Jodie put the car in neutral and climbed out, her alarm turning to despair as she saw that one of the rear wheels was stuck fast in a deep rut and looked as though it had a flat tyre.

Now what was she going to do? She certainly couldn't drive anywhere in it.

She went back to the car, massaging her aching leg as she did so. She was tired, and hungry, and thoroughly miserable. Opening her bag, she reached for her mobile phone, and the wallet in which she had placed all the details of her travel arrangements and car hire.

As she picked up the phone her eyes widened in dismay. Her phone was already on, and by the looks of it there was no signal. Not only that, but when she attempted to dial a number anyway the phone gave an ominous bleep and the display light died. She must have left it on, and now the battery was flat. How could she have been so stupid? She needed help, but what was she going to do? Stay here and wait for someone to drive past? She hadn't seen another sign of life, never mind another vehicle, for miles. Walk? To where? Back down the hundreds of kilometres to the last village she had passed through what felt like hours ago? The pain in her leg was gnawing at her now. Should she walk on up into the mountains? She gave a small shiver.

She hadn't seen another driver in the whole of the time she had been on this road, but someone must use it because she could see tyre tracks in the dust. She looked up towards the mountains, and, as though somehow her own despair had conjured it up, she saw the distant lights of another vehicle racing towards her.

The relief made her feel almost giddily weak.

Savagely Lorenzo depressed the accelerator of the black Ferrari, letting the powerful car take his anger and turn it into a speed that demanded every ounce of his driving skill as he negotiated the twisting road in front of him.

Caterina had been very clever, working on his grandmother in the way that she had. Had he been here... But he had not. He had been abroad, visiting the scene of the latest world disaster, helping to find ways of alleviating the misery of those who had been caught in it via his unofficial and voluntary role within the government, unifying different charities and providing hands-on administrative practical help and expertise.

The severity of this particular crisis had meant that he had not even been able to return to Italy for his grandmother's funeral, although he had managed to find time within his meeting-packed day to go into a local place of worship and add his prayers to those of her other mourners.

A gentle, unsophisticated woman, who had once told him she had hoped as a young girl to become a nun, she had died peacefully in her sleep.

The Castillo had come to her through her first husband who, in the way of things in aristocratic circles, had also been the second cousin of her second husband, Lorenzo's own father, which was why the Castillo had been hers to leave as she wished.

He had always been her favourite out of her two grandsons, Lorenzo knew. He had spent his holidays with her after the divorce of his parents, and it had been his grandmother he had turned to when his mother had announced that she was marrying her lover—a man Lorenzo detested.

He had never been able to bring himself to forgive his mother for that. Not even now when she, like his father, was dead. Her actions had opened his eyes to the deceitful, self-serving ways of the female sex, and their determination to put themselves first whilst laying claim to a sanctity they did not possess. His mother had always insisted that her decision to divorce his father had been taken to spare him the pain of growing up in an unhappy home. She had lied, of course. His feelings had been the last thing on her mind when she had lain in the arms of her lover and chosen him above her husband and her son.

The Ferrari snarled and bucked at the bad condition of the road. Lorenzo ignored its complaints and changed gear, hurling it into a sharp corner, and then cursed beneath his breath as, right in front of him, he saw a car blocking the road and a young woman standing beside it.

Jodie winced as she heard the screech of brakes, choking on the dust raised by the Ferrari's tyres as it skidded to a halt only inches away from the side of the hire car. Automatically she had made herself stand upright, instead of leaning on her vehicle for support, the moment she had seen the other car.

What kind of madman drove like that down a road like this—and in the dark, too? she wondered shakily, holding on to the door of the car for support as she watched him uncoil himself from the driver's seat and come towards her.

'*Disgraziata!*' A stream of Italian followed the snarlingly contemptuous word he had already hurled at her. But Jodie was not going to let herself be cowed by him—or by any man—ever again.

'When you've quite finished...' Jodie interrupted him, her own voice every bit as hostile as his. 'For a start, I'm not Italian. I'm English. And—'

'English?' He made it sound as though he had never heard the word before. 'What are you doing here? Why are you on this road? It is a private road and leads only to the Castillo.' The questions were thrown at her like so many deadly sharp stiletto knives.

'I took a wrong turning,' Jodie defended herself. 'I

was trying to turn round, but a wheel got stuck, and now the tyre is flat.'

She was pale and thin, her eyes huge in the exhausted triangle of her small face, her fair hair scraped back. She looked about sixteen, and an underfed sixteen at that, Lorenzo decided unflatteringly, as he swept her from head to toe with an experienced male glance that took in the droop of her shoulders, the hardly discernible shape of her breasts, the narrowness of her waist and her hips, and the unexpected length of the denim-clad legs attached to such a small frame. Was she wearing heels, or were they really as long as they looked?

'How old are you?' he demanded.

How old was she? Why on earth was he asking her that?

'I'm twenty-six,' Jodie responded stiffly, tilting her chin as she looked up at him, determined not to be intimidated by him despite the fact that she was already aware that he was so spectacularly good-looking she wanted to run away and hide before he realised how pathetically inferior as a woman she was to him as a man. Automatically, her hand went to her bad leg. It was really hurting her now.

Twenty-six! Lorenzo frowned as he looked down at her hands. No rings. 'Why are you here on your own?'

Jodie was beginning to feel she had had enough. 'Because I *am* on my own. Not that it is any business of yours,' she informed him.

'On the contrary, it is very much my business— since you have seen fit to trespass on my land.'

His land? Of course it would be his land; it possessed exactly the same harsh, arrogant inhospitality as he did.

'And what do you mean, you are on your own?' she heard him demanding. 'Surely you have a...a husband, or a lover. A man, a *partner*, in your life.'

Jodie winced, and then laughed bitterly. He didn't know about the still tender nerves he was brutalising. 'I thought I did,' she agreed angrily, 'but unfortunately for me he decided he wanted to marry someone else. This—' she gestured towards the landscape and the car '—was supposed to be our honeymoon. But now...' Just saying the words still hurt, but strangely there was also a savage sense of relief in being able to vent her emotions instead of having to keep them locked inside her for the sake of others, as she had had to do at home.

'Now what?' Lorenzo challenged her. 'Now you are travelling alone and looking for someone to replace him in your bed? The coastal resorts are the best hunting ground for that. Not the mountains.'

Jodie drew in her breath in outraged fury. 'How dare you say that? I am most certainly not looking for *anyone*, let alone someone to replace him. In fact, that is the last thing I want to do,' she found herself adding. 'I shall never let another man into my life to hurt me. Never. From now on I intend to live by myself and for myself.' Bold words, but she meant every single one of them!

Lorenzo frowned as he heard in her voice the passionate intensity of her determination.

'You still want him so much?'

'No!' Jodie told him fiercely, without stopping to wonder why he was asking such a personal thing. 'I don't want him at all—not now.'

'So why are you here—running away?'

'I am not running away! I just don't want to be there to see him marry someone else,' she added defensively when she saw the way he was looking at her. 'Especially when she's all the things I'm not. Exciting, glamorous, sexy...' Jodie lifted her hand to her face to rub away the tears that had suddenly filled her eyes. She had no idea why she was telling this stranger all of this, admitting to him things she had not even admitted to herself before.

'It is the man who determines whether or not a woman is "sexy", as you put it,' Lorenzo decreed dismissively, as caught up in this strangely intimate exchange as Jodie. 'A skilled lover has it in his power to create a full flowering of even the most tightly closed bud.'

A shock of tingling awareness quivered through her belly as Jodie absorbed the meaning of his astoundingly arrogant statement.

'Not that many young women are tightly closed buds in this day and age,' Lorenzo added sardonically, as he watched the colour come and go in the pale face that was so shadowed with tiredness.

'Modern women have claimed the right to their own sexuality,' Jodie responded fiercely. 'They do not—'

'It does not sound to me as though you have been very effective in claiming yours,' Lorenzo told her derisively. 'In fact, if I were to make an assessment of it, I would guess that your experience is extremely limited—otherwise you would not have lost your man to another woman.'

His sheer arrogant machismo both astounded and infuriated her. But she was forced to admit that *non-*

existent would have been a more accurate estimation of her sexual expertise. Painfully she released the pent-up breath his words had caused her to hold, in shaky relief that he had not added to her existing humiliation by somehow recognising that she was still a virgin. Not by choice, though. All those months in hospital, after the car crash in which her parents had been killed and she had been so badly injured that at one point it had been feared she would not survive, had stolen a large chunk out of her life.

'Which, presumably, is why you are confusing physical lust with love—a word, an *emotion*, your sex has laid claim to and downvalued to the extent that is now worthless,' Lorenzo continued harshly.

'*My* sex?' Jodie took up the challenge immediately, the gold-hued warmth of her eyes heating to an indignant dark amber.

'Yes, your sex! Do you deny that women have now become as much serial adulterers as they once claimed only men could be? That their reasons for marriage are based on their own selfish and shallow emotions and needs—needs which in their eyes come before the needs of anyone else, even the children they bear?'

The bitterness she could hear in his voice momentarily shocked Jodie into silence. But she rallied quickly to defend her sex, pointing out, 'If that is your consistent experience of women, then maybe *you* are the common factor—and the one to blame.'

'I? So you believe that if a child is abandoned by its mother, it is the child who is at fault? A novel mindset—which only underlines what I have just been saying!'

'No, that is not what I meant—' Jodie began.

But it was too late. He was ignoring her words to demand autocratically, 'What is your name?'

'Jodie. Jodie Oliver. What is *your* name?' she asked equally firmly, not to be outdone.

For the first time since he had stopped his car she sensed a momentary hesitation in him before he said coolly, 'Lorenzo.'

'The Magnificent?' Jodie quipped, and then went bright red as he looked at her.

Il Magnifico. That had always been Gino's teasing way of addressing him, claiming that it was no wonder he had been so successful when he carried the same name as one of Florence's most famous Medici rulers.

'You know the history of the Medici?' he shot at Jodie.

'Some of it,' she said neutrally, suddenly not wanting any more argument with a stranger. She was beginning to feel very tired and weak. 'Look, I need to get in touch with the car hire firm and tell them about the car, but my mobile isn't working. Could you possibly…?' He must surely be going back through the village she had driven through—there was nowhere else to go. If he would take her there she might be able to find a room for the night and telephone the car rental people.

'Could I possibly what?' Lorenzo demanded. 'Help you? Certainly.' She had just started to sag with relief when he added softly, 'Provided that *you* agree to help *me*.'

Instantly warning signals flashed their messages inside her head, causing her to tense.

'Help you?' she repeated cautiously.

'Yes. I need a wife.'

He was mad. Completely and utterly insane. She was stuck on a deserted road with a madman.

'You…want me to help you find a wife?' she managed to ask, as though it were the most natural request in the world.

Lorenzo's mouth compressed, and he gave her a look of cold derision. 'Don't be ridiculous. No, I do not want you to help me find a wife. I want you to *become* my wife,' he told her coolly.

CHAPTER THREE

SHE was being ridiculous?

'You want me to be your wife?' Jodie repeated slowly. 'I'm sorry, but—'

'You don't want to marry—ever. Yes, I know,' Lorenzo interrupted dismissively. 'But this would not be an ordinary marriage. I need a wife, and I need one within the next few weeks. I have as little real desire for a wife as you have for a husband—although for different reasons. Therefore it seems to me that you and I could come to a mutually beneficial arrangement. I get the wife I need, and you, after we have been married for twelve months, get a divorce and…shall we say one million pounds?'

Jodie blinked and shook her head, not sure that she had actually heard him correctly.

'You want me to agree to marry you and stay with you for twelve months?'

'You will be well reimbursed for your time—and it is only your time and your status as my wife that I shall require. Your presence in my bed will not be part of the arrangement.'

'You're crazy,' Jodie told him flatly. 'I don't know anything about you, and I—'

'You know that I am prepared to pay you a million pounds to be my wife. As for the rest…' He gave an arrogant shrug of his powerful shoulders, and told her, briefly and dismissively, 'There will be time later for me to explain to you everything you need to know.'

By rights she ought to be scared to death, Jodie decided. But, despite the fact that she was obviously in the presence of a madman, for some reason the main emotion that filled her was not fear but bemusement. Bemusement and a certain sense that fate had listened in to her secret thoughts and decided to take a hand in her life. Here was the opportunity—the man—her pride had ached for...

Was she mad? She surely couldn't be thinking of accepting his ridiculous proposition?

'If you want a wife that badly, surely there must be someone—'

'Many someones,' Lorenzo stopped her sardonically. 'Unfortunately they would all want what I do not want to give—it is amazing how easily your sex claims undying love when money and social position are involved.'

'You mean you would be targeted by fortune-hunters?' Jodie guessed shrewdly. It was obvious, after all—not just from his car and his clothes, but more betrayingly from his manner—that he was wealthy. 'Is that why you want to marry me, because a fake marriage will keep them at bay?'

'Not exactly.'

'Then why?'

'It's a condition of my late grandmother's will that I either marry within a certain time of her death or I forfeit...something that means a great deal to me.'

Jodie's forehead crinkled into a small frown.

'But why on earth would she do that? I mean, either she wanted you to inherit whatever it is or she didn't.'

'The situation is more complex than that, and involves...other issues. Let us just say that my grandmother was persuaded to do something that she thought was in my best interests by someone who was following their own agenda.'

Jodie waited for him to continue, but instead he reached for her hand. 'Give me your car keys and—'

She gave a small, determined shake of her head. 'No.' If she wasn't already totally off men for life, this man and his unbelievable arrogance would surely be enough to put her off them, she decided angrily.

But at the same time an insidiously tempting possibility had begun to form inside her head. What if she were to agree, on condition that Lorenzo escorted her to John and Louise's wedding? With the whole village invited, two extra guests wouldn't cause any problems...and, yes, she admitted it, there was a part of her that was sore enough and woman enough to want to be there, showing the world and the newly married couple that not only did she not care about their betrayal, but that she had a new partner of her own. Wasn't there a saying, 'Living well is the best revenge'? And how much better could a discarded and unwanted fiancée live than by showing off her new, better-looking and far more eligible man? A man, moreover, who desperately wanted to marry her!

She was wrenched out of this mental triumphant return to the scene of her humiliation by Lorenzo's arrogantly disbelieving voice. 'No?'

It was ridiculous that she could even contemplate

doing something so shallow, and it showed the effect that just a few minutes in the company of a man like Lorenzo was having on her. She was not going to let herself listen to the urgings of her pride. Leaving it and her conscience to wage war on one another with an undignified exchange of inner accusations, she tried to do the sensible thing, and told Lorenzo firmly, 'Even someone as…as arrogant and used to getting what they want as you seem to be must see that what you're suggesting just isn't—'

'A million isn't enough? Is that what you're trying to say?'

Her face burned. 'The money has nothing to do with it.' The cynical look he gave her at that made her burst out angrily, 'I can't be bought. Not by John, and certainly not by you.'

'John?'

He hadn't pounced so much as leapt on her small betrayal, and now he was looking at her as she imagined a large sleek cat might look at a mouse it was enjoying tormenting.

But she was not a mouse, and she wasn't going to be either bullied or tormented by any man ever again.

She lifted her head and told him coolly, 'My ex-fiancé. He offered me money, too, but he was offering it out of guilt, because he didn't want to marry me, not as a bribe because he did. He wanted me to be the one to break off our engagement, so that no one could accuse him of dumping me. Obviously you both share the same male mindset. Like you, he thought that he could buy what he wanted, regardless of what I might be feeling.' Despite her attempt to appear unaffected by what she was revealing, a mixture of sadness and cynicism shadowed her eyes. Her mouth twisted slightly as she added, 'In a way, I suppose he did me a favour. Knowing that he thought so little of me that he would buy his way out of our relationship made me realise that I was better off without him.'

'But, despite that, you still want him.'

The unemotional statement made her heart thud nauseatingly inside her chest.

'No!' she said quickly. 'I do not ''still want him''.'

'So why have you run away, if it is not because you are afraid of what you still feel for him?'

'I have not run away! I'm having a holiday, and when I go back...' The small involuntary movement that caused her shoulders to droop as she contemplated returning home was more telling that she realised. When she went back—what? She had no job to go back to. Not now. And no home—she had, after all, sold her cottage, and even if she had not done so she doubted that she would have wanted to live there, with all its memories of her false happiness. But she could go back with her head held high and on the arm of a man she could truthfully say was going to become her husband, she reminded herself.

And then what? He had already told her the marriage was only to last twelve months.

Then she would shrug her shoulders and say, as so many others did, that it hadn't worked out. There was far less shame in that than there was in being labelled as a dumped reject.

'In twelve months' time you could go back with a

million pounds in your bank account,' she heard Lorenzo saying, as though he had read her mind.

It was so tempting to give in and agree. And she resented him for putting her in a position where she was tempted. What had she promised herself about never being manipulated by a man again? Gritting her teeth, Jodie pushed herself back from the edge of giving in.

'If you really want a wife,' she told him crossly, 'then why don't try finding one *without* using your money? Someone who wants to marry you because she loves you, and believes that in you she has found a man who loves her back, a man she can respect and trust, and…' She saw the way he was looking at her and shook her head. 'Oh, what's the use? Men like you and John are all the same. He only values the kind of woman he can show off, the kind of woman who makes other men envy him, and you only want the kind of woman you can buy so that you can control her and your relationship with her. Well, I am not that kind of woman. And, no, I will not marry you.'

As she turned away from him Lorenzo could feel the anger surging through him. She was *refusing* him? This…this too-thin *nobody* of a tourist—a woman who had been rejected publicly by the man who had promised to marry her? Didn't she realise just what he was offering her or how fortunate she was? Marriage to him would transform her instantly from an unwanted dab of a woman into the wife of someone wealthy enough to buy her ex-fiancé a hundred thousand times over. She would instantly be raised to a social height most women could only dream of, she would be courted by the famous and the rich, and, if she was intelligent enough to capitalise on what he would be giving her when their marriage was over, she could find herself a new husband. Any amount of men would be only too willing to marry the woman who had been selected by a man like him. All she had to do in order to totally transform her life was agree to be his wife.

And yet, instead of recognising her good fortune, she was actually daring to take it upon herself to lecture him! Well, she was no loss to him. She wouldn't have lasted a day, not even twelve hours once Caterina had got her claws into her, and he was a fool to have wasted his time on her in the first place. He could drive down to the coast and find a dozen women within one hour who would jump at the opportunity she had turned down.

'Fine,' he snapped, turning his back on Jodie as he strode back towards the Ferrari.

He was leaving her here? He couldn't—he wouldn't! Jodie's eyes widened in mute shock as she watched him walk away from her.

'No, wait!' she called out, as she stumbled anxiously after him, gasping at the pain in her weak leg, her anger giving way to a fear that was only slightly alleviated when he eventually stopped and turned round. 'I need to get in touch with the car hire firm and let them know what's happened.'

'They won't be very happy about the fact that you have damaged their vehicle. I hope you have brought plenty of money with you,' Lorenzo warned her coldly.

'I'm insured,' Jodie protested, but a cold, hard knot of anxiety gripped her stomach as she remembered her cousin warning her about the problems she would face if she were to be involved in an accident.

'I doubt that will benefit you, especially when I inform the authorities that you were driving on a private road, and in doing so that you endangered not just your own life but mine as well. You are going to need a very good solicitor, and that will be very expensive.'

'But that's not true!' she protested. 'You weren't even here when...'

Her voice trailed away as she saw the look in his eyes.

'You're trying to frighten me and—and blackmail me!' she accused him.

He shrugged and continued to walk back to his car. She watched helplessly as he opened the door, whilst her emotions raged in impotent fury. He was the most hateful, horrible man she had ever met—arrogant, selfish, and the very last kind of man she would have wanted to marry for any kind of reason. But a logical, practical voice inside her head was pointing out that it was late at night and she was miles from anywhere down a private road, wholly dependent on the goodwill of the man now about to leave her here.

He had started the engine and was pulling out to drive past her. Panic filled her. She started to run towards the car, gasping at the pain in her weak leg as she flung herself at the driver's door and banged on it.

Expressionlessly, Lorenzo opened the window.

'All right, I'll do it,' she told him recklessly. 'I'll marry you.'

He was staring at her so impassively that she wondered if he had changed his mind. Her heart started hammering uncomfortably fast, making her feel slightly sick.

'You're agreeing to marry me?'

Jodie nodded her head, and then exhaled shakily in relief as he pushed open the passenger door of the car and said brusquely, 'Give me your keys and wait here whilst I get your things.'

It was a warm night, but anxiety and exhaustion were making her shiver slightly, so that her fingers trembled against the impersonal hand he had stretched out for her car keys. A prickle of unwanted sensation raced up her arm, causing her to recoil from her physical contact from him. He had long, elegant hands, with lean, strong fingers—unlike John, who had had somewhat plump hands with short fingers. The knowledge that the stroke of those hands against a woman's body would deliver a dangerous level of sensual pleasure pierced the thin skin of her defences, making her emotional recoil from it even more intense than her physical recoil from his touch.

Lorenzo frowned as he got out of the Ferrari and strode over to Jodie's hire car, unlocking the boot. Her recoil from him had the hallmark of a kind of sexual inexperience he had imagined no longer existed. In fact, the last time he had seen a grown woman recoil like that from a man's casual touch had been the last time he had visited his grandmother, when he had sat with her watching one of the old-fashioned black and white films she'd loved so much. He lived in a world peopled by the sophisticated, the blasé, the experienced, the rich and the aristocratic: a world driven by cynicism and greed, by self-interest and envy. Power did not go hand in hand with goodness, as he had every reason to know. Jodie Oliver wouldn't survive a month in that world.

He shrugged away his thoughts. Her survival was not his concern. He had other matters, another kind of survival, to worry about, and she was merely the instrument by which he would achieve that. Had he genuinely wanted to marry her... His frown deepened. What kind of thought was that? He had no desire to marry anyone, much less a thin, wan-faced young woman who had 'broken heart' written all over her.

He glanced down at the small case he had removed from the boot of the car, and then went to check the interior of the car itself.

'How long did you say you intended to stay away from your home for?' he asked Jodie wryly as he carried her things back to the Ferrari.

Jodie flushed at the implication she could hear in his voice. 'I have enough with me for my needs,' she told him defensively, adding with angry dignity, 'And there are such things as laundries, you know.' She wasn't going to tell him that she had chosen her small trolley case specifically because it was light enough for her to lift, and that the last thing she had felt like when she was packing had been bringing with her all the pretty things she had bought for her honeymoon.

She felt the increase in weight of the car as Lorenzo

got back into the driver's seat. There was a disconcerting intimacy about being in a machine like this one with a man who was so very much a man.

The scent of expensive leather reminded her poignantly of an afternoon she had spent with John, when he had gone to buy a new car and taken her with him. They had visited showroom after showroom as he admiringly inspected their top-of-the-range vehicles. But none of them, no matter how expensive, had come anywhere near being as luxurious as this car, she thought now, her senses suddenly picking up on the cool, subtle woody scent of male cologne mixed with the very sensual smell of living, breathing male flesh.

By the time she had finished absorbing the messages with which her senses were bombarding her, Lorenzo had reversed the Ferrari and turned it round.

'Where are we going?' she demanded uncertainly.

'To the Castillo.'

The Castillo. It sounded impossibly grand. But five minutes later, when she saw its steep escarpments rising sharply up out of the rock face, she decided that it was more barbaric than grand—like something left over from another less civilised age. An age where might was more valued than right; an age where a man could take what he wanted simply because he chose to do so. An age surely well suited to the man seated next to her, she decided a little sourly.

They drove into the Castillo through a narrow arched entrance, so evocative of the Middle Ages that Jodie had to blink to dismiss her mental images of chainmailed men at arms and heralds announcing their arrival.

The empty courtyard was lit by the flames from large metal sconces that threw moving shadows against the imposing stone walls with their watching narrow slit windows.

'What an extraordinary place,' Jodie heard herself saying apprehensively.

'The Castillo is a relic left over from a time when men built fortresses rather than homes. I warn you, it is every bit as inhospitable inside as it is out.'

'You live here?' She couldn't keep the dismay out of her voice.

'I don't, but my grandmother did.'

'So where…?' Jodie began, and then stopped uncertainly as she saw the way his mouth was compressing. It was obvious that he did not like her asking so many questions. He had opened the door of the car and she wrinkled her nose as she caught the pungent smell of something burning. 'Something's on fire,' she told him.

Lorenzo shook his head. 'It is merely the mixture of wood and pitch that is used in the sconces. After a while you will grow so accustomed to it that you won't even notice it,' he added in a matter-of-fact voice.

After a while? Did that mean that she was to *live* here? Without electricity?

As though he had read her mind, Lorenzo informed her, 'My grandmother preferred the old-fashioned way of life. Fortunately I was able to persuade her to have a generator installed to provide electricity inside the Castillo.'

When one thought of an Italian castle one thought of something out of a fairy tale, but this place was nothing like that. Bleak and brooding, it made her shudder just to look up at the granite walls.

'Come…'

Sitting in the Ferrari had caused her weak leg to stiffen and seize up. Jodie could feel her face burning as Lorenzo waited impatiently for her to get out of her seat whilst he held the door open for her. The agonising pain that shot through her leg as she finally managed to do so made her bite down hard on her bottom lip to stop herself from betraying what she was feeling. John had hated anything that drew attention to her infirmity, insisting that she always wore jeans or trousers to hide the thinness of her leg with its tell-tale scars.

'If you wear trousers no one is going to know that there's anything wrong with you,' he had told her more than once. Jodie could feel her throat closing with painful tears. She had wanted so desperately to hear him say to her that he didn't care what she wore, because he loved her so very much that every part of her was equally precious to him. But, of course, men were not like that. Louise had said as much when she had explained to Jodie just why John preferred *her*.

'The trouble is, sweetie, that men don't like all that disfigurement stuff. It makes them feel uncomfortable. Plus, they want a woman they can show off— not one they've got to apologise for.'

'You mean *some* men don't,' Jodie had corrected her, with as much dignity as she could muster.

'*Most* men,' Louise had insisted, before adding bluntly, 'After all, how many men besides John have actually wanted so much as a date with you, Jodie? Think about it. And let's not forget,' she had added, pressing home her advantage, 'any man is bound to worry about what he's going to have to face in the future, with a wife who's got health problems, from a financial point of view alone.'

'I haven't got health problems,' Jodie had objected. 'The hospital has given me a complete all-clear—'

'Because they can't do any more for you. You told me that yourself. Your leg is never going to be as it was, is it? You get tired if you have to walk any distance now—imagine how awful it would be for poor John if in, say, ten years you needed to be in a wheelchair. How would he cope? With the business booming the way it is, John needs a wife who is a social asset to him, not one who is going to be a handicap. You really mustn't be so selfish, Jodie. John and I are trying to make this as easy for you as we can.'

It was the 'John and I' that had done it, igniting Jodie's temper so that she had exploded and told her one-time friend in no uncertain terms exactly what she thought of both her and of John, ending up with, 'And, personally, the last kind of man I would want to commit to is one so shallow that all he sees is what lies on the surface. To be honest with you, Louise, you've done me a big favour. If it hadn't been for you I might have gone ahead and married John without knowing how weak and unreliable he is. You obviously aren't as fussy in that regard as I am.' She had finished pointedly, 'But I should be careful, if I were you. After all, you won't be young and glamorous for ever, will you? And, since you've said yourself that looks are so immensely important to John, you're going to have to live with the knowledge that ultimately he may dump you for someone younger and prettier.'

She had been shaking from head to foot as she walked away from Louise. And when John had turned up on her doorstep less than an hour later, accusing her of upsetting Louise, she hadn't known whether to laugh or to cry. In the end she had laughed. Somehow it had seemed the better option.

It was then she had gone out and bought herself the shortest denim miniskirt she could find. The accident had not been her parents' fault, and she had fought long and hard to be able to overcome her own injuries. From now on, she had decided, she was going to wear her scars with pride, and no man was ever, ever again going to tell her to cover up her legs because of them.

For ease of travelling, though, right now she was wearing a pair of jeans—an old, faded pair of jeans that made her look totally out of place next to Lorenzo in his beautifully tailored suit, she thought, as he propelled her across the courtyard and into a cavernous baronial hall, his hand resting firmly on the middle of her back.

CHAPTER FOUR

THE room they entered was furnished with several pieces of intricately carved dark wooden furniture. A coat of arms had been cut into the stone lintel above the huge fireplace. The carpet on the stone floor beneath her feet looked worn and shabby, and she could see where the film of dust on a table in the middle of the room had been disturbed by something thrown down on it with such force that it had skidded through it.

A door in the far wall was thrown open, and a woman stood there, framed in the opening. Immediately Jodie forgot her surroundings as she focused on her. Tall and soignée, she was everything one imagined a wealthy and elegant Italian woman should be. Her dark hair was pulled back in a smooth knot to reveal the perfect bone structure of her face. Dark eyes flashed a look of triumphant possessive mockery towards Lorenzo—the same kind of predatory female look Jodie had seen in Louise's eyes when she had looked at John. The other woman hadn't even seen her, hidden as she was in the shadows. Who was she?

A sense of disquiet started to seep through her; an awareness of deep and dark waters driven by dangerous unseen currents that could suck her down into their icy depths if she wasn't careful. Instinctively Jodie sensed that Louise and this woman were two of a kind, and that knowledge was enough to rub against the still painfully raw emotional nerves inside herself.

She looked at Lorenzo. He looked relaxed, but she could feel his tension in the sudden increased pressure of his fingers, where they were splayed across her back. Something was going on here that she wasn't privy to—but what? So many unanswered questions, and they were destined to remain unanswered, Jodie guessed, as she watched the full mouth thin, crimson with carefully applied lipgloss, and the delicate nostrils flare. A huge diamond flashed blindingly as the woman raised one hand to touch the deep vee neckline of the expensive black dress she was wearing in a deliberate gesture of enticement. What man could resist following with his gaze the scarlet glisten of the long nails as they rested briefly in the valley between the tight, high fullness of her perfectly shaped breasts?

Her dress moulded to a waist so small that Jodie guessed it must be the result of a tightly laced corset, before curving lushly over rounded hips. Its hemline revealed a pair of long, slender, warmly tanned legs, whilst her feet, with their scarlet-painted toenails, were adorned with the highest and most delicate pair of strappy sandals Jodie had ever seen. She looked like someone who was about to walk into the most sophisticated and luxurious kind of setting there was, instead of being here in this dilapidated fortress in the middle of nowhere.

A look of open triumph lit the Italian woman's face as she sashayed towards Lorenzo. But her brown eyes lacked any kind of warmth, Jodie noticed, and as she walked, talking quickly, her voice sounded harsh and slightly flat, jarring against Jodie's ears, rather than warm and musical as she had expected.

She had almost reached them when Lorenzo held

up a commanding hand and said smoothly, 'In English, if you please, Caterina. That way, my wife-to-be will be able to understand you.'

The effect of his words on the woman was cataclysmic. She stopped moving and turned to look at Jodie, who discovered that she was being propelled forward out of the shadows and anchored to Lorenzo's side by means of his almost manacle-like grip on her wrist.

A furious, disbelieving female glare savaged Jodie where she stood, followed by an equally furious outburst of Italian.

'This way,' Lorenzo instructed Jodie, ignoring her.

'No!' The woman placed herself in front of them, and said in English, 'You will not do this to me. You cannot! Who is she?'

'I have just told you. My wife-to-be,' Lorenzo answered her dismissively.

'No. You cannot do this.' The flat, metallic voice was filled with fury. 'No. No!' She was shaking her head from side to side so violently that Jodie felt dizzy, but not one single strand of the immaculately coiffed hair escaped. 'No,' she repeated. 'You will not make such a nothing your *duchessa*, Lorenzo?'

His *duchess*?

'You will not speak so of my intended wife,' she heard Lorenzo saying coldly.

Dear God, what on earth had she got herself into?

'Where has she come from? What gutter did you—?'

Immediately a look of haughty rejection stiffened Lorenzo's expression, but Caterina ignored it, grabbing hold of his arm and insisting, 'Answer me, Lorenzo, or I will...'

'Or you will what, Caterina?' he demanded unkindly, removing her hand from his arm. 'As it happens, Jodie and I met some months ago. It was my intention to bring her to the Castillo to meet my grandmother, but unfortunately she died before I was able to do so. Knowing now, though, that it was her dearest wish that I should marry, I intend to follow the dictates of my own heart as well as fulfil the terms of her will by marrying Jodie as soon as possible.'

Jodie blinked in disbelief as she listened to his entirely fictitious account of their 'relationship'.

'You're lying. None of that is true. I know the truth, and I shall—'

'You know nothing, and you will do nothing.' Lorenzo stopped her immediately, adding grimly, 'And let me warn you now against any attempt on your part to spread gossip or rumours about either my wife-to-be or my marriage.'

'You cannot threaten me, Lorenzo,' Caterina almost screamed at him. 'Does she know why you are marrying her? Does she know that it was your grandmother's dying wish that you should marry me? Does she know that you—?'

'*Silencio!*' Lorenzo commanded harshly, his icy, furious glare slicing down in front of her like a jagged-toothed portcullis slicing into an enemy force.

'No. I will not be silent!' She swung round to give Jodie a contemptuously hostile look. 'Has he told you that the only reason he is marrying you is because of this place? Because unless he marries he cannot inherit it?'

This woman must surely be the person with their own agenda he had spoken of earlier, Jodie thought. Somehow she managed to stop her expression from betraying what she was feeling—a legacy, no doubt, from all those hospital visits, and her determination not to let others see her in pain and pity her for it. Was Lorenzo really prepared to marry a woman he didn't know simply to inherit this grim, crumbling fortress?

'It is impossible that he would want to marry a woman like you,' Caterina told her venomously.

Pain jerked through her. Caterina's words were so similar in content to the words Louise had said to her—just as Caterina's brunette beauty was also very much like Louise's. They ignited a surge of angry pride inside Jodie that burned along her veins. She took a deep breath, and then heard herself saying recklessly, 'But he *is* marrying me.'

For a few seconds Jodie was so lost in the heady euphoria of delivering the very words she had so longed to deliver to Louise that nothing else mattered—least of all the small inner voice trying desperately to beg her to be more cautious.

Even when she heard Caterina's infuriated shriek and caught the scent of her alcohol-laden breath she still didn't realise her danger, and the other woman's scarlet-tipped hand was already raised to rake savagely down the soft flesh of her face when Lorenzo suddenly released Jodie and took hold of Caterina, forcing her back from Jodie as he snapped, '*Basta!* Enough.'

'You cannot do this to me. I will not let you!' Caterina screamed at Lorenzo.

Jodie's head was ringing with the shock of listening to her, and her body shook in the aftermath of Caterina's attempt to physically attack her.

'You will pack your things and leave the Castillo immediately,' she heard Lorenzo order bitingly.

'You cannot make me. I have as much right to be here as you. Remember, until you are married the Castillo belongs as much to me as it does to you. Only when you are married does it become yours. And you will not—'

'*Basta!*'

The command cracked across her outburst like a whip against naked flesh, causing Jodie herself to wince and shudder as she watched Lorenzo give the other woman a hard shake before releasing her.

Ignoring Jodie, Caterina complained to Lorenzo, 'You have hurt me. Tomorrow there will be a bruise...' She switched to Italian and said something softly to him, then laughed mockingly.

Jodie waited impassively. Her female instincts, honed now by the belated recognition of all those glances and soft, not-quite-caught words she had witnessed John and Louise exchanging in the weeks before they had admitted their betrayal of her, were immediately suspicious that what Caterina had said to Lorenzo had been both intimate and sexual. Why? Because their relationship had once been intimate and sexual? *Had been*...or still was? There was clearly animosity between them now—animosity and contempt where Lorenzo was concerned—or at least that was the way it seemed.

'He is using you. You know that, don't you? And once he has what he wants he will discard you,' Caterina told Jodie venomously, and then as abruptly as she had arrived she was gone, banging the door shut behind her as she left.

Completely ignoring what had just happened, Lorenzo announced autocratically, 'This way. I will show you to our apartments.'

The scene with Caterina had left her feeling slightly sick and shaky now that it was over, Jodie realized. Much as she had felt in the aftermath of Louise's revelations. But Lorenzo was already halfway towards the door through which Caterina had disappeared, and Jodie had to hurry to catch up with him. Beyond the door was another hallway, this one containing an imposing and unexpectedly elegant marble staircase.

'This part of the interior of the Castillo was remodelled during the Renaissance,' Lorenzo explained when he saw her surprise.

At the top of the stairs a wide corridor branched to the right and left. Lorenzo took the right fork, which was dimly lit with old-fashioned electric wall lights, beyond which Jodie could see a pair of ornate double doors.

'My grandmother made this part of the Castillo over to me for my own use after the divorce of my parents,' Lorenzo announced as he opened the doors. 'Gino always said—'

'Gino?' Jodie questioned, her thoughts still seething with curiosity.

'My cousin, and Caterina's late husband.'

'She is a widow, then?' Jodie couldn't help asking him.

'Yes, she is a widow.'

'And she lives here?'

A cynical grimace touched his mouth and then disappeared, to be replaced by a look of bitterness.

'She has an apartment in Milan, but she moved here when my grandmother became ill.' He frowned, and then said abruptly, 'You ask too many questions. It is late now, and I have things to do. I will explain everything that you need to know tomorrow. Just remember that so far as everyone else is concerned our relationship is of some duration, as are our plans to marry.'

'Caterina said that your grandmother wanted you to marry her,' Jodie couldn't help commenting.

His mouth hardened, and Jodie began to regret her challenge.

'She was lying,' he told her harshly. 'She is the one who desires a marriage between us, because she covets my title and my wealth. Caterina is a bloodsucker and a leech, a woman who has proved beyond any doubt that she is happy to sell herself to the highest bidder.'

Jodie was curious to know more, but there was a look on his face which said that the subject was now closed. Cautiously she walked through the doors he had just opened, and once she had done so her curiosity about Caterina was pushed to one side by her surprise. The room into which she had walked was surprisingly modern, and furnished very simply. Plain plastered walls had been painted a soft cream, and a heavy-textured natural-coloured carpet covered the floor, on which stood two large leather sofas.

'The original panelling was taken from this room during the war, when the Castillo was occupied,' Lorenzo informed her. 'That was when my grandmother's first husband was killed.' Jodie gave a small shudder without knowing why she should suddenly feel chilled.

'Where...where are Caterina's rooms?' she asked him uncertainly.

'She is occupying the state rooms, as did my grandmother,' Lorenzo informed her dismissively, continuing briskly before Jodie could ask any more questions, 'I shall arrange for my lawyer to come here tomorrow so that we can draw up a contract and make the necessary arrangements for our marriage.'

Jodie tensed. 'I've been thinking…'

'Caterina has alarmed you—is that it? You are afraid of her?'

'No!' Jodie denied the charge vigorously. 'I'm not afraid of her at all.'

Lorenzo lifted one dark eyebrow as though in disbelief.

'It isn't that,' Jodie insisted again, 'but if you are serious about this marriage between us, then I want…'

'Yes?' Lorenzo invited her. It was just as he had thought. Already she was working out how much she could get out of him. 'You want what? Two million instead of one?'

Jodie flashed him an angry look. 'No. I've already told you I don't want your money.'

'But you do want something?'

'Yes,' she agreed, and took a deep breath. 'I want you to go with me to John and Louise's wedding.'

She held her breath, waiting for him to refuse, telling herself that this would be the get-out, her reason for insisting that she was not going to be dragged any further into whatever devious plans he was hatching.

But, instead of refusing her, Lorenzo accused softly, 'So you do still want him?'

'No! I just want…' She paused and shook her head. 'I don't have to explain my reasons to you. Those are my terms for marrying you. It is up to you whether or not you accept them.' *Please, let him refuse…*

'Very well, then. We will go to your ex-fiancé's wedding, but it will be as husband and wife.'

Jodie could feel her body sag with relief. Relief? Because of a fatalistic sense of having any more decisions taken out of her hands? Because she had weakly handed over control of her life to an arrogant stranger?

'Come with me...'

Tiredly, Jodie followed him through another set of doors that led into a very male study, and from there into an ante-room from which two doors opened. 'This is my room,' Lorenzo informed her, indicating one door, 'and this is the guest room.'

He was looking at her almost as though he was testing her, as though he was waiting for her to make a choice. Determinedly she stepped towards the door to the guest room and turned the handle.

Like the other rooms, it was decorated and furnished in a plain, modern style, but all Jodie was interested in was the wonderful large bed. Her leg was hurting so much she was beginning to drag it slightly.

'Those doors on either side of the bed lead into a dressing room and a bathroom,' she could hear Lorenzo explaining. 'I shall have your bag sent up. Are you hungry?'

Jodie shook her head. She had gone beyond that. All she wanted was to lie down and feel the pain easing out of her leg. She took a step forward and her weak leg, already overtired from the long drive, buckled and started to give way. Automatically she put out her hands to try and save herself as she fell. She heard Lorenzo cursing, and then he was reaching for her, just managing to catch her before she hit the floor, yanking her back to her feet so sharply that the pain slicing into her made her cry out.

'*Diablo!* What is it? What's wrong?'

'Nothing. It's just my leg,' Jodie told him, pushing him away and trying to stand up straight. But it was too late. Her leg had had enough and was refusing to support her properly. She could see the way Lorenzo was frowning. Immediately her chin tilted proudly.

'I have a problem with my leg. I was in an accident and it was damaged. Sometimes when it gets over-tired…' She looked away from him. 'If you don't want to marry me because of it, then—'

'Is that what he told you? The man you were to marry?' Lorenzo guessed. 'That he didn't want you because of it?'

Jodie's face burned. She had said too much—a mistake she could only put down to her tiredness and the stress of everything that had happened to her.

'No.'

'But it was a cause of some conflict between you?' Lorenzo continued to probe.

'He didn't like the fact that it was…damaged.' She made an attempt at a dismissive shrug. 'But then, that's only natural, isn't it? Men do like beautiful women, and—'

'It is an intrinsic part of human nature to value beauty,' Lorenzo told her. 'But sometimes the greatest beauty of all comes only through suffering and pain.'

Jodie looked at him uncertainly. She was too tired to try and analyse such a cryptic, sombre remark. Instead, she looked longingly towards the bed. Lorenzo followed the direction of her gaze.

'I'll leave you now. You should find everything you need in the bathroom, but if you do not then just ask Pietro when he brings up your case. He will inform Maria, and she will attend to it.'

'Pietro and Maria,' she said, carefully repeating their names. 'Your servants?'

'They look after the Castillo. Originally they were employed by my grandmother. By rights they should both retire, but this has always been their home and it would be a cruelty to send them away now—or to imply that they are not able to be of any use,' he added warningly. 'Once I have spoken with my lawyer, and put in hand the arrangements for our marriage, I shall address the matter of making this place more habitable.'

They were going to be living *here*? There were so many questions she knew she ought to be asking, but right now she was too exhausted to care about anything other than getting some sleep.

CHAPTER FIVE

AT LEAST the bath water was hot, and the towels Maria had brought for her, bustling importantly into the bedroom on a stream of incomprehensible Italian whilst she inspected Jodie with her sharp gaze, were deliciously soft and thick.

As in the bedroom, the decor in her *en suite* bathroom was very plain, but there was no mistaking the quality of the sanitaryware or the cool smartness of the marble covering the floor and walls.

Wrapped in one of the towels, Jodie padded barefoot back to her bedroom and opened her case, quickly searching through it for the nightshirt she knew she had packed. But when she lifted her neatly packed tops out of the case she started to frown. Her nightshirt was there, all right, but so also was the deliciously frivolous new underwear she had bought for her honeymoon: bras and short knickers in floral patterns; silk thongs that fastened with satin bows; a sheer floral mini-slip that was so pretty she hadn't been able to resist it; even the cream lace and satin basque she had bought on a sudden impulse one lunchtime after yet another evening spent with John refusing to do anything more than indulge in gentle 'petting'.

She hadn't known then, of course, that the reason he had not taken their intimacy to its logical conclusion had not been because he had loved her so much, but because he had loved her so little. Now, thanks to Louise, she knew that all the time she had been aching for him and admiring his restraint he had secretly been turned off by her.

What on earth was this stuff doing in her case? She found the answer in a small note from her cousin-in-law, tucked in between the folds of her nightshirt.

It seemed such a pity not to take these with you. You never know, you might meet someone who will appreciate them—and you.

Jodie almost laughed out loud. Andrea had had more of a presentiment than even she could have guessed! As a bride-to-be, she ought to be able to find a use for such frivolous items, but she knew that Lorenzo would be even less appreciative of both them and her than John had been.

She pulled on her nightgown and closed the case, placing it on the floor before crawling into the middle of the huge bed and switching off the light.

By rights she ought to be thinking about the situation she had put herself into and working out how best to extricate herself from it, but she was far, far too tired.

Lorenzo shut down his computer and got up from the desk where he had been working. He had e-mailed several people: his lawyer, explaining to him his plans—or at least as much of them as he wanted him to know; a certain very highly placed diplomat who owed him several favours, requesting his help in cutting through the normal procedures so that he could marry his British fiancée as quickly as possible; and the Cardinal, who was his second cousin once re-

moved. Fortuitously he already had in his possession
Jodie's passport, having found it in the wallet of
travel documents she had left on the passenger seat
of her car, and he had faxed its details to all three
men. His instructions to his lawyer were that he
should draw up a marriage agreement with the utmost
haste, and at the same time to make arrangements for
the sole ownership of the Castillo to be transferred to
Lorenzo, in accordance with the terms of his grandmother's will.

He then left his apartments and headed downstairs,
striding through the warren of unused rooms with
their old-fashioned furnishings and musty air until he
reached the door he wanted. Already the tension was
building inside him, and along with it the excitement;
already his senses were anticipating the pleasure that
lay ahead of him. He would marry a dozen pale-faced,
too-thin English women if necessary, in order to satisfy the desire that had driven him for so long.

The cramping pain seizing her leg muscles was savage and unrelenting, wrenching Jodie out of her deep
sleep with a sharp cry of pain.

Lorenzo heard it as he walked out of his bathroom,
his forehead pleating into a frown when it was repeated. Securing his towel round his hips, he strode
towards the guest room, thrusting open the door and
switching on the light.

Jodie was lying in the middle of the bed, desperately trying to massage the pain out of her locked
muscles.

Lorenzo recognised immediately what was happening. Going over to the bed, he took hold of her by
her shoulders, demanding curtly, 'What is it? Cramp?'

Jodie nodded her head, and managed to gasp painfully, 'Yes. In my leg...'

The intensity of the pain had turned her face bonegrey, and Lorenzo could see the small beads of perspiration forming on her forehead.

'Do you suffer like this often?'

Why was he asking her that? Was he afraid of saddling himself with a wife who would be a liability even if she was only a twelve-month wife?

'No, only when I get overtired—oh!' Jodie winced and cried out as his strong fingers found the exact spot on her leg where the pain was bunched.

'Lie still,' Lorenzo instructed her. 'It's all right.' He added, when she looked warily at him, 'I do know what I'm doing.'

Jodie would have continued to resist if a second bout of cramp hadn't seized her, leaving her with no energy to do anything other than focus on coping with the searing pain. Lorenzo cursed out loud and then lifted her up, ignoring her protests as he turned her over and placed her back on the bed.

Now, with her legs exposed by the ridiculously infantile elongated tee shirt she was wearing, he could see that he had been right about their length, and that she had not been wearing heels. He could also see that one of her legs was slightly more slender than the other, and that on the inside of its knee there was a delicate silver tracery of scars.

With the cramp continuing its brutal assault on her, Jodie wasn't even aware that she was digging her fingers into Lorenzo's arm as she willed herself not to cry out. This was the worst she could ever remember it being.

Lorenzo waited until her grip had started to relax

before releasing himself and going quickly to work, his long, lean fingers probing the knot of locked muscle until Jodie wanted to scream in agony. She tried to drag her leg free of his fingers, but then slowly, blissfully, they started to take away the pain, kneading and stroking until the muscle began to relax. A tiny quiver jerked through her muscle and automatically she clenched it, waiting for a fresh onslaught, her whole body shaking.

'Relax...' Lorenzo was still massaging her leg, but now the long, firm strokes of his hands were moving upwards, and the tension that was gripping her as she felt his fingers brushing against the hem of her nightshirt was caused by the cramping sensation in her stomach, not her leg. And it had nothing whatsoever to do with over-tiredness.

'To judge from these scars you must have had several operations?'

Jodie tensed again. She wanted to pull her leg away, but she was afraid to move in case in doing so she caused the hem of her nightshirt to ride even higher. It was too late now to wish she had put on some underwear as well as the nightshirt.

'Yes,' she said briefly.

'How many?'

She exhaled. 'Does it matter? It isn't as if you're going to be left having to look after me if I end up in a wheelchair or anything, is it?'

'Is that a possibility?' He was still massaging her leg, but now his fingers were slowly stroking over the tight scar tissue itself. For some odd reason Jodie discovered that she badly wanted to cry. No one had ever touched her scars with anything other than clinical detachment. The long months in hospital had inured her to physical examinations, to doctors discussing her as though she were a piece of broken equipment they were trying to piece together again and put in working order. Which, of course, to them, was exactly what she had been. She was grateful to them for everything they had done for her—how could she not be?—but at the same time…

At the same time what? Secretly, she had craved a more personal touch, a comforting, knowing touch that neither flinched from her scars nor made a dramatic fuss about them.

But not a touch that made her feel the way Lorenzo's touch was making her feel!

'No. My leg is always going to be weak, but it has healed properly now,' she blurted out, then bit her lip, not wanting to remember those horrifying days when the doctors had feared they might have to amputate. 'Thank you. You can stop now. The cramp has gone,' she told him as she forced herself to concentrate on something—anything—other than on the smooth gliding stroke of his fingers against her skin. No lover could have… No *lover*? Now what was she thinking?

She rolled over so that she could face him, all too conscious of the warm weight of his hand where it still lay across her bare thigh, her eyes widening as she took in what she hadn't realised before: namely that all he was wearing was a towel, wrapped low on his hips, and that the body it revealed was enough to make any right-thinking woman go weak with female appreciation. But from now on she was not going to allow herself to want any man, she reminded herself fiercely, and certainly not a man like this one. Every instinct she possessed told her he was far too dangerous. He was an autocratic alpha male who was determined to get what he wanted, no matter who he had to use in order to do so, and it was that she ought to be concentrating her attention on—not the taut muscles of his flat belly, or the distracting maleness of the body hair that arrowed downwards to where his towel had slipped slightly to reveal where it began thickening out. Jodie touched her tongue-tip to her lips and sucked in a shaky gulp of air.

Lorenzo removed his hand from her thigh and straightened, pausing in the act of resecuring his towel to watch as Jodie focused on the movement of his hands, her breathing accelerating.

'If you keep on looking at me like that,' he began in a warning tone, 'I'm going to think—'

'What do you mean?' Jodie protested, her face burning.

'You were looking at me like a girl looking at her first man,' Lorenzo said mockingly. 'Which leads me to wonder what kind of woman you are that you look at me like that—and what kind of man this ex-fiancé of yours was to give you that need.'

'I wasn't looking at you like anything,' Jodie argued frantically. 'You're imagining it. No modern woman needs to wonder what a man's body looks like.'

'So it wouldn't bother you, then, if I weren't wearing this?' Lorenzo suggested, his fingers resting against the top of his towel.

Jodie made a valiant attempt at a small nonchalant shrug. 'No—why should it? One naked male body is much like any other.'

'Was your ex-fiancé circumcised?'

Jodie opened her mouth and then closed it again, her face slowly turning a deep shade of pink whilst her heart skidded and bounced around inside her chest cavity as though seeking the same invisible escape route as her thoughts. Was he asking her that because he had guessed that she simply didn't know? Because he wanted to humiliate her by making her admit how limited her sexual experience really was?

'Er…why do you ask?'

'Why don't you answer?'

'I'm not questioning you about your past sex life. And if we're going to get married—'

'If? There is no *if* about it. I've already contacted my lawyer. He'll be here in the morning.'

'It will take quite a long time to go through all the legal formalities, I expect.'

'Not for us. Once we have seen Alfredo we shall be leaving for Florence.'

'Florence?'

'I have some business to attend to there, and you will want to buy a wedding outfit.'

'A wedding outfit?'

The dark eyebrows lifted. 'I take it that you didn't bring your bridal gown with you when you ran away?'

Jodie looked away from him. 'No, I didn't,' she agreed quietly. Her wedding dress was still hanging up in the shop where she had bought it, paid for but never collected.

Lorenzo watched her impassively. 'There are any number of designer shops in Florence. You are bound to find something in one of them.'

Designer shops? Finding something would be the easy bit, Jodie reflected; paying for it at designer shop prices with her limited budget would be the hard part.

She moistened her lips with the tip of her tongue.

'What if…? What if I've changed my mind?'

'I shan't let you.'

'But you can't stop me.'

The way he was looking at her brought it home to her that she was trapped here in this ancient stronghold, where no doubt his ancestors had once held their prisoners captive in the depths of its dank dungeons.

'What is it exactly that you are so afraid of?' he asked.

'I'm not afraid of anything—or anyone,' Jodie lied.

'So there is no reason why we should not be married, then, is there? It is an arrangement from which we both stand to gain something of importance to us. When is this ex-fiancé of yours to marry?'

'The middle of next month.'

'*Bene.* We will be married ourselves by then, so you will have the pleasure of introducing me to him as your husband. Now, it is late, and tomorrow there is much to be done.'

'Why don't you want to marry Caterina?'

Immediately his face hardened. 'That is no concern of yours,' he told her dauntingly. 'I shall leave you now to sleep. With any luck the cramp will not return.'

In other words, mind your own business, Jodie reflected ruefully as she watched him leave.

CHAPTER SIX

THE sound of her bedroom door opening and the rattle of crockery brought Jodie out of a complicated dream in which she had been forced to watch as John walked down the aisle towards his waiting bride. But when he reached her it wasn't John who was marrying someone else but Lorenzo. Bizarrely, instead of feeling relieved, she had actually felt searingly jealous.

'*Buongiorno,*' Maria greeted her cheerfully as she put down the tray she was carrying and then walked over to the windows to draw back the heavy curtains. Sunshine immediately flooded the room, followed by deliciously soft warm air as Maria opened the windows to reveal a small balcony.

The smell of fresh coffee and the sight of rolls and fruit made Jodie salivate with hunger.

'*Grazie, Maria.*' She thanked the elderly maid with a warm smile, pushing back the bedclothes as Maria turned to leave the room.

She hadn't realised her room had a balcony, and when she hurried over to investigate it she discovered that it looked out onto an enclosed courtyard garden that was almost Moorish in style. Fretted archways were swathed with tumbling masses of pink roses, and from her vantage point above them she could look down into the heart of the garden to a fish pond, where an ornate fountain sent sprays of water jetting upwards before they fell back to dimple the surface of the pond, disturbing the fat goldfish basking in the morning sunshine.

Returning to the bedroom, Jodie poured herself a cup of coffee and then headed back to the balcony. It was wide enough to hold a small wrought-iron table and two chairs, and she was just about to sit down on one of them when her bedroom door opened a second time. Thinking that Maria had come back, she looked up with a smile that faded as she saw that it was not Maria who had come in but Lorenzo.

'*Bene*, you are awake. Alfredo has telephoned to say that he is on his way and will be here within the hour. I trust you slept well, with no return of your cramp?'

'No—I mean, yes—I did sleep well, and, no, the cramp didn't come back.' It hadn't come back, but the faint tingle in her flesh where he had massaged it had kept her awake for a long time after he had gone.

Unlike her, Lorenzo was fully dressed, making her feel acutely conscious of the brevity of her nightshirt. Not that he was looking at her. Instead he was frowning as he stared at something on the floor beside her bed, next to the case she had been too tired to unpack last night.

Striding over to it, he leaned down and retrieved the basque she had forgotten to put back in the case, holding it up between his thumb and forefingers and looking at her with a query in his scowl.

'What is this?'

'What does it look like?' Jodie challenged him crossly

'It looks like something a certain type of showgirl might wear.'

'It…it was part of my trousseau,' Jodie told him

reluctantly. She certainly didn't want him thinking it was something she had brought with her to wear on holiday. 'It got into my case by…by mistake.'

'Your trousseau? You mean you were going to wear *this* as a means of enticing your husband to make love to you? What was he? Some kind of bondage fetishist?'

It took several seconds for his meaning to hit her defences.

'It's a chainstore basque, that's all,' she told him furiously. 'If you want to give it some kind of sleazy, sordid interpretation, then that's up to you.' She was perilously close to angry tears of humiliation as she remembered the shy uncertainty with which she had purchased the boned and lace-tied item of underwear, hoping that it might tempt John to behave more passionately towards her. 'Right now they're a fashion item. Some women even wear them as outerwear.'

'Yes, I have seen them. They display their breasts as crudely as whores, offering up their wares for any man who feels like examining them.'

Whores? Was he suggesting…? 'I suppose the way you like your women dressed is—' Jodie began angrily, only to have Lorenzo interrupt her.

'The way I like to see a woman dressed is in something that hints subtly at her sexuality instead of flaunting it, and in fabrics as sensual as her skin. Not clothes that make her look like either a child or a whore,' he told her and he dropped her basque onto the bed.

A *child*? Was he referring to her nightshirt?

'How is your leg this morning?' he added calmly, as he helped himself to a cup of coffee and walked over to the balcony to join her.

Suddenly what had seemed like a pleasant spot to
enjoy the morning air had become an intensely intimate and very small space. Had he deliberately referred to her leg now because he guessed how sen-
sitively aware she was that its weakness made her less
desirable as a woman? If she hadn't already sworn
off men and love for ever, Jodie decided bitterly, then
surely Lorenzo would have been enough to make her
do so.

'It's fine. Anyone can get cramp, you know,' she
told him defensively. 'Even someone with two perfectly normal legs.'

'Which you think yours are not? There are many
places in the world where people, often children, subjected to the injustice of wars they don't understand,
have been left with injuries, including the loss of
limbs, that make a mere weakness such as yours
something they would welcome.'

Jodie listened to him in disbelieving fury. Was he
actually daring to preach at her? When he lived the
kind of privileged life isolated from reality he obviously did?

'What would you know about other people's suffering?' she demanded scornfully. 'I bet the closest
you have ever been to witnessing the ravages of war
is in a newspaper or on a television screen.'

She put her cup down on the small table with a
small angry movement and made to walk past him
back into the bedroom. But Lorenzo, who had become
engrossed in looking down into the garden, put his
hand on her arm to stop her.

'Caterina is watching us from the garden,' he told
Jodie quietly.

'So?'

Putting down his own cup, he turned towards her, saying softly, 'So this...'

He was closing the distance between them and there was nowhere for her to go. His arms locked round her, imprisoning her, their warmth pressing through the thin fabric of her nightshirt. His hands spread against her back, curving her into his own body as though she were completely formless and malleable, his to do with as he chose. One hand remained flat against the small of her back, arching her against him—draping her against him, she recognised dizzily—whilst the other slid up to her neck, his fingers burrowing into the soft thickness of her hair, tangling in it that he could draw her head back and lift her face towards his own.

Trembling from head to foot with furious outrage, Jodie glared up at him.

His head blotted out the sunlight as he lowered it so that his mouth could take possession of hers. Jodi stiffened defensively, not daring to move. His lips felt cool and firm against her own. She could smell the fresh scent of soap and clean linen. Stubbornly she refused to return his kiss. The pad of his thumb stroked caressingly behind her ear and against the vulnerable flesh of her neck, and a small betraying shudder of reaction galvanised her whole body.

His lips brushed hers, the silver-grey eyes glinting with a knowledge that made her whole body burn as he demanded silkily, 'Don't you even know how to kiss properly? And you were betrothed! Open your mouth.'

Faced with a choice of being branded as a woman so sexually inept that she couldn't even kiss, or giving in to his arrogant demand, Jodie chose female pride over anger. Her lips softened and parted, the golden shimmer of her gaze meshing recklessly with the hypnotic silver of Lorenzo's as though it were a lodestone luring her to a destiny she couldn't escape. Her mouth clung to his and her arms lifted to wrap around his neck. She could feel the warmth of the sun on her back, but it was the heat of Lorenzo's touch that her flesh was responding to, the sensation of his hand spread flat against the bare skin of her back beneath her nightshirt, whilst she stood on tiptoe, arched against him, kissing him with a sensual intimacy that would normally have shocked her.

She could feel his hand shaping her waist and then moving upwards to cup her bare breast beneath the nightshirt, his thumb-pad brushing with deliberate emphasis against her suddenly tight nipple, making it and her quiver as readily as a bow drawn by an expert archer. His other hand was massaging the base of her spine and then moving lower, pushing aside her briefs so that he could stroke the naked rounded curve of her bottom.

The sudden fierce sexual thrust of Lorenzo's tongue against her own brought her up intimately against him, her breath escaping on a soft, shivered rush of pleasure. 'What is it?' Lorenzo whispered. 'Do you want me to stroke your breasts? To kiss them and caress them? Do you want me to take your nipple into my mouth and bring it and you to the highest pinnacle of pleasure? Is that what you are asking me for with that wanton thrust of your hips against mine?' As he was whispering to her Lorenzo's hand moved round to caress the soft swell of her sex.

This was what she had longed for so much from John—desire, intimacy, sensuality—and she absorbed it into herself with each and every one of her senses, lost in a private world of erotic pleasure.

It was the sound of angry footsteps crunching across the gravel beneath the balcony that brought her back to reality, her body stiffening in outraged rebuttal as she wrenched her mouth from beneath Lorenzo's.

'You had no right to do that,' she told him angrily.

'So why didn't you stop me?' Lorenzo shrugged, infuriatingly matter-of-fact.

She hadn't stopped him because she had been enjoying what was happening too much to want to, Jodie realised guiltily. 'You said there would be no...no intimacy between us,' she retorted, sidestepping Lorenzo's charge.

'That wasn't intimacy,' Lorenzo informed her. 'If I'd wanted intimacy with you, I'd have taken you somewhere where we couldn't be overheard, and right now, instead of standing here glowering at me, you'd be lying under me, and the only words you'd be uttering would be your eager pleas for my possession. As I warned you, I was simply demonstrating for Caterina's benefit the fact that you and I are to marry. Or is that glower you are giving me because you are *not* lying beneath me right now, while I show that virginal body of yours what sex is all about?'

'I am not—'

'You are not a virgin? Is that what you were going to tell me?'

'I wasn't going to say that. I was going to say that I'm not interested in having sex with you.'

'So you *are* a virgin?'

'What if I am? Is it a crime?'

'In law, no. Against nature, yes. Where is the pleasure in a closed book that has never been read? A song that that never been sung? A scent that has never filled the air with its fragrance or a woman who has never cried out her fulfilment to the lover who has taken her to it?'

Beneath them the golden silence of the morning was suddenly broken by the sound of a car arriving in the adjacent courtyard.

'That will be Alfredo,' Lorenzo told her, suddenly businesslike. 'Come through into my office as soon as you are dressed. Alfredo will want to go through all the necessary paperwork for our marriage.'

As she watched him leave, Jodie wanted very badly to tell him that she had changed her mind; to break through his arrogance and to pierce his pride the way he had pierced hers. How could she possibly have reacted to him as she had? How could she have let her guard down so far that she had actually physically responded to him? Now he obviously thought that he could use her own vulnerability against her to make her do anything he wanted her to do. *Anything.* Every word he had just said to her, every look he had given her, had said quite plainly that he now believed she was his for the taking.

But she wasn't, and she never, ever would be. She knew that, and she was going to make sure that he knew it as well. And if she couldn't? How much did she really want to bolster her pride and appear at John and Louise's wedding with her own brand-new husband? Enough to take that risk?

More than enough, Jodie decided with renewed determination as she gathered up some clean clothes and headed for the shower. Especially since she already knew that, no matter what Lorenzo said or did, or even fleetingly made her feel, nothing could alter the fact that she simply did not want an intimate one-to-one emotional or physical relationship with a man ever again. John had shown her that she could not trust his sex, and if John could not be trusted to mean it when he said that he loved her and wanted to marry her, then she certainly wasn't going to risk trusting a man like Lorenzo!

Fifteen minutes later, showered and dressed, and with her still damp hair caught back off her face, Jodie hesitated outside the door to the study-cum-office Lorenzo had shown her the previous night.

She could have sworn she hadn't betrayed her presence by the smallest sound, much less even raised her hand to knock politely on the door, but somehow Lorenzo must have divined it, because before she could do so he was opening the door and taking her by the arm to draw her into the room. Taking her by the arm or imprisoning her? Certainly to any onlooker the way the strong, lean fingers were curling round her wrist might look both protective and possessive— the hold of a lover wanting to establish the exclusivity of a relationship—but she, of course, knew better.

'I was just beginning to wonder what was keeping you,' he told her.

'I've only been half an hour,' Jodie protested defensively.

'A lifetime for us to be apart,' he told her softly, giving her a look of such sexually explicit hunger that her own eyes widened and darkened before she could stop herself from reacting to it. She was awed by the impact of a look that somehow managed to convey a desire to strip every item of clothing from her body and explore and pleasure it in the most intimate way possible, but at the same time made it fiercely clear that he also wanted to wrap that same body in the protection of his love and adoration, to keep it and her for himself alone. What on earth must it be like to be truly loved and desired by a man who looked at one like that? A man who was not either afraid of or embarrassed to show his feelings? But Lorenzo had no feelings for her, she reminded herself, and nor did she want him to.

'Alfredo, come and let me introduce you to my wife-to-be.'

Lorenzo's lawyer was about the same age as Lorenzo himself, but nothing like so tall or so awesomely good-looking, Jodie thought. He did, though, have very nice, warm brown twinkling eyes, and a kind smile.

'Lorenzo has just been telling me about you. I thought he must be exaggerating, in that deranged way that lovers have, but now I see that he was not doing you justice,' Alfredo complimented Jodie warmly.

Lorenzo's lawyer was just being courteous, that was clear, albeit in a flattering, slightly over-the-top way. Jodie knew that, but she still couldn't help dimpling him a laughing smile, immediately feeling at ease with him.

'No wonder you are so anxious to rush her to the altar, Lorenzo,' Alfredo continued. 'In your shoes—'

'But you are not in my shoes, are you?' Lorenzo pointed out, with what Jodie thought was almost insufferable arrogance.

The lawyer, though, did not seem to be offended. Instead he laughed and said, 'There is no need to be jealous, my friend. I can see that Jodie only has eyes for you.' Whilst Jodie was still digesting this untruth, he continued, 'I was just asking Lorenzo where you met. I assume it must have been when he was out of the country, in the aftermath of that dreadful earthquake. I know that Lorenzo was there in his capacity of adviser to those government officials who run our own aid programmes. Which reminds me, Lorenzo— I have, as you instructed, ensured that sufficient money has been put aside to cover the medical fees of the children who are to join the prosthetic limb replacement programme.' Alfredo turned to Jodie and gave her a charming smile accompanied by a small rueful shrug. 'You will already know that your husband-to-be has a soft heart and digs deep into his pockets to help those in need. Did you meet him through his charitable work?'

Jodie could feel her face starting to burn as she remembered her earlier accusatory comments to Lorenzo. And she couldn't even allow herself the satisfaction of inwardly believing that Lorenzo had primed his lawyer to speak as he had. One look at Lorenzo's grim expression was enough to make it plain that Alfredo's unwitting revelations had not pleased him.

'Jodie does not work in any capacity for any of the aid programmes, Alfredo.' Lorenzo stopped him. 'As it happens I met her some time ago, when I was in England. I had planned to bring her here to meet my grandmother, but unfortunately Nonna died before I could do so…which brings me to the matter of my late cousin's widow, Caterina.'

'She can have no claim on the Castillo once you have complied with the terms of your grandmother's will and are married,' Alfredo assured Lorenzo immediately.

'No claim on the Castillo, no, but it seems that Caterina feels she has the right to make a claim on me,' Lorenzo told him cynically.

Alfredo started to frown. 'But that is impossible.'

'Indeed. But Caterina, as we both know, is somewhat prone to exaggeration. Ridiculously, she has even suggested that my grandmother wished me to marry *her*! Having run through Gino's money, and dragged his name in the gutter, it seems she desires to do the same with mine.'

'There has been gossip about her,' Alfredo agreed uncomfortably.

'Indeed. And I do not wish there to be any about my marriage or my future wife, so perhaps a few words in the right ears to warn them to ignore anything Caterina might have to say?' Lorenzo suggested smoothly.

'An excellent idea,' Alfredo agreed, whilst Jodie listened and silently digested the suavely subtle, lethal way in which Lorenzo was dismantling Caterina's power base. When it came to getting what he wanted, Lorenzo was obviously a ruthless opponent. A ruthless, arrogant, dangerous man—who voluntarily gave both his time and his wealth to help the young victims of far-off wars and disasters. That wasn't just one man, it was two very different men inside the same skin—like Janus, the double-faced Roman god of beginnings and endings, from whom the month of January took its name. Lorenzo was an enigma of a man, and the polar differences within himself made him toxically dangerous. But not to her. No man would ever again be a danger to her.

'I have brought with me all the various documents you will both need to sign in preparation for your marriage. The Cardinal was most helpful. He suggested the Church of the Madonna in Florence for the service, and he has undertaken to arrange for the banns to be read from this Sunday. Since the law is that they must be read on two consecutive Sundays before the marriage can be conducted, that means that you can be married just over two weeks from today.'

Banns? And a church service? Their marriage was to be just a temporary business arrangement: it didn't need to be celebrated in church. A simple civil ceremony was all that was necessary. Jodie started to step forward, but somehow Lorenzo had managed to get between her and Alfredo. She could feel his fingers curling determinedly around her wrist, and she could see the warning in his eyes as he lifted her now tightly clenched palm towards his lips.

'You have done well, Alfredo,' he said approvingly, without shifting his gaze from Jodie. 'Hasn't he, *cara*?'

His lips were caressing her knuckles, each individual one in turn, until, helplessly, she could feel her fingers uncurling from her palm, as though eager for more.

'I have also prepared the necessary papers for you both to sign with regard to the financial agreement. There is one for you to sign, Jodie, renouncing any future financial claim you might have against Lorenzo in the event of a divorce, and the other which you asked me to draw up, Lorenzo, stating that in the event of the marriage breaking down within twelve months of the ceremony you will pay Jodie one million pounds sterling, plus a further million pounds for every year after that that you remain married.'

'I'll sign the papers renouncing any future claim I might have against Lorenzo, but I don't want his money.' The words were spoken before Jodie could stop herself. She could see that Alfredo looked both rueful and slightly embarrassed.

'Of course it is unpleasant to have to talk about such things now, before you are even married, but—'

'I don't want the money,' Jodie repeated.

'This is something we can discuss in private later,' Lorenzo informed her in a warning tone, before turning to smile at Alfredo and telling him, 'You have a long journey back to Rome, so the sooner we get all the paperwork dealt with, the better.'

'Why do we have to have a church service instead of just a civil ceremony?'

It was over an hour since Alfredo had left, but Jodie's system was still in full adrenalin-producing mode as she confronted Lorenzo across the width of his desk.

'Why should we not? It is customary within my family, and will be expected.'

'You should have told me before. I thought we would just be having a civil wedding. Being married in church will make it seem so real…'

Lorenzo was frowning now.

'Our marriage will be real,' he informed her. 'That is the whole point of undertaking it. It has to be "real", as you put it, in order for me to fulfil the terms of my grandmother's will. Or at least, "real" in the sense that it will be conducted as a real wedding. We shall not, of course, be consummating it.'

'No, we most certainly won't,' Jodie agreed vehemently. 'I'm beginning to wish that I had never got involved in any of this.'

'It is too late for that now, and besides, you will be well remunerated.'

'I've already told you I don't want your money. All I want is for you to attend John and Louise's wedding with me.'

'I could hardly have that put in the marriage contract. As it is, there is bound to be some degree of gossip and speculation about our relationship. You have Alfredo on your side, though. He was obviously afraid that your feelings had been hurt by the necessity of legalising the financial aspects of our marriage.'

'You could never hurt my feelings. You aren't important enough to me, and I intend to make sure that no man ever is from now on.'

'You intend to die a virgin?'

He was mocking her, Jodie knew.

'And if I do? There are more important things in life than sex!'

'How would you know? By your own admission, you have never truly experienced it.'

Jodie had had enough.

'A woman does not need to have penetration in order to experience sexual pleasure. Nor does she need a man,' she told him frankly.

'Is that the only way you feel able to allow yourself to reach fulfilment? Either by your own hand or through the use of some battery-driven device that cannot—?'

'No! I wasn't talking about me. I just meant... I'm not listening to any more of this.' Jodie could feel her face burning with self-conscious colour as she covered her ears with her hands.

'I am simply making the point that you are rejecting something without having experienced it.'

'What about you? You're rejecting marriage, aren't you—at least a proper marriage? And you haven't been married, have you?'

'I haven't been married myself, but I have witnessed the marriages of others and seen what a destructive sham the state of marriage is—how it is used to cover greed and selfishness, and how children born into it are left to deal with the fall-out from their parents' deceit.'

'That isn't true of all marriages. Some don't work out, yes, but there are happy marriages. My cousin and his wife love one another very deeply, and my parents were happy together...'

'Really? So how come this wonderful gene that has enabled them to achieve the rare state of bliss by-passed you?'

'It's all down to having the ability to pick the right partner. I realised with John that I don't have that ability, and that is why I never intend to let myself fall in love again. But that doesn't mean I don't believe marriage can work or that some people—other people—have the ability to make the right partner choice and to share commitment.'

'Only a fool believes that sexual love can be permanent,' Lorenzo told her challengingly, as though he expected her to disagree with him. But Jodie was wary of getting involved in any more arguments that featured sex. Every time she did, a funny little sensation deep inside her sprang into life and pulsed in such an intimate and demanding way that she could barely concentrate on what she was saying because of it.

'Oh, and by the way,' Lorenzo continued, 'don't think that I was taken in by that artful comment of yours about not wanting the million pounds. What are you hoping? That if you refuse it now then later, when we divorce, you will be in a much stronger position to claim far more? If that is the case, let me warn you—'

Jodie had had enough. 'No, let *me* warn *you* that the only reason I am marrying you is so that I can show John he isn't the only man in the world, and so that I can hold my head up high at home, instead of being pitied. It's my pride that's motivating me, not any desire for money. I do not want your money! And I certainly don't want your...your sexual expertise, either!'

'That's just as well, because you aren't going to be offered it,' Lorenzo said unkindly. 'It amazes me that still in this modern day the myth persists that adult, sexually mature men have a secret yearning for the untutored body of a virgin. Personally I can think of nothing more unenticing. Maybe that was why your ex-fiancé chose someone else over you. Have you thought of that?'

Had she thought of it? There had been endless nights and days when she had thought of nothing else in those early weeks. Nights when she had lain in bed, feverishly wondering how she might suddenly transform herself from a virgin into an alluringly experienced woman who could seduce him away from Louise just as Louise had seduced John away from her. But that had been in the maddening furnace of new rejection, and those fires, with their dangerous, damaging compulsion to prove herself as a woman, had now cooled. And they certainly weren't going to be re-ignited by a man like Lorenzo—a man who looked and behaved as though he knew everything there was to know about a woman's sensuality and a man's ability to rouse and enjoy it.

The pulsing inside her body suddenly became sharply intense. Not just a pulse now, but a deep-seated ache as well.

CHAPTER SEVEN

'THERE is something I want to say to you.'

Caterina stood in front of Jodie, blocking her exit from the pretty garden she had left her room to explore.

'Alfredo was here earlier. Why?'

'Isn't that something you should be asking Lorenzo, not me?' Jodie tried to head her off.

'He doesn't want to marry you really. It's me he wants. He's always wanted me and he always will. Always and for ever. I was his first woman and I shall be his last. But, because I chose to marry his cousin, Lorenzo feels he has to punish me, and to show me that he no longer cares. But he does. He still wants me, and I can prove it any time I like.'

Jodie could feel herself wanting to reject the intimacy of the information being forced on her, along with the shockingly graphic images that were already forming inside her head. She was no voyeur, she told herself angrily, and the last thing she wanted to imagine was Lorenzo making love to Caterina.

'Whatever he may have told you, the only reason he's marrying you is because his own stubborn pride makes him believe that he has to resist his feelings for me to prove how strong he is. The truth is that Lorenzo is afraid of his need for me,' Caterina boasted, adding mockingly, 'When he beds you it will be me he is imagining he is holding, and me he secretly wishes he were holding.' She gave Jodie a contemptuous look, the same kind of look that Louise had given her. Her heart seemed to miss a beat, and she could feel what must surely only be an echo of remembered pain and rejection stealing away her self-confidence and hard-won self-belief.

'You and Lorenzo may once have been lovers—' she began bravely.

'May? There is no "may" about it. We were.' Caterina stopped her. 'He adored me, worshipped me. He could not resist me.'

Jodie's stomach rolled queasily. Inside her head she could hear Louise saying triumphantly to her, 'John can't resist me.'

'There was a quarrel—a misunderstanding. Lorenzo was young and hot-headed. I could not allow him to treat me thus, so to teach him a lesson I left him.'

Jodie could well imagine how Lorenzo must have reacted to that kind of treatment. His pride would certainly have been outraged. But surely true love was stronger than pride?

'He is only marrying you because he does not have any feelings for you. Lorenzo is afraid of his feelings for me and that makes him fight against them. But he will not fight them for ever. He cannot. His desire for me is too strong.'

'That's ridiculous,' Jodie forced herself to protest. 'After all, there is nothing to stop him marrying you if he wanted to do so.'

'It is his mother who is to blame for his ridiculous refusal to marry me,' Caterina insisted angrily. 'It is because of her that he fears to publicly acknowledge his love for me. Because of her he tries to deny and reject it. But I can still make him want me.'

'Isn't his mother dead?' Jodie pointed out.

'Lorenzo has never forgiven his mother for betraying his father and leaving them both when she went off with her lover.' Caterina gave a small, almost contemptuous shrug. 'Such a fuss about nothing. He was a child of seven, with a father rich enough to provide him with all the care he needed. But, no, that was not good enough for Lorenzo. He wanted his mother to come back…he even pleaded with her to come back. Gino told me. He adored her. They both did— Lorenzo and his father. She could do no wrong. To them she was a madonna. I have told Lorenzo many times that it is crazy for him to still brood now on what happened when he was a child. Women leave their husbands and their children all the time, and Lorenzo will leave your bed for mine if you are fool enough to marry him,' she warned Jodie. 'I shall make sure of it. And I promise you, when I do, he will not be able to resist me.'

Just as John had not been able to resist Louise. What was it about women like Louise and Caterina that made men so vulnerable to them and so impervious to their selfishness?

For a woman who professed to love Lorenzo as much as Caterina was doing, Jodie reflected, she didn't seem to have very much sympathy with him. For a seven-year-old boy to lose the mother he loved as intensely as Caterina had said Lorenzo did must have had a deeply psychological effect on him. And if he had actually loved Caterina, her marriage to his cousin must surely have intensified his belief that women were not to be trusted, and that they were amoral, shallow and selfish cheats.

What am I doing? Jodie asked herself wryly. Surely she wasn't actually feeling sympathy for Lorenzo?

As she watched Caterina walk away, Jodie told herself that it was a good job she was not marrying Lorenzo for love.

Jodie turned to look at the granite hulk of the Castillo walls. She was alone in the garden now, Caterina apparently having grown tired of issuing her dark warnings. She would not have entered an unwanted marriage in order to possess such a place, Jodie thought wryly, but she was not Lorenzo. It must be a matter of family pride to him that he was its master.

She tensed as she heard footsteps on the gravel, recognising them immediately as Lorenzo's. A tiny feathering of sensation started to uncurl slowly inside her: a potent blend of danger, excitement, and challenge pumped intoxicatingly throughout her whole body by the jerky, speeded-up bursts of her heartbeat. It was reassuring to compare what she was feeling now with the emotions and sensations she had felt when she had first met John. The two reactions had nothing in common, and therefore this feeling she had now was not a sign that she was in any way attracted to Lorenzo.

'I saw Caterina speaking with you earlier. Tell me what she was saying.'

It was typical of him, of course, that he should not only make such a demand but actually expect it to be met—as though he had the right to question her, and also to be answered.

Jodie answered him as bluntly. 'She told me that you were lovers.'

'And what else?' he demanded, refusing to react.

Jodie shrugged her shoulders. 'Only that you would do anything to gain possession of the Castillo—but then I already knew that. And that your mother deserted you and your father when you were a small child—which of course I did not.'

Now she had the reaction she had not had before. Immediately Lorenzo's expression hardened. 'My childhood is in the past and has no bearing on either the present or the future.'

He was wrong about that, Jodie decided. It was obvious from the way he was reacting that his childhood held painful issues which had never been resolved.

'How is your leg? I noticed that you were rubbing it earlier, when Alfredo was here.'

What had motivated that comment? Concern for her? Or a deliberate attempt to change the subject? Jodie knew which she believed was the more likely reason, but that wasn't enough to stop her answering him.

'That's just a...a habit I have. It doesn't mean... My leg's fine.' She was behaving in as flustered a manner as though he had paid her some kind of unexpected compliment, she realised angrily. John's rejection might have battered her self-esteem, but it certainly hadn't reduced her to the pathetic state where she was grateful to a man for asking after her health! But Lorenzo's comment had reminded her of something she knew she had to do.

And now was probably a good time to do it, she thought, since the fading light meant that Lorenzo wouldn't be able to see her red face.

'I—I owe you an apology,' she told him abruptly. 'I realise from what Alfredo said that I was wrong to suggest that you knew nothing about the horrors of war.'

'You are apologising to me for an error of judgement?'

Jodie risked a quick glance up at him through the indigo-tinted evening air, and discovered that the downward curve of his mouth was revealing the same cynical disbelief she could hear in his voice.

'Yes, I am,' she said. 'But if you'd told me about your aid work in the first place, I wouldn't have needed to, would I?'

'Ah, I thought so. I've yet to meet any woman who will genuinely admit that she could be to blame for anything.'

'That's the most ridiculous exaggeration I have ever heard!' Jodie objected immediately. 'It's like saying that—'

'That you're never going to trust another man because one man has let you down?' Lorenzo suggested silkily.

'No! That's a personal decision I've made about my own future. It doesn't mean—and I have never said—that all men can't be trusted. Maybe you should look more closely at why you think the way you do, instead of making unfounded accusations against my sex!' she told him recklessly.

'*That* was an *apology*?' Lorenzo said derisively.

She felt so tempted to tell him that she had changed her mind, and he would have to find someone else to help him to secure his wretched Castillo. But her determination to salve her pride with the possession of a husband to replace the one she had so humiliatingly lost was stubbornly refusing to let her do so. She would withstand whatever she had to in order to enjoy the sweet satisfaction of seeing John and Louise's expression when she introduced them to her 'husband'.

She didn't want revenge, or money—such negative aspirations were empty and worthless—but she so badly did want the ego-boosting experience of seeing everyone's faces when she turned up at the wedding with Lorenzo.

With a handsome, multi-millionaire, titled husband at her side, no one was going to pity her, or glance at her leg when they thought she wasn't looking, or whisper about her, explaining who she was and what had happened. Yes, it was shallow. Yes, it was foolish. Yes, a part of her felt ashamed that she should give in to such a need. But she was still going to do it. And if it turned out that she ended up upstaging the bride? Tough!

A small shiver of shocked awareness of her own growing strength tingled over her skin. Two months ago she had been so low she couldn't even have contemplated feeling like this. Who knew what she could achieve once the wedding was behind her? She could begin a whole new life, a life doing the things she wanted to do, without having to worry about pleasing any man ever again.

'What are you hoping for? That he will turn round at the altar, see you and leave her?' Lorenzo demanded harshly.

Jodie stared at him and blurted out, 'How did you know I was thinking about John?'

'There is a certain look in your eyes when you do so.'

'Well, you're wrong,' she fibbed. 'I wasn't thinking about him. I was thinking about what I am going to do in the future. I wasn't well enough to go to university, or to train to do anything after the accident, but there is nothing to stop me doing so now.'

'Most admirable,' Lorenzo said, making it clear that he found her mission statement for the future anything but. 'Now, if we don't go in soon Maria will be coming to warn us that it is time for dinner. I hope you like pasta, because that is all you are likely to get. Her cooking is of the plain and simple variety, but at least it might add some flesh to your bones.'

Perhaps she was a little bit on the thin side—emotional pain did that to a person, after all—but there was no need for him to keep on pointing it out to her, was there? Jodie decided crossly as she turned away from him.

'Be careful,' he warned her sharply. 'There is a step here—'

But it was already too late, and Jodie gave a small cry as she missed it in the darkness and stumbled forward.

Powerful hands seized her waist, and, as he had done before, Lorenzo caught her before she hit the ground, lifting her back onto her feet and steadying her there.

When was it that her instincts registered and recognised the subtle shift in the way those hands were holding her? The movement that took their hold on her body and turned it from the impersonal dig of his fingers into the curve of her waist as he supported her into an explorative search for the femaleness of that curve? Was it really after it was too late to check or reject his instinctive male reaction? Had he really drawn her closer? Or had she been the one to move towards him?

In the shadowy darkness it was impossible for her to see his face, or to judge which of them had promoted the body-to-body intimacy they were now sharing, and she hoped it was equally impossible for him to read her expression.

He bent his head towards her and took her mouth in a shockingly intimate kiss of hard passion that was over almost as soon as it had begun. Then, without a word of either apology or explanation, he released her.

She was in more danger of stumbling now than she had been before, Jodie realised, as her suddenly shaky legs carried her unsteadily towards the light of the Castillo.

Jodie was on the verge of falling asleep when she heard the sound of Lorenzo's bedroom door opening. Sucking in her breath, she tensed her body, her concentration focused on her own door, but the firm footsteps were already fading as Lorenzo walked past her room without even hesitating.

Jodie sat up and looked at her watch. It was gone midnight. Where was he going? To Caterina? And if he was there was no reason for her to be concerned, was there? And certainly not enough to lie here wide awake, checking her watch every few minutes, her ears stretched for the sound of his return, like a jealous lover.

CHAPTER EIGHT

FLORENCE! How well its medieval ruler Lorenzo de Medici had loved his city, and how willingly he had shown that love, commissioning the best of the Renaissance's gifted artists to embellish and enhance both its glory and his own.

Jodie could only catch her breath as she sat beside Lorenzo in the Ferrari whilst he edged it through the city's busy traffic, stretching every sense she could to take in as much as possible of the wonders all around her. Lorenzo turned off the busy main road that ran alongside the River Arno and drove the Ferrari down a street lined with elegant seventeenth-century buildings.

'My apartment is in the block above us,' he informed Jodie casually, as he turned into a narrow alleyway and then down into an underground car park.

Jodie's eyes adjusted to the gloom of the car park after the brilliance of the sunlit street. He had already informed her that he lived in Florence, but he hadn't said as yet just where they would be living once they were married. Given the choice she would far rather be in Florence than the Castillo, Jodie thought as they left the car.

Lorenzo guided her towards a door which opened onto a flight of stairs that took them up to an impressive entrance hall, with an equally impressive coat of arms prominently displayed above its main doorway. The same coat of arms, surely, which she had seen carved into the fireplace lintel in the great hall of the Castillo?

'Come—the lift is this way,' Lorenzo instructed her. 'My apartment is on the top two floors. I chose it when I had the Palazzo remodelled because of its views—although my grandmother used to complain that she wished I had chosen one at ground level. She did not care for enclosed spaces or lifts.'

'The Palazzo?' Jodie questioned suspiciously 'Does that mean that the whole of this building—?'

'Was originally the home of my family? Yes. The Palazzo was built for the tenth Duce, who had many business interests in Florence. During my grandfather's lifetime it fell into disrepair—much like the Castillo. When I inherited it I was faced with two choices. Either I abandoned it and sold it, or I restored it and found a way to make it pay for itself. Converting it into apartments seemed the most sensible option. That way I could retain control over any work to be done.'

'Is this where we will be living, then?' Jodie asked as they got out of the lift and she followed him across an elegant marble-floored outer hallway to a pair of intricately carved heavy wooden doors.

'There will be times when we will live here in Florence, yes, which is why—' He broke off from whatever he had been about to say to unlock the doors before opening them for her.

The room beyond them was another hallway: a long, rectangular double-height space, with a gallery around the whole of the upper storey. Its ceiling was domed in the centre and painted with allegorical scenes from mythology, whilst its walls were hung with paintings.

'My family were at one time renowned patrons of the arts. The eleventh Duce enjoyed entertaining the English visitors who came to Florence in the seventeenth and eighteenth centuries. He held court here in the Palazzo, and his mistress's salons were famous.'

'His *mistress's* salons?' Jodie queried uncertainly.

'The eleventh Duce was something of a rebel. While he stayed here in Florence, and set up home with his mistress, his wife and children were banished to a villa outside the city. He was a great patron of beauty in all its forms. He caused something of a scandal in Florence by having his mistress depicted in a series of paintings, each one portraying her readiness to receive him in a different sexual position. It is rumoured, in fact, that in order for the artist to faithfully portray the correct angles of her body, the original sketches were made whilst she and the Duce were in the act of making love. But the Duce's figure was removed by the artist for her final painting, so that her patron could visualise his lover's body as she waited to receive him.'

'Oh,' said Jodie weakly. 'The artist was a woman?'

Lorenzo shrugged. 'My ancestor was probably concerned that a male artist might find such an erotic commission too much for his self-control. And rumour has it that Cosimo himself was not averse to persuading his artist to abandon her work in order to join them in their pursuit of sexual pleasure.'

When Jodie couldn't help glancing at the walls, Lorenzo told her grimly, 'You will not find any of the paintings here—they vanished a long time ago—looted, so it is believed, on Napoleon's instructions. He had heard of them and wanted them. If they still exist they will be in the possession of some private

collector.' Lorenzo give another shrug. 'Their value
was not in the hand of the artist who painted them so
much as in their notoriety.' He flicked back the cuff
of the linen jacket he was wearing and glanced at his
watch.

'It is now almost four o'clock. I telephoned ahead
and arranged for you to have a private showing at a
designer salon on Via Tornabuoni. The manager there
understands the situation, and she will help you to
select a suitable wardrobe—including a wedding
dress. It isn't very far from here, and—'

'No!' Jodie could see the look of hauteur darkening
Lorenzo's eyes. He obviously didn't like having his
plans questioned. Tough, she decided grittily. No way
was she going to be treated like some kind of mindless doll he could have dressed up in over-priced designer clothes to suit his own idea of how his wife
should look.

'I agree that I need to buy something suitable to be
married in, but I am perfectly capable of making my
own choice and paying for whatever I need with my
own money. Think of how much medical care you
could donate to those children in need, instead of
wasting money on designer clothes for me,' she urged
him.

'You have a valid point,' he agreed. 'But Italian
society, like any other society, has its rules and its
obligations. For you as my wife not to be dressed as
the other wives will cause questions to be asked—
which could raise doubts as to the true validity of our
marriage. That in turn could lead to a legal challenge
that the terms of my grandmother's will are not being
met. Indeed, I wouldn't put it past Caterina to do
everything she can to achieve just that. And, since the

whole purpose of this marriage is to meet those terms, it is necessary that we both conform to society's expectations. If it will make you feel any better, I shall undertake to donate an equal amount to charity as you spend on clothes.'

'That's bribery,' Jodie told him, but Lorenzo was already walking away from her, leaving her no choice but to follow him.

To her surprise the gallery opened out into a second, even longer single-storey rectangular space, this one housing more modern paintings and sculptures.

'Like my ancestors, I substitute my own lack of artistic skill by taking an interest in and supporting those who do have it,' Lorenzo was explaining dryly. But Jodie wasn't fully listening to him. Instead her attention had been caught by the large wall space in the middle of the gallery, which was filled with what seemed to be unsophisticated, childlike drawings.

'Ah, my most valued commissions,' Lorenzo told her quietly.

Jodie looked at him uncertainly. 'They look like children's drawings.'

'That is exactly what they are. These drawings were all produced by children who have lost limbs—sometimes but not always a dominant hand—as victims of a variety of wars. These drawings were done after they had been fitted with their new limbs, as part of their ongoing therapy. The very special paintings in the middle of the wall are painted with those new limbs.'

Jodie discovered that emotional tears had suddenly rushed to fill her eyes. Blinking them away, she told Lorenzo huskily, 'No wonder you value them so much.'

He turned away. 'I shall introduce you to Assunta, who is my housekeeper here, and she will show you over the rest of the apartment while I make some telephone calls.'

In other words, he was bored with her company and wanted to be free of it. Well, that certainly did not bother her, Jodie assured herself ten minutes later, as she was handed over into the care of a shrewd-eyed middle-aged woman who subjected her to open scrutiny and then inclined her head. In excellent English, she said calmly, 'If you will come this way, please…'

Half an hour later Jodie had seen every room in the apartment, which covered not one but two floors of the Palazzo and included an astonishingly luxuriant roof garden.

It was plain that Lorenzo favoured modern design and furnishings over antiques, but she had to admit that the strong lines of the furniture complemented the large rooms with their high ceilings.

Her bedroom was across the corridor from Lorenzo's, and had its own dressing room and bathroom. To Jodie's relief, Assunta unbent enough to explain that she had worked in London for a time at a restaurant owned by a cousin of her father, which was where she had learned her English. Now a widow, who prized her independence, she added that working for Lorenzo had up until now suited her very nicely.

'I shan't be wanting to interfere in the way you manage things,' Jodie assured her, picking up her cue. Indeed, she would not! She doubted that Lorenzo would thank her if she were to be the cause of his housekeeper handing in her notice.

'It is my cousin Theresa who is housekeeper at the Duce's villa near Sienna. It is a very good place for *bambini* there, with much space and fresh air.'

Another hint? Jodie wondered as she stood beneath the welcome spray of the shower, mentally revising their conversation. Well, she certainly wouldn't be providing Lorenzo with his *bambini*. The shower continued to pound her skin with its needle-sharp spray whilst Jodie stood perfectly still and let images of small dark haired children stampede over her defences and trample them into nothing.

There was a sharp rap on her bathroom door and she heard Lorenzo calling out briskly, 'It is time for us to leave.'

'I'm nearly ready,' she fibbed, and then gave a small gasp as he took her at her word and walked into the bathroom.

Was it possible to be caught at any worse disadvantage than naked and dripping wet? Jodie wondered, pink-cheeked, as Lorenzo folded his arms and leaned against the now closed door.

'*That* is nearly ready?' he demanded pithily.

'It won't take me long to dry myself and get dressed…' And it would take her even less time if he wasn't standing between her and the thick warm towels on the towel rail on the other side of the bathroom. Why didn't he leave? Did he really expect her to walk past him stark naked while he subjected her to more of that steely scrutiny with which he was already openly studying her legs? Out of habit she turned to one side, trying to tuck her injured leg out of sight, more anxious to conceal that from him than either her breasts or the neat soft triangle of damp curls covering her sex.

'Do you want to have a closer look at my leg?' she demanded tartly. 'I know the scars aren't a pretty sight, but don't worry—I can cover them up.'

Lorenzo took his time about lifting his gaze from her legs to her face, and when he eventually did so her heart thumped heavily against her ribs.

'Perhaps I should have you painted like this,' he told her softly. 'A fair-haired Northern water nymph, with legs long enough to encourage a man to imagine how it would feel to have them wrapped around him. Or maybe spread on a silk-covered bed, with them wantonly open, begging for the touch of your lover's lips against their tender flesh. There are sexual positions that require... No! Do not look at me with that hungry virgin look in your eyes,' he told her sharply. 'Otherwise I might be tempted to satisfy that hunger for you.'

'You were the one who came in here,' Jodie reminded him. 'I didn't invite you.'

'Liar. You invite me every time you look at me, with those virginal half-glances that say how curious you are to know what it is like to lie with a man.'

'That is not true!' Jodie said hotly. 'If I wanted to have sex with a man, which I do not, then you are the last man I would choose.'

She realised immediately that she had gone too far—Lorenzo was so arrogantly male that there was no way he would allow her to get away with that kind of challenge to his masculinity. But it was too late. He was striding towards her, ignoring both her shocked cry of protest and the effect her wet body was having on his clothes as he hauled her out of the shower and picked her up in his arms.

'Put me down,' Jodi demanded, but Lorenzo wasn't

listening to her. Instead he was carrying her through her bedroom and towards the bed, where he put her down against the pale green silk coverlet and held her there.

He knelt over her and demanded softly, 'So, what is it you want to know most? How it feels to have a man caress you here, like this?' Still holding her shoulder with his left hand, he trailed the fingers of his right hand down the whole length of her body to her knee, and then slowly stroked up the inside of her clenched thigh.

Helplessly, Jodie closed her eyes as her flesh absorbed the intimacy of his touch and then reacted with a series of sensual shudders that ricocheted relentlessly through her.

'Ah, so you like that? And this?' His lips were caressing the sensitive spot just behind her ear, causing the ache deep inside her body to become a fiercely urgent eager pulse.

Jodie moaned in outraged protest. He had no right to be doing this to her.

But Lorenzo had obviously mistaken the cause of her moan, because he murmured, 'More curiosity? Very well, then—you shall have your answer.' His hand swept up over her body to her breast, shaping it and then rubbing the pad of his thumb over the erect swelling of her nipple until all she could visualise inside her head was his tongue curling round her nipple and then lapping rhythmically at it.

Knowing her own desire had never been an issue for her; it was having that desire not just satisfied but aroused to the pitch it was being aroused to now that had always been her problem. She had imagined she might feel like this, but her imagination had fallen way short of the reality, she acknowledged dizzily as she locked her fingers in the thick darkness of Lorenzo's hair and urged his head down towards her eager nipple. In the afternoon sunshine that filled the room through the slats in the window blind, she could see the telltale hardness of Lorenzo's erection, and her senses twisted with sweet triumph at the sight of his arousal.

'Still curious?' Lorenzo's tongue stroked the sensitive flesh of her nipple and her body arched up towards him for more. His hand dipped between her legs, his palm warm against the eager swelling of her mound. Instinctively Jodie held her breath, willing him to part the closed lips of her sex and find the wet heat waiting so urgently for him. Reality, reason, responsibility were forgotten. She was like someone possessed by a sudden fever—taken over by it so that it overruled every other control system within her. The knowing fingers answered her silent plea, parting the soft pads of flesh and then stroking her with intimately long, slow strokes that made her cry out whilst her body jerked in frantic response.

'Now you see what your curiosity has brought you to,' she heard Lorenzo saying thickly. But he wasn't making any attempt to stop giving her the pleasure his touch was inciting. Instead his touch became stronger and deeper, until—suddenly and shockingly—the ache inside her became a fierce convulsion that gripped her and then exploded into an intense orgasm.

Jodie lay stiffly on the bed, refusing to look at Lorenzo. She felt scorched by the humiliation of what had happened, and too close to tears to risk allowing herself to speak. Not because she had had an or-

gasm—it wasn't her first, after all—but because of
the way she had had it. And because of the man who
had called it up out of her body so effortlessly.

'You shouldn't have done that,' she finally managed to say.

'No,' Lorenzo agreed heavily. 'I should not.'

Jodie closed her eyes. She could feel him with-
drawing from her as he stood up.

'I'll go and ring the salon and tell them we shall
be later than arranged.'

Why had she let that happen? Why hadn't she
stopped him straight away? Her post-orgasm lethargy
clung heavily to her body as she showered again and
dressed as quickly as she could, promising herself that
it was never, ever going to happen again. Lorenzo
was a man—and an Italian—he was probably driven
by machismo and all those other things that gave such
men their powerful sexuality. And of course her unwitting challenge had meant that he had had to make
his point to her. Other than that she had no idea why
he had done what he had—only that he must not be
allowed to do so again.

Lorenzo stood in his study and looked broodingly
out of the window. He had never been the kind of
man who allowed himself to be driven or ridden by
the needs of his body, so why, *why* had he allowed
himself to give in to them now? She was just another
woman, that was all, and not even an obviously sexually available woman.

Not sexually available, no, but sexually responsive... Lorenzo closed his eyes and immediately saw
Jodie as he had seen her minutes before, lying naked
on the bed, giving herself up to her pleasure...the
pleasure he had given her. Immediately his body, still

half tumescent from its earlier unsatisfied arousal, stiffened into a painfully hard erection. He couldn't possibly want her as badly as that. Wanting the woman—the virgin—he had chosen to marry for purely practical reasons was a complication he did not need in his life right now.

How had he managed to find a woman who was still a virgin—a hungry sexually curious virgin—who looked at him with a question in her eyes as old as Eve? But he couldn't afford the time it would take to find someone to replace her now. At the moment Caterina was still shocked enough for him to gain the upper hand in the war between them, but once she had time to recover from that shock she would be back to her plots and the subtle, mind-poisoning tricks at which she excelled. And besides, by now the whole of Florence probably knew the identity of his bride-to-be.

What did one wear to buy clothes sold in a designer showroom? Jodie wondered ruefully. Probably not what *she* was wearing—which was her spare pair of clean jeans and a clean top—but since she had brought only the bare necessities to Italy with her, they would have to do.

Lorenzo was waiting for her when she found her way back to the main salon. As soon as she walked into the room he announced grimly, as he ushered her towards the main door, 'What happened earlier in your room must not be allowed to happen again.'

He was looking at her, speaking to her—lecturing her, almost!—as though it had been her fault, Jodie recognised indignantly as they stepped into the lift.

'It certainly mustn't,' she agreed fiercely. 'But I wasn't the one who instigated it.'

'Maybe not. But you didn't stop me, did you?' The lift had reached the ground floor.

'Why do men always blame women when it is they who—?' Jodie began heatedly, only to be stopped by Lorenzo.

'It was Eve who offered Adam the apple,' he reminded her flatly, as he held open the lift door for her.

'Man's eternal get-out,' Jodie seethed. '"The woman tempted me…"'

'So you admit that you did?' Lorenzo demanded as he guided her towards the street exit.

'I admit no such thing,' Jodie retorted angrily, blinking in the fierce sunlight.

'It will take less time if we walk to Via Tornabuoni,' Lorenzo informed her as he took hold of her arm and nodded in the direction they were to walk, ignoring her fury. 'It is this way. We will cut through this alleyway here, which brings us out into this square.'

Jodie forgot her annoyance and caught her breath in awed delight at her surroundings. She longed to be able to take her time and absorb everything around her, but Lorenzo was hurrying her through the square and down another narrow street, where an ancient church crouched between the other buildings, its doors open in welcome.

Via Tornabuoni turned out to be a wide street filled with imposing buildings and even more imposing shops—so much so that Jodie found herself hanging back a little when they reached one store. A uniformed doorman opened the door for them and

Lorenzo ushered her inside. Almost immediately a soignée, pencil-thin, immaculately groomed young woman who looked more like a model than a sales assistant glided towards them, her attention focused on Lorenzo rather than Jodie. Of course Jodie couldn't understand what Lorenzo was saying to her, but there was no mistaking its impact. They were ushered towards the back of the store and into an enclosed private area, where Ms Soignée disappeared and was replaced by a slightly older, even more dauntingly stunning woman, who quickly introduced herself as the *direttrice* of the store.

'I received your message and conveyed it to the *maestro*,' she informed them reverently in English. 'The designer has himself selected several gowns for your consideration, and they have been couriered here from Milano.'

They were being left in no doubt as to the great honour being bestowed on them, Jodie reflected, but she had to admit that it was equally obvious that the *direttrice* was very impressed by Lorenzo.

She turned to look anxiously at Jodie and then exhaled slightly. '*Bene*, your fiancée is not tall, it is true, but she has the right slenderness for our clothes. If you will come with me…'

'I am afraid that I have several business appointments I must keep,' Lorenzo apologised. 'But I know I can leave my fiancée safely in your hands. I shall return for her in two hours.'

The *direttrice* looked disappointed, but resigned, whilst Jodie watched Lorenzo leave and told herself that it was ridiculous for her to feel somehow abandoned.

She was taken to a private room, where she perched

on a small gilt chair as label-clad acolytes reverently presented her with a selection of wedding gowns from what she understood from the *direttrice* was the very latest collection.

Jodie was no designer label junkie, but these were very special, and she was forced to admit that she was in danger of losing her heart to them all. But in the end there could only be one choice, and she made it, rebelliously selecting a gown that was in fact a tightly fitting corset bodice with an elegantly draped skirt that fitted it so perfectly it looked as though it were actually a dress and not two pieces.

The *direttrice* beamed her approval.

'Yes, that is the one I would have chosen for you. It is very simple, but very elegant, very regal—truly a wedding gown for a princess. We have guessed your size from the Duce's description of you. So many times a man tells us one thing and we discover...' She gave a small resigned shrug. 'But fortunately the Duce was correct.'

Half an hour later, Jodie faced her own reflection in the mirror. A young woman who was almost a stranger to her looked back. Jodie blinked and felt her eyes blur with emotional tears. If only her parents, her mother, could have seen her dressed like this. The gown made her look taller, and emphasised her tiny waist. A fitted lace jacket with three-quarter sleeves concealed any bare flesh. The train was so long and so heavy that Jodie worried that she wouldn't be able to manage it.

'It is perfect for you,' the *direttrice* sighed ecstatically. 'The *maestro* will be so pleased. Now, for the other things you will need...'

It was another hour before the *direttrice* finally declared herself satisfied, by which time Jodie had been provided with a deliciously curvy suit that could be dressed up for evening or worn more simply during the daytime, along with a selection of tops to go with it, two pairs of impossibly flatteringly cut trousers, a summer-weight coat with a matching skirt, two pretty silky dresses, plus shoes and handbags, and what seemed like an enormous amount of 'everyday things', as the *direttrice* had called them, from the designer's more casual jeans-based range. The only way she could assuage her guilt over such blatant consumerism would be to insist that Lorenzo made good his promise to make a charity donation equivalent to the cost of her new clothes, Jodie reflected.

She was just beginning to get tired, and felt relieved when the door to the private room opened and Lorenzo walked in.

'You have everything you need?' he asked her.

Jodie nodded her head.

Thanking the *direttrice*, who promised that those items that were in need of small alterations would be delivered to the apartment by the following afternoon, Lorenzo ushered her back out onto the now dark street.

'Are you hungry?' he asked.

'Very,' Jodie admitted.

'There is a restaurant a short distance from here where they serve simple but excellent local food.'

The restaurant was down a narrow street, its tables set out on the pavement, and they had to edge their way to one of the few tables that was empty.

'If you would like me to recommend something for you?' Lorenzo offered once they were seated and the waiter had brought menus.

'Yes, please—but nothing too heavy,' Jodie begged him, 'otherwise I won't be able to sleep.'

'Very well, then. Perhaps not the *affettati misti* to start with, which is a traditional selection of cold meats, but instead *pinzimonio*, which is fresh vegetables with olive oil?'

'That sounds perfect,' Jodie agreed.

'Then, if it will not be too heavy for you, you should try the *lasagne al forno*—it is a speciality of Florence and like no other lasagne you will ever have tasted,' he assured her.

Smiling, Jodie nodded her head. 'What are you going to have?' she asked him.

'I shall start with the *affettati misti* and then I think *calamari in zimino*—stewed squid,' he explained, and Jodie pulled a face.

All around them other diners were talking and laughing, whole families eating together, Jodie noticed slightly enviously. Her only family were her cousin David and his wife Andrea, and though she and David had always got on well, there was a nine-year gap between them. David had already been married when her parents had been killed, and his parents—her father's brother and his wife—had returned to her aunt's home country of Canada.

'Tomorrow morning I have arranged for us to visit my bank,' Lorenzo was telling her. 'There are some papers there it is necessary for you to sign. I have opened a bank account for you, and the family betrothal ring is in the bank's vaults, along with certain other pieces of jewellery. The ring will have to be cleaned, and possibly resized—although, like you, my mother had very slender fingers.'

Their first course had arrived, but Jodie discovered that she had lost her appetite a little.

'What's wrong?' Lorenzo asked her.

'I don't feel happy about the idea of wearing a valuable piece of jewellery,' she told him truthfully. 'Especially not some kind of family heirloom. What if I were to lose it?'

'I am the head of my family and you are to be my bride. It will be expected that you will wear the family betrothal ring,' Lorenzo told her firmly.

'Couldn't you have a copy made or something?' Jodie persisted.

Lorenzo started to frown. 'If it concerns you so much, then I shall think about it. Now, eat your dinner—otherwise Carlo will think that you do not like his food, and to a Florentine that is a very great insult.'

The next morning Lorenzo allowed Jodie a little more time to gaze in awe at her surroundings as they walked through the city to his bank. She was wearing some of her new clothes—an outfit she had privately labelled *Roman Holiday*, because it comprised a pair of linen Capri pants in a mixture of creams and tans that sat low on her hips, teamed with a plain tan top. Woven wedges with tan ties and a quirky little bag completed the outfit, to which Jodie had been forced by the bright morning sunshine to add her own sunglasses.

Although she was too engrossed in her surroundings to be aware of the admiring male glances she was collecting, Lorenzo most certainly wasn't. Remembered bitterness darkened his eyes. Women were too vulnerable to the flattery of other men and their own egos, as he already knew. But it didn't matter to him how many other men found Jodie desirable, did it? He had no feelings for her, and nor was he going to allow himself to develop any.

'This way.'

Lorenzo's curt instruction reminded Jodie of how much she disliked and resented his arrogance. She felt nothing but pity for the poor woman who did eventually become his 'real' wife, she decided.

Nowadays Florence might be famous for its works of art, but there had been a time when its fame had rested on the reputation of its bankers—of whom the Medici family had been members, Jodie remembered as they stepped into the cool, cathedral-like sombreness of Lorenzo's bank.

The formalities appertaining to the opening of a bank account for her were soon dealt with, allowing them to be taken down a marble stairway to an impressive pillared and gilded room patrolled by two armed guards. They were given a key and escorted to one of several small private rooms, furnished with a table and several chairs. Here they had to wait for the vault manager and one of the armed guards to return with a locked safety deposit box, which was put on the desk in front of Lorenzo. He then produced a key and inserted it into the lock. Only then did the manager and the guard leave them to lock themselves in the small room.

Only the hum of the air-conditioning broke the silence as Lorenzo turned the key. She was, Jodie discovered, actually holding her breath.

Lorenzo lifted the lid of the box. Quickly Jodie looked away. She had very mixed feelings about old and priceless jewellery. For one thing, it always seemed to possess a dark and tainted history—if not because of the way it had been mined, then often because of the acts of cruelty and greed of those people who had wanted to possess it. No wonder priceless stones were so often said to be cursed.

Lorenzo looked down into the box. The last time it had been opened had been following the death of his mother. He had a savage impulse to slam the lid shut, to take Jodie by the hand and to go out into the bright warmth of the sunshine. But he could not do that. He was a Montesavro, and the head of his family, and besides, what ghosts—if there were such things—could possibly lurk here, in this piece of metal? His fingers closed round the familiar faded velvet box he remembered from his childhood.

'Here it is,' he told Jodie brusquely, closing the safety deposit box and relocking it before opening the ring box.

'There is a legend that when the woman who wears this ring is pure the stone glows with a particular clarity. My mother always claimed that it was the stone itself that was clouded,' he added cynically, as Jodie stared in disbelief at the huge rectangular emerald surrounded by white flashing diamonds.

'I can't possibly wear that,' she protested. 'I'd be terrified of losing it. I wouldn't feel safe unless I had an armed guard with me. It must be worth...' She shook her head, and Lorenzo frowned, recognising not awed excitement in her voice at the thought of the ring's value but instead shocked distaste. A woman who felt distaste rather than excitement at the thought of wearing expensive jewellery? Such a woman was so far removed from his own experience that he hadn't imagined one might exist.

'Let's see if it fits before we start arguing about whether or not you will wear it,' he told her coolly.

Jodie could feel her hand starting to shake when Lorenzo gripped her wrist and then slid the ring down onto her ring finger. The very weight of it felt uncomfortable. Jodie frowned, and immediately went to tug it off.

'No, leave it!'

The peremptory bite of Lorenzo's voice shocked her into stillness.

Lorenzo's frown deepened as he studied the ring, lifting her hand so that he could inspect it more closely.

'What's wrong?' she asked him uncertainly.

'Look into it and tell me what you can see,' Lorenzo instructed her.

Reluctantly Jodie did so. 'I can't see anything,' she told him, confused.

And neither could he, Lorenzo acknowledged. The ring was totally free of the vague cloudiness which he remembered had so dissatisfied his mother. A freak of chance? A difference in chemical reactions between one woman's skin and another's? There had to be a logical reason for the clarity of the emerald when Jodie wore it.

Oblivious to the conflicting emotions Lorenzo was trying to repress, Jodie tugged off the ring and handed it back to him.

'I meant what I said. I'm not wearing it,' she told him hardily.

'We shall see. Certainly you will have to wear it on Sunday, when we attend church for the first reading of our banns,' Lorenzo informed her.

She knew someone who would be envious of her

supposed betrothal ring, Jodie thought half an hour later, after they had left the bank. And that was Louise. Jodie could well imagine her reaction were she to turn up at John's wedding wearing it! Automatically, to cheer herself up, she tried to conjure up some satisfying images of her moment of triumph—but somehow the sense of elation she wanted just wasn't there. But that was the only reason she was putting herself through this whole palaver, allowing herself to be bullied and hectored…and made love to…by Lorenzo. Wasn't it?

CHAPTER NINE

THERE could be far, far worse ways in which to spend the next twelve months than exploring this wonderful city, Jodie thought happily as she took her reluctant leave of the Medici Palace and headed for the Piazza Signoria.

She had the day to herself, Lorenzo having announced earlier that he had some business to attend to and would be gone until after lunch. Not that she minded—not one little bit. It was just the sight of so many couples strolling hand in hand that was making her aware of not having his imperious, imposing presence at her side, and nothing at all personal. How could it be? She was determined not to let down her emotional guard with any man ever again, and even if she hadn't been she would have to be a complete fool to fall in love with a man like Lorenzo.

No, it was just the warmth of the summer sun and the effect of Florence itself on her emotions that was giving her that inner feeling of sadness. Of course if Lorenzo had been with her he would have been able to tell her much more about the city than any guidebook. But determinedly she reminded herself firmly of how the tension that had somehow crept into even their most mundane conversational exchanges made her feel on edge—as though somehow she was on a constant adrenalin surge, her body waiting... For what? For him to touch her again? Her thoughts were drifting down dangerous pathways, she warned herself.

She tried to focus on the square and its famous sculptures, pausing to check the guidebook she had bought earlier. While she was living here she could even try to learn Italian and turn her year of marriage into a means of adding to her future CV. That would give her something far better to occupy her thoughts than these dangerous sensual longings that had begun to creep up on her so disturbingly. Of course Lorenzo would be a good lover, she told herself scathingly. She didn't need to experience his lovemaking at first hand to know that!

The city was busy with other tourists, and by the time she had walked as far as the Uffizi, having decided to leave exploring the Palazzo Vecchio for another occasion, she was beginning to feel both tired and thirsty. There was a café-bar in the square near to the apartment, she remembered, and it would not take her long to walk there.

When she got there, the small square was so busy that at first she thought she wouldn't be able to get a table. But finally she found one, and sat down with a small sigh of relief.

Half an hour later, she was just finishing her second cup of coffee when a handsome young Italian approached her table.

'*Scusi, signorina,*' he apologised, giving her a boldly flattering smile. 'May I share your table? Only the café is full and…'

He was very good-looking, and quite obviously an expert at recognising solitary female tourists, Jodie reflected in rueful amusement as she looked back at him.

From the other side of the square Lorenzo watched the age-old tableau being played out in front of him. Young male Florentines traditionally spent the summer months flirting with gullible female tourists—so much so, in fact, that it was an accepted rite of passage that moved from the discreet pick-up, via walks through the city, to the speedy conclusion of sex in the tourist's hotel and another notch in her partner's belt. And of course Jodie, with her woman's body so eager to make up for her lost teenage years, even if she was not prepared to acknowledge it, would no doubt fall into this particular young Florentine's hands like a ripe peach.

Lorenzo could already see how openly responsive she was to her admirer, tilting her head back to look up at him, no doubt smiling at him... How often had he seen his mother give that same smile to her lover when as a young boy she had used him to camouflage those early meetings. When he had also smiled guilelessly at the man with whom she'd planned to betray his father. Well, Jodie was not going to get the opportunity to follow his mother's example, no matter how clinically businesslike their own marriage was to be. Purposefully he started to make his way toward the café.

'Please do have the table,' Jodie told the waiting young man gently. 'I was just about to leave anyway.'

'No—why don't you stay and allow me to buy you another cup of coffee?' he suggested, leaning towards her, his hand reaching to her arm.

Immediately Jodie stood up and stepped back from him, shaking her head as she refused politely. 'No, thank you.' She could see the confusion and disbelief in his eyes and had to struggle not to laugh. He was very good-looking, and no doubt used to having his overtures met with far more acceptances than refusals.

Lorenzo came to an abrupt halt as he saw the way Jodie got up from the table and then shook her head. Her body language made her feelings quite plain, and he could see from the sag of the young man's shoulders that he was as aware as Lorenzo that he had been turned down.

Jodie took her bill to the cash desk and, having paid it, started to head back towards Lorenzo's apartment. Lorenzo turned the small incident over inside his head, frowning as he did so. He tried to visualise either his mother or Caterina doing what Jodie had just done in the same situation, knowing that neither of them would have walked away as she had. Could Jodie be different from them? Could she be that rare woman—at least in his experience—who was not driven by ego and vanity, who did not need a constant influx of new and admiring male attention?

As he walked past the café his young fellow citizen was already eyeing up another tourist, who, to judge from the way she was smiling back at him, was rather more appreciative of his endeavours than Jodie had been.

It had become impossible for her to walk into the apartment without having to go and stand in front of Lorenzo's 'children of courage' gallery, Jodie knew, and each time she did she saw something new in the artwork that she hadn't seen before. On a low table beneath the drawings there was an expensive leather-bound album in which Lorenzo had placed details of every child whose work hung in the gallery. She was studying it when Lorenzo walked in.

'Tired of sightseeing?' he asked her.

'My feet are,' Jodie admitted ruefully. 'So I thought I'd come back and do some reading instead. I bought lots of books about Florence while I was out. Some of them have descriptions in several different languages, but I was thinking, while I'm here, I'd like to try to learn Italian.'

'Since we shall be moving between Florence and the Castillo, it might not be wise for you to enrol in a formal language school, if that is what you were thinking. But it would certainly be possible to hire a private tutor if you wish,' Lorenzo offered, adding, 'Have you had lunch yet?'

Jodie shook her head. 'No. I stopped for a cup of coffee at the café in the square.' She paused and wrinkled her nose.

'You didn't enjoy it?'

'The coffee was fine, but I got hit on by one of those professional flirty types. I suppose that's one of the downsides of being alone.'

'Some women enjoy the attention.'

Jodie closed the album and stood up. 'Well, I didn't.'

Lorenzo could see that she meant what she was saying.

'Why don't I ask Assunta to make us some lunch and bring it up to the roof garden? You can read your guidebooks to me if you wish—in Italian.'

Jodie was staring at him in astonishment, and Lorenzo had to admit he was just as startled by his own suggestion. He had intended to spend the afternoon working, not playing at being a language tutor.

She really, really did not want to do this, Jodie realised, hesitating in front of the entrance to the church where their banns were to be read for the first time this morning.

As though he sensed her reluctance, Lorenzo stepped forward and took hold of her arm, so that she had no option other than to step forward with him. She had had to guess at what to wear, opting in the end for a plain black linen skirt and a short-sleeved chocolate-brown tee-shirt, over which she had draped one of the beautiful multicoloured silk squares she had found tucked away with her new clothes as a small gift from the store, thinking that if necessary she could adjust the square and cover her head.

She had been glad she had opted for dark colours when she had seen Lorenzo, wearing a formal dark suit complete with a crisp white shirt and a tie. Now, unable to stop herself looking slightly anxiously towards him, she stepped with him into a world that was totally unfamiliar to her. She recognised how forbidding and arrogant he looked. Take away the suit and clothe him in the costume of a Medici warlord, and he could have been a Renaissance soldier prince, she decided with a small shudder.

The huge emerald on her ring finger flashed green fire in the sunlight, and someone in the small congregation filing in through the narrow door gasped—although whether in awe or shock, Jodie didn't know. Although no one spoke, it was obvious from the looks that were exchanged that the other worshippers knew Lorenzo, and Jodie could feel the sharp weight of their speculation resting almost as heavily on her as the betrothal ring.

People entered the dark interior of the church and slipped into pews, kneeling immediately in prayer, and Jodie turned towards the nearest pew herself, only to find that Lorenzo was shaking his head and walking past. Their footsteps echoed on the cold stone floor, the stones themselves worn and slippery with use. Ahead of them at the altar the priest kneeled, head bowed in prayer, whilst smoke from the incense drifted lazily upwards in the beam of light coming in through the narrow stained glass windows.

They had reached the last pew, and Jodie's eyes widened a little when she recognised Lorenzo's family crest carved into the wood. A little uncomfortably she bowed her own head in prayer. A prayer for her parents, and for David and Andrea, for her friends and for all those in need, and then to her own astonishment she found herself suddenly praying fiercely that Lorenzo might find some way of making peace with his own past.

Even though she knew why they were here in the church, she was still not prepared for the effect hearing their banns read had on her—or the emotional poignancy and turmoil she felt. Unconnected images blurred her vision—a sunny day, and her parents laughing down at her as they walked together; the shock of learning of their deaths; her aunt and uncle's unhappy faces as they struggled to explain to her what had happened, and that she herself might still lose her leg; the first time she stood up properly after the accident; the first time John had asked her out, standing awkwardly beside her desk in the small office where she had worked for his father; the first time he had kissed her, and the let-down feeling of disappointment she had had because she didn't feel more excited.

The small ceremony they had just been part of should surely be about more than fulfilling the demands of someone's pride, or gaining material possessions, and she should now be standing here outside the church feeling uplifted by the promise of future shared love—instead of which she actually felt slightly guilty and shabby.

The priest was heading towards them, smiling warmly as he congratulated them, his warmth increasing Jodie's discomfort. He was tall and unexpectedly vigorously male, with an intent gaze.

'If there are any matters you feel you wish to discuss with me, my child, I am at your disposal,' he told Jodie gently, in excellent English.

'My grandmother's will has meant that we have had to change our plans to marry in England and bring our wedding forward,' Lorenzo informed him, slightly coolly. 'And we are grateful to you for your co-operation.'

The priest inclined his head gravely, and Lorenzo placed his hand in the middle of Jodie's back in what she bemusedly recognised as a classic male possessive gesture, firmly ushering her away. She could feel the warmth of his hand through her top, and the wilful thought crept into her mind, like the incense smoke rising to the light, that had they truly been in love she might have turned to look up at him and smile at him, and his hand might have stroked her flesh in mute promise as he returned her smile. But they were not in love, and she had absolutely no wish for them to be in love!

'I wish we didn't have to get married in church,' she told him uncomfortably as they made their way back to the Palazzo. 'It made me feel so guilty when Father Ignatius prayed for us and for our marriage, knowing that it isn't going to be a real marriage.'

'A real marriage as in a sexual marriage, I assume you mean?'

'No.' Jodie denied it immediately, but she could see from his expression that he didn't believe her. 'Real marriage is about much more than just sex,' she persisted.

'But sex is a part of it—and you, as we both know, are dangerously curious to know the reality of a man's possession.'

'You keep saying that, but it isn't true!'

'Your lips say one thing,' Lorenzo told her softly, 'but your eyes say another.'

She might be a virgin, but she could still recognise the growing sexual tension between them for what it was, Jodie decided shakily.

'I need to return to the Castillo for a few days,' Lorenzo added abruptly. 'It would be easier to leave you here in Florence, but, since we are so newly betrothed, it would be better if you were to accompany me. When is your next fitting for the wedding dress?'

'On Thursday.'

'*Bene*, we shall be back by then.'

Jodie looked at the emerald ring she had just removed and replaced in its box, prior to getting ready for bed.

The apartment was well set up with burglar alarms, she knew that, but even so she didn't feel happy about the thought of the ring being in her room overnight, and would far rather it were in Lorenzo's keeping.

Closing the box, she picked it up and hurried out of her own room and across the corridor, hesitating briefly before she knocked on Lorenzo's bedroom door.

His brisk '*Si?*' had her opening the door and stepping into the room, explaining, 'I've brought you the ring. I wanted to...' Her voice trailed away as her gaze slid helplessly over the smooth golden flesh of his torso, where it was revealed by the unbuttoned shirt he was removing.

'You wanted to what?' he prompted silkily, walking past her to close the door before shrugging off his shirt completely. The gold strap of his watch gleamed subtly in the lamplight, the dark vee of his body hair a silky mesh of male sexuality that riveted and trapped her spellbound gaze.

Her mouth had gone dry. She touched her tongue-tip to her lips, unable to focus properly on answering him, her senses too overwhelmed by the sight of him. He was so arrogantly, so devastatingly, so *magnificently* male.

If just the sight of those broad shoulders and that solidly muscled chest could make her feel like this, what would it do to her to see him fully naked? She drew a deep, juddering breath of silent recognition at the ache uncoiling inside her.

'The ring,' she managed to tell him unsteadily, stretching out the hand in which she was holding the small box. 'I want you to have it.'

'Do you? Or do you mean you want me to have *you*, to satisfy that curiosity of yours and to satisfy you along with it?'

Beneath her angry outrage a shiver of something sensual and excited stroked her senses. Was he right? Was that secretly why she had come to his room? Because she had wanted...hoped...?

Lorenzo watched as her expression reflected her feelings. Somehow she was burrowing deeper and deeper into his thoughts, causing him to question things—beliefs—he did not want to question. He might be better at concealing his desire than she was, but that didn't mean he was any better at controlling it, he knew.

'I didn't come here for that reason at all,' Jodie protested belatedly. 'I just didn't want to be responsible for looking after the ring.' Could he hear in her voice, as she could, her own uncertainty about her subconscious motivation?

'As you don't want to be responsible for "looking after" your own virginity any more?' Lorenzo suggested harshly. 'You are overwhelmed by your virginal curiosity—admit it! It eats at you, and aches deep inside you, keeping you awake at night, wondering…wanting…'

'No,' Jodie breathed, but she knew she might just as well have been saying yes. 'I don't want you,' she said fiercely, trying to cling on to some kind of reality.

'Not me,' Lorenzo agreed. 'But you do want what I can give you—the knowledge your time in hospital has denied you. You want to know what it feels like to know a man's body, to know a man's possession. You can deny it with these,' he told her mockingly, reaching out and rubbing the pad of his thumb against her parted lips, 'as much as you wish, but I could take them now with my own and they would tell me something very different.'

'No,' Jodie repeated, but she was looking helplessly up into his eyes, just standing there without moving as he came to her and slowly slid his hands up over her arms, from her wrists to her shoulders, and she trembled almost violently with sensual pleasure and anticipation. He was drawing her closer, so close that the hot, primitive male scent of him engulfed her. She put her lips to the bare flesh of his collarbone with a small moan, and then pressed eager open-mouthed kisses the length of his throat, greedily tasting his flesh before running her tongue-tip over his Adam's apple whilst her fingers dug into the hard muscles of his shoulders and she strained against him.

Was this what happened when a woman was a virgin? Lorenzo wondered, as he struggled to control his sudden savage longing to feel her mouth on every part of him. This wild, wanton outpouring of need—not for male possession, but for the right to take her own pleasure in whatever way she wished? And why should he stop her? Why should he not let her take her pleasure where she wished and in whatever way she wished?

He looked down at her, to where he could see outlined by her strappy top the stiff thrust of her nipples, and his male instincts surged in feral need. He cupped her face and took her mouth with his own, driving into it with the slow rhythmic thrust of his tongue as he tugged down her top with his free hand until her breasts spilled over the fabric, creamily fleshed, with warm brown nipples already swollen hard with desire.

Jodie didn't even hear herself moan with hot delight at the feel of Lorenzo's naked flesh against her own. She was lost in her own arousal. His silky dark body hair sensitised her already eager nipples while the stroke of his tongue in the hollow behind her ear brought her arching compulsively into him, into him and against him, grinding her hips against his body in a frenzy of eager longing.

Jodie could see their twinned images in the bedroom mirrors, and she watched passion-bound as

Lorenzo cupped her breast and readied the dark peak of her nipple for the downward descent of his head and the deliberately erotic caress of his tongue.

This time as she arched her body up to his, willingly sacrificing it to her growing pleasure, Jodie did hear herself cry out in female longing. But the sound of her own desire only increased the fevered beat of her blood as it surged through her veins, heating her belly and spreading through it an ache that weakened her muscles and softened her flesh into warm, wet compliance.

When Lorenzo picked her up bodily, she wrapped her arms around him and gasped in pleasure to feel him suckling on the taut peak of her nipple whilst he tugged off the rest of her clothes.

By the time he placed her on the bed they were both naked, and he was leaning over her whilst he trailed slow kisses over her openly eager body. Jodie could see how the thick strength of his erection rose stiffly toward his belly, and she yearned to reach out and touch it.

The sensation of Lorenzo circling her navel with his tongue-tip as his hand stroked slowly up the inside of her thigh was melting away whatever desire she might have had to conjure up some kind of resistance. Her rapt gaze was fixed unashamedly and avidly on his erection.

Lorenzo lifted his head to watch her as she reached out half hesitantly and took him in her hand, her eyes widening as she absorbed the texture and heat. A soft slow burn of excited colour warmed her skin when she registered the pulse that flooded his darkly engorged thickness. She stroked him with fervent female appreciation and approval, and Lorenzo closed his eyes and exhaled, unable to withstand his body's longing to enjoy her wondering exploration.

How powerful it made her feel to touch Lorenzo like this, and how eternally female, in a way that somehow connected her with the whole of her sex from the dawn of time. It was woman who aroused this maleness in a man, woman who controlled and commanded it, drawing from it her own pleasure as well as allowing man to take his. Her fingers explored and stroked, and her lips parted and her breath caught on a small whisper of soft wanton pleasure as she felt the response Lorenzo couldn't quite control. He felt so rigid, and yet at the same time so malleable. Silky desire flushed her, tempted her to bend her head and…

'No!'

The harshness of Lorenzo's refusal sent a shock through her. Confusion and disappointment darkened her gaze as it met his, and then returned to cling to his now openly pulsing stiffness.

If he let her place her lips against him now, he wouldn't be able to control himself, Lorenzo knew. She had already aroused him well beyond his own personal safety limit. If he let her caress him so intimately, he wouldn't be able to stop himself from taking her.

'Why not?' Jodie protested.

'We can't have full sex,' he answered her curtly.

With her own arousal an unsatisfied ache that physically hurt, Jodie persisted doggedly, 'Why not?'

'I don't have any condoms, and there's no way I intend to fall into the trap of fathering a child I don't want and which ultimately I would have to pay for,' he told her harshly.

'Wouldn't it have been better to have thought of that earlier?' Jodie asked him pointedly as she moved away from him and got off the bed, retrieving her clothes and redressing with clumsy haste.

No way was she going to let him guess how much his rejection of her reminded her of John's, or how much it and he had hurt her. And she certainly didn't want him to know how shamingly and how very, very much she was aching deep inside herself for what he was not going to give her.

How foolish she had been to think that she was in control of his desire. In this relationship she wasn't in control of anything, she decided bitterly, as she almost ran for the door, desperate for the sanctuary of her own bedroom.

CHAPTER TEN

JODIE tensed as she heard the sound she had been lying awake waiting for. The now familiar click of Lorenzo's bedroom door being opened very quietly, and then closed again equally secretively.

In two days' time they would be getting married, but on no less than four occasions now Jodie had been aware of Lorenzo leaving his bedroom late at night and not returning to it for at least an hour. And Caterina was still living at the Castillo, in Lorenzo's late grandmother's rooms. If Caterina had made good her threat to get Lorenzo back into her bed, then surely *she* had a right to know about it? Even though she was only going to be a temporary wife.

Getting out of bed, Jodie pulled on her robe and slipped her feet into a pair of soft-soled shoes. She was determined to confront Lorenzo with her suspicions. Being a business arrangement wife was one thing, but being the unwanted wife of a man who had a mistress was very definitely another. And the kind of humiliating situation she had no intention of allowing Lorenzo to put her in.

She hurried along the landing to the top of the stairs, and as she looked anxiously down them she saw Lorenzo's shadow moving swiftly along the hallway below. Determinedly she hurried after him, wondering why he had not simply used the upper corridor that led to Caterina's apartments.

Several narrow passageways led off the hallway

which linked the old part of the Castillo to this newer wing, which had been added in the seventeenth century. Which passage had Lorenzo taken? There was a light burning on the stairs that led down to a lower level. Exhaling nervously, Jodie turned down them. The stairs were directly under Caterina's apartment, so perhaps—

She gave a small shocked scream as suddenly, out of the shadows, a hand curled round her wrist.

'What the hell do you think you're doing?'

'Lorenzo!'

He must have realised that she was following him and waited to trap her.

'I wanted to know where you were going. This is the fourth time I've heard you leave your room late at night,' she told him boldly, lifting her chin.

'You were spying on me?'

The narrow-eyed look he was giving her was making her feel acutely uncomfortable, but she wasn't going to let him see that.

'If I'm going to marry you then I have a right to know if you're having sex with Caterina.'

'*What?*'

'I won't marry you if you are,' Jodie told him fiercely. 'And I mean that.'

'You mean you're snooping around following me because you thought you were going to find me in Caterina's bed?'

Put that way, he made it sound as though her behaviour was verging on the bunny-boiling, Jodie realised guiltily. How could she tell him that his rejection of her, so closely mirroring John's lack of sexual interest in her, had not only heightened her own insecurities but had also led to her wondering if, like

John, Lorenzo was actually finding sexual satisfaction with someone else?

'You can't deny that you and she have been lovers,' she told him stubbornly.

'Have been, yes,' he agreed tersely. 'But that was nearly twenty years ago, when I was a boy.'

'She says you still want her.'

'She may choose to think that, but it is most certainly not true,' Lorenzo told her firmly. His fingers were still clamped round her wrist, and suddenly he cursed beneath his breath, saying grimly, 'You want to know where I go? Very well, then—come with me.'

He was walking so fast along the narrow, tunnel-like corridor in front of them that Jodie almost had to run to keep up with him. She could smell damp, and see it too on the vaulted curve of the ancient stone walls. She gave a small shiver, and then a shocked gasp as they reached a heavy oak door and Lorenzo told her emotionlessly, 'The corridor beyond here was once know as the *via eternal*, because it led to the Castillo's dungeons and torture chambers.'

'The torture chambers?' Jodie could hear the horrified revulsion in her own voice.

Lorenzo gave a dismissive shrug as he unlocked and then opened the heavy oak door. 'They were considered a necessary part of warfare.'

'In medieval times, perhaps,' Jodie acknowledged. 'But—'

'No, not merely in medieval times,' Lorenzo interrupted, his voice and his expression both so savagely forbidding that she shivered.

Beyond the door lay a large cavernous room with a low, vaulted ceiling. Wine racks leaned emptily against one wall, whilst moisture dripped onto the floor from the ceiling.

'It's all right,' Lorenzo told her following her anxious upward glance. 'The ceiling is quite safe, and the coldness of the air, although unpleasant, does have certain merits.'

'More torture for the prisoners?' Jodie suggested sharply.

'My grandmother's first husband was imprisoned down here for a time.'

The unexpectedness of Lorenzo's low-voiced comment sent a shock through her.

'He was against Mussolini and made the mistake of saying so; for that he was imprisoned and tortured in his own home. My grandmother never really got over it. Oh, she remarried after his death, but her heart wasn't really in it. She often told me herself that, given a free choice, she would have preferred to retire to the contemplative life of a convent—but she had promised him that she would provide his house with an heir. Her marriage to my own grandfather was arranged by her first husband as he lay dying from the damage inflicted on his body by his torturers. They stole many works of art from the Castillo—and emptied the wine racks,' he added grimly, nodding in the direction of the empty racks. 'But there was one treasure they were not able to take.'

Jodie looked round the bleak, cold underground room in bewilderment.

'Down here?'

Lorenzo shook his head. 'No. Come with me.'

He led her over to a small door that opened onto another set of stairs. 'These lead up to the main salon of what used to be the state apartments.'

'Caterina's rooms?' Jodie questioned him uncertainly.

'She sleeps in what was my grandmother's room, which forms part of the state apartments, yes—which is why I use these stairs to reach the salon instead of the main corridor stairs.'

They had reached the top of the stairs and another door.

'Through here, in the main salon, concealed by the fabric which my grandmother's first husband had specially applied to the walls, is a series of wall paintings by a pupil of Leonardo. Although, according to my grandmother, family legend insists that the Master himself had a hand in their execution.'

As he spoke he was ushering her into a large elegant room, its walls hung with green silk fabric. The room was shabby and slightly neglected, with dust motes hanging in the air along with the faint smell of roses.

'The Duce was afraid that Mussolini's men would lay claim to the Castillo because of the paintings, and so he had them covered up. It was his dream that one day they would be fully restored. Our family is a large one, and there are some members of it who feel that the Castillo should be sold and the proceeds shared. My grandmother wanted to leave the Castillo to me because she knew I would fulfil on her behalf the promise she made to her dying first husband.'

'So why did she make it condition of her will that you must marry?'

'That was through Caterina's interference. My grandmother was a gentle person who thought only good of others. Caterina seized her chance after Gino died and managed to convince Nonna that we were star-crossed lovers and I wanted to marry her. She is what one might term an adventuress, to whom marriage to my cousin Gino gave social standing. She had hoped to raise herself even higher by trapping me into marriage with her. Money and social position are all that matter to her.'

Jodie frowned. Her instincts were telling her that what he was saying was the truth, and that Caterina had lied to her.

'Caterina knows how important the Castillo is to me,' Lorenzo continued. 'Gino had told her of my promise to our grandmother, and she thought she could use that to force my hand. Fortunately for me, my grandmother's notary managed to conceal from Caterina the fact that he had omitted her name from the final signed copy of the will, so that it read merely that I had to marry, instead of stating that I had to marry Caterina. And, as if the situation weren't complicated enough already, she has been encouraging some Russian syndicate to believe that the Castillo will be available to buy. They wish to convert it into a luxury hotel.'

'But why do you come here at night?'

'Because I cannot do so during the day, when Caterina is here, and because I have a need to commune with the past, to assure the man who gave his life to preserve it that I will do my best to fulfil his dream.' He gave a small shrug. 'At the same time, I have dreams of my own. I would like to see the Castillo turned into a rehabilitation centre for the young victims of war—a place where they can recover physically and emotionally. I want it to be a centre for young artists and artisans, gifted craftspeople who will work on the restoration that is needed and train their young apprentices to follow in their footsteps. I want to banish from the Castillo, and from the lives of young victims of war, at least some of the shadows and dark places, and to fill them instead with light and the pleasure of living. The meetings I have been having in Florence are connected with my plans for the Castillo. As soon as we are married, and the Castillo is legally mine, my first and most important duty is to put in hand the restoration of the paintings.'

Jodie had to blink fiercely to disperse her foolish tears, her earlier antagonistic suspicions of him swept away by a sudden surge of admiration.

'It sounds wonderful—a truly noble enterprise,' she told him huskily, looking up at him, her admiration warming her eyes.

Lorenzo looked back at her and Jodie caught her breath as he took a step towards her, quickly disentangling her gaze from his whilst her heart raced and thudded.

'Caterina does not think so. She would far rather the place was sold and my money was hers to do with as she chooses. She drove my cousin to his death, and even if I loved her rather than loathed her I could never forgive her for that,' Lorenzo told her harshly.

Jodie gave a small shiver.

'But you must have loved her once…'

'Why? Because I had sex with her?' Lorenzo shook his head. 'I was eighteen and driven by the desires of my body, that was all.' As he was being driven by them right now, if he was honest, to take hold of Jodie and take her back to his bed, so that he could finish what had been started the night she had returned the betrothal ring to him. There hadn't been a single night

since then when he had not thought of doing so—
ached to do so. She'd got under his skin in a way that
no other woman had, mental images of her filling his
head and stealing away his thoughts whilst his body
raged and pulsed. Angrily he fought against the longing taking hold of him.

Every bride felt nervous—it went with the territory,
Jodie assured herself as the alarmingly efficient stylist
the designer salon had insisted on sending to help her,
plus a seamstress and a dresser, bustled round her
bedroom.

Who would have thought that a small, quiet wedding would involve so much strategic planning? A
little ruefully, Jodie suspected that it was her gown
rather than her that was the cause of the stylist's relentless insistence on overseeing every detail of her
wedding-day appearance—right down to the spa treat-
ments she had arranged for Jodie the previous day.
Now, massaged plucked, waxed and tinted to within
an inch of her life, Jodie tried to imagine how she
might be feeling if this was the real thing, a real wedding, and she was standing here nervously being laced
into her corset in anticipation of making her vows to
a man she really loved and who really loved her.

But of course that was never going to happen.
Because she was never going to love a man, was she?
Was she? she repeated insistently, when her question
was met by a stubborn silence from the reassuring
inner voice that should have acknowledged and
agreed.

'No, you must pull it tighter,' she could hear the
stylist instructing the dresser, and she winced as the
breath was squeezed out of her lungs.

Her hair had been arranged in an artless mix of loose plaits coiled softly into an 'up do' and then threaded with invisible thread strung with diamonds to complement the pearl and diamond embroidery on her gown. A make-up artist had spent what felt like hours working on her face to make it look as though she wasn't actually wearing any make-up at all, merely a soft glow, although her eyelids had been brushed with a subtle gold-green powder which made them look enormous as well as reflecting the green glitter of the emerald.

By the time the stylist was satisfied with the narrowness of her waist, Jodie was afraid she might pass out from an inability to breathe.

'Come and look,' the stylist insisted, taking her to stand in front of the full-length mirror.

The reflection gazing back at her was totally unfamiliar. Huge gold eyes ringed with curling black lashes looked at her, soft rose lips surely much fuller than hers parted to show pearly white teeth. The cream corset bodice of her gown revealed lushly curved breasts and an impossibly narrow waist, whilst silky fine cream hold-ups covered legs that seemed to go on for ever, thanks to the height of the heels she was having to wear.

'*Bene,*' the stylist pronounced, beckoning to the dresser. 'Now for the skirt.'

Heaven knew how she would have managed to dress herself, Jodie reflected half an hour afterwards, when both skirt and train had finally been arranged to the stylist's satisfaction, and the cream lace veil and bodice had been slipped on to cover her hair and bare skin.

There was a knock on the door, and some flurried conversation out of Jodie's earshot, and then the stylist was handing her flowers and telling her urgently, 'It is time for you to leave...'

CHAPTER ELEVEN

FINALLY it was over: the church service, the walk-about she hadn't realised she would be expected to make, greeting the well-wishers, the friends of Lorenzo's, who had included his lawyer and his charming wife, and the impromptu wedding lunch which Carlo had insisted on preparing for them whilst everyone else in the restaurant joined in the celebration. Nine hours of it in all, during which Jodie had not dared to attempt to eat or drink, never mind sit down.

And now they were finally alone, Assunta having prepared and left them a cold supper before coming to the church to see them married. Jodie was so exhausted she could barely stand. The corset had become a form of excruciating torture from which she ached to be free with every muscle in her body that hadn't been numbed by its pressure.

In the hallway of the apartment, she headed for the stairs, picking up her long skirts.

'You are tired?' Lorenzo guessed.

She could barely nod her head. Tired didn't even begin to describe her physical and emotional exhaustion. *Emotional* exhaustion? Because of what, exactly? She felt like kicking the unwanted inner voice for probing and prodding—it, after all, knew as well as she did exactly how she had felt standing next to Lorenzo whilst the priest spoke the words of the marriage ceremony. The light from the windows had illuminated her face, but the inner light illuminating her understanding of a truth she hadn't wanted to recognise had been far more powerful. She had hated the feeling of deceit that had clung to her, the sense of guilt and shame at the way they were using vows that should have been sacred to suit their own purposes.

'I'll come up with you,' she heard Lorenzo saying.

How could a mere dress weigh so much? By the time she reached the top of the stairs her heart was pounding nauseatingly, and she was feeling oddly light-headed.

Outside the door to her bedroom, Lorenzo touched her lightly on the shoulder and said coolly, 'If you've got a minute…?'

They had only just been married, and he was asking her if she had got a minute as though they were no more than acquaintances. But then, wasn't that exactly what they were?

She could see that he was waiting for her to cross the corridor and follow him into his room. Her leg was aching painfully, but she refused to let it drag.

She stepped into his bedroom and stood as close to the door as she could, refusing to look at the bed.

Lorenzo had walked over to the tallboy, where he'd picked up something, and now he was walking back towards her.

'Knowing how you feel about the emerald, I thought you might prefer to wear this instead. Oh, and you can keep it afterwards if you wish,' he told her with a dismissive shrug.

Silently Jodie took the small box from him and opened it. Inside was a perfect pear-shaped solitaire diamond. Mutely, she looked at it.

'I couldn't possibly keep that. It must have been very expensive.'

Lorenzo was frowning at her as though her refusal displeased him. 'As you wish,' he agreed curtly. 'It isn't of any real consequence.'

'Like our marriage,' Jodie heard herself saying shakily. 'I really would have preferred not to have had a church ceremony. It made me feel—' She broke off and shook her head as she realised the impossibility of making Lorenzo understand how she had felt.

The sudden action caused a wave of dizziness to swamp her, followed by the shocked realisation that she was about to faint. Instinctively she made grab for the nearest solid object, which just happened to be Lorenzo. As she swayed towards him Lorenzo caught hold of her.

'It's the dress,' she managed to tell him. 'It's laced so very tightly...'

The next minute he was turning her round, supporting her with one arm whilst he inspected the fastenings of her bodice and demanded grimly, 'Why didn't you say something? How the hell does this thing come off?'

'The skirt and the train have to come off first, before I can remove the bodice,' Jodie told him weakly. 'They're just hooked onto it.'

Before she could stop him he was feeling for the tiny fastenings, unsnapping them with ruthless speed. When they were all free the train and skirt sighed softly to the floor, leaving Jodie standing in her silk stockings, high heels, tiny boy-short briefs—and the unbearably tight bodice.

'What on earth possessed you to wear something so tight?' Lorenzo demanded.

'It wasn't my idea. It was the stylist's,' Jodie admitted. 'She insisted on it being so tightly laced.'

'How does it fasten?'

'It's laced on the inside, and then fastened with hooks and eyes.' Just the effort of speaking was making her feel sick from her inability to draw enough air into her lungs.

'Don't move,' Lorenzo told her, leaving her standing in the middle of the floor as he went over to the tallboy and opened a drawer. When he came back he was holding a pair of scissors.

'No, you can't—' Jodie protested weakly, but it was too late. He was already cutting into the fabric, ignoring her protests.

She almost cried from the sheer bliss of simply being able to breathe naturally as the corset fell away.

'*Dio!* It's a wonder your flesh is not numbed and dead,' Lorenzo said critically as he studied the red marks on her pale skin where the corset had cut into her. 'And why did you not say before now that your leg is paining you?'

'Because it isn't,' Jodie fibbed.

'Yes, it is. Go and lie down on the bed. I will massage it for you.'

'There's no need for you to do that,' she protested. 'I'll be fine now that I'm free of the corset.' She folded her arms over her breasts, suddenly, now that she didn't have to worry about taking her next breath, acutely conscious her state of undress, but as she shifted her weight from one foot to the other a sharp pain shot up her injured leg, causing her to smother a gasp of pain.

Lorenzo muttered something she couldn't translate

and then picked her up, ignoring her tired protest as he carried her over to the bed.

'You are the most stubborn woman I have ever met,' he told her grimly as he put her down. 'Now, lie down and I will massage your leg for you.'

She wanted to refuse—out of pride if nothing else—but the truth was that her leg was really hurting, and the thought of having the pain massaged away was too tempting to refuse.

Silently she lay down on her front and closed her eyes. She had forgotten about the stockings she was still wearing, and tensed as Lorenzo removed them— as clinically and efficiently as though she were made of plastic rather than female flesh and blood, she acknowledged wryly. But her flesh knew that *he* was male, and its response to the firm massaging movement of his fingers against the aching muscles in her thigh was most definitely not clinical.

She had originally lain on her stomach to conceal from him both her naked breasts and her expression— not so much out of modesty, but out of fear of what they might reveal to him. Now, as she felt her nipples hardening when his fingers stroked and kneaded her aching flesh, she was very glad that she had done so. As his fingers drew the pain out of her flesh their touch replaced it with a very different kind of ache, beginning deep inside her with a small fluttering pulse that quickly grew stronger until the desire it generated was spreading outwards into every nerve-ending. Uncomfortably she pulled away, and moved to sit up, fearing that somehow Lorenzo might guess what she was experiencing.

'What's the matter?' he demanded. 'Are you worried that I might try to seduce you?'

He was mocking her, she knew that. 'No, of course not. Why would I think that? After all, I already know that you don't desire me.'

She had rolled over now, and was sitting up. But she couldn't get off the bed because Lorenzo was standing immediately in front of her.

'And you want me to desire you?'

'No!' she said fiercely.

'You're lying.' Lorenzo accused her, shocking her as he suddenly drew her up to stand virtually body-to-body with him. 'But then, lying is second nature to your sex, isn't it?'

Yes, she was lying, Jodie admitted. Because she had no other alternative, no other way to protect herself. Why was he behaving like this towards her? She'd realised from what Caterina had told her that his childhood experiences with his mother and her unfaithfulness to his father had given him a low opinion of her sex, and a need to protect himself from emotional pain, but that was no reason for him to punish her. Just as she had no real reason to brand all men as faithless, shallow cheats because of the way John had behaved towards her? She swallowed uncomfortably, unable to ignore her own inner critical voice.

'You're lying,' Lorenzo repeated. 'Admit it.'

'Admit what?' Jodie challenged him recklessly. 'That I want you? Why? What purpose or benefit is there in my doing that? You don't want me. All you want is for me to give you an excuse to go on telling yourself that all women are like your mother and Caterina. Well, we aren't. You want me to lie to you because that way you can keep on telling yourself that all women are the same. Because you're afraid of wanting—'

'Enough!'

Jodie tried to protest, but it was too late. His mouth was already covering hers, his hands almost bruising the tender flesh of her upper arms as he held her to him so hard that she could feel the buttons on his shirt pressing into her skin.

'I am afraid of nothing,' Lorenzo whispered fiercely against her mouth. 'Least of all of wanting you. And to prove it…'

Before she could evade him he was kissing her, deeply and intimately, whilst his hands stroked over her body to cup her breasts.

She should stop him. She knew that. But her own desire was stronger than her will-power. The anger that had flared up between them had unleashed a passion in Lorenzo that ignited her own and overwhelmed her careful restraint. He lifted one hand to her head, sliding his fingers into her hair and exposing the slender vulnerability of her neck to the sensual assault of his lips.

Shudders of hot, illicit pleasure that began where his mouth caressed her skin and ended deep inside the female heart of hers seized her, took her to a place where reality didn't exist and all that mattered was following the lure of the primitive surge of her own desire for him.

He had captured her nipple between the long lean finger and thumb of his free hand and was playing softly with it, then less softly when both it and its partner stiffened with excitement. The erotic sensation of him tugging sensually on it was relayed to her through what felt like a million tiny nerve-endings, magnifying the pleasure so much that she was racked helplessly by its domination as it took her and filled her, weakening her will-power along with her bones, and focusing all of her straining concentration not on the urgent warnings of her defences, but instead on the wet heat between her legs, and the desire-swollen flesh she ached for Lorenzo to touch.

Had she actually verbally said what she wanted? She had communicated it to him somehow, Jodie realised dizzily, as his fingers untangled from her hair and his hand stroked down her body, moulding her hipbone, his fingers pressing into the curves of her bottom as he held her with both hands and pulled her into his own body so that she could feel how hard and aroused he was. He kissed her with shockingly deliberate intimacy as he caressed the quivering flesh of her stomach, then stroked his fingers along the hip-hugging line of her silky knickers, teasing her eager flesh with a softly tantalising touch that made her press closer to him until he responded to her need and slipped his hand into the softly fluted leg of her underwear to cover her sex.

Completely lost, Jodie made a small delirious sound of pleasure into his kiss that turned to a broken exclamation of shocked delight when he slid his fingers into her waiting wetness. The feel of the slow movement of his fingers over her aroused flesh was both an exquisite pleasure and an almost unbearable torment. She wanted him to go on doing what he was doing, but she wanted him inside her as well, filling her, satisfying the need that was tightening round her. She moaned out loud as he plucked softly at the aroused nub of her clitoris, her own hand going immediately to the thick thrust of his own erection, easily visible beneath his clothes but frustratingly separated from the full intimacy of her touch by them.

'Wait,' she heard him tell her thickly, and then he was lifting her, placing her back on the bed before swiftly removing his clothes. She lay back, her head on the pillows, watching him with an absorbed, hungry, unashamed eagerness, her breath coming in soft little panting gasps of need, her hand resting over her own sex, not to protect it, but to quieten it as it pulsed its clamouring message of readiness.

His nakedness excited her so much. She couldn't drag her gaze away from the stiff length of his erection as it thrust upwards from the soft dark mat of his body hair. It crossed her mind that she should be feeling virginal fear instead of such a delirious sense of eager excitement. He was leaning over her, removing her briefs, watching her as he did so. Heat and shock suffused her as he slowly slid one finger the length of her wetness. Greedily her body lifted towards him and his finger traced her again, stroking and lingering, caressing the hard little nub of excitement clamouring for his attention and then slowly, very deliberately, sliding inside her. Jodie gasped and then moaned in delight as she felt him stretching her gently, still caressing her.

His body was covering hers now, and he was kissing her. Eagerly she kissed him back, only stopping when she felt the loss of his pleasure-giving fingers. Her eyes rounded and her face burned when he lifted his hand towards her lips and told her thickly, 'Taste yourself on me.' Hesitantly she opened her mouth and let him place his fingers within it, closing her eyes and obeying his whispered, 'Suck them,' as she drew in the taste of her own arousal mingled with the taste of his skin and felt the power of the aphrodisiac he was giving her.

Now she was totally lost, a mindless slave to her own sexuality and need as his hands and his mouth caressed every part of her. Her shoulder, the inner flesh of her arm, her breasts, her belly, and she writhed and moaned and reached for him with her own hands and mouth, savouring the sharp taste of him as she breathed in his intimate man scent and felt its erotic impact on her senses. She ached to let her tongue-tip circle the stiff shiny head of his sex, but Lorenzo wouldn't let her. Instead his tongue was exploring her, tracing a sensual pathway of fiery pleasure over her wetness, stroking firmly against her clitoris, taking her far, far beyond the furthermost reaches of her own sensual imaginings. She wanted him so much. Too much...

Abruptly, reality pierced her sexual arousal and she tensed, pushing Lorenzo away whilst her body screamed its pain at her denial of its pleasure.

Lorenzo sat up, frowning, and made to take her in his arms, but Jodie resisted him and shook her head, telling him fiercely, 'No!'

'What? What are you saying? You want me—you were giving yourself to me...' he insisted fiercely.

'And you want to prove that all women are like your mother—that we all lie and cheat. Yes, I do want you,' she agreed shakily. 'But I want my self-respect more.'

As she spoke she was wriggling away from his restraining arm and getting off the bed, hurriedly gathering up her scattered clothes, fully aware that

Lorenzo was watching her but not daring to look back at him in case her resolve wasn't able to withstand her doing so.

Lorenzo lay on his bed and stared up at the ceiling. The ache he could feel inside himself was just physical, that was all. And the emotion burning inside him was just furious anger that Jodie should dare to say to him what she had. She meant nothing to him. Nothing!

The emptiness of his bed without her was something that he welcomed, rather than regretted. As he would welcome the emptiness of his life once she had gone from it, he assured himself fiercely.

The reason he had been so sexually aroused by her, so sexually lost in the sweetness of her, was simply that it had been too long since there had been a woman in his bed. And that was a need he could easily satisfy. Right now, if necessary, simply by making a phone call. And if he couldn't reach any of the many women whom he knew would be pleased to receive his summons—well, he knew, although not from personal experience, that Florence, like any other city, had its high-priced and high-class hookers, women who knew how to please a man without making any demands on him other than their fee.

But why pay a hooker when remembering one was enough to cool his sexual desire? When he had first met Caterina she had made no secret of the fact that she had several rich lovers, even if later she had claimed that it was not true and that he had misunderstood her. And his mother, with the expensive gifts she had received...a reward for her infidelity, even if they had only been from one lover. His heart started to thud angrily.

He got up off the bed. Five minutes later, standing beneath the lash of the shower, he could feel his heartbeat returning to normal.

What really infuriated him was that Jodie, whom he had begun to consider someone whose thinking was sound and rational, should start making such ridiculous and unfounded accusations. How dared she accuse him of being so emotionally damaged that he *wanted* her to lie to him to reinforce his belief that her sex could not be trusted? He had proved that he trusted her, had talked to her about things that were so close to his heart he had never discussed them with anyone else. Did she really think that he would do that and then try to create a reason to mistrust her? It was totally illogical that he should do such a thing— like a panicking child trying to protect itself from being hurt because it feared to love.

After all, it wasn't as though he was afraid he might be falling in love with her and was fighting desperately against doing so, was it? *Was it?*

He turned off the shower and reached for a towel.

CHAPTER TWELVE

THEY had been married for nearly a week, during which time no mention had been made by either of them of the night of their wedding. Lorenzo was icily polite and indifferent towards her when they were together, and Jodie had taken to spending so much time sightseeing that at night she simply fell into an exhausted sleep the moment she went to bed.

But now they were back at the Castillo, the final paperwork having been dealt with to transfer its ownership to Lorenzo.

'I have not forgotten that I still have to fulfil my part of our bargain,' he told Jodie crisply as they crossed the Castillo's courtyard. 'I have put in hand the necessary arrangements for us to fly to London at the end of the week for your ex-fiancé's wedding. The Cotswolds hotel I have booked us into is in a place named Lower Slaughter?'

'Oh, yes. I know it,' Jodie acknowledged. If it was the hotel she thought it must be, it was very exclusive and expensive.

'I thought you would want to keep some distance between ourselves and your former home.'

'Yes, I do,' Jodie agreed colourlessly. She certainly did not want anyone realising that she and her brand-new husband were sleeping in separate rooms. Especially not when she was going to be flaunting her happily married state under everyone's nose. She exhaled hesitantly.

'I've been thinking,' she told Lorenzo quietly. 'I'm not sure that it's such a good idea for me to...to go ahead with what I'd planned.'

'But that was your whole purpose in agreeing to marrying me.'

'Yes, I know.'

They had reached the hallway now, and Lorenzo was frowning as he studied the untidy pile of suitcases and boxes heaped in the middle of the floor.

'We'll discuss this later,' he told Jodie as an inner door opened.

Caterina swept in, declaring dramatically, 'So, you have arrived to flaunt your triumph and throw me out, have you? Well, you're too late. I am leaving of my own accord. You think you have gained a victory, Lorenzo. But in truth you have gained nothing other than this crumbling ruin and a wife you do not want. And all for what? For the sake of some old paintings and so that you can keep a promise made to an old woman,' she taunted him bitterly. 'We could have had so much together, but now it is too late. Ilya will be here for me soon.'

'Ilya?' Lorenzo questioned sharply.

'Yes. We met when he was interested in buying this place. He has been a good...friend to me. And now...' She pouted and then smiled rapaciously.

'You mean he's your lover?' Lorenzo checked her curtly.

'Why should I answer you? But, yes, we are lovers, and we will be married once his divorce comes through. He is sending a driver for me, and someone to collect my things.'

She turned and looked at Jodie. 'Be careful that Lorenzo doesn't use you as he did me. And, if he does, make sure that he doesn't impregnate you. Because he will force you to abort your child, just as he forced me to abort mine.'

Jodie could feel the blood leaving her face. She looked wildly towards Lorenzo, expecting to hear him deny Caterina's horrific accusations, but instead he simply turned on his heel and left.

'That's not true,' Jodie whispered. 'It can't possibly be. Lorenzo would never—'

'What? Have you fallen in love with him already?' Caterina mocked her. 'You little fool. You mean nothing to him, and you never will. And it is true. Lorenzo forced me to abort my child. If you don't believe me, go and ask him. He will not spare you by lying to you about it. Not Lorenzo. His pride wouldn't let him.' She started to laugh, stepping past Jodie as a car swept into the courtyard.

Jodie had no idea how long she had been out here, sitting alone in the Castillo garden, trying to cope with the violence of her turbulent emotions.

It wasn't true what Caterina had said to her, she told herself stubbornly. She had not fallen in love with Lorenzo. *But she wanted him.* Physical desire was not love. *But it was a manifestation of it.* She could not love a man who not only did not love her, but who did not even recognise what love was. *But what if she did?*

'It's getting dark, and if you stay out here much longer you'll risk ending up with your leg aching.'

She hadn't heard Lorenzo come into the garden, and automatically she moved deeper into the shadows, because she was afraid of what he might read in her expression. She tensed as he sat down beside her.

'You're right. I'd better go in,' she told him in a thin, emotionless voice.

'Why don't you want to go back to England?'

'What?' Jodie looked at him blankly. She had almost forgotten their earlier conversation, thanks to the inner turmoil Caterina's comments had caused her.

'There must be some reason,' Lorenzo persisted.

'I'm not sure that it's something that I want to do any more,' she admitted reluctantly. 'It seemed a good idea at the time, and…and it even gave me a sense of purpose—something to focus on. But now…' Now her old life seemed a million years away, and she didn't care what John and Louise did or thought, because now… Because now what? A fear that she didn't want to give any room to was uncurling inside her with all the clinging tenacity of a killer vine. Was this seismic shift in her emotional focus because she was falling in love with Lorenzo?

Falling in love? That implied that she was in the middle of an act she could halt, she decided with relief, clinging to that thought in desperation. And she would halt it, she decided fiercely.

'I think we should go.'

'Do you?' If she argued with him now, would he start thinking that it was because she might be falling in love with him? No way did she want that.

'Yes. It will help you to find closure and be a way to draw a line under your relationship with both of them. Then you will be able to move on.'

'Mmm. I suppose you're right.'

'I know that I'm right,' Lorenzo said. 'I just wish…'

'What? That you had married Caterina?'

'No,' he denied sharply.

'Did you...? Was it...? Was it true what she said about—about the baby?' Jodie whispered, unable to stop herself from asking the question that had been splintering and festering inside her since Caterina had made her accusation.

'Yes,' Lorenzo admitted heavily.

Jodie shuddered. 'Your own child!' she protested with revulsion. 'How—?'

'No! Caterina was not... It was not my child. But that does not diminish my guilt. I hadn't thought... That was the trouble. I didn't think. I just assumed, with the arrogance and stupidity of youth, that—' He broke off and Jodie could see the tension in his jaw. 'Caterina and Gino had been engaged for about six months when she boasted to me that she had a new lover. She had never forgiven me for ending our brief relationship, and I think she thought she could make me jealous. She told me that she was to have his child, but she had told Gino the child was his. I was angry on behalf of my cousin, whom I knew loved her deeply, with all the self-righteous anger of the very young. I tried to force her hand. I told her she must tell Gino the truth or I would do so myself. I wanted Gino to know what she was—and, yes, it is true I hoped he would end the engagement. For his own sake. But instead of telling Gino the truth she had her pregnancy terminated—and told Gino she had lost the child. He was devastated, and immediately insisted on marrying her. So, through my interference, one life was lost and another destroyed.'

Jodie had to swallow as she heard the raw emotion in his voice. 'You weren't responsible.'

'Yes, I was. If I had not interfered she would have had the child.'

'And she would have gone on lying to your cousin.'

'I tried to play at being God, and no man should do that. I tried to control her behaviour because I had not been able to control my mother's. She left my father and she left me, too, to be with her lover. Caterina stayed with Gino, but, like my mother, she sacrificed her child for her own ends. It felt like I had murdered my own brother.'

As she heard the pain in his voice it occurred to Jodie that Caterina must have known how he would react, and that her decision would have been motivated by her desire to inflict that pain and guilt on him.

'I can never forgive myself for it—never!'

'It was Caterina who made the decision—not you,' Jodie pointed out quietly. 'It was her child, and her body. You weren't even the father.'

'If I had been there is no way she would have been allowed to do what she did,' Lorenzo told Jodie passionately. 'Not even if I had to lock her up for nine months to make sure of it.' He fell silent for a moment, then spoke more quietly. 'My mother once told me that she hadn't wanted me. She hadn't even really wanted to marry my father. There had been family pressure, and she had decided that marriage to him was at least a form of escape from the strict control of her parents.' Lorenzo's voice was bleak.

'I was so lucky to have two parents who loved one another, and me,' Jodie commented softly. She couldn't begin to image what it must have been like for a young child to be told by his mother that he wasn't wanted.

'She was little more than a child when she got married. Seventeen, and my father was twenty-four. He loved her intensely. Too much. Her lover was a racing driver she met through a friend. So much more exciting than my father. She used to take me with her when she went to meet him. I had no idea then of the truth. I thought... He showed me his car and...'

And you liked him, Jodie recognised compassionately. *You liked him, and then you felt you had betrayed your father—just as your mother had done.*

'They ran away together in the end, and my mother died of blood poisoning in South America, where he was racing. My father never got over losing her, and I swore then that I would never...'

'Trust another woman?' Jodie finished for him.

'Let my emotions control me,' Lorenzo corrected her.

'Do we really have to stay married for a year?' she asked him. 'After all, you've got the Castillo now, and Caterina has left...'

'Our arrangement was that we would remain married for one year,' he reminded her curtly. 'To change that now would give rise to gossip and speculation, and although Caterina has left she could decide to challenge the will if she thought she might win such a case. I don't want that.'

'Twelve months seems such a long time.'

'No longer than it was when you agreed to remain with me for that period.'

But then she hadn't known what she knew now, had she? Then she hadn't known that she would be in danger of falling in love with him, that every extra day she had to spend close to him would increase her danger. But she could hardly tell him that.

'What will happen with the Castillo now?' Jodie

asked, knowing that there was nothing she could say to explain her reluctance to stay with him that would not give her away.

'I am arranging for several experts to come out and inspect the paintings so that we can discuss how best to restore them, and I also intend to put in hand the necessary work to convert the Castillo into a centre for rehabilitation and artistic excellence. I have spoken already with several of Florence's master guilders and other craftsmen— But none of this can be of much interest to you,' he told her tersely.

Jodie dipped her head so that he couldn't see how much his careless words had hurt her. But of course he didn't see her as a part of the future he was planning. Why should he?

What was the matter with him? Lorenzo derided himself. Just because he felt a connection with Jodie that he had never experienced with anyone else, a closeness to her, it didn't mean anything. And it certainly didn't mean that he was falling in love with her. He could feel himself tensing, outwardly and inwardly, as though he were trying to lock out his thoughts and feelings—and not just lock them out, but squeeze the very life out of them as well.

Because he was too afraid of them to allow them to exist? For centuries, out of ignorance and prejudice, man had sought to control what it feared by destroying it. Was he doing the same? If he was really so afraid of the effect Jodie was having on him, then why hadn't he seized the chance she had offered to get rid of her? Because he wasn't afraid at all. Why should he be? What was there to fear? Jodie meant nothing to him, and when the time came for them to go their separate ways he would be able to do so without a single qualm or regret.

CHAPTER THIRTEEN

THEIR flight from Florence by executive jet, followed by a helicopter pick-up from Heathrow to their hotel, had been accomplished with so much speed and in so much luxury that Jodie felt as though she were taking part in some kind of TV extravaganza rather than real life. They'd been escorted from the helicopter to their suite with a focused concentration on their comfort that had bemused her and made Lorenzo look even more saturnine and arrogant than ever.

The stunningly beautiful seventeenth-century Cotswold stone hotel had originally been a private house. Now owned by a consortium of wealthy entrepreneurs, who had originally bought and remodelled it as an exclusive private members' country club, it catered for the wealthy and demanding. Its Michelin-starred restaurant was fabled and notoriously selective about its clientele, its spa was a favourite haunt of the A-list celebrity set, and it was *the* favourite venue for private events in that same set. A coterie of very wealthy clients were said to have set up a private gambling club there, in which fortunes were lost and made, and the world's style critics had declared it the place they would most like to be.

From the welcoming hallway, with its antiques and air of a country seat home, to the decor of their suite, complete with vases of exactly the same flowers she had had at their wedding and the latest Italian business magazines, everything breathed exclusivity and attention to detail.

This truly was a different world, Jodie thought, as their personal butler assured her that her clothes would be unpacked and pressed within an hour.

'I've arranged for us to have a hire car delivered here today, so that I can familiarise myself with the area ahead of the wedding,' Lorenzo remarked.

'John's parents are holding an open house party tonight. The whole village is invited.'

'We shall be attending?'

Did she really want to? Somehow the heat that had scorched her pride and driven her to long to be able to stand tall amongst those who knew her with a new man at her side had cooled to an indifference that made her wonder why she was here at all.

John, Louise, and the pain they had caused her, had lost their power over her emotions. The life she had known and lived before she had met Lorenzo felt so distant from her now. Already she was making new friends in Florence; she was developing new interests, a wider outlook on life. She could not see herself coming back here at the end of her year of marriage to Lorenzo. But what would she do? Stay in Florence? No, that would be too painful.

Painful? Why? But of course she already knew the answer to that question. She had suspected it the night he had told her about the history of Castillo's hidden paintings. And she had known it the evening she had sat in the Castillo garden and listened to him telling her about his childhood, his feelings.

'I'm not sure that this is a good idea any more,' she told Lorenzo uncomfortably.

'Why not? Because you're afraid of what you might learn about your own feelings?'

'No! There isn't anything to learn about them. I already know how I feel.' How true that was!

She still loved this blind fool of a man who had so stupidly chosen another woman over her, Lorenzo thought angrily.

'You are afraid that when you see this ex-fiancé of yours you will be so overcome that you won't be able to stop yourself from running to him and begging him to take you back?' he suggested grimly.

'That's ridiculous,' Jodie objected. 'Apart from anything else, I'm a married woman now.'

'And you're naïve enough to believe your wedding ring will prove an effective barrier to your emotions?'

'It doesn't have to. I don't have any emotions for John any more. He means nothing to me now. That's why I don't want to go.'

Her voice rang with conviction, and Lorenzo felt his heart slam into his ribs, urging him to ask the question it so badly wanted answered. Ignoring it, he flicked back the sleeve of his jacket without allowing her to reply and told her curtly, 'It's almost lunchtime. I suggest we have something to eat, then we can collect the car and I can familiarise myself with this evening's route.'

The Cotswolds lay drowsing under the warmth of the summer sunshine, its villages filled with coachloads of tourists. And, as she did every summer, Jodie wondered what those drovers who had once brought their sheep to market along these traditional roads would have thought if they could be transported to modern times.

The small market town of Lower Uffington, where Jodie had grown up, was slightly off the normal tourist track, fortunately, and Jodie felt her stomach muscles start to clench with tension as she sat stiffly in the passenger seat of the hired Bentley. Lorenzo negotiated the narrow lanes as they dipped down between familiar grey stone walls and passed the sign that marked the boundary to the town.

Up ahead of them lay the pretty town square, with its traditional wool merchants' houses lining its narrow streets, beyond which the road started to rise towards the Cotswold uplands where sheep still grazed, as they had done for so many centuries. Its wool market had made the town prosperous, and that prosperity was still evident in its buildings.

Her own little cottage was hidden out of sight down a narrow lane, its garden tucking its feet into the small river that ran behind the main street. A pang of mingled pain and nostalgia gripped her, but it wasn't so severe as she had dreaded. Anywhere could be home if it was shared with the person you loved, she realised.

A small sign indicated the opening between two houses that led to the yard belonging to John's father's building business, and Jodie exhaled sharply as she saw John's car parked at the side of the road close to it.

'What is it?' Lorenzo demanded.

'Nothing.'

And that was the truth. The sight of John's car, which in the early days of their break-up would have filled her with aching pain and loss, now didn't affect her at all—apart from a slight feeling of relief once they had driven past it, in case John himself should have appeared and seen her.

At the end of the town, set in its own pretty green, was the church, small and squat, its stained glass windows picked out by the sunlight. Preparations were obviously already in hand for tomorrow's wedding, Jodie recognised as she saw bunches of white flowers tied up with white ribbon and netting ornamenting the old-fashioned gate.

John's family, like her own, had been here for many generations. John's parents were relatively well to do, and their converted farmhouse with its large garden was just outside the town.

'Can we stop?' Jodie asked Lorenzo.

'If you wish.' He swung the car round into the small car park, and brought it to a halt.

There was one thing she did want to do, Jodie acknowledged. One very personal visit she had to make.

'There's no need to come with me,' she told Lorenzo as she reached to open the car door. 'I shan't be very long.'

'I may as well. I need to stretch my legs,' Lorenzo answered her.

She could see him frowning when she headed for the church. And his frown deepened when, instead of using the main gate, with its floral decorations, she chose to make a small detour and open a much smaller gate which led across the immaculate green and then behind the church to the graveyard.

No one else seemed to be around, but even if there had been, and she had seen someone she knew, Jodie would not have allowed herself to be detained. She had known when she stood in the church in Florence, making her vows to Lorenzo, that this was something she wanted to do.

She took the familiar narrow path that wove its way between large mossed grey tombstones, so ancient that their engraving had almost worn away, heading deeper into the graveyard until she came to the place she wanted.

There, set into the mown grass beneath a canopy of soft leaves, was the small plaque that marked a shared grave.

'My parents,' she told Lorenzo simply.

Tears blurred her eyes, and her hand shook slightly as she reached into her handbag and carefully withdrew the small box in which she had stored the petals from her wedding bouquet. Taking them out, she scattered them tenderly on her parents' grave.

When she turned to look at Lorenzo a huge lump formed in her throat. His head was bowed in prayer.

'It's silly, I know, but I wanted them to know…' She stopped and bit her lip.

'Do you want to go inside the church?' Lorenzo asked.

Jodie shook her head. 'No. They'll be getting it ready for the wedding and I don't want…'

'You don't want what? To confront the friend who stole your fiancé? I thought that was why we are here?'

'John's an adult. No one forced him to break his engagement to me for Louise.' Her head had begun to ache slightly. 'Can we go back to the car?'

Lorenzo shrugged. 'If that is what you want.'

What she wanted was for Lorenzo to love her as she had discovered she loved him. What she wanted was to be back in Florence with him, living her life with him, creating a future with him.

'I'm getting a headache,' she told him instead.

'It is probably anxiety. What exactly are you hoping for tonight, Jodie?'

You. I'm hoping for you to look at me and love me.

'I'm not hoping for anything.'

'No? You're not hoping secretly that John will see you and recognise that it is you he wants after all?'

'That's not going to happen.'

'But you want it to?'

'No.'

They were back at the car, and Jodie was so engrossed in rejecting Lorenzo's suggestion that she didn't notice the woman looking sharply at her until a familiar voice announced in surprise, 'Jodie? Good heavens! I thought you were still away.'

Lucy Hartley—whose husband worked for John's father!

Somehow or other Jodie managed to produce the necessary smile. 'It's just a flying visit,' she explained. 'I wanted to show my...my husband—'

'Your husband? You're *married*?'

To Jodie's relief, Lorenzo stepped forward and extended his hand. Quickly Jodie performed the introductions, watching Lucy's eyes widen as she did so.

'You'll be going to John's parents' open house party this evening, will you?' she enquired.

'We certainly hope to do so,' Lorenzo answered smoothly, before Jodie could say anything. 'If we won't be encroaching. Jodie has told me so much about her home and her friends, and I'm looking forward to meeting them.'

'Oh, no. I'm sure that Sheila and Bill will be only

too delighted.' Lucy was beaming. 'I'll certainly tell them I've seen you. Where are you staying, just in case anyone asks?'

Reluctantly Jodie told her, and saw how her eyes widened a little more in recognition of the exclusivity of the hotel.

'My! You have gone up in the world, Jodie!'

Jodie could feel her face starting to burn.

'We must go—but hopefully we shall see you this evening,' Lorenzo offered politely, quickly steering Jodie away before she could give vent to her feelings.

'That woman is such a snob,' she complained angrily as Lorenzo unlocked the car and opened the door for her. 'The moment I mentioned the hotel she was all over us like a rash. And she doesn't even know about your title.'

Lorenzo closed the passenger door and walked round to get into his own side of the car.

As soon as he had started the engine, Jodie told him fiercely, 'Lorenzo, I don't want to go tonight. When I first said that I wanted to, I wasn't thinking things through properly. I don't think we should go.'

'We can hardly not go now,' Lorenzo pointed out calmly. 'We will be expected.'

She ought to be grateful to Lorenzo, Jodie knew. He had rearranged his schedule in order to accommodate this visit for her, and now here she was, telling him that she didn't want to be here.

Lorenzo looked at Jodie's averted profile. He could see the effect the thought of seeing her ex-fiancé and his bride-to-be was having on her, and how much it was upsetting her. So why was he insisting on her doing so? What was he trying to prove that was worth proving? Why didn't he put his foot down on the accelerator, head for the hotel and take her back to Italy before she could change her mind? Once there, he would have nearly a whole year...

A year in which to what? To persuade her to remain married to him? That was what he wanted, was it?

What if it was? It didn't mean anything other than that he was beginning to feel that it would be easier to remain married to her than not to do so. Marriage gave a man a certain sense of purpose and stability. Just because previously he had not considered the value of an old-fashioned arranged marriage, that did not mean he was so inflexible in his thinking that he could not recognise it now. He and Jodie were married, after all; there was much to be said from a practical point of view for them staying married.

He would still be able to maintain his emotional barriers. Once he had assured himself that she accepted that this ex-fiancé of hers was now unavailable to her, and a part of her past, he felt confident that they could develop a working relationship.

And a sexual relationship? His body tightened in betrayal.

Jodie in turn would have the protection of a husband and a life of comfort. There could even be children, if she wished. He frowned sharply as this magnanimous thought provoked a reaction within his body and his emotions that went a whole lot farther than any mere sense of self-laudatory approval of his generosity. He had never previously considered the production of children an essential part of his life plan—he had more than enough male relatives to produce the next Duce—but with the future of the Castillo to be considered it made sense for him to have heirs of his own to hand it on to. And Jodie would not desert her children.

He braked sharply to avoid a cyclist, mentally denying that his immediate and instinctive belief was a rash emotional reaction rather than one based on logic.

He wouldn't, he decided as he turned into the hotel grounds, make any firm decision until after tonight, when he had seen how Jodie reacted to the sight of her ex-fiancé. If after that, and further careful thought, he was convinced that their marriage had a future, once they were back in Italy he would tell her so.

She really wished she hadn't ever said she wanted to do this. Jodie studied her reflection in the bedroom mirror and smoothed a nervous hand over her beautifully cut cream crêpe trousers.

'Ready?'

Numbly she nodded her head as Lorenzo walked into her bedroom. He looked exactly what he was: a tall, dark, impossibly handsome and even more impossibly arrogant, totally male man—the kind of man any woman would be attracted to. The kind of man any woman could see would make her emotionally vulnerable if she wasn't careful. What a pity *she* hadn't been woman enough to recognise that right from the start.

She could see the way he was looking at her, but if she had been hoping for a compliment about her appearance she was in for a disappointment, she realised.

As she started to head for the bedroom door he reached out and stopped her. For one wild heartbeat her head was filled with impossible images and even more implausible scenarios—Lorenzo taking her into his arms and refusing to let her go; Lorenzo insisting that he wanted to keep her here in this room and make love to her; Lorenzo telling her passionately that he loved her. Weakly she refused to admit how much she wished they could actually happen, and tried to focus instead on what Lorenzo was saying to her.

'I think you should wear this tonight.'

She looked down at the familiar emerald ring.

'It is, after all, your betrothal ring,' Lorenzo pointed out, 'and a symbol of our relationship.'

Wordlessly Jodie reached out to take it from him, but he shook his head slightly and took hold of her hand, sliding the ring onto her finger himself.

Tears stung her eyes. Foolish, foolish tears that betrayed to her just how badly she had misjudged her own vulnerability. Only a woman deeply in love could feel the way she felt right now.

It didn't take them very long to reach John's parents' home. A marquee had been set up in the garden, and the field adjacent to the house already contained several rows of neatly parked cars.

They were greeted at the gate by a young dinner-suited cousin of John's, who recognised Jodie and gaped slightly at her, then blushed.

'I suppose we ought to try and find John's parents first,' Jodie told Lorenzo.

'That sounds a good idea,' he agreed.

'What's that you've got?' Jodie asked curiously, noticing the small parcel he was carrying.

'Hand-made chocolates for our hostess,' he informed her, adding, 'I'll have a dozen bottles of wine sent to our host later.'

Jodie gave him a rueful look and reached into her

bag, producing an almost identically wrapped box. 'Snap,' she told him, laughing up at him, smiling naturally for the first time since they had arrived in England.

'Jodie! Lucy said that she'd seen you in town this afternoon.'

Jodie's smile vanished as she saw John's mother standing in front of them.

Instinctively she moved closer to Lorenzo. John's mother was scrutinising them both very sharply, Jodie saw, and her chin suddenly lifted as she looked back at her.

'I hope we aren't gatecrashing?' she said calmly. 'May I introduce my husband to you, Sheila?'

'Your husband? Lucy did say, but I wasn't sure... My goodness, this is a surprise.' John's mother gave a small tinkling laugh. 'And there we were, worrying about you being upset and broken-hearted.'

'Jodie recognised very quickly that calf love means nothing when one finds the real thing.' Lorenzo's smile might have taken some of the sting out of his words, but Jodie still gave him a sharp look, and wasn't surprised to see the cold gleam in his eyes.

'Well, I hope the two of you will be very happy, Mr...' Sheila began insincerely.

'Lorenzo Niccolo d'Este, Duce di Montesavro,' Lorenzo introduced himself, with cool, insouciant confidence.

'You're a duke?' Sheila asked faintly.

Lorenzo inclined his head in assent, and said suavely, 'But please do call me Lorenzo.'

Suddenly Jodie was almost beginning to enjoy herself.

'And how is Councillor Higgins?' she asked

sweetly, turning to explain to Lorenzo, 'John's father is a local councillor.'

John's mother had, she noticed, begun to turn an unflattering shade of pink. It was funny how Jodie was beginning to remember all those occasions on which John's parents had let her know that they considered her to be just that little bit inferior to them.

Of course she was behaving very badly, she knew, but sometimes behaving badly could be fun!

'That's one of the benefits of being married to you and not to John,' she murmured to Lorenzo as they moved away to allow Sheila to greet some new arrivals.

'What is?'

'No mother-in-law,' she said succinctly.

By now they had begun to attract rather a lot of attention, as people recognised her and did a small double take before turning to look more closely and curiously.

Lorenzo had put his hand beneath her elbow in a very solicitous manner—probably because he was afraid that she might trip in her high heels and end up flat on her face and thus disgrace them both, Jodie reflected as she managed to negotiate the unlevel ground.

'Jodie...'

She spun round with a genuine smile as she heard the warmth and pleasure in the voice of the local doctor.

'Dr Philips!'

He gave her an enthusiastic hug and then smiled down at her. 'You're looking well.'

'Italian food, Italian sunshine—'

'And an Italian husband,' Lorenzo cut in, making the doctor laugh.

'I shouldn't say this,' the doctor whispered with a grin, 'but I always thought you were wasted on young John. A nice enough lad, but a bit on the weak side—and very much under his mother's thumb.'

'Poor John—that's not very kind,' Jodie protested, but she still laughed.

Lorenzo lifted two glasses of wine from a passing waiter's tray and handed Jodie one.

She still hadn't seen either Louise or John, although she thought she had caught sight of Louise's parents. She had always liked Louise's mother, but she had no wish to see her now. Naturally, as a mother, she would support her daughter no matter what that daughter might have done.

And besides, honesty compelled Jodie to admit that if Louise and John did love one another, then surely it was only right and proper that they should be together. She no longer cared what they did, because her own life and her own feelings had moved on. She looked at Lorenzo and allowed herself the pleasure of a private fantasy in which she would suggest to him that they leave and go back to their hotel. He'd agree with satisfying alacrity and an even more satisfyingly intimate smile because of the sensual pleasures to come. She gave a small sigh as she relinquished this unlikely but, oh, so alluring scenario.

'Your leg?' Lorenzo questioned immediately, misunderstanding the reason for her sigh.

Should she fib and pretend that it was bothering her so that they could leave?

But before she could say anything the vicar and his

wife had joined them, and Lorenzo had become involved in a discussion with them about Florence.

Jodie took a small sip of her drink, and was looking for somewhere to put her glass when she heard Louise saying sharply, 'I want a word with you!'

Louise was on her own, and there was no sign of John.

'Don't think I don't know what you're up to and what you're doing here,' her ex-friend whispered angrily.

Jodie could feel her face starting to burn. She was guiltily aware of her original motive in coming here. But perhaps there was a chance, instead, to forgive—to end the bitterness between them?

'This is real life, Jodie, not some romantic novel,' Louise was saying. 'John isn't going to take one look at you and throw me over to come back to you.'

'Good. Because I honestly don't want him to,' Jodie told her. 'Louise, I'm married now, and I—'

'Married? You?' Louise gave her a contemptuous look. 'You might have taken everyone else in, but I don't believe it for one minute. My guess is that you aren't married at all—you certainly don't look it—and I think your supposed "husband" is some actor you've hired.' She glared at Jodie angrily. 'No man as good-looking as he is would want you, with that leg of yours. Everyone's laughing at you. You know that, don't you? Pretending that you've married a duke. As if! And that ridiculous ring that you're wearing,' she added, her lip curling. 'It's so obvious that it's fake—just like you and just like your marriage. I'll bet you're still that same pathetic little virgin you were when John dumped you.'

Instinctively Jodie looked towards Lorenzo, a silent plea in her eyes. He looked back at her.

And then he was coming towards them, responding to the silent emotional message she had sent him. Relief filled her. It was all she could do not to throw herself into his arms and beg him to take her away.

Lorenzo felt Jodie's pain in his own heart. Fury and an instinctive desire to protect her boiled through him. He had heard what Louise had said to her, and he hadn't needed the silent plea she had sent him, begging for his help, to take him to her side. He wanted to snatch her up and take her away from these people who did not appreciate her, from the man who had not loved her as she so deserved to be loved…as he in his stupidity had tried to refuse to love her. But now that love was filling him and driving out everything else, everyone else. Nothing, no one mattered other than Jodie and her happiness.

He reached her and took hold of her hand, watching as relief shone emotionally in her eyes.

'For your information,' he told Louise coldly, 'I am not an actor. Jodie and I are married, and I worship the beauty of her body almost as much as I love the sweetness of her nature. And as for the authenticity of both my title and my family betrothal ring…' The look he gave Louise was so withering that Jodie was surprised it didn't shrivel her to nothing on the spot.

'Since you are engaged to a man who obviously cannot tell what is genuine and what is not, I suppose one might *expect* to hear you expressing ill-informed and ignorant opinions,' he continued levelly. 'And so far as our reason for being here goes…' Lorenzo now raised his voice slightly, as a curious crowd gathered around them. 'That was my decision. I wanted to see where Jodie had grown up, to meet the people she had grown up amongst. And I confess I also wanted to meet the man who was foolish enough to give her up. Jodie merely wanted to offer you both her best wishes.'

Lorenzo was still holding her hand, Jodie recognised, and what was more he was holding it very firmly in his own as he moved protectively closer to her. Automatically she leaned in to him, welcoming the sensation of his body absorbing the sick, trembling shock of her own.

'What a pitiful creature you are,' Lorenzo said to Louise in a very quiet voice, inaudible to most of those around them. 'You steal a friend's fiancé, and then, because of your inadequacy and lack of emotional depth, you are forced to live in fear of losing him back to her.'

Louise turned from red to white as Lorenzo's cutting words hit home, and suddenly the woman Jodie had always thought of as such a beauty actually looked ugly.

John had come hurrying over to Louise's side and was looking helplessly back and forth between the women. When she looked at him Jodie recognised how poorly he compared with Lorenzo, and how weak he was as a man. If she hadn't already realised she didn't love him any more, she surely would have done so now.

'Are you ready to leave?' Lorenzo asked Jodie.

Silently she nodded her head.

CHAPTER FOURTEEN

THEY had driven back to their hotel in silence, and Jodie was only thankful that Lorenzo wasn't saying anything. Now that they were back in their suite she realised how shocked and distressed Louise's spiteful attack had left her feeling.

All she wanted was the privacy of her room, so that she could give way to the tears that weren't far off, and to her relief Lorenzo made no comment when she said quickly, 'My head aches. I…I think I might as well have an early night.'

In her room she undressed and then showered, drying herself quickly before padding across to the bed and slipping between the cool clean sheets, reflecting that it was just as well that Louise had not known she and Lorenzo were sleeping in separate rooms.

She tensed as she heard a firm tap on her bedroom door and Lorenzo calling out, 'I've ordered you some supper. I'll bring it in for you.'

It was too late to tell him that she didn't want it. He was already opening the door and pushing a heavily laden trolley into the room.

'It's just a cold salad and a pot of tea. I remember you said you liked to drink tea when you had a headache. Or is your pain that of a heartache?' he asked her dryly.

Jodie bit her lip and struggled to sit up, whilst holding on to the protective cover of the bedding. Taking a deep breath, she said huskily, 'Lorenzo, I haven't thanked you yet for...for...for supporting me with what you said to Louise.'

'You are my wife. When it comes to the validity of our marriage being questioned, naturally you have my support. Equally naturally, I could not allow that foolish woman to make her ridiculous accusations unchecked.'

Jodie shook her head. 'We both know it wasn't your idea that we should come here.'

'No, it was yours, because you wanted to see your ex-fiancé. You are better off without him, you know,' he told her coolly. 'The impression I gained from the people I spoke with is that he is a rather weak and shallow young man, very much still dominated by his mother.'

'Louise's family are quite well off, and I suppose that, coupled with Sheila's concerns about my health, would have made her think Louise would be a better wife for John—not that I want him. He means nothing to me now. I can see him for what he is, and I think I'm lucky not to be marrying him.'

Lorenzo frowned. 'You sound as though you really mean that.'

'I do. I'd stopped loving him before I left England. Coming back has just confirmed what I already knew.' In more ways than one, she admitted, but of course she couldn't tell Lorenzo that coming back and seeing John had shown her just how strong her love for Lorenzo was compared with the feelings she had once thought she had for John. She still had her pride, and that pride was stinging badly now from Louise's attack on her.

She chewed on her bottom lip and then said unhappily, 'I should have realised that people would guess that our marriage isn't real and that you don't want me.' She laughed a little wildly. 'I suppose I must have "unwanted virgin" written all over me, what with my leg, and—'

'What nonsense is this?' Lorenzo demanded, putting down the cup of tea he had been pouring for her and coming over to stand beside the bed.

'It isn't nonsense,' Jodie persisted miserably. 'John rejected me because of my leg, and it's because of it that I'm still a virgin. I hate knowing that other people pity me, and…and look down on me because of it,' she told him fiercely. 'And I just wish that…'

'That what?'

'That when Louise looked at me she had seen a true woman.'

Lorenzo sat down on the bed next to her.

'If that is really what you want, it is achieved easily enough,' he told her smokily. 'Because, far from sharing your idiotic ex-fiancé's opinion, I happen to desire you very much.'

Jodie swallowed and squeaked uncertainly, 'You…you do?'

'Yes. And, what's more, I'm more than willing to prove it to you. We've got tonight,' Lorenzo told her. 'And if you wish tomorrow you can witness their wretched marriage with all the bloom of a woman whose sexual curiosity has been answered and whose sexual hunger has been satisfied.'

Lorenzo was offering to make love to her?

A little apprehensively, she wetted her lips with her tongue tip. 'But…but before you said that we couldn't because—'

'The hotel management here are most forward thinking.'

When Jodie looked puzzled he explained, 'There is a pack of condoms with the other toiletries they have supplied.'

'Oh. Oh, I see…'

'The choice is yours,' Lorenzo told her.

His willingness to have sex with her meant nothing in any real sense, Jodie knew. It was sex he was offering her, that was all. Not the love she longed for, and certainly not the future and the permanence. But still she wanted what he was offering.

Jodie swallowed hard and looked at him.

'Then I choose to say yes.'

When he got up off the bed and walked away from her all she could think was that the pain was a million times worse, in a million different ways, than it had been when John had walked away from her. But then she saw that instead of going to the door Lorenzo had stopped beside the trolley. He had removed a bottle of champagne from an ice bucket and was opening it to fill two glasses.

He walked back to the bed with them and handed her one.

'To tonight and what we will give one another. May it be everything you wish it to be,' he toasted her softly.

Apprehensively Jodie took a sip of the sparkling champagne, and then trembled as Lorenzo took the glass from her and kissed her.

His mouth tasted of champagne and of him, and she clung to that thought whilst his tongue-tip stroked her lips and then teased them apart.

He kissed her until she couldn't think beyond the pleasure of their shared intimacy and her own desire for more; until she had reached out to him and wrapped her arms around his neck whilst her lips parted eagerly under his; until they were lying together on the bed and his hands were caressing her naked body as he removed the unwanted barriers between them.

Skin on skin with the man she loved: could there be anything more sensual or more desire-inducing? Jodie wondered deliriously as she allowed herself the luxury of exploring the warm flesh padding Lorenzo's muscles whilst his hands skimmed and then shaped her body with slow, purposeful sensuality.

He kissed the hollow at the base of her throat, and then the hollow between her breasts, rimming the indentation of her navel whilst she shivered with pleasure and sighed softly.

Only when he caressed her injured leg did she tense and waver, shuddering anxiously and trying to pull away. But Lorenzo refused to release her, bending his head to kiss the criss-cross pattern of her scars.

'No...' It was the first time she had spoken, her plea sharp and filled with pain.

Ignoring her, Lorenzo told her softly, 'I thought the first time I saw you that you had the most wonderfully long legs. I knew then that I wanted to feel them wrapped around me whilst I possessed you.'

'You couldn't have thought that,' Jodie protested. 'You were so angry!'

She saw his mouth curve into a genuinely amused smile. 'Didn't you know, little virgin, that a man can be both angry and aroused? Your ex-friend is a fool. No man worthy of the name would ever reject you, Jodie.'

'My leg,' she protested.

Lorenzo kissed her scar a second time.

'Your leg is all the more beautiful because it carries the evidence of your courage.'

Emotional tears filled her eyes, but before she could shed them Lorenzo had started to kiss his way up the inside of her thigh, and other, more intense emotions were gripping her.

His hand covered her sex. Slowly he began to caress it, until she was arching up to press herself closer to his touch, her fingers digging into the warm flesh of his shoulders as her legs opened wider for him and his tongue joined his fingers in an erotic exploration of her arousal.

She moaned with pleasure when she felt him penetrate her wetness to ease one finger inside her, stroking her and then slowly moving deeper. Immediately her muscles tightened eagerly around it and her body pulsed fiercely. Lorenzo positioned himself so that he could kiss her breasts whilst he slowly stroked her intimately, a second finger joining the first, the pleasure of their movement inside her making her cry out, then cry out again as Lorenzo answered her appeal with the sensual rake of his teeth against her stiff nipple.

Her body was moving of its own accord, seeking an intimate rhythm that came from deep inside her, accompanied by a small growl of female frustration.

'You want me inside you?' Lorenzo asked her thickly.

Jodie nodded her head and dug her fingers into his flesh more tightly as he positioned her, lifting her and then reaching for a pillow, which he eased beneath her hips whilst the frustration inside her grew.

She had no apprehensions, no reservations, only an aching female hunger, and she watched openly as he positioned himself over her, her senses delighting in the sight of him, so thick and strong.

More easing himself into her than thrusting, Lorenzo watched the expressions chase one another across her face as her muscles accepted his thickness, closing tightly round it.

'Do you want more?' he asked.

Jodie took a deep breath and whispered fiercely, 'Yes. All of you. I want all of you...'

She could feel him filling her so completely that the sensation of him within her made her catch her breath, and then rake her nails against his back as he moved out and then in deeper, with rhythmic thrusts that took her breath and drove her to want more and still more, until she was moving with him, eagerly giving up her own control to him, as her body became his to fit to himself and pleasure until she could not endure that pleasure any more.

She felt the onset of her orgasm gripping her, so much more intense than what she was already used to, so very different, and it took her pleasure into a different dimension that was filled with the feel of him inside her. She cried out to him, and then cried out again, as he filled her with his own release, clinging to him as she murmured words of love and pleasure.

Lorenzo looked towards the bed where Jodie still lay sleeping, and wondered despairingly how it was possible for his whole life to have changed between one heartbeat and the next.

He had looked at her in that English garden, seen the pain and despair in her eyes, and known immediately that his savage need to protect her was born of love.

Love. Had it been there from their first meeting, unrecognised by him because he had not wanted to recognise it? Or had it grown as his knowledge of her had grown? Did it even matter?

Jodie opened her eyes.

'Lorenzo.' She smiled, and then blushed a little.

'Are you okay? No regrets?'

Jodie shook her head. 'No regrets.'

'You don't wish that it had been John?' Lorenzo questioned wryly.

'No. I wanted it to be you.'

'Mmm. Well, since it was me, I think we need to talk about the future.' He took a deep breath and looked away from her. 'How would you feel about us making this marriage permanent?'

When she didn't reply he turned round, frowning, only to see the tears spilling from her eyes.

'I can't say yes,' Jodie wept. 'I want to, but it wouldn't be fair to you. Not when…'

'Not when what?'

'Not when I know that I love you,' she admitted, very softly.

Lorenzo went over to the bed and sat down on it next to her.

'Would it make any difference if I admitted that I've fallen in love with you?'

'Only if it's true,' Jodie answered him gravely.

He had reached for her hand and twined his fingers through her own, and now he was lifting their inter-locked hands to his lips so that he could kiss her palm. Her heart was thudding heavily, slamming against her chest wall. She wanted so much to believe him, but she was afraid to do so.

'I didn't use a condom,' he told her quietly.

Jodie swallowed. 'You mean you forgot?'

'No, I mean I chose not to. Because I wanted our pleasure to be skin to skin, with no barriers between us, and because I can't think of anything more wonderful than knowing we could have created our child.'

'You trust me enough for that?'

'Yes, and more than that. I trust you enough to admit that I love you. I saw the way you looked at me when Louise was insulting you. I saw that you were asking not just for my help but for me.'

He leaned forward and kissed her softly, then drew back from her. Jodie gave a small murmur of protest and moved closer, pressing her lips to his.

'Tell me properly that you love me,' she whispered. 'Show me.'

EPILOGUE

'Look at their faces,' Jodie whispered to Lorenzo as they stood side by side in the Castillo courtyard, watching the expressions of the children who were just being helped from the specially adapted bus that had brought them from the airport. The first of the young victims of war to come to the Castillo under the scheme Lorenzo had initiated.

It was a year almost to the day since they had returned from England, committed to one another and their marriage, and to the accomplishment of Lorenzo's dream.

In the state apartments the restored paintings glowed with the richness of their vibrant colours. In the newly painted and furnished dormitories, beds waited for the children and trained therapists waited in the new extension housing the swimming pool, treatment rooms and gym.

'This is such a wonderful thing you are doing, Lorenzo,' Jodie told him emotionally. 'You are giving so much to so many, bringing so much joy to their lives.'

'No more than the joy you have brought to mine,' he told her, bending his head to kiss her, and then laughing as their three-month-old son, whom she was holding in her arms, reached out to grip his finger.

The City-Girl
Bride

PENNY JORDAN

PROLOGUE

THE head of the Perfect Matches Department, English Speaking Division, scratched the top of his wing in irritation.

'Now look what's happened,' he complained to his newest and least experienced recruit. 'They've called a summit meeting of all the top angels in Cupid Department to discuss the current state of romance. Far too many people are refusing to fall in love and make commitments. If this continues we shall be out of business and a fine thing that would be. Of course they would call this wretched conference when I'm already short-staffed and I've just finished drawing up this session's list of ideally matched pairs. It's too late to put things on hold now, and besides—' he glowered darkly '—this session I'm determined that we're going to meet our target, I am not having that pompous idiot from the Third Agers Section telling me yet again that he's matched up more couples than us. But there's just no one to do the work.'

'There's me.' His newest assistant reminded him eagerly.

The head of the department sighed as he studied the hopeful smile of his trainee recruit. Enthusiasm for one's job was all very well, and to be applauded of course,

5

but in this particular recruit's case that enthusiasm needed to be tempered by the caution of experience and time. However, right now... Right now he had six couples to get together: couples who as yet had no idea that they were meant for one another, couples whose romances needed to be set in motion asap.

Reluctantly he acknowledged that on this occasion he would have to bow to expediency and ignore his forebodings. Handing over his carefully compiled list, he told his junior 'Every one of these couples has been carefully vetted and checked for compatibility. In this department we do not put couples together unless we are sure they will stay together. Everything is set in place and nothing can go wrong. All you have to do is make sure that each and every one of them is in the right place at the right time. You must follow my instructions exactly. No experimentation or short cuts. Do you understand?'

All students had to learn, of course, but it was, to say the least, unfortunate that this particular student's experimentation had led to a New York socialite's pedigree chow falling desperately in love with her neighbour's prize-winning Burmese cat. Luckily the outcome had not been totally without merit, and the marriage which had ensued between the socialite and her neighbour had been a very satisfactory conclusion to the whole affair. He had been working towards pairing her off with someone very different, but there you are...

*　　*　　*

'Hi there. What are you doing?'

The new recruit grimaced as one of the naughtiest zephyrs blew playfully on his wings.

'I'm busy,' he responded loftily. 'So go away and bother someone else.'

With hindsight he acknowledged that it had probably been the wrong thing to say. It was common knowledge that this particular zephyr positively enjoyed her reputation for boisterous behaviour, and perhaps it was silly of him to have spread out all the head of department's carefully written notes and instructions, along with the slips on which the names of the humans they related to were written.

'Go away like this, do you mean?' she challenged him, taking a deep breath and sending all his precious papers flying as she exhaled noisily over them.

Of course afterwards she was contrite, and helped him to gather everything up. It was surprising just how much power there was in that ethereal frame, and by the time they had finally collected everything he was feeling out of breath himself.

But that was nothing to the feeling of dread filling him as he tried frantically to remember which couples had been paired together.

The zephyr did what she could, and in the end he was as sure as he could be that he knew what he was supposed to do.

'So, which couple are you going to do first?' she asked him.

He took a deep breath. 'This one,' he told her, showing her their names.

She frowned as she looked at the names and their addresses. 'But how are they going to meet?' she asked him.

'I don't know,' he admitted. 'I'll think of something.'

'Can I help?' she begged eagerly. This was so much more fun than blowing a few leaves off trees, which was all she was ever allowed to do.

'No,' he denied firmly, quickly changing his mind when he saw her taking another deep breath.

As a first step in bringing the two ideally matched partners together, his job was to engineer a meeting between them according to the instructions he had been left.

Engineer a meeting... Right...

CHAPTER ONE

MAGGIE stared in disbelief at the downpour which had suddenly appeared out of nowhere, turning the road she had been driving along into a vast puddle and making her head ache with the tension of concentrating. From the moment she had seen the sale advertised she had been determined to buy the house. She was sure that it was exactly what her adored grandmother needed to lift her out of her current unhappiness.

Of course Maggie knew that nothing and no one could ever replace her grandfather in her grandmother's life, but Maggie was convinced that returning to live in the house where her grandparents had started their married life, a house that was filled with memories of their shared love, would help to take her grandmother's mind off the sadness of her loss. And Maggie was a woman who, once her mind was made up about anything or anyone, refused to change it. Which was why she was such a successful businesswoman—successful enough to be able to attend the auction being held to sell off the large Shropshire estate on which her grandparents had begun their married lives, in the rented house which was now being auctioned for sale.

Maggie had grown up hearing stores of Shropshire and its rich farmlands, but Maggie was a city girl; farms, rain, mud, animals, farmers—they were not for her. The company she owned and ran as a headhunter, her modern city apartment, her friends—single career woman like her—these were the things she enjoyed and valued. But her love for her grandparents was something else, something special. They had provided her with a secure and loving home when her own parents had split up, they had encouraged and praised her, supported her emotionally, loved her, and it both hurt and frightened her to see her once strong grandmother looking so frail and lost.

Until Maggie had seen the Shopcutte estate advertised for sale—its Georgian mansion, farmlands and estate properties, including the pretty Dower House where her grandparents had spent the first years of their marriage—she had been in despair, not knowing how to lift her grandmother's spirits and terrified, if she was honest, that she might actually lose her. But now she knew she had found the perfect means of cheering her up. It was imperative that she was successful at the sale auction, that she acquired the house. And she was determined that she would.

But for this appalling and unforecasted torrential rain she would have reached her destination by now—the small country town adjacent to the estate, where the auction was to be held and where she had booked herself a room at the town's only decent hotel.

When the rain had first started, appearing from nowhere out of a hitherto cloudless sky, she had had to slow her speed down to a crawl. The sky was far from blue now, in fact it was nearly black, and the road was empty of any other traffic as it narrowed and dipped at a perilously acute angle.

Was this really the A-class road she had been following? Impossible, surely, that she might have made a wrong turning. She simply did not do things like that. If there was one thing that Maggie prided herself on it was being in control.

From the top of her glossily groomed, perfectly cut blonde hair to the tips of her equally perfectly pedicured and painted toes Maggie epitomised feminine elegance and self-discipline. Her size eight figure was the envy of her friends—and that flawless skin, that equally flawless personal life, as devoid of the untidiness of emotional entanglements as Maggie's home was devoid of clutter. Yes, Maggie was a woman to be reckoned with: a woman no man would dare not to respect or would risk tangling antagonistically with. After seeing the havoc and mess caused by her parents' various sexual and emotional relationships, Maggie had decided that she intended to remain safely and tidily single. And so far none of the many men she had met had done anything to make her change that decision.

'But you are far too gorgeous to be alone,' one would-be suitor had told her, only to be given one of her most scathing and dismissive looks.

Perhaps somewhere deep down inside herself she did sometimes secretly wonder just why she should be so immune to the dangerous intensity of emotional and physical desire experienced by other women, but she refused to allow herself to dwell on such thoughts. Why should she? She was happy the way she was. Or at least she would be once she had got this auction out of the way and was the owner of the Dower House.

It was ridiculous that she should have had to come out here at all, she fumed as she began a steep descent. She had tried to buy the house prior to the auction, but the agent had refused to sell it. So here she was, and...

'Oh, no. I don't believe it,' she protested out loud as the road turned sharply and she saw in front of her a sign marked 'Ford'.

Ford...as in fording a river, as in some archaic means of crossing it surely more suitable to the Middle Ages rather than the current century. But that was what the sign said, and there in front of her was a shallow river, with the road running right through it and up the hill on its opposite side.

And this was an A road? Irritably Maggie started to drive through the water. That was the country for you, she fumed grittily.

She could hear above the noise of her car engine a loud rushing sound that for some reason made the hair at the back of her neck prickle, and then she saw why. Coming towards her at an unbelievable speed along the course of the river was a wall of water almost as high as the car itself.

For the first time in her life, Maggie panicked. The car's wheels spun as she depressed the accelerator, but the car itself didn't move, and the wall of water...

*   *   *

Finn was not in a good mood. His meeting had taken much longer than he had planned and now he was going to be late getting back. His mind was preoccupied with his own thoughts, so it gave him a shock to see the unfamiliar car motionless in the middle of the ford, but it gave him even more of a shock to see the swollen race of river threatening to overwhelm it.

He was in no mood to rescue unwanted and uninvited visitors with no more sense than to try to attempt to cross the river during what had to be the worst cloudburst the area had known in living memory, and in such an unsuitable vehicle. He frowned ominously as he dropped the Land Rover into its lowest gear.

He might have made the fortune which had enabled him to retire from the world of commerce by using what his mentor had once told him was the keenest and shrewdest financial brain he had ever come across, but that world and everything it encompassed was not one he ever wanted to return to. This was his *métiere*—what he wanted. But he wanted it permanently. And the lease on Ryle Farm could not be renewed when it ran out in three months' time, which was why he had decided to bid for the Shopcutte estate. He knew that the house, the land and the other properties were being auctioned off in separate lots, but Finn wanted them all. He wanted and he intended to keep the estate intact, and with it his own privacy.

Protecting his privacy; guarding his solitude was vitally important to Finn, and fortunately, thanks to those hectic years he had spent working as one of the City's most successful money market dealers, he had the financial means to buy that privacy and solitude—in the shape of the Shopcutte estate.

Those people who had known him in his early twenties wouldn't be able to reconcile the man he had been then with the man he was now. He was a decade older now, of course, and in those days... In those days his high earning power had gained him an entrée into a fast-living world of trust fund socialites, models, money and drugs. But, as he had quickly come to discover, it was a world driven by greed and filled with insincerity. He had been too hardheaded to succumb to the easy availability of sex and drugs, but others he had known had not been so wise, or so lucky.

Already disenchanted with what had been going on around him, Finn had been filled with a sense of revulsion for the life he was living after the death of one of his colleagues from an accidental drug overdose. Finn had been openly and brazenly propositioned by girls crazed with need by their addiction, had attended parties thrown by clients where those same girls and the drugs that had ruined their lives had been handed round like sweets. It was a world that valued material wealth and held human beings cheap, and one day Finn had woken up and known that it could no longer be his world.

Perhaps unfairly, he had come to blame big city culture for sins that should have more appropriately been apportioned to his fellow human beings. But his own needs had forced him to question what he really wanted out of life, filling him with a craving for peace and a simpler, cleaner, more natural way of life, as well as a loathing for city life and, if he was honest, a wary hostility towards those who lauded it.

His mother had come from farming stock and he had obviously inherited those genes. He had made his plans, taken a calculated gamble on his own judgement which had netted him a profit that had run into millions. His employers had pleaded with him to stay, telling him he could name his own terms, but he had made his decision. Owning his own land would give him the opportunity to grow organic crops as well as breed cattle and increase his small herd of alpaca.

Unlike Maggie, the moment Finn heard the sound of the water thundering towards the ford he knew what it was, and immediately stopped his Land Rover, cursing under his breath as he realised that the huge flood of water filling the riverbed would mean that the ford would be impassable, even for his sturdy four-wheel drive, and that he would end up being marooned on the wrong side of the river. Angrily he looked at Maggie's car. A trendy, top-of-the-range convertible that only a fool would possibly have attempted to take across a flooded ford.

The dangerously fast-flowing water was halfway up the side of the car—and rising. In another few minutes the car would be in danger of being swept completely away, and its blonde-haired driver with it.

Grimly Finn restarted his own vehicle and drove slowly and carefully through the swilling water towards Maggie, gritting his teeth as he felt the powerful surge of the water buffeting the side of the Land Rover and trying to force it downstream.

In her own car, Maggie could not believe what was happening to her. Things like this simply did not happen...especially not to her. How could she possibly be here, in the middle of a flooding river with water creeping higher and higher? She gave a shocked gasp as the car started to move, slewing sideways. She was going to be swept away completely. She might even drown. But she had seen the Land Rover coming up behind her and told herself that she was panicking unnecessarily. If its driver could cross the ford then so could she. Determinedly she tried to restart her car.

Finn simply could not believe his eyes. As he saw Maggie's shiny blonde hair swing across her face when she leaned forward to restart her car he thought he must be hallucinating. What on earth was she doing? Surely she must realise that her car was not going to start? And even if by some remote chance it did...

Drawing alongside her, he carefully brought the Land Rover to a halt and wound down his window.

Maggie saw what he was doing and gave him a supercilious look, which Finn ignored. He could see now that she was a city woman, and his irritation and exasperation with her grew. Gesturing to her to wind down her own window, he returned her look with darkly bitter dislike.

Initially Maggie had intended to ignore his arrogant command—in the City a woman never responded to overtures from unknown men—but then she felt her car move again.

'What the hell do you think you're doing?' Finn demanded irascibly once Maggie had lowered her window. 'You're driving a car, not a submarine.'

His obvious irritation and contempt infuriated Maggie, who was not used to being verbally mauled by the male sex. Normally her looks alone were enough to guarantee that they treated her gently.

'What I am doing,' she responded acidly, 'is trying to ford the river.'

'In this—a flood?' Finn couldn't keep the ire out of his voice.

'There was no flood when I started to cross,' Maggie retaliated hotly, and then gasped as her car started to move again.

'You're going to have to get out of the car,' Finn told her. Any moment now, he suspected, the car would be completely swept away with her in it, if she didn't move quickly, but he was worried that she would start to panic and make the situation even worse than it already was.

'And how do you suggest I do that?' Maggie asked him with a sharp frostiness icing her voice and her eyes. 'Open the door and swim for it?'

'Too dangerous—the current's too strong,' Finn informed her brusquely, ignoring her attempt at sarcasm. Giving her slender body a brisk inspection, he told her crisply, 'You'll have to climb out through the window; there should be enough room. I'm parked close enough

for you to be able to crawl into the back of the Land
Rover through the rear passenger window.'

'What? You expect me—?' Maggie was almost lost
for words. 'I am wearing a designer suit and a pair of
very expensive shoes, and there is no way I am going
to ruin them by crawling anywhere—least of all into an
extremely muddy Land Rover.'

Finn could feel his blood pressure rising, and along
with it his temper. He had never met anyone who had
irritated him as much as this impossible woman was doing. 'Well, if you stay where you are it won't just be
your shoes you'll be in danger of losing. It could be your
life as well—and not just your own. Have you any idea
of the—?' Finn broke off as her car rocked with the
force of the water buffeting it. He had had enough.

'Move. Now,' he ordered her, and to her own shock
Maggie found that even before he had finished speaking
she was scrambling through her car window.

The feel of two strong male hands supporting her,
almost heaving her towards the Land Rover's open window as though she were a…a sack of potatoes, only
increased her sense of outrage. As she wriggled and
slipped head-first into the rear of the Land Rover the
breath whooshed out of her lungs at precisely the same
time as her shoes slid off her feet.

Without even having the courtesy to check that she
was all right her rescuer was continuing to cross the
river, his vehicle somehow pushing its way through the
flood which had threatened her own car. As she struggled to sit up Maggie saw her car start to move down-

stream as the flooding river finally overwhelmed it. She was shivering with shock and reaction, but the driver of the Land Rover seemed totally unconcerned about her as they finally emerged onto dry land and he started to drive up the hill.

Another few seconds and that idiotic woman would have been swept away with her car, Finn fumed once he had safely negotiated their passage back onto dry land. Now, until the river went down, the farm was effectively marooned. There was no other road off the property, which was enclosed on both sides by steep hills.

'You can drop me in the centre of the town,' Maggie informed him in a dismissive clipped voice. 'Preferably opposite a shoe shop, since I now have no shoes.' And not anything else, she recognised. No luggage, no handbag, no credit cards...

'The centre of *what*?' Finn demanded incredulously. 'Where the hell do you think you are?'

'On the A road, five or so miles from Lampton,' Maggie told him promptly.

'On an A road... Does this look like an A road?' Finn's voice was loaded with male disbelief.

Now that she looked at it—properly—Maggie could see that it didn't. For one thing it was barely more than single track, which meant...which meant that somehow or other she must have taken a wrong turning. But she never took wrong turnings—in any area of her life.

'Things are different in the country,' she informed Finn contentiously. 'Any old road can be an A road.'

Her arrogance infuriated him.

'For your information this is a private road, leading only to a farm…my farm.'

Maggie's soft brown eyes widened. She studied the back of Finn's head whilst she tried to assimilate what he had told her. He had a strong bone structure, and thick, very dark brown hair. His hair needed cutting. It covered the collar of his shirt. She wrinkled her nose fastidiously as she took in the shabbiness of his worn coat. She could almost see the forcefield of male anger and hostility that surrounded him, and she felt equally antagonistic towards him.

'So I must have made a wrong turning somewhere.' She gave a small shrug. Only she knew just how much it cost her to admit that she might have got something wrong.

'If you hadn't virtually hijacked me I would have been able to turn round and—'

'Turn round?' Finn interrupted her with a derisive snort. 'If I hadn't turned up you'd have been damned lucky to be alive right now.'

The brutality of his harsh words sent a shiver running through her, but Maggie refused to let him see it. Instead she did what she had trained herself to do, which was to focus on her ultimate goal and ignore everything else.

'How long will it be before the river goes down?' she asked him. 'If we wait here?'

'Wait…?' Finn couldn't keep the disbelief out of his voice. 'Lady, a river like this could take days to subside,' he told her, impatient of her naivety. People like her shouldn't be let loose in the country. They had as much idea of how dangerous nature could be as a child had of crossing a motorway.

'Days…?'

In his driving mirror Finn saw the panic flaring briefly in Maggie's eyes, and against his will he wondered what had caused it. What the hell was he doing, getting curious about her?

'How…how many days?' Maggie asked, fighting not to betray her concern.

Finn shrugged. 'That depends. The last time we had a flood like this it was well over a week.'

'A week…' Now there was no hiding the despair in Maggie's voice. And, if the road really did lead only to the man's farm, it looked as if she had no choice but to spend that week with *him*.

They were almost at the top of the hill now, and automatically she turned round in her seat to look back the way they had come. The Tarmac glistened wetly, a narrow black ribbon against the autumn landscape, and as for her car—she could just about see its roof above the floodwater as it lay at an angle, wedged against a tree.

With the initial shock of what had happened over, Maggie was filled with unfamiliar panic and anxiety. Her clothes, her mobile phone, her bag—with her money and credit cards and all those taken-for-granted things that reaffirmed who and what she was—had gone, swept away from her by the flood with her car. She was, she recognized with stomach-dropping resentment, totally dependent on her rescuer.

In his rearview mirror Finn carefully monitored the

emotions shadowing Maggie's eyes. He knew how to
read people, and how to second-guess their thoughts;
city life had taught him that. City life, like this city
woman. What was a woman like this one doing in such
an out-of-the-way country area? Everything about her
screamed that she was not a country-lover. And every
instinct he had was telling him that she was trouble.

Finn knew danger when he saw it, right enough, but
for some reason he couldn't understand he had an overwhelming urge to go ahead and walk right into it, he
recognised, with a grim disbelief at his own totally uncharacteristic behaviour as he heard himself saying, 'If
you've got friends in the area you can ring them from
the farm to tell them what's happened.'

What the hell was he doing, practically inviting her
to involve him in her life? Finn asked himself angrily.
There was no way he wanted to be there. She irritated
and antagonised him to the point where... To the point
where he just knew he had to take her in his arms and
see if that deliciously full soft mouth felt as good as it
looked.

Finn clenched his jaw. What the hell was happening
to him? To think...to imagine...to want... He shook his
head, appalled by the sheer inappropriateness of his unwelcome thoughts.

'I'm not visiting friends,' Maggie denied tersely.

Finn waited, expecting her to elaborate, and then
when she didn't wondered why he should find her refusal to confide in him so intensely aggravating. By

rights he should have been pleased that she was so determined to keep her distance from him.

Maggie could feel herself starting to bristle with irritation as she recognised that her rescuer was expecting her to tell him what she was doing in Shropshire. As though she was a child being called to account by an adult. Well, her business was none of his, and besides, the very nature of Maggie's career meant that secrecy and discretion were of prime importance—so much so that they were now second nature to her. Anyway, why should she divulge her very private reasons for being in the area to this...this farmer?

They had crested the hill now, and the lane narrowed even more ahead of them, meandering through pastureland towards a pretty Tudor farmhouse. A small herd of animals grazing in one of the fields was disturbed by the Land Rover and raced away from the fence, capturing Maggie's bemused attention.

'What are those? Llamas?' she asked, unable to check her curiosity.

'No, llamas are much larger. These are alpaca. I keep them for their wool.'

'Their wool?' Maggie repeated, watching as the small herd stopped and one of its braver members craned its long neck to stare at them.

'Yes, their wool,' Finn repeated, adding sardonically, 'It's highly prized and very expensive—and I wouldn't be surprised if your 'designer' hasn't used it in his clothes.'

The way he'd said the word 'designer' was so challenging that Maggie itched to retaliate, but before she could do so he had put the Land Rover in a higher gear and switched on the radio, so that any attempt she might have made to talk would have been drowned out by the sound of the announcer.

'Sounds like we're not the only ones to be caught out by this freak storm,' Finn commented.

'Thank you,' Maggie told him tartly. 'But I don't need a translation. I do speak English.'

The auction was in six days time—the river had to have gone back to normal by then. She wished now that she had not given herself this extra time, but she had hoped to be able to convince the agent, when she talked with him face to face, to accept her offer for the Dower House prior to the auction taking place. She was fully prepared to pay, and to pay generously to secure the house. Anything to see her grandmother smile again.

They were driving into the farmyard now—in the paddock beyond it Maggie could see hens scratching in the grass and ducks on the pond. An idyllic scene, no doubt, to some people. But not to her, no way, and especially not when it came inhabited by a man like the one who was now turning round in his seat towards her.

'Let's just get one thing straight,' he was telling her grimly, 'I don't like this situation any more than you do, and, moreover, I was not the one who stupidly drove my car into a river which was plainly in full flood. Neither was I the one who made a wrong turning and ended up—'

'There was no flood when I tried to cross the ford,'

Maggie interrupted him sharply. 'It just seemed to come out of nowhere—as though…' As though some malign fate had been waiting for her, she wanted to say, but of course she was far too sensible to make such a silly comment. 'And, since you apparently own this wretched place, I should have thought you would have a legal obligation to warn motorists of just how dangerous it is to use the supposed ford.'

Ignoring her mistaken belief that he owned the farm—this was no time to become involved in minor details—Finn barred his teeth savagely in an unfriendly smile whilst he reminded Maggie unkindly, 'Since this road is private, and on privately owned land, there isn't any need.'

'That's all very well,' Maggie countered immediately, 'but perhaps you could explain to me just how a person is supposed to know that, if there isn't a sign to tell them so?'

'There doesn't need to be a sign,' Finn told her through gritted teeth. 'It's perfectly plain from any map that this is virtually a single-track road which leads to a dead end. Women,' he exploded sardonically. 'Why is it they seem pathologically incapable of reading maps?'

Maggie had had enough—all the more so because of the small inner logical voice that was trying to tell her unwantedly that her adversary had a point.

'I can read a map perfectly well, thank you, and I can read human beings even better. You are the rudest, most arrogant, most…irritating man I have ever met,' she told him forcefully.

'And you are the most impossible woman I have ever met,' Finn retaliated.

Silently they looked at one another in mutual hostility.

CHAPTER TWO

MAGGIE finished the call she had just made to her assistant explaining to her what had happened and asking her to organise the cancellation and reissue of her credit cards.

'Do you want them sent direct to you where you are?' Gayle had asked her.

'Er, no… Get them to send them to the hotel for me instead, please Gayle. Oh, and when you report what's happened to my insurance company and the garage make sure they know I'm going to need a courtesy car, will you?'

She had kept the details of what had happened brief, cutting through Gayle's shocked exclamations after she had retreated to the room Finn Gordon had shown her to, clutching the mobile telephone he had loaned her. It galled her to have to ask him for anything, and she frowned now as she quickly dialled her grandmother's number. She hadn't told her what she was planning to do, had simply fibbed instead that she was going away on business for a few days.

The fraility in Arabella Russell's voice when she answered Maggie's call choked Maggie's own voice with emotion.

*   *   *

27

Standing outside the partially open door, with the cup of tea he had made for his unexpected and unwanted guest, Finn heard the soft liquid note of love in her voice as she asked, 'Are you all right, darling?'

Stepping back sharply from the door, he wondered why the knowledge that there was a man, a lover in Maggie's life should be so unwelcome.

They had exchanged names earlier, with a reluctance and formality which in other circumstances he would have found ruefully amusing. Despite her bedraggled state, Maggie still managed to look far too desirable for his comfort. He had tried to reassure himself that his preference was and always had been for brunettes, and that he preferred blue eyes to brown, but he had still found himself staring at her for just that little bit too long.

Her call to her grandmother over, Maggie examined her surroundings. The room Finn had shown her to was large, and mercifully possessed its own bathroom. Its dormer windows looked out onto fields, beyond which lay some awesomely steep hills clothed in trees. The autumn light was already fading. What on earth was she going to do, stuck here until the river subsided? Maggie wondered bitterly.

Her request to her 'host' for access to his computer so that she could e-mail Gayle had met with a grim and uncompromising, 'I don't have one. I prefer to choose whom I allow to intrude into my life.'

Which had been a dig at her as well as a reinforcement

of his dislike of technology, Maggie suspected. The man was positively Neanderthal. Everyone had a computer. Everyone, that was, but this farmer she had managed to get herself trapped with. Crossly Maggie acknowledged that if fate had done it deliberately to annoy her it couldn't have produced a man who would antagonise and irritate her more, or whose lifestyle was so much the opposite of hers. So far as she was concerned the river could not go down fast enough—and not just because of the impending auction.

In his kitchen, Finn was listening to the local weather forecast on the radio. As yet no one had been able to come up with any an explanation for the freak storm that had been so oddly localised and which, it seemed, had caused chaos which was only limited to within a few miles of the farm.

Finn hoped the river would be crossable in time for the auction. He preferred to bid in person rather than by phone; he liked to see the faces of his competitors so that he could gauge their strengths and weaknesses. Not that he was expecting to have much competition for the estate so far as the main house and the agricultural land went. However, when it came to the estate cottages it was a different matter. There was no way he wanted second home owners or holidaymakers living on his land. No, what he wanted was his privacy. What he wanted—

He turned round as the kitchen door opened and Maggie walked in. She had removed the jacket of her suit and the thin silk blouse she was wearing revealed the soft swell of her breasts, surprisingly well rounded in such an otherwise fragile fine-boned woman. The sight of her in silk shirt, plain gold earrings and straight tailored black skirt, but minus her shoes, caused Finn to smile slightly.

Immediately her chin came up, her eyes flashing warningly. 'One word,' she cautioned him. 'Just one word and I'll…'

Finn couldn't resist. 'You'll what?' he goaded her. 'Throw something at me? A shoe, perhaps?'

'I'm a mature woman,' Maggie told him through gritted teeth. 'I do not throw things…ever.'

'What? Not even caution to the winds, in the arms of your lover?' Finn derided her. 'How very disappointing that must be for him.'

Maggie couldn't believe her ears. How on earth had they managed to get on such personal ground?

'I do not have a lover,' she heard herself telling Finn sharply.

Finn digested her too-quick denial with silent cynicism. He already knew that she was lying. She embodied everything he most disliked about the life he had left behind him. So why did he feel this virtual compulsion just to stand and look at her? He had seen more beautiful women, and he had certainly known far more sexually encouraging women. She had an almost visible ten-foot-high fence around her, warning him to keep his distance—which was exactly what he wanted and intended to do. So why was a reckless part of him hungrily wondering what it would feel like to hold her, to kiss her, to…?

Compressing his mouth against the folly of such thoughts, he said curtly, 'I'm going out to lock up the fowl for the night. If you want something to eat help yourself from the fridge.'

Help herself? Eat on her own? Well, he certainly believed in being hospitable, Maggie reflected waspishly as she watched him walk out into the yard. If she'd been in the City now she would still have been working. She rarely finished work before eight, often leaving her office even later, and most evenings she either had dinner with clients or friends; if with friends at one of the City's high-profile restaurants, if with clients somewhere equally expensive but far more discreet.

Her apartment possessed a state-of-the-art stainless steel kitchen, but Maggie had never cooked in it. She could cook, of course. Well, sort of. Her grandmother was a wonderful cook and had always encouraged Maggie to concentrate on her studies whilst she was growing up, and somehow there had never been time for Maggie to learn domestic skills from her.

Well, at least if she had something to eat now she could retreat to her room and stay there. Who knew? By tomorrow the river might be fordable again. Certainly if it was possible for a person to will that to happen then that person would be Maggie.

Skirting the large table in the middle of the room, she looked disparagingly at the untidy mess of books and papers cluttering it. An old-fashioned chair complete with a snoozing cat was pulled up in front of the Aga, not a bright shiny new Aga, Maggie noticed, but an ancient chipped cream one. The whole house had a run-down air about it, a sad shabbiness that evoked feelings in her she didn't want to examine.

Maggie had spent the early years of her childhood being dragged from one set of rented lodgings to another by her mother after the break-up of her parents' marriage. Every time her mother had met a new man they had moved, and inevitably, when the romance ended, they had moved again. In some people such a life might have created a deep-seated need for stability and the comfort and reassurance of a close loving relationship with a partner, in Maggie it had created instead a ferocious determination to make herself completely and totally independent.

This house reminded her of those days and that life and she didn't like it. Nothing in Maggie's life now— the life she had created for herself—was shabby or needy, nothing was impermanent or entered into impulsively without cautious and careful thought. Everything she surrounded herself with was like her: shiny, clean, groomed, planned, ordered and controlled.

Or rather like she normally was, she corrected herself, as she looked down at her unshod feet in their expensive designer tights. Maggie never went barefoot—not even in the privacy of her own home—and most certainly never in anyone else's home. To her being barefoot was surely synonymous with being poor, and vulnerable, and either of those things made her feel weak and afraid and angry with herself for feeling that way.

Quickly she went to open the fridge door. She was becoming far too dangerously introspective. As she looked into the fridge her eyes widened.

Finn pushed open the back door and removed his boots. The paddock was a quagmire of mud, partially due to the activities of the ducks and partially to the recent downpour. He had had the devil of a time catching one of the bantams, and had even got to the point of consigning the little wretch to the devil and the nightly marauding fox, but in the end his inherent concern for its safety had won out and he had persevered, finally managing to lock it up safely.

He was cold and hungry and his afternoon's unscheduled meeting with the alpaca breeder had meant that he hadn't made the chilli he had intended to prepare for his supper. He had an evening's worth of paperwork in front of him, which he wasn't looking forward to. Perhaps he was making life harder for himself than it needed to be by refusing to install a computer. It would certainly make his paperwork easier.

As he kicked off his muddy boots he could see Maggie staring into the open fridge.

'What's wrong?' he demanded as he walked across to her.

'Everything in here's raw,' Maggie responded in consternation. Like him, she was hungry, and had somehow been expecting…well, if not the kind of meal that would be served at one of London's stylish restaurants, then at least a pizza.

An answering frown of disapproval furrowed Finn's own forehead, as he listened to her.

'What else did you expect? This is a farm, not a supermarket,' he told her dryly. 'We live at the beginning of the food chain, not at its end.'

'But it all needs cooking,' Maggie protested. She was looking at him with a mixture of hauteur and disdain that made Finn long to shake her.

'Look, this isn't some fancy city restaurant; of course it needs cooking.'

To his astonishment Maggie slammed the fridge door shut and stepped back from it. 'I've decided that I'm not hungry,' she told him coolly.

'Well, no, I don't suppose you are. You look as though you don't live on much more than a few overrated radicchio leaves,' Finn told her unkindly.

Maggie wasn't sure what infuriated her most, his contempt for her figure or his contempt for her lifestyle. And anyway, how did a man like him know to name the City's current of-the-moment salad ingredient? Maggie wondered sourly.

'Well, you may not be hungry, but I most certainly am,' he told her, reaching past her to re-open the fridge door.

At such close quarters Maggie could actually feel the male heat coming off his body as well as see its unwantedly disturbing male strength. What on earth was the matter with her? She had never been the kind of woman who had been interested in or affected by the sight of a well-defined muscular torso. And he had the kind of facial bone structure that any male model would pay a plastic surgeon thousands for, she decided unkindly, driven by a raw need to somehow punish him for making her aware of him at all, even if it was only in the privacy of her own thoughts. He was all taut male planes and angles, and as for his eyes—surely it was impossible for a man with such dark brown hair to have such shockingly dangerous steel-blue eyes?

'Changed your mind?' she heard Finn asking her.

'What...? I...?' As she started to stammer with unfamiliar self-consciousness she wondered how on earth he could have guessed that she was unexpectedly being forced to revise her first impression of him as a man she found physically unappealing, despite his good looks.

'You look hungry,' Finn explained patiently.

She looked hungry! Maggie felt her face start to burn, and then realised that Finn couldn't possibly mean what she had thought he meant, that he couldn't possibly know what she was thinking and feeling...yes, feeling... For a man she hardly knew—a man she didn't want to know. What on earth was happening to her? The thoughts she was having—they were...they were impossible, inadmissible, unthinkable. But as they stood facing one another, with the fridge door open between them, the most peculiar feeling was sweeping over Maggie, an odd sort of light-headedness combined with an awareness of Finn as a man in the most shockingly intimate sort of way, so shocking, in fact, that—Maggie shook her head, trying to dispel her riotously erotic thoughts, her face growing pink at their temerity and inventiveness. This was totally alien to her. She had never before imagined, dreamed, nor wanted to imagine or dream such things, such needs, such desires. Even the air she was breathing seemed to be filled with a sense of urgency and excitement—of expectation, almost—that she was totally at a loss to understand. It was almost as though someone or something outside herself was forcing her to see Finn in a different light...

Finn's eyes narrowed assessingly as he saw Maggie's pupils dilate. She had started to breathe more quickly, her lips parting, her breasts rising and falling in a way that made it impossible for him not to be aware of her femininity. He had the most extraordinarily intense desire to close the fridge door and to take her in his arms and...

Grimly he turned away from her.

'I intended to cook a chilli for my own supper; there'll be more than enough for two.'

He sounded curtly dismissive, as though he was secretly hoping she would refuse. Well, tough—why should she? She wasn't going to go to bed supperless just to please some arrogant, impossible man. No way.

'I take it you won't be cooking dinner wearing that?' she said tartly, determined to wrest control of the situation into her own domain as she flicked a deliberately disparaging glance at his ancient coat.

The look Finn gave her sent a prickle of alluring excitement that was totally alien to her racing down her spine.

'No, I won't be,' he agreed, his voice mock affable as he added carelessly, 'In fact you could get the chilli started whilst I go up and have a shower. Here's the mince,' he informed her as he removed a covered container from the bottom of the fridge. 'I shan't be long.'

Helplessly Maggie stared at the container he had given her before going over to the worktop and reluctantly opening it. What she should have done was tell him in no uncertain terms before he had left the kitchen that there was no way she was going to be turned into some kind of unpaid domestic help and that he could make his own supper. But, having missed that opportunity to put him in his place and save her own face, she had no option other than to try to cook the wretched stuff. There was no way, not ever in a hundred years, a thousand years, that she was going to admit to him that she had no idea how to cook it.

Anyway, it couldn't be that difficult, could it? She had seen her grandmother cooking whilst she worked on her homework at the kitchen table. It was surely just a matter of putting it in a pan and... Her forehead furrowed into a frown of concentration as she tried to remember just what her grandmother had done, mentally picturing her in the comfortable kitchen of the home that she had made Maggie's. She could visualise her grandmother plainly enough, smiling, bustling between the cooker and

the sink whilst delicious mouthwatering smells filled the
room. But as to what she had actually been doing…

Maggie mentally squared her shoulders. She could do
it. She had to do it. There was no way she would ever
concede victory to that…that farmer.

She needed a pan first, and the logical place for that
had to be in a cupboard close to the Aga. Pleased with
her own intelligence, she went towards it.

Five minutes later, when she had checked every cupboard in the kitchen, red-faced and fuming, she finally
found what she was looking for on the opposite side of
the room. And men had the audacity to claim that
women were illogical. Ha!

Decanting the contents of the container into the pan,
she grimaced in distaste. It looked unappealingly raw.
She carried the pan over to the Aga and stood non-
plussed in front of it before tentatively lifting one of the
covers. The heat coming off the hotplate made her wince
before hastily putting the pan down on it and stepping
back. Now all she had to do was to wait for the stuff to
cook. Good.

Upstairs in his bedroom, Finn rubbed his damp hair dry
and then dropped the towel to reach for a clean shirt to
pull over his naked torso. He didn't want to analyse why
he had found it necessary not just to shower but to shave
as well, and he wasn't going to.

A pungent smell was beginning to fill the air. He
sniffed it warily and then frowned. Something was burn-

ing. Without bothering to put on his shirt, he made for the door.

In the kitchen, Maggie couldn't understand what was happening. A horrid pall of smoke was filling the room—and as for the smell! The mince couldn't be cooked yet, surely? She had a memory, admittedly vague, of her grandmother spending far longer than a mere few minutes cooking hers!

Cautiously she approached the Aga, and was just about to lift the lid off the pan when Finn came bursting into the kitchen.

'What the hell are you doing?' he was demanding as he strode past her and grabbed the pan off the stove, carrying it over to the sink, where he dumped it unceremoniously then removed its lid to peer in disgust at its smoking contents before turning on the tap.

'It's not my fault if your cooker isn't reliable,' Maggie informed him with a bravado she was far from feeling.

'My cooker!' Finn exclaimed through gritted teeth. 'It isn't the cooker that's unreliable, it's the cook. Why on earth didn't you add some more water to it?'

Some *more* water. Maggie gulped and looked away, feigning disdain, but obviously her acting wasn't good enough, because to her chagrin she heard Finn saying in an oh, so dangerously soft voice, 'You did add water, didn't you?'

Maggie swallowed. Her grandmother had had very strong views about lying, but surely on this occasion...

'You didn't, did you?' Finn breathed in disbelief.

Maggie affected a nonchalant shrug. 'So we favour different schools of cooking...'

'Different schools?' His eyes narrowed. 'You haven't a clue, have you?' He scoffed sardonically. 'Thank you, fate. Not only have I got to house her; I've got to feed her as well. Tell me,' he invited unkindly, 'just how many other non-skills do you possess that are likely to bring havoc to my life? You can't read a map, you can't cook, you—'

'Stop it.'

Maggie wasn't sure which of them was the more shocked by the sound of her tear-filled voice.

The silence it caused seemed to stretch for ever, hostility giving way to shock, shock to a soft little prickle of sensual tension which in turn led...

'I'm sorry.' It was the gruff note of real apology in Finn's voice that did it, Maggie assured herself later. That and the fact that she had really been intending to walk past him and out of the room—would have walked past him if her eyes hadn't been blurred by tears of shame and anger causing her instead to walk into him, into him and into...into his arms.

CHAPTER THREE

'I'M SORRY. I didn't mean to hurt you,' Finn apologised gruffly, as he pushed the silky hair back off Maggie's face, his fingertips enjoying the soft delicacy of her skin. Her throat seemed to fit the curve of his hand perfectly. She was trembling slightly, and in his own body...

'You haven't. You didn't,' Maggie responded huskily. She couldn't stop looking at him; their glances were meeting, meshing, mating; she didn't want to stop looking at him.

'I'll make us something else to eat,' Finn offered. He knew he should release her, but he didn't want to, couldn't bear to.

Maggie shook her head. 'It's you I'm hungry for,' she whispered softly. 'Not food. Just you. Only you, Finn.'

As she lifted her face towards his Maggie knew that she had never done anything in the whole of her life that felt more right than this, more right than Finn.

Finn tried to apply the brakes of caution and common sense to the escalating urgency of his response to her, but one look into the dark haze of her passion-filled eyes had much the same effect on those brakes as the wall of water sweeping down the river had had on Maggie's car.

His kiss was tentative at first, his lips exploring the soft curves of hers, but then she moved closer to him, nestling into his arms, her breathing quickening, the look in her eyes making Finn groan out loud.

'Kiss me, Finn,' Maggie whispered insistently, adding with a shaky urgency that made Finn catch his own breath in fierce longing, 'Properly this time.'

'Like this, do you mean?'

Finn's hand slid beneath her hair, supporting her head as they gazed helplessly at one another. They kissed quickly, as though equally wary of what they were doing, equally wary of their mutual hunger for one another. Brief, fierce kisses were snatched, as though they were starving, in fear of being deprived of the means of satisfying their hunger. But slowly their kisses became longer, deeper.

Behind her closed eyelids, Maggie savoured the richness of the texture of Finn's mouth. His kisses were the most extraordinarily sensual she had ever experienced. Without doing anything more than holding her and kissing her he had made her whole body come alive with longing for him. Everything about him was having the most erotic aphrodisiacal effect on her, making her think things, want things, want him, with a female ardour and urgency that left her breathless. Breathless and aching, eager, hungry, and wanting him. Just as he wanted her. Finn was a man, and even if his kisses hadn't shown her that he wanted her as passionately as she did him his body would have given him away.

Experimentally she slid her tongue-tip into his mouth. The arm he had wrapped around her body tightened and she felt him shudder, felt too the corresponding quiver of reaction that set her own limbs shaking.

'Don't do that unless you mean it,' Finn warned her rawly. Heat flamed in his eyes, and beneath her explorative fingertips the hard high planes of his cheekbones burned.

'I do mean it,' Maggie responded. Automatically she looked round the kitchen, and, correctly sensing what she was seeking, what she was thinking, Finn released her from his arms and took hold of her hand, silently leading her out of the kitchen and towards the stairs.

His bedroom was on the opposite side of the landing to the room he had given her. Silently he drew her into it, and equally silently Maggie went with him. It was simply and traditionally furnished, and at any other time she would have turned her nose up its shabbiness and lack of style. But the bed was large, with heavy iron head and footboards.

The air in the room was clean and slightly cold, so that Maggie shivered a little.

Watching her, Finn remembered how cold he too had found the farmhouse when he had first moved in. It didn't possess any central heating, but he had grown used to its lack of modern conveniences.

As she shivered again Maggie instinctively moved closer to Finn, seeking the warmth of his body. The sensation of his arms closing around her was so intense that it rocked her on her heels. As they kissed Maggie felt as though Finn's warmth was wrapping itself all around her, enfolding her. She could feel his hands moving over her body and she started to tremble. Not with cold now, but with a growing ache of need.

Unable to resist their temptation, Finn explored the taut shape of Maggie's breasts. Her nipples, tight and erect, pressed into his palms through the fine silk of her shirt. Opening his eyes, he absorbed the eroticism of their tautness pushing against the fabric before slowly circling them with his thumb-tip.

Maggie had forgotten that she had ever been cold now. Feverishly she slid her palms over Finn's naked torso. She ached to see all of him. To touch all of him, and now, oh yes, right now.

She had just made the very interesting discovery that when she trailed her fingertips across his collarbone and then down his arm his whole body shuddered in sharp response, and when she placed her hand flat against his chest and then moved it lower, so low that it was resting on the belt of his jeans, that shudder became a whole lot more intense.

His own hand was travelling the length of her spine, taking her mind off the way he was reacting and focusing it instead on the way she was feeling. Arousal, hot and sharp, lifted her skin in tiny goosebumps against his touch, as though it just couldn't get close enough to him.

She exhaled softly as Finn's hand moved to the buttons on her shirt, and then found that the sensation of his fingertips brushing against her naked skin as he unfastened them was making it impossible for her to breathe in again.

As he pulled the fabric back from Maggie's body Finn

acknowledged that what was happening between them was destroying virtually every belief he had about what he wanted from life.

Watching him, and seeing the open, raw male sensuality blazing out of his heavily-lidded eyes, Maggie exhaled.

The feel of her soft sweet breath gusting warmly against his bare skin made Finn grit his teeth against the ferocity of his reaction to her. The air ached with the sexual tension stretching between them.

As Finn leaned forward to kiss first one of her naked breasts and then the other, Maggie moaned sharply, her body arching towards him in mute supplication.

It was too much for Finn's self-control; she was too much for his self-control. Quickly removing the rest of her clothes and his own, Finn lifted Maggie onto the bed.

The coldness of the cotton duvet beneath her bare back made Maggie shiver, but the heat of her desire for Finn soon burned away that cold. Her body throbbed with longing for him, and the feel of his hands on her skin as he lowered himself against her and slid them beneath her to lift her hips to meet his own made her cry out, a wild tormented female sound of need that echoed the turbulence darkening her eyes.

'Finn,' she cried out his name as she wrapped herself around him, pressing wild hot kisses against his skin, his throat, his jaw, his mouth, holding it captive with her own whilst her body shook. 'Now, Finn,' she begged him passionately. 'Now.'

It was the force of the river at full flood, the warmth of the sun on a tropical beach, the cool magical clarity of a frosty sky married to the purity of newly fallen snow; it was every pleasure she had ever know intensified a million times. He filled her body with joy and her heart with an emotion so intense that it spilled from her eyes in pure gleaming tears and from her mouth in a golden sound of loving words. It was a revelation, and somehow an affirmation. It was a world she had always stubbornly refused to believe could exist and at the same time a world a secret part of her had always longed to inhabit. It was. It was Finn and it was love. And as her body came down from the heights his had taken it to and she lay drifting on the soft safe warm afterswell of pleasure, lying at peace in his arms, Maggie turned to look at the man who had just totally changed her life.

Gazing deep into his eyes, she lifted her fingertips to his face, tracing its contours wonderingly. Looking back at her, Finn took her hand and held it against his lips, tenderly kissing her fingers.

'I love you.'

Maggie could see shock followed by an intense burn of emotion darkening Finn's eyes as she said the simple words.

Saying them had shocked her as well—so much so, in fact, that she immediately longed to call them back, wondering frantically why she had ever uttered them, furiously angry with herself for the vulnerability they were now causing her to feel. As though desperate to escape them she tried to turn away from Finn, but he refused to allow her to do so, taking hold of her instead, his hands gentle on the tense resistance of her body.

'What is it? What's wrong?' he asked her quietly.

'Nothing,' Maggie lied sharply as she tried to evade the quiet depth of his searching gaze.

'Yes, there is.' Finn contradicted her. 'You're angry because you said you love me.'

'No,' Maggie denied fiercely, but she could tell from the expression in Finn's eyes that he didn't believe her.

'I don't know why I said it.' She tried to cover herself. 'It must have been some kind of knee-jerk adolescent reaction to the fact that we...'

When she stopped Finn supplied softly for her, 'That we made love? Is that what you're trying to say?'

Maggie shook her head. She had been intending to use the words 'had sex', if for no other reason than to remind herself of just what the reality of their situation was. But something in Finn's eyes had warned her against doing so.

'We're both adults, Maggie,' Finn was telling her gently. 'Why should it be so difficult for us to use the word 'love' about what we've just shared, about one another? There was love between us. And to deny that...'

He paused and shook his head, whilst Maggie, thoroughly unnerved by what he was saying burst out sharply, 'We hardly know one another. We can't.'

'We can't what?' Finn challenged her. 'We can't tell one another that we've fallen in love, even though it's true? We can't mention it? Show it to one another...like this?' And then he was reaching for her, wrapping her in his arms and holding her so tightly that she could hardly breathe as he told her with fierce raw male intensity, 'I don't know how this has happened to us or why, Maggie, but I do know that now that it has…'

As his fingers stroked through her hair Maggie revelled in the mute tenderness of his touch, its confirmation of his admission of love. 'Now that it has what?' she asked him.

'Now that it has…this…' Finn responded.

As he started to kiss her his fingertips slid seductively down her spine. Voluptuously Maggie closed her eyes on a tiny moan of helpless resignation. There would be time later for her to analyse her feelings and get them back under her own control. For now…

For now there was nothing she wanted more than the feel of Finn's flesh against her fingertips, the feel of Finn himself against her.

A triumphant smile curved Maggie's mouth as she lifted the lid from the casserole she had just removed from the Aga and sniffed the delicious aroma emanating from it. For this evening's supper they would be eating *coq au vin,* thanks to the slightly battered cookbook she had unearthed from deep inside one of the kitchen cupboards.

Or chicken casserole, as Finn would no doubt describe it.

Finn. Helplessly, knowing how much she would regret her foolishness and berate herself mentally for it, Maggie closed her eyes and succumbed to the temptation to slowly and lovingly mentally recreate every single inch of him.

Four days ago she hadn't even known he existed, and wouldn't have cared if she had; three days ago she had known, but could have quite definitely contemplated a world without him. But now... Now... A loving dreamy smile softened her mouth, her emotions too powerful for her to ignore. She still felt bemused by the speed with which they had fallen in love—bemused by it when she wasn't desperately trying to remind herself of all the reasons why it was impossible for her to behave in such an irrational and impulsive way, allowing her emotions to control her instead of the other way around—and completely, totally enchanted, enthralled and enraptured by Finn himself.

And somehow, without knowing quite how, and totally against her better judgement, she had allowed Finn to convince her that what they felt for one another was too wonderfully special to be ignored. They were in love. They whispered it to one another in the sleepy relaxed closeness of shared spent passion, moaned it to one another in its tumultuous throes, cried it out to one another as they climbed its heights together, vowed it to one another in barely spoken tender triumphant post orgasmic mutual bliss. They were in love.

Cautiously Maggie had allowed herself to wriggle out of the protective straitjacket of emotional denial she had cocooned herself in for her own safety, to begin to believe in what she was feeling, to make plans...

This morning she had woken up to find Finn leaning over her, his head propped up on one hand whilst he looked at her.

'What is it? What are you doing?' she had asked him sleepily as she reached up to touch the rough stubble on his jaw with one delicate fingertip.

'Watching you,' had been his husky reply. 'Did you know that you twitch your nose when you're asleep?'

'No, I don't,' Maggie had denied.

'Yes, you do,' Finn had told her lovingly. 'And you part your lips just a little, so that I'm irresistibly tempted to kiss them to see if they taste as soft and warm as they look.'

'If you don't know that by now,' Maggie had begun to challenge him teasingly, 'when you've had enough opportunity to find out…'

'No. Never, never, ever could I have enough of you,' Finn had told her, adding with a dangerous glint in his eyes, 'Want me to prove it?'

Laughing, she had pretended to try to escape as he reached for her and wrapped her in his arms.

'Oh, I know it,' Finn had confirmed, giving her a sexily smouldering dark-eyed look that had made her stomach muscles quiver in delicious anticipation. 'And I know too that if I touch you here…' His fingertips had brushed against her already taut nipple and Maggie had raised her hand to his collarbone, tracing its length with fingers that trembled slightly.

It had been gone ten o'clock when they had finally

got up. An appallingly late hour for a farmer, Finn had told her.

He was out checking on the animals now. Soon he would be back, and then...

Maggie replaced the casserole in the Aga, concentrating on the weather forecast being broadcast on the radio.

The freak flood was subsiding, the forecaster announced, and no further cloudbursts were expected.

Which meant—which meant that she would be able to make it to the auction, Maggie decided in relief.

All morning whilst she prepared her *coq au vin* she had been making plans. The farm was only rented, Finn had told her that, which meant that Finn was free to return to the City with her. She closed the Aga door and frowned slightly. It did concern her a little, if she was honest, that a man of Finn's age should only be renting a property—and as for his lack of ambition... But that could be remedied, she felt sure.

He was an intelligent man and she was convinced that with her encouragement and support he could soon gain enough qualifications to get a proper job in the City. Heavens, if she, with her connections, couldn't help him then no one could. And she was fully prepared to support him financially whilst he retrained. It was true that it was a little hard for her to visualise him living in her small apartment, with its minimalistic elegance, but somehow they would manage. She would take him to a suitable shop and get him a decent suit, and then she would organise a get-together at one of her favourite 'in' restaurants so that he could meet her friends, perhaps

one or two people with the right connections, so that he
could begin networking.

Her mind working busily, Maggie continued to plan.
They would have a small elegant wedding—thanks, perhaps, to her grandmother she was old-fashioned enough
to want to give their love the commitment of marriage—
perhaps at one of the City's newly licensed and breath-
takingly beautiful National Trust properties. They would
honeymoon somewhere far, far away and ridiculously
romantic, and frighten each other by remembering how
easily they might not have met.

Happily engrossed in her thoughts, Maggie didn't hear
Finn come into the kitchen. Removing his boots, he
stood for a few seconds watching her. Was it really only
four days ago that he had considered her the most in-
furiating woman he had ever met? Smiling ruefully, he
walked up behind her, wrapping his arms around her as
he lowered his head to gently nuzzle the side of her neck.

'Mmm…something smells good,' he told her appreciatively.

'My perfume,' Maggie responded huskily. What was
it about that touch of a certain man's lips and only his
that had the power to reduce a woman to this state of
sweetly intense longing, to make her want to…?

'No, I meant the dinner,' Finn informed her.

Maggie pretended indignation as she leaned back in
his arms. 'It said on the radio that the river is going
down,' she told him, closing her eyes, wanting to purr
with sensuality as his fingertips stroked down her arm
and found the deliciously sensitive little spot just inside

her elbow where last night the touch of his mouth had made her moan softly with pleasure as her body arched languidly into his.

'Yes, I know. I heard it too,' he confirmed.

Still looking at him with eyes liquid with pleasure, Maggie reluctantly reminded herself of something she had to do. She hadn't been able to speak with her grandmother—her grandmother was used to Maggie going away on business and being incommunicado for a couple of days or so, but Maggie wanted to telephone Gayle and ask her to let her know that she would soon be in touch.

Ringing herself was too fraught with potential hazards for Maggie to contemplate right now. Whilst Arabella Russell had never been the kind of person to sit in judgement on others, nor was someone who believed in imposing her own moral values on them, Maggie wanted to be in a position to explain to her grandmother just how she felt, as well as what had happened, in person. And, just as she did not feel comfortable with her grandmother worrying about what she was doing, neither did she feel comfortable with the prospect of Finn perhaps teasing her for worrying about an old lady's sensibilities.

For an adult woman to be worrying about how her grandmother might react to the fact that she had made love with a man she had only known a matter of hours might seem justifiably risible in this day and age, but Maggie was not going to expose either herself or her grandmother to Finn's potential amusement.

As he watched Maggie's eyes darken and the expressions of concern and anxiety chase one another across her face, Finn was forced to acknowledge what he had determinedly pushed to the back of his mind ever since he'd overheard her phone call that first day. Namely, that he wasn't the only man in Maggie's life. Initially he had told himself that it didn't matter, but of course it did, and it had mattered from the first moment he had kissed her; from the first moment he had wanted to kiss her, he corrected himself grimly.

There was nothing he wanted more than for them to be completely honest with one another. The love he felt for her demanded it. What would happen if he told her that he already knew? Perhaps…

'Finn? May I use your telephone? There's a phone call I need to make.' Maggie could see Finn frowning as she blurted out her request.

'Someone special?' Finn asked her as lightly as he could, inwardly praying that she would open up to him, tell him about the someone else she shared her life with, and tell him too that what *they* now shared meant that her relationship with her existing lover would have to end.

Someone special. Maggie tensed. Her grandmother was special, but she wasn't ready yet to tell Finn about her, or to explain to him just why Arabella Russell mattered so much to her. The caution that had guarded her for so much of her life hadn't entirely lifted its heavy barrier from her heart.

'No…I just need to speak to my…my assistant.'

Finn knew immediately that there was something she

was concealing from him. Silently he prayed that she
would tell him what it was before…

Confused, Maggie waited for Finn to answer her.
What on earth was it about a simple request to use his
telephone that had brought such a darkly brooding look
to his face?

There was nothing else for it, Finn acknowledged. If
Maggie wasn't going to tell him of her own accord then
he was going to have to force the issue, to make his own
position plain, put his cards on the table and tell her here
and now what he was looking for from their relationship—that nothing less than total and complete commitment from her would satisfy him.

He knew that taking such a step was a gamble, a gamble which would have been dangerous even without the
hidden presence of another man in her life, given the
brevity of the time they had known one another. Still, it
was a gamble he had to take; his love for her was forcing
him to take it. He hoped that once Maggie knew just
what he wanted from her she would drop her guard and
tell him the truth.

Finn took a deep breath, and then, his hands cupping
Maggie's shoulders with firmly tender strength, he
looked down into her eyes. 'Before you do anything else,
speak to anyone else,' he emphasised, hoping she would
guess that he knew who it was she really wanted to
speak to, 'there's something I have to say to you—something I've never said or wanted to say to any other
woman.'

He paused whilst Maggie tried to guess what was

coming, impatient to get her phone call out of the way, let Gayle know that with the river no longer flooding she would soon be back in London, so that she could tell Finn about the exciting plans she had been making for both of them. Plans that meant that the sooner she did get back to the City, the sooner she could be starting to work on the wonderful life they would be sharing together.

'Yes?' she urged Finn curiously. They had already told one another of their love, so it couldn't be that

'I want you to move in here with me, Maggie.'

Finn could see the shock that Maggie wasn't quite quick enough to banish from her eyes and his heart felt like granite inside his chest, a heavy leaden weight of black, bleak disillusionment.

'Maggie?' he pleaded rawly, when she continued to look at him in silence. 'I know you've got your city life, your city commitments…' He turned away from her a little, not wanting her to guess what he was thinking. She had told him about her business, her headhunting agency, and somehow he had managed not to betray to her his own feelings of distaste for the way of life she was reminding him of.

For a moment Maggie thought that he was just teasing her, that his suggestion was some kind of unfathomable male joke, but then she realised that he was actually serious. A fierce rush of emotion seized her—panic, fear, anger—forcing a deep chasm between her and her earlier feeling of love. In its place was a sense of betrayal, of disillusionment, a shocking and unwanted return from the idealistic world she had been creating in her own thoughts to one of reality.

'Me move in here? No, that's impossible,' she told Finn immediately, shaking her head as she pulled back from him. 'How could you possibly think—?' She stopped and looked round the kitchen and then back at him, unable to vocalise the full extent of her disbelief.

'Impossible?' Finn challenged her flatly. 'Why?' But of course he already knew the answer to his own question, just as he also knew that she was unlikely to give it to him, to be honest with him. His knowledge of her duplicity lay heavily against his heart. She had said that she loved him, but he himself had heard her call another man 'darling', with a note of soft tenderness in her voice that had said how much he meant to her.

He had hoped, prayed, that she might tell him about her lover, that she might say something, anything that would explain, excuse her lack of honesty, but she had said nothing, had given herself to him with a sweet hot passion that he had been totally unable to resist even whilst he had been despising himself for not being able to do so. For the first time in his life he had had to admit that he was unable to control his own feelings, unable to stop himself from loving her even whilst all the time knowing that she was committed to someone else.

When she had claimed to love him she'd been lying to him. When he had asked her to come and live with him she had refused—because of that someone else and the commitment she already shared with him. But she was obviously not prepared to tell him any of this. And if that made her a liar then what did it make him? What had he wanted her to tell him? That there was another man in her life but that because of what they had shared he now meant nothing to her whilst he, Finn, meant everything? Where the hell did he think he was living? Certainly not on planet earth. Cloud cuckoo-land was more like it.

A quick fling, a few days of sexual excitement with a stranger—that was all he was to her. He had known so many women like her in the old days, known them and felt sorry for them, for all that was missing from their lives, never imagining that one day he would fall in love with one of them.

Silently his stubborn heart begged her to confide in him, to justify its belief in her against the cynical contempt of his brain.

Maggie felt as though she was in shock. How could Finn possibly have imagined that she could live here? Angrily she blamed him for the destruction of her happy plans. And yet instead of exhibiting guilt, as he ought to be doing, something in Finn's manner was suggesting that he felt *she* was the one who was at fault. If he really loved her, as he had claimed to do, he would know instinctively how impossible it was for her to live somewhere like this.

The cold weight of his own disillusionment and pain lay like lead against Finn's heart, entombing it. Bitterness filled him, darkening his eyes and hardening his mouth in a curt line of contempt.

'You're right,' he agreed savagely. 'It is impossible.

What were you planning to do, Maggie? Just disappear without a word, without a Thank you for having me? I should have remembered, shouldn't I, that city women like you get a thrill out of indulging in a little bit of rough now and again—especially when it can be kept hidden away…walked away from? Well, perhaps before you do go I should really give you something to remember me by.'

Before Maggie could escape Finn moved, trapping her between the kitchen wall and his body and placing his hands on the wall either side of her as he deliberately lowered his mouth towards her own and began to kiss her with a savage passion that stripped away any veneer of polite social convention, revealing the raw, naked intensity of his anger—and his desire.

And hers she admitted bitterly as the sheer physical strength of her own need burned through her. Beneath his mouth she opened her own, taking angry biting kisses from his lips, her hands curling into small fists that clawed at the front of his shirt as she both clung to him and tried to force him away. The weight of his body as he lowered it against hers to imprison her made her want to fight against what he was doing and at the same time not merely to succumb to it but to feed it, until they were both consumed in the flames of their mutual hatred. She hated him and she wanted him. She wanted to destroy him and she wanted to wrap her body around him, draw him deep into it and keep him there, her prisoner, to do with as she willed, to make him helpless and dependent on her, to make him ache for her, need her, want her, to make—

The shock of Finn abruptly releasing her almost made her stumble, and that he should be the one to reject her made bitter passion burn in her eyes as they faced one another in silence.

It was Finn who broke that silence, speaking in a voice so empty of emotion that it caught at a vulnerable nerve ending she hadn't known she possessed, thickening her throat with tears of loss she would have died rather than let him see.

'I don't know which of us I despise the more.'

'I thought it was my sex that was supposed to be changeable,' Maggie responded, keeping her voice as light and indifferent as she could. 'This morning you swore you loved me, and now—'

'It wasn't love,' Finn interrupted her harshly. 'God knows just what it was, but it bore as much resemblance to love as the devil does to an angel.' Only he knew, thank God, just what it cost him to deny his feelings, to put pride and reality before the intensity and vulnerability of his love, the love he had now sworn to himself he must destroy.

Afraid of what she might, say, what she might betray if she allowed herself to speak, Maggie turned on her heel and left.

CHAPTER FOUR

MAGGIE hadn't realised that Shrewsbury was such a busy town. No, not a town, a city, she reminded herself, remembering her earlier phone call with her assistant Gayle. She had driven here in the hire car Gayle had organised for her and, having parked it, had set out to find the small designer shop Gayle had informed her the city possessed in order to buy herself some clothes. The city itself, though, had proved more distracting than she had expected. More than three-quarters enclosed by the loop in the river within which it was built, it possessed a strong sense of itself and its history.

It was here that the Welsh marauders had been held at bay, here too that the rich sheep farmers had brought their flocks. Maggie stopped, the bleakness of her own thoughts momentarily suspended as she caught sight of an entrancingly pretty courtyard down one of the city's medieval wynds. And then, as she turned the corner, she saw the shop she had been looking for, its windows as artfully temptingly dressed as any one of its London peers.

Pushing open the door, Maggie went inside, and a warmly smiling assistant came towards her. Giving her a quick shrewd look, Maggie recognised in the black suit she was wearing the cut of one of the fashion scene's most cherished designers. Quickly she explained what had happened and what she was looking for.

'I think we've got the very thing,' the assistant told her. 'It's a bit late in the season, but one of our regular clients, who is your size, cancelled part of her reserve order.' She gave Maggie a small smile. 'She met someone whilst she was working in New York and she's gone over there to be with him.'

Whilst she chatted she was moving through the clothes rails, deftly removing several items which she displayed for Maggie to examine. There was a mouth-watering honey-coloured full-length cashmere coat, butter-soft and blissfully warm, that Maggie fell immediately in love with even before she tried it on. When she did so, the gleam of approval in the assistant's eyes made Maggie wonder what Finn would think if he could see her in it—a weakness which she instantly tried to wall up behind a defensive barrier of sternly abrasive thoughts as she warned herself of the folly of allowing herself to think about him.

Why should she want to or need to anyway? Need to? The appalled expression that crossed her face as she slipped off the coat and handed it back to the assistant had the latter misguidedly assuming that it was caused by the cost of the coat, which she quickly explained was an exclusive designer model.

'It's fine. I love it,' Maggie assured her, and then winced at her own casual use of a word which had caused her so much anguish when it was applied to Finn.

Finn. Finn. Why on earth couldn't she stop thinking

about him? Why was she driven by this self-destructive urge to link everything she was doing with him? Maggie berated herself an hour later as she left the shop, wearing not just the cashmere coat but the suit she had bought as well.

For once a self-indulgent bout of retail therapy had failed to have its normal recuperative effect on her senses, and despite the warmth of the shop, and the restorative powers of the delicious cappuccino the assistant had produced for her, there was a cold emptiness inside Maggie, a feeling of misery and deprivation that reminded her unwantedly of the child she had once been, an outsider envying her peers who had all seemed to belong to happy loving families.

But that had been before she had gone to live permanently with her grandparents and become secure in their love, before she had taught herself that solitude and independence, both financial and emotional, were of far more value to her than an emotion which, like those who claimed to give it, could never be totally relied on. Now, back in the security of her own personal space, she couldn't understand why on earth she had behaved in the way she had And as for believing that she had fallen in love. She just didn't know how she could have thought such a thing. Love was far too unstable, untrustworthy and volatile to ever form part of her life-plan.

Firmly she congratulated herself on having come to her senses. What had happened was regrettable, and had revealed a previously unsuspected weakness within herself, but at least no lasting harm had been done. No

doubt to Finn, undeniably good-looking and possessed
of such sexual dynamism and power, she was simply
another foolish woman who had made a fool of herself
over him. Her face burned as she forced herself to remember just how much of a fool and how explicitly.
Thank goodness she was never likely to see him again,
she told herself as she checked her watch and hurried
down the windswept street towards the car park where
she had left her car.

It would only take her half an hour or so to drive back
to the hotel in Lampton. She had arrived there the previous afternoon, dropped off by the taxi which had collected her from Finn's farmhouse. It had taken a consid-
erable amount of patience and all of her many business
skills before she had been able to persuade the manager
of the hotel to lend her the money to pay her taxi fare—
that and a telephone call to Gayle, who had not only
vouched for her but also given the hotel manager her
own credit card number to cover both the fare and a
small cash loan to Maggie, to tide her over until the new
cards Gayle had ordered for her arrived. Much to
Maggie's relief, these had been delivered by hand to the
hotel this morning.

Momentarily her footsteps faltered. She could still see
and feel Finn's angry hostility towards her as he had
watched her leave. Finn. What had happened between
them had been an aberration, a totally inexplicable act
completely contrary to her nature, and she was just
thankful that reality had brought things to an end when
it had.

Despite the warmth of her newly acquired cashmere coat Maggie gave a little shiver, so totally engrossed in her own thoughts that it was a handful of heart-stopping seconds before her brain registered what her body had already recognised: namely that the man standing in the middle of the street, as immobile as any statue, less than five metres away from her, was none other than Finn himself.

'Finn.' As she whispered his name Maggie could feel the physical reaction overwhelming her body, a cold drenching icy sense of shock as potentially dangerous as any floodwater could ever be, and an equally devastating blast of hot searing yearning as uncontrollable as a forest fire

'Maggie!' Caught off guard, Finn felt the shock of seeing her crash through his defences. The urge to wrap her in his arms and carry her away somewhere private, where he could show her in all the ways that his rebellious body wanted to show her just what they could have together, was so strong that he had taken a step towards her before he realised what he was doing.

The sight of Finn striding purposefully towards her sent a wave of panic over Maggie. Immediately she looked for some means of escape. She just wasn't up to any kind of conversation with him right now, not with her emotions in such chaotic disarray. There was a narrow street to the side of her. Quickly she dived into it, her heart hammering against her ribs as she heard Finn calling out to her to wait.

After Maggie's departure from the farm Finn had told

himself that he was glad she had gone, reminding himself of all the reasons why a relationship between them could never work. But last night he had dreamed of her, ached for her, woken at six o'clock in the morning not just physically hungry for her but emotionally bereft without her—and furiously, bitterly contemptuous of himself for being so.

Finn could not possibly have known that she was in Shrewsbury; Maggie knew that. But nevertheless there was a sense of fatefulness in the fact that she had seen him, a sense of intensity that made her feel both frightened and angry, as though somehow she herself was to blame for his appearance, having conjured him up by her own thoughts. And even as she hurried away from him a certain part of her was feeling hectically excited at the thought that he might pursue her, catch up with her, and...

And what? Take her in his arms and swear that he was never going to let her go? Somehow magically turn back time so that...? Was she going completely mad? He was a farmer, not a wizard, she reminded herself sternly.

Ignoring the inner voice that warned him that nothing could be gained by prolonging his own agony, Finn made for the narrow lane Maggie had hurried down. But just as he was about to enter it he heard the familiar voice of his closest neighbour, an elderly farmer, who blocked Finn's access to the lane as he proceeded to complain to him about current farming conditions. Knowing that beneath the older man's complaints lay loneliness, Finn felt obliged to listen, even whilst he was inwardly cursing his appearance for preventing him from following Maggie.

What was she doing in Shrewsbury? Why hadn't she gone straight back to London? She had never told him exactly what it was that had brought her to Shropshire—they had been engrossed in discoveries about one another of a far more intimate and exciting nature than any mere mundane exchanges concerning their day-to-day lives.

Maggie... Finn closed his eyes as his ache for her throbbed through every single one of his senses.

As she reached out to unlock her car, Maggie gave a swift look over her shoulder. There was no sign of Finn anywhere in the car park. She told herself that she was glad he hadn't followed her. And if he had done she would naturally have told him that he was wasting his time. Wouldn't she? She started the car, then paused, giving the car park a final sweeping visual search before slowly driving away.

The auction wasn't due to take place until the following morning, but the agent for the sale of the estate had agreed to see her, and Maggie was still hoping that she might be able to persuade him to allow her to buy the Dower House before it went to auction. She was prepared to pay over and above its reserve price if necessary. She had to buy the house for her grandmother, who had sounded even more quietly unhappy than before when Maggie had rung her from the hotel.

Lambton was only small, a traditional country town with a mixture of various styles of architecture showing it had grown and developed over the centuries, and as she parked outside the agent's office Maggie realised that she could probably have walked there from the hotel faster than she had driven. Or at least in theory, she reflected with a rueful look down at the ravishingly pretty and impossibly high-heeled shoes she was wearing.

Finn would have taken one look at them and immediately rejected them as ridiculous and impractical—which no doubt meant that in his eyes at least she and the shoes were a good match.

Finn. Why on earth was she allowing herself to think about him—again? Had she forgotten already what he had said to her? Had she forgotten too that he had actually expected her to move into that remote farmhouse? A clever ruse, of course; he must have known that what he was suggesting was totally impossible, and would no doubt have been caught totally off guard if she had agreed. Still, from what she heard from her girlfriends, as being dumped went it had at least been original.

As she pushed open the door to the agent's office she had to battle against a dangerous feeling of loss that had somehow insidiously and unwarrantedly found its way into her thoughts, and she warned herself that she should be thinking about the reality of the situation instead of grieving for some foolish fantasy that she was very fortunate to have walked away from.

'I really am sorry,' Philip Crabtree, the agent, told Maggie ruefully, 'but we have strict instructions that the estate is to be auctioned and not sold prior to auction,'

'But why?' Maggie protested. 'Especially when I'm prepared to pay well over the reserve price.'

The agent sympathised with her. It was plain how important it was to her to acquire the Dower House, but as he had already explained there really was nothing he could do.

'I can't give you an answer to that other than to say that those are the instructions of the present owner.'

'Who is the present owner?' Maggie asked him—perhaps if she were to approach him or her direct she might be able to persuade them to sell outright to her.

'An American who unexpectedly inherited not just this estate but also a much larger one in another part of the country. He's been very specific about how he wants the sale to be handled. In fact originally he planned to attend the auction himself, but it seems that some unforeseen circumstances have cropped up that prevent him from doing so. I am sorry,' he commiserated when he saw Maggie's face. 'I can see how much you want the house.'

Maggie shook her head at his misconception. 'I don't want it for myself,' she told him. 'It's for my grandmother.' Briefly she explained her grandparents' connection with the property.

He was immediately even more sympathetic. 'I wish I could do more to help you,' he told her, 'but I have to follow our client's instructions. Perhaps I shouldn't tell you this, but we haven't had an awful lot of interest in the properties, so I don't think you need to worry about too much competition from other bidders.'

Thanking him for his time, Maggie made to leave. She knew she should have found his reassurances comforting, but she would far rather have preferred to know that the Dower House was going to be hers now rather than have to wait until after the auction.

Aspects of her life over which she was not in full control did not appeal to her one little bit, and besides…

As she hurried back to her car, huddled into her coat, she admitted reluctantly that she was anxious to leave Shropshire as quickly as she could—just in case. Just in case what? Just in case she should see Finn again, and he should have come to his senses and realised how wrong he had been; he'd tell her that he had had to find her to admit as much, declaring undying love for her, apologising to her and pleading with her to give him a second chance…

Just for a moment she allowed herself to dwell on this gratifying scenario—not because she wanted to see him again. No, of course not. No, it was simply a matter of knowing that she was in the right and feeling that he should concede as much. That was all. Nothing more. In fact so far as she was concerned it was actually a relief knowing that she was not going to see him again. Yes, quite definitely. Very definitely, in fact, she decided as she drove back to the hotel.

As she turned off the main road and into the long tree-lined drive that led to the Georgian mansion house of the estate, where the auction was to take place, Maggie reluctantly acknowledged the impressive grandeur of her surroundings. The trees were at the full height of their autumn glory, and the parkland stretching to either side of them was warmed by the morning sunshine. The house itself, which she could see ahead of her, was everything that was best about Georgian architecture, neither institutionally large, nor spoiled by any later unworthy additions.

She had a girlfriend in London, newly married and in her mid-thirties, who was desperate for just such a house—and desperate too, Maggie suspected, to remove her very wealthy and notoriously very susceptible new husband from the London scene and the attentions of other women. When Maggie had expressed her doubts about the wisdom of her friend turning her back on the successful career she had built up in the City, she had been told, smugly, that her friend had already made plans to work from the country, and that all she now needed to complete her happiness was the right house. And the right house apparently would have to be Georgian. Just like the one in front of her.

Undeniably it was beautiful, Maggie admitted as she parked her car at the end of a row of three other cars on the gravel forecourt to the house and got out.

The front door to the house was open, a notice there directing potential bidders to the room where the auction was to be held, and inside the hall on a dusty table was a pile of brochures the same as the one already in Maggie's possession, which listed the items to be auctioned.

The main house itself, along with its gardens, the farmland and estate buildings, were of no interest to Maggie—even if she had been able to afford them, which she most certainly could not. It would take a very, very wealthy person to be able to buy in full such an estate, she knew. No, her interest lay exclusively in the Dower House, which was listed as Lot 4 in the brochure, Lots 1, 2 and 3 being, respectively, the Georgian House she was now standing in, along with the stables and garages attached to it and its garden; the farmland; and the estate buildings which comprised barns and a pair of cottages. The Dower House was over a mile away from the main house, set in its own pretty garden and with its own private drive to the main road. Maggie could see as she walked into the large and once elegant, now slightly shabby drawing room, that Philip Crabtree had been correct when he had told her that there would be very few other bidders. Apart from the agent himself, and a young woman who was obviously working with him, there were only another six people in the room.

Gratifyingly, as soon as he saw her, Philip came hurrying over to greet her, introducing his assistant to her as he did so and explaining that the heavily built be-suited man standing studying the faded yellow silk covering the drawing room walls was a builder, and the man with him his accountant, and that he was hoping to buy the main house and the stables and garages for development purposes. The older man standing staring out of the window was, as Maggie had guessed for herself, a farmer who wanted to buy the farmland, the younger man with him being his son, and the young couple standing a little nervously side by side were hoping to bid successfully for one of the cottages.

'Normally when we hold auctions in town we get a lot of interested spectators who are there simply for the entertainment value an auction provides, and if we'd been auctioning off household goods we would undoubtedly have had far more people here, but the furniture, such as it is, goes with the house, and is not of any particular value.'

Philip stopped speaking and looked at his watch, whilst Maggie waited. The auction was almost due to start, and she could tell that the agent was slightly on edge and preoccupied. Thanking him for the information he had given her, she moved away.

The drawing room's yellow silk was faded where the sun had touched it, and despite the existence of some heavy old fashioned radiators the room felt cold and smelled old and musty. Even so, to her own surprise, Maggie found that something about it was giving her an unfamiliar feeling of concern and compassion, almost as though in some odd way the house itself was reaching out to her, to tell her how much it wanted to be loved and cherished and brought back to life.

Such unexpectedly intense and emotional thoughts made her frown, engrossing her so much that it caught her off guard to hear the agent announce that the auction was about to begin.

As she went to join the small semicircle forming in front of him, Maggie was suddenly conscious of the way Philip was looking over her head and past her, as though…

Automatically she looked round, and then froze in disbelief as she saw Finn standing just inside the door. Her heart gave a fierce jolt and lurched against her ribs as emotions she couldn't control escaped from the captivity of her will-power. How had he found her? How had he known…? Fiercely she fought for self-control, sternly telling herself what she ought to be feeling and how she ought to be reacting, and it certainly wasn't with that dangerous mixture of sweetly painful anguish and joy she had now thankfully managed to subdue. How dared he seek her out like this? Here…now, when he knew she would be forced to acknowledge him. Yes, that was better. That was more the reaction she ought to be feeling.

But underneath her anger she could still feel all too keenly that sharp frisson of excitement and pleasure her body had given as it registered his presence. She wasn't going to speak to him now. He must wait until after the auction, until she was ready, prepared, her defences firmly in place…

'Ah, Finn, good. I was just beginning to think you weren't going to make it.'

The warmth and relief with which the agent was greeting Finn, the recognition his arrival produced, startled Maggie, putting a brake on her own thoughts. It was unpleasantly obvious that Philip had been expecting Finn

to arrive—had been waiting for him to arrive, she recognised with sudden stark insight.

'Sorry I'm late,' Finn was apologising easily, switching his gaze from Maggie to the agent. But as soon as
he had finished speaking to him he switched it back to
her again, and any delusions she might have been foolish
enough to entertain that he had come to the auction to
see her would very quickly have been banished by the
look of frowning wariness he was giving her, Maggie
recognised.

The agent's assistant, obviously desperately anxious
to make contact with Finn, all but knocked Maggie over
as she hurried towards him, smiling up at him and standing so close that had she got any closer she would have
been in actual bodily contact with him, Maggie reflected
sourly as she monitored the other girl's openly awed and
flirtatious manner.

And Finn, of course was enjoying every minute of her
attention. What man wouldn't?

As she glowered at them both—a glower that was
caused by distaste and her relief that she was far too in
control of herself and had far too much self-respect to
ever behave so needily to any man, Maggie quickly assured herself—Finn looked up and towards her, his gaze
trapping hers before she had time to look away.

Just what was it she could see in those winter-blue
eyes? Mockery, conceit, contempt, anger—all of those,
plus a hostility and suspicion that infused her own gaze
with a reciprocal hot resentment and pride. Yet, despite
that, she still could not bring herself to drag her gaze

from him, leaving it to him to be the one to end their fiercely silent visual engagement.

The auction had started, and Maggie concentrated determinedly on what was happening. The builder had started the bidding for the main house at a figure that made Maggie's eyes water a little, but her shock at realising the value of the property was nowhere near the shock she got when she saw the auctioneer looking past her and, unable to stop herself from turning round, realised that Finn was bidding for the house against the builder. Finn, a property-less farmer, bidding for a house which a nod of the builder's square-shaped head was already taking swiftly to the two million pound mark.

As the battle between Finn and the builder pushed the house up even further, Maggie could only look on in disbelief whilst Finn, a man whom she had assumed had to struggle financially, continued to bid for a property which was climbing inexorably towards three million.

At three and a quarter million the builder and his accountant exchanged looks, and Maggie saw the builder's mouth twist angrily as he conceded defeat.

As she battled with her disbelief Maggie saw the agent congratulate Finn with obvious pleasure before starting the bidding for the land.

Well, if Finn thought *she* was going to congratulate him he was going to be disappointed, Maggie told herself fiercely, and she deliberately turned her back on him. Surely he would leave now that he had got what he wanted? Her face grew hot as she remembered unwillingly her foolish assumption that he had come to the auction to seek out her. Thank goodness she hadn't said anything to him that might have betrayed that misconception—and her with it—to his scorn and rejection.

Finn watched grimly as Maggie turned her back on him. He was still battling with the sense of shock he had experienced on seeing her—and with the savagery of his unwanted pain when he had realised that she wasn't there, as his initial heart-wrenching belief had been, because of him.

Almost absently he nodded in the auctioneer's direction, signalling his interest in the land. It was entirely Maggie's fault that he had so nearly been late for the auction in the first place. A night of broken sleep interspersed with graphically emotional and physical dreams about her had resulted in him doing something he never did—oversleeping. Ever since he had first heard that this estate was coming up for auction he had been determined to buy it. Owning it would be the fulfilment of a decade long search. And yet now, instead of concentrating on the bidding, his thoughts were focused almost exclusively on Maggie.

What was she doing here? Bidding for one of the lots; that much was obvious from her intent concentration on the auctioneer and the sale brochure she was holding. But which lot? Not the main house, nor the land...

Finn frowned as he automatically raised his bid to meet that of Audley Slater. Audley was a local farmer whose family connection with the area went back over several generations. His land ran next to that of the estate, and Finn could well understand why he wanted to buy it, but Audley believed in intensive farming, and Finn knew that if he was successful he would drain the estate's water meadows, and probably sell the river's fishing rights. He wanted to retain the water meadows and if possible restore them to their original form.

No, Maggie couldn't be interested in the land—which left the cottages and the barns that went with them, and the Dower House.

Finn's frown deepened. Philip Crabtree, the agent, had been scrupulous about not discussing any other potential buyers with him, other than to say that both the Dower House and the cottages had attracted some interest. And, cautious about not revealing too much of his own plans, Finn had allowed Philip to believe that his bidding would be for the main house itself and the land.

Out of the corner of his eye Finn saw Audley Slater shaking his head as Finn raised his bid yet again.

Five minutes later, coming over to Finn after the auctioneer had finally signalled that Finn's bid for the land was successful, Audley told him bluntly, 'It will take one hell of a long time for you to make a profit out of the land at that price.'

Maggie could see Finn talking to the farmer he had just outbid. Next to her the young couple were huddled together, holding a whispered conversation.

'Not long now,' the agent told Maggie reassuringly as he walked past her.

The bidding for the cottages didn't take long. The moment the young couple realised that Finn was entering the bidding they virtually gave up. Maggie felt angry on their behalf as she saw their disappointment. Her stomach started to churn nervously as she heard the auctioneer announce the final lot for sale: The Dower House.

'This is a very pretty little Georgian house, with a good-sized garden, in an excellent situation, although in need of a certain amount of renovation and repair. I shall start the bidding at two hundred thousand pounds.'

Refusing to look at Finn, Maggie raised her brochure. 'Two hundred thousand,' she offered, hating the cracked anxious note she could hear in her own voice.

So Maggie was bidding for the Dower House. He should have guessed, Finn acknowledged bitterly. It would make a perfect 'weekend retreat' for Maggie and her partner—her lover. The lover she had denied to him existed; the lover he would never have known she possessed, given her sensual responsiveness to him, if he hadn't heard her himself on the telephone to him. He could just imagine what would happen if Maggie were to be successful in her bid to buy it. The house would be gutted. An expensive team of architects would be brought in to renovate the whole place, followed by equally expensive builders, and then no doubt one of the City's most trendy interior designers,

But the Dower House belonged rightfully to the estate, it was a part of its history, and there was no way Finn had ever intended to have city weekenders living right under his nose—any weekenders, but most definitely not

Maggie and her lover. Angrily he raised her bid. No matter how much it cost him there was no way he was going to have Maggie buy the Dower House. No way he could endure having her living there, no matter how infrequently, reminding him of certain things he had no wish whatsoever to be reminded of.

Maggie gritted her teeth and tried not to let her hostility show as she topped Finn's bid. He was doing this deliberately; she knew it. The auctioneer had virtually assured her that the Dower House was hers, that no one else was interested in bidding for it. She tensed as she heard Finn's clipped response to her bid. Three hundred thousand pounds—they had reached the house's reserve price, but there was no way she was going to stop now...

Oblivious to the interest the battle between them was now causing the others in the room, Finn and Maggie continued to outbid one another, taking the price of the Dower House higher and higher. Three hundred and fifty thousand, three hundred and seventy-five thousand, four hundred thousand...

When Maggie reacted sharply and fiercely to Finn's four hundred thousand with her own four hundred and twenty-five thousand, she could see the look of concern on the agent's face. The knowledge that he felt sorry for her, that he obviously felt she was getting out of her depth, only spurred her on. Four hundred and fifty thousand came and went, and four hundred and seventy-five. Maggie was way over her top limit now, but she no longer cared. All she cared about was winning... All she cared about was refusing to allow Finn to best her, to defeat her.

They were standing less than two metres apart and, unable to help herself, Maggie turned towards Finn.

'Why are you doing this?' she mouthed bitterly at him.

'Why do you think I'm doing it?' he mouthed equally bitterly back. 'There is no way I'm going to let you get the Dower House. No way, Maggie. No matter how much it costs me.'

No matter how much! The apprehension flooding Maggie almost overwhelmed her fury.

'Five hundred thousand pounds!'

A cold rush of icy shock rushed through Maggie as she heard Finn make his bid, his voice, like his demeanour, stern and unyielding. When he turned away from her to face the auctioneer an unfamiliar recklessness tore through her, totally obliterating the anxious voice of caution begging her to think about what she was doing. Instead of listening to it, Maggie started to make frantic mental calculations. She would have to remortgage her London flat, and borrow against the business as well as empty her savings accounts...

The reality of the financial ruin she could be facing if she allowed her pride its head finally got through to her, like a blast of cold air in an overheated room, making her shudder as she recognised her own danger.

She could sense the tension in the room, the sense of appalled fascination their duel was creating amongst the onlookers. Her pride urged her not to give in, but reality forced her to acknowledge that she could not continue. Her awareness of her own vulnerability tasted bitter, made her eyes sting with angry emotions she furiously refused to acknowledge. Holding her head high, she looked across at Finn properly, for the first time since the bidding had begun. Silently he looked back at her. His eyes were inimical and cold, his mouth a hard tight line of angry rejection

The auctioneer was waiting for her response to Finn's last bid. Reluctantly she shook her head, appalled by the unexpected and unwanted rush of hot tears choking her. Unable to face any more, she turned on her heel, heading for the exit.

She had just reached her car when Finn caught up with her. He had wanted to go to her before, but he had needed to speak with the young couple who he knew had been planning to bid for one of the cottages. He had learned that they were local youngsters, and that the young man had only recently left agricultural collage with excellent qualifications. It had immediately occurred to Finn that, since he would be in need of agricultural workers for the estate, he could both offer the young man a job and throw in the rental of the cottage at a suitably low rate, and he had wanted to make this offer to them before they left the house.

So far as Maggie and her desire to buy the Dower House went, he knew he had done the right thing, the only thing he could have done, but something about the way Maggie had looked at him as she conceded defeat had made him feel as though... As though what? As though he had behaved badly, unfairly?

'Maggie...'

The moment she heard his voice Maggie felt her emotions swamping her. Swinging round, her back against the door of her car, she glared at him. 'If you've come to crow over your victory, Finn, don't bother.' She gave a bitter laugh. 'I suppose I should have known that you would never allow me to win. How nice to be able to throw so much money away without counting the cost. I hope you consider it was worth it.'

'It was,' Finn assured her, suddenly equally angry, forgetting now, as he heard and felt her antagonism, the look of aching disappointment and pain he had seen in her eyes as she had acknowledged her inability to bid any higher. 'I would have paid twice as much to keep the likes of you from owning the Dower House, Maggie...'

'The likes of me?' Maggie was too incensed to conceal her feelings.

'City people. Weekenders,' Finn elucidated in a curt voice. 'The countryside should be for living in full time, not treated as some kind of manicured playground.'

'Oh, I see,' Maggie retaliated furiously. 'I'm good enough to take to bed, but apparently not good enough to have as a neighbour. Is that what you're trying to say? Well, for your information—' She stopped in disbelief as for the second time in less than half an hour the intensity of her emotions brought her dangerously close to tears.

'The fact that we went to bed together has nothing to do with the Dower House,' Finn denied—untruthfully. He could feel the tinge of colour creeping up under his skin as his conscience forced him to admit to himself that, contrary to his verbal claim, the fact that they had been lovers had everything to do with the fact that he didn't want her living in the Dower House. Not when he knew she would be sharing it—and her bed—with the man she had called 'darling', not when last night— all night, virtually—he had ached and longed for her, not when against everything he knew about himself a part of him still stubbornly refused to accept that there was no way there could ever be a proper relationship between them.

'You bid for the Dower House to spite me,' Maggie accused him once she had herself back under control.

'No,' Finn denied sharply. 'I had always intended to bid for the whole estate…'

'That's not what the agent told me,' Maggie argued, shaking her head. 'He told me that no one else was going to bid for the Dower House.'

'He may have believed that,' Finn acknowledged 'But—'

'But the moment you realised I wanted it you were determined that you were going to stop me,' Maggie cut in bitterly, too angry to conceal her feelings.

'There are other houses,' Finn pointed out.

'Not for me,' Maggie rejected grimly.

She looked white-faced and anguished, and ridiculously Finn found himself aching to comfort her. She

had plainly replenished her wardrobe since she had left
the farm. She was wearing the soft creamy cashmere
coat he had seen her in in Shrewsbury, and a toning pair
of trousers, with a fine knit top that clung to her breasts.
She looked both elegant and expensive, and somehow
softly vulnerable as well, the delicacy of her small heart-
shaped face and huge brown eyes driving him to anger
against himself for what he was feeling.

As she started to turn away from him a sudden fierce
gust of wind caught at Maggie's unfastened coat, sending it swirling around her and virtually blinding her. As
she reached to push it away so automatically did Finn.
Their hands touched, Maggie's retracting as though it
had been burned, leaving Finn's to somehow drop to her
body, cupping her hipbone beneath the heavy folds of
her coat.

Its fragility and the memories the feel of it evoked
sent desire rocketing through Finn in a way that caught
him completely off guard.

'Maggie.'

The urgency in his voice hit her senses with the same
devastating impact as alcohol on an empty stomach. She
could feel herself swaying in response to the desire she
could hear running through that roughly urgent utterance
of her name. She could almost see the images compressed in it. The two of them lying naked on his bed
whilst he...

'Let go of me,' she demanded as she was deluged with
panic—panic caused not by a fear of him but of herself

and what she might do, what she might reveal if he continued to stay where he was.

But as she pulled back from him she realised there was nowhere for her to go, that she was already backed up against the car. Inside her she could feel her anger and excitement battling for supremacy. Finn was leaning towards her.

Her lips framed the word 'no' but it was too late. The kiss they exchanged was mutually hostile and denying, a fierce pressure of lips on lips, mouth on mouth, tongue battling with tongue as they fought to overcome one another and their own unwanted feelings.

If the time she had spent in Finn's arms had opened her eyes to the danger of her own susceptibility to his sensuality, then the kiss they were exchanging now was confirming just how right she had been to reject her feelings for him.

To feel such an intensity of emotion frightened her. To know that she was capable of wanting so passionately a man who made her feel so angry, of wanting him so intensely that a part of her was actually relishing the furious savagery of their intimacy, shocked and appalled her. And to know that she of all people was capable of being totally overwhelmed by emotions in a way that ran contrary to everything that was important to her filled her with a blind panic that somehow gave her the strength to wrench her mouth away from Finn's, to push him out of the way long enough for her to be able to pull open her car door and get inside.

As she drove off in a furious spray of gravel Finn

stared after her, fighting to regulate his breathing and his feelings. Where the hell had that come from? Absently he lifted his hand to his jaw, and then winced as his thumb pad brushed his bottom lip and found the place where Maggie had briefly savaged it with her teeth. He had never known such a passionate, contrary, downright dangerous woman—and he wished he didn't know her now.

Not when that woman was Maggie—and most definitely not when she was involved with another man.

CHAPTER FIVE

'I'M REALLY glad I managed to catch you before you left town,' Philip exclaimed as he came rushing into the foyer of the hotel just as Maggie was on the point of leaving. 'I'm really sorry about the Dower House,' he plunged on, ignoring Maggie's cool reception.

'You virtually told me that there were not going to be any other serious bidders for the property,' Maggie burst out, unable to keep her feelings to herself as she had promised herself she would do when she had first seen him hurrying towards her. After all, a humiliation like the one she had endured at Finn's hands was hardly something anyone would want to dwell on.

Unable to endure the thought of spending another night in Shropshire, she had decided to travel back to London immediately.

'I didn't think there were going to be,' the agent insisted.

He looked so anxious for her to believe him that Maggie knew he was telling the truth.

'Finn had told me that he intended to bid for the house, and the land, but I assumed that they were all that he was interested in. Like you, he asked me about the possibility of pre-empting the auction, but of course I told him that the owner was insistent on the property being broken up into lots and sold separately. We very often find a large house with land sells for more as separate lots, as indeed was the case. Finn has been looking to buy either a farm or a small estate locally for some time.' He paused and shrugged, looking uncomfortable as he told her, 'I really am sorry. I had no idea he intended to bid for the Dower House.'

Maggie gave him a thin smile. She suspected she knew exactly what had prompted Finn's unexpected decision to bid. The minute he had realised she wanted it he had obviously decided he was going to prevent her from getting it, no matter what it cost him.

Feigning a casual disregard she did not feel, she told the agent truthfully, 'Well, there was certainly no way I could have afforded to outbid him.'

Maybe not, but she had certainly tried hard enough, Phillip reflected inwardly. The Dower House had gone for more than twice its real market value.

Of course, he was very familiar with the red mist that could so easily overwhelm rival bidders, each determined to better the other, however, he could not remember ever experiencing such a charged atmosphere as the one generated by Finn and Maggie as they had fought for possession of the Dower House. It had been his concern for her ashen-faced despair as she had left that had prompted him to come in search of her, to assure her that he had had no prior knowledge of Finn's intentions.

'I know how much securing the Dower House meant to you,' Philip continued. There had been, he was sure, a sheen of tears in her eyes earlier as she had conceded defeat to Finn. 'Finn is a very generous man, something of a philanthropist. Perhaps if you were to approach him he might be prepared to rent the house to you... I know that he's offered to rent one of the cottages to Linda and Pete Hardy—they were at the auction. They're both over the moon and singing Finn's praises to whoever will listen to them, and now Pete is going to be working for Finn as well.' The agent chuckled. 'One of the reasons they had hoped to pick up the cottage cheaply was because whilst Linda works full time as a nurse, Pete didn't have a job.'

Even as she was digesting the agent's surprising news about Finn's generosity to the young couple who had wanted to bid for one of the cottages, Maggie's reaction to his suggestion that she throw herself on Finn's charity was as immediate as it was instinctive.

'No.'

Maggie could see that the harshness of her denial had shocked him. Forcing her lips to part in poor imitation of her normal smile, she told him in a less emotional voice, 'I wanted to give the house itself to my grandmother, not a rental agreement.'

She knew her excuse was not exactly logical, but there was no way she could tell the agent the real reason why she knew that Finn would refuse any request from her— for anything.

'Well, if you're sure, I'd better go and see Finn,' Philip was telling her a little awkwardly. 'Buying the estate is going to leave his bank account several million pounds lighter. Not that he can't afford it, of course.'

He was talking about Finn as though Maggie herself knew his circumstances, and even though she knew she would regret giving in to the temptation Maggie found it impossible not to say a little acerbically, 'I hadn't realised there was so much money in farming.'

The agent laughed. 'There isn't. And I'm afraid Finn's plans to extend the scope of his organic farming venture are not very popular with the likes of Audley Slater. But then of course Finn is not reliant on the land financially. He made a fortune as a City trader in the boom, and he had the foresight to take a large proportion of his bonuses in share options. He's worth millions,' he told Maggie.

Finn had been a city trader. Maggie fought to conceal her disbelief—she found it almost impossible to equate the man Finn had seemed to be with the stories she had heard about groups of wild young men who had become almost a byword for all types of excess. Things were different now, of course; there had been too many falls from grace for it to be otherwise.

The agent's revelation had affected her more deeply than she wanted to acknowledge, but somehow she managed to force a polite smile as he shook her hand before turning to leave.

Why hadn't Finn said anything? Told her—told her... Why had he let her think that the City was an alien concept to him? The certainty that she had known so little about him, been so wrong about his background, reinforced the fear she had fought so determinedly to subdue that with Finn, both he and their relationship would be outside her control.

The square was virtually empty as she hurried towards her car. What had she expected? To see Finn's Land Rover parked there? A dirty muddy old Land Rover! City traders drove up-market gleaming sports cars, the faster and more expensive the better. They dated models and actresses, and they loved city life and city women. But Finn did not. Finn felt only contempt for city women...

City women...or just one city woman...just her?

Sombrely Maggie got into her car. She had a long drive ahead of her, and the one thing she was determined she was not going to do was spend it thinking about Finn Gordon. Why should she? After all, he meant nothing to her. Nothing at all.

Finn didn't know why on earth he was bothering wasting his time like this. After all, he had far better things to do. And why should he apologise anyway? Grimly he crashed the Land Rover's gears, his attention more on his thoughts than what he was doing as he drove through the small town's narrow streets, heading for Maggie's hotel. Anyone would think he was looking for any excuse he could find just to see her And there was no way he was fool enough to do anything like that. She already had a man in her life, and even if she hadn't she had made it more than plain that she wasn't prepared to give up her city lifestyle.

Swinging into a convenient car park space, he reminded himself that he had had to come into the town anyway, to see Philip.

'Finn, I was just on my way back to the office to ring you.'

Cursing under his breath as Philip hailed him, Finn couldn't resist looking past him and across the square to the hotel. The memory of the angry kiss he and Maggie had exchanged outside the house still burned at danger heat...

'I'm just on my way back to the office now,' Philip was telling him. 'I've just been to see Maggie Russell— I felt I ought to. I hadn't realised that you were intending to bid for the Dower House, and I'm afraid I encouraged her to believe she had every chance of bidding successfully for it herself. Luckily I just managed to catch her before she left.'

Left? Maggie had gone?

That wasn't some crazy desire to go after her that had him half turning back towards the parked Land Rover was it?

'I did suggest that she should ask if you would be willing to rent the house to her,' Philip continued, as Finn checked his reckless impulse. 'After all, from your point of view it would make much more sense to have it tenanted than left empty, especially with such a potentially good tenant—an elderly widow living on her own, and...'

'A what?'

All thoughts of going after Maggie gone, Finn stared

at the agent, the brusque sharpness of his voice causing the younger man to look confused.

'An elderly widow,' he repeated, persisting when Finn continued to look sternly at him, 'Maggie's grandmother. Maggie told me the story when she came to my office to ask if she could buy the house prior to auction at the reserve price. I'm sure she won't mind me repeating it to you.'

Finn had his doubts about that, but he quelled his conscience and gave Phillip an encouraging look.

'It seems that her grandparents lived in the Dower House as a young married couple. Maggie's grandfather has recently died, and she is concerned about the effect his loss is having on her grandmother. When she saw that the Dower House was coming up for auction she hoped that if she could buy it for her grandmother it might help to cheer her up a bit.'

Her grandmother. Maggie had wanted the house for her grandmother! Silently Finn digested the information Philip had given him. Equally silently he recalled Maggie's stricken look when she had realised that he was not going to allow her to outbid him.

The story the agent had told him was forcing him to see Maggie in a different light; to see her as someone who cared very deeply about those she loved. There had been no mention of her grandmother when she had told him about her successful business, but then there had been no mention of a lover either; in fact she had denied flatly that she had one.

Later that afternoon, as he drove back to the farm,

Finn discovered that he was still thinking about Maggie. As he drove across the ford he found he was actually looking down into the water, as though he might see one of her ridiculously impractical shoes there. He had noticed that she was wearing another pair of impossibly high-heeled shoes again today—only instead of seeing the choice of such footwear in the country and in such weather as gross folly, rather dangerously it had taken on an almost endearing quality, a special something that made her wholly and uniquely Maggie.

The fact that he had no close family of his own was something that Finn felt very keenly. His parents had married late in life, when their own parents had been elderly, so Finn had never known his grandparents. His father had died of a heart attack shortly after Finn's eighteenth birthday and his mother had died less than a year later. His own experiences had taught Finn how important family was. And as he drove into the farmyard he was deep in thought.

'And then Bas said that he didn't care how long it was going to take, he was going to keep on proposing until I gave in and agreed to marry him. So I thought I might as well save us both a lot of time and hassle and give in there and then.'

Politely Maggie joined in the others' laughter as they all listened to Lisa, drolly explaining how she came to be wearing a huge solitaire diamond engagement ring having sworn only weeks earlier that she was never ever going to get married.

The eight of them had been meeting up once a month for the last five years, all of them dedicated career women, all of them independent twenty to thirty-somethings, with their own flats, cars, accountants, and the wherewithal to buy their own diamond rings if they wanted them, and all of them determined to stay single. But gradually things had started to change.

Maggie wasn't sure she could pinpoint exactly how or when that change had started to happen. She just knew that it had, and from being earnest occasions on which they discussed their ambitions and successes over a meal at whichever of London's trendy eateries they were currently favouring, their get-togethers had begun to take on a much more personal note. The names of family members had begun to creep into their conversation, along with shamefaced confessions of parental or sibling pressure regarding their lack of partner and/or offspring, and a bonding at a much deeper level had come into being. Maggie had relished that closeness. Her friends were very important to her and she knew she wasn't alone in that feeling. Friends, as anyone who read a magazine or newspaper knew, were the new 'family'.

But now once again things were changing, and this time Maggie did not like it.

Caitlin had started it, returning from a holiday in Ireland to announce out of the blue that she was moving in with her boyfriend.

'My sister has this gorgeous baby,' was how she'd limply explained her change of heart, 'and I suddenly realised that I'm five years older than she is and that if I'm not careful...'

'It's your biological clock ticking away,' Lisa had told her knowledgeably, and that had been the start of it.

Now all of them had partners—all of them but her, Maggie realised as she listened to the others' laughter as they teased Lisa. But they were the ones who had changed, not her; just as they were the ones who sometimes looked a little self-conscious when they talked about their altered goals. As she talked to her friends right now, the unwelcome thought struck Maggie that it was almost as though Finn, with his back-to-nature, downshifting lifestyle, was more akin to them than she was herself. She felt...she felt almost as though she was an outsider, she recognised indignantly. And for some reason she was not prepared to analyse she felt like putting the blame for this on Finn's shoulders. And why shouldn't she? After all he was to blame for the fact that she was sitting here thinking about him.

'Of course Ma's jumped on the bandwagon now,' Lisa was telling them. 'I think I'm going to have to physically restrain her from organising a full-works wedding—and Bas isn't much help. He's virtually egging her on. Mind you, if he had his way there'd be no way I'd be decently fit to walk down the aisle. Waddle down perhaps; I've never known a man so desperate to become a father...'

'It's the new thing,' Charlotte interrupted. 'Men are baby-mad. Everywhere you look men are downscaling, cutting back their working hours, insisting that they want to spend more time with their families. I've lost count of the number of couples I know who've moved out of the City in the last year, and all of them because they either have or want to start families.' She gave a small shrug. 'And after all what could be more cosy than a huge country house big enough for you to work from home, and to house a family? Loads of people are trying to persuade their parents to move in with them, too. I mean, you just couldn't get any better childcare than your own parents, could you?'

As Maggie listened to the heated debate that followed she felt a cold sharp pang of alienness. But these were her friends, women she had shared her hopes and dreams with for the last five years—women who, after her grandmother, formed her closest relationship circle.

'Well, moving out to the country is quite definitely a hot new trend,' Tanya confirmed. 'I mean look at Greta and Nigel. Of course those with the financial resources to do so have always aimed to own a house in the country along with a city *pièd-a-terre*, but...'

As another heated flurry of exchanges broke out Maggie remained silent, locked in the pain of her own thoughts.

'You're quiet Maggie,' Charlotte noticed, turning to look at her. But before Maggie could make any response Lisa was laughing.

'Oh, Maggie thoroughly disapproves of us all. She thinks we're traitoresses to the cause, don't you?'

'No, of course I don't,' Maggie denied, but she could see that they didn't believe her. And she could see, too, that suddenly she was excluded from their new shared closeness.

'Putting relationships first is the really happening thing now, Maggie,' Tanya told her gently.

Tanya worked in PR and knew all about 'happening' things. She had gone on holiday six months earlier—a tiny private island one could only visit by invitation—fallen in love with a fellow guest, and was now planning to give up her job and join him on his planned trek across the Andes.

Not that Maggie really needed anyone to underline for her what she already knew. She had lost count of the number of people she had 'relocated' recently who had insisted on 'time out for family' clauses being built into their contracts.

In the past their evenings out had ended late, but now it seemed everyone had things they needed to go on to—everyone but her, Maggie acknowledged. She could walk to her apartment from the wine bar where they had met. Halfway there she stopped outside a small super-market, and somehow or other she found she was walk-ing into it…

It was only when she was back outside that Maggie allowed herself to question just why she had found it necessary to buy the ingredients to make a chilli.

'Gran, why don't you come back to London with me? We could shop, and there's a wonderful new show we could go and see,' Maggie suggested to Arabella Russell that weekend.

'No…no. It's kind of you to think of me, Maggie, but I just don't feel in the mood. At least in this house I feel as though I'm still close to your grandfather, even though he was only here for a few short months.'

Her grandparents had moved into a smaller house six months before her grandfather's death, and Maggie could feel her throat aching with tears as she listened to her grandmother. In the few weeks since Maggie had last seen her she seemed to have become so frail. She looked frighteningly tired and defeated, as if…as though…

Thoughts Maggie dared not let herself form sent a sickening weave of panic through her. If Finn hadn't stopped her from buying the Dower House right now she could have been telling her grandmother that she had a special surprise for her. She could have been anticipating the pleasure and happiness in her eyes as she walked into the house she had known as a young wife. And Maggie just knew that in that house her grandmother would 'see' her grandfather as he had been when they had been young together, and that she would draw strength from their shared past happiness.

Finn… Finn…

She got up and hurried into her grandmother's kitchen, opening cupboard doors, searching…

'Maggie, what on earth are you doing?'

Guiltily Maggie looked round as her grandmother followed her into the kitchen.

'Umm…I was going to make some chilli.'

'What…?'

Red-faced, Maggie closed the cupboard doors. What on earth was happening to her? Why was it every time she thought about Finn she had this peculiar desire to make chilli?

Subliminal association was one thing; taking it to the ridiculous lengths of being physically compelled to make chilli just because the act of doing so brought her closer to her memories of the time she had spent at the farm with Finn was something else—and a very worrying and unwanted something else at that. Why on earth should she need to cling to those memories, as if…as if they were some sort of comfort blanket that she simply could not get through any anxiety without?

It was over a month since she had last seen Finn—well, five weeks, two days and seven and three-quarter hours, actually. Not that she was counting. Or cared. No, indeed not. Why should she? She didn't. No way. No way at all. She was perfectly happy as she was—more than happy. She was ecstatic. Her life was perfect…everything she had ever wanted it to be. At least it would have been if only her grandmother…

Damn Finn. Damn him and his ridiculous antagonism towards city people buying country property. What right did he have to dictate what others could and could not do? No right at all…other than the power that having far too much money gave him, to pay more than twice its value for a house just to stop another person owning it. Well, she just hoped he would be happy in his huge mansion, with his land and his alpaca and his empty Dower House… No, she didn't; she hoped he would be thoroughly miserable, because that was what he deserved. Unlike her beloved grandmother, who did not deserve to be unhappy at all.

Finn looked grimly at his surroundings. He had taken possession of the estate three days ago, his livestock had been moved to their new home, and he had successfully interviewed a first-class team of workers to help him put his plans into practice. So why wasn't he feeling more happy? Why, in fact, was he feeling distinctly unhappy?

From the library of the house, which was the room he intended to work from, he could see across the parkland to where the empty Dower House lay behind its high brick wall. Despite the warmth of the room—the house's ancient heating system had proved surprisingly efficient once it had been coaxed into life—the house had an air of chill emptiness about it.

According to Philip's assistant, it needed a woman's touch, and Finn knew exactly which woman's touch she had envisaged it having. But she wasn't his type. She was…not Maggie.

Angrily he dismissed the taunting voice whispering the words inside his head. He had been down to see the Dower House the previous day. Structurally it was sound and weather proof, but, like the main house, inside it needed modernising.

'Pity to let a place like this stand empty.' Shane Farrell, the man he had taken on as his gamekeeper, had commented. 'Wouldn't mind living here myself,' he had added hintingly.

'I'd planned to offer you the cottage next to Pete's,' Finn had told him, referring to the second of the pair of empty estate cottages he had bought at the auction. But Shane was right. It would be shameful to allow the Dower House to stand empty and deteriorate, especially when...

Walking back over to his desk, Finn picked up the telephone and searched the directory for the number of his solicitor.

The letter was waiting for Maggie when she arrived home at nine o'clock in the evening after a particularly trying day. Gayle was off work, ill with bronchitis, and the person Maggie had been discreetly courting on behalf of one of her best clients had telephoned her in a furious temper, from her home, to announce to Maggie that she had just been informed by her current employers that they knew what was going on—when she had specifically stressed to Maggie how vitally important it was that their discussions were kept a secret. Maggie suspected that it must have been the woman's partner who had leaked the information; they worked in the same field, but the partner was less well thought of. However, there was no way she could voice such a suspicion.

She had then had an equally irate call from her clients, who had been informed of what had happened by the woman herself. Appeasing them had made her late for lunch with another client—one who had a thing about punctuality. And then after lunch she had tried to ring her grandmother, and panicked when she had not been able to raise her either on the house phone or the mobile Maggie had insisted on giving her.

She had virtually been on the point of driving into Sussex to find out if she was all right when her grandmother had finally answered her mobile, explaining that she never liked to take it with her when she went to visit Maggie's grandfather's grave, which she did every week, because she felt that it was the wrong thing to do.

Without Gayle's capable hands controlling the day-to-day running of the office Maggie had found herself becoming bogged down in paperwork, and the last thing she had needed had been a long complaining telephone call from a man she had headhunted unsuccessfully the previous year and who had now decided that he had made the wrong move in electing to take a job competitive with the one she had been authorised to offer him. He had wanted her, in his own words, to 'fix things' so that he could accept her client's offer after all.

It was only sheer professionalism that had allowed her to grit her teeth and bite back her instinctive response to his patronising manner—that and the satisfaction it had given her to tell him sweetly that, unfortunately, 'fixing things' was quite simply beyond her capability.

Having opened her apartment door, she picked up her post before closing it again and then locking it. The block her apartment occupied was in a part of the City that had certain and specific restrictions on alterations to the elegant late-Georgian buildings, which meant that it was devoid of any kind of modern high-tech security features—much to Maggie's grandmother's relief.

'I'm sorry, Maggie, but I just don't trust those horrid little "speak into me" things—they never seem to be able to hear me properly,' she had complained, whilst Maggie had stifled her giggles. 'And I certainly feel much happier knowing that you are properly protected by a good old-fashioned doorman and that your apartment door has a proper kind of lock on it. Modern technology is all very well, but you just can't beat a real lock,' Arabella Russell had pronounced firmly. And Maggie had known better than to argue with her.

Whenever her grandmother visited Maggie's apartment she invariably brought a little 'home-made something' with her—not just for Maggie, who she was convinced did not eat properly, but also for Bill, the commissionaire, a widower who lived in a small apartment in the basement with a large ginger cat, and who seemed to conduct a running battle with the block's central heating and air-conditioning systems.

The arid heat of the central heating system felt stifling to Maggie after the cold outside, and just recently the apartment's silence had begun to grate a little on her nerves. She had even actually dreamed about waking up to birdsong and the sounds of the countryside.

Ridiculous, of course. She hated the countryside. It was dirty, and wet, and filled with impossible men wearing boots and driving battered old Land Rovers, masquerading as poor farmers whilst all the time owning squillions of pounds which they used to stop people like her from buying any of their wretched countryside.

Shrugging off her coat, Maggie started to open her

mail. And then stopped, dropping the letter she was reading in furious disbelief. What on earth…? How could…? Angrily she walked into her small kitchen and then walked back again, picking up the letter she had thrown aside and rereading it.

Finn understood that she had wanted to buy the Dower House for her grandmother, and on that understanding, and on condition that she never at any time moved into it herself with her lover, he was prepared to rent the property to her at a favourable peppercorn annual rental, to be agreed. If she would write back to him confirming her agreement to these terms then he would instruct his solicitor to begin the necessary legal proceedings and to draw up a lease.

Maggie couldn't believe what she was reading. The arrogance. To dare to…

Did he think she would actually…? And what did he mean, on condition that she never at any time moved into it herself with her lover? She did not have a lover. How could he possibly think that when he…when she… Oh, yes, now she could see the City trader coming out in him. Of course to him the idea of sexual exclusivity would be laughable.

Write back to him! Maggie was seething. Oh, no. She had a far, far better idea than that!

CHAPTER SIX

AS SHE drove west along the motorway Maggie was mentally rehearsing just what she intended to say to Finn. The 'time out' effect of a night to sleep on her fury had done nothing to lessen it. That he should dare to patronise her in such a way! And what had he hoped to gain from changing his mind? Her eternal grovelling gratitude? After that condition he had so insultingly outlined? Did he really think that if she had been involved with another man she would have behaved with him as she had, never mind allow him to dictate to her how, when or where she saw her lover?

Engrossed in her fury, she let the miles fly by, and it was only the sharp pangs of hunger gripping her stomach that reminded her how long it was since she had last eaten. Last night she had been too tired and then too furious to even contemplate eating. This morning she had been too busy thinking about what she intended to say to Finn and how she intended to make sure that he never made the mistake of trying to patronise her again to bother with any breakfast. A cup of coffee had been enough, but now her body was insisting that it needed nourishment!

Irritably Maggie drove more slowly, looking for somewhere to eat. It seemed a sensible idea to drive straight into Shrewsbury rather than waste time driving down country lanes, even it did mean a detour.

The smart wine bar where she eventually ended up having her lunch reminded her very much of her City haunts. As she waited for her meal to be served she studied the eager group of young men and women seated at a table close by. Absently eavesdropping on their conversation, she was forced to acknowledge that there was very little difference other than that of location between them and their London peers. She had even heard one of the young men announcing that he had turned down a move to London, though it would have meant a higher income, because he didn't want to leave his friends or his family.

Maggie gave a small shiver. Had Tanya been right when she had teasingly claimed that Maggie was getting out of touch, that she was clinging to values and beliefs that were no longer viable? The girls had told her that commitment with a capital 'C' was the new buzzword, that it was generating an excitement, a sense of expectation and hope that everyone was eagerly reaching out to.

'Deep down inside everyone wants to be loved,' Lisa had claimed. 'It's just that our generation has had a hard time getting round to admitting it. We were almost born cynical. We looked at our parents and their lifestyles and said, "No way, thanks. We'd rather be self-reliant and single than risk what they put themselves through." But now it's different—we're different. We can see where they got it wrong and we can see how important and valuable, how empowering the values they misguidedly thought unimportant actually are. Although naturally they do need a little fine tuning,' she had acknowledged without the slightest trace of any irony. 'And best of all,' she had added mischievously, 'it's men who are getting the commitment bug really badly this time round. Love, marriage, babies, families—that's where it is now, Maggie. The "me" generation and everything it represented is gone. Right now the big thing is the "us factor"—sharing, caring, being. And I think it's wonderful.'

'I never realised your second name was Pollyanna,' had been Maggie's dry response, but deep down inside she had registered Lisa's comments—registered them and wanted to reject them because of the way they made her feel.

Unwilling to pursue her thoughts, Maggie paid for her lunch and left the wine bar. It would take her just over an hour to drive to the estate. The pithy observations she intended to make to Finn on his letter to her would not take very long to deliver and, since she had no intention of hanging around whilst he responded to them, she should be back on the road and on her way back to London before dark.

As she hurried to where she had parked her car she was aware of a sharp drop in temperature, and huddled protectively into her coat.

'I've searched all over London for that coat,' one of her friends had complained indignantly when she had seen her wearing it. 'There's a two-month waiting list for it. Where on earth did you get it?'

Smugly, Maggie had told her.

'Shrewsbury? Where on earth is that?' her friend had demanded.

As she left the cathedral city behind Maggie could see the grey-white clouds piling up slowly against the horizon. The countryside looked cold and bare, sheep huddling together motionlessly as she drove past them. At least Finn's alpaca should be used to winter weather with their heritage. Maggie started to smile as she remembered their cute small faces and huge dark eyes, their long necks weaving from side to side as they had watched her approach them curiously.

Was she going mad, grinning inanely to herself over the actions of farm animals? And worse still worrying about them?

This time she found her A road without any difficulty at all; indeed, she didn't even need to refer to her map in order to find the turn off for the Shopcutte estate.

The first thing she noticed as she turned into the drive was how much barer of leaves the trees now were; the second was that outside the house, right in front of the front door, she could see Finn's four-wheel drive.

That seriously stomach-churning feeling she was getting couldn't possibly be caused by doubts about the wisdom of what she was doing, by second thoughts, could it? No, of course not...

Of course not!

Even so, was it really necessary for her to spend so

much time carefully parking her car, reversing it so that it faced the drive—for a speedy and dignified exit—and then straightening it not once but three times until she was finally satisfied.

As a small confidence-booster she had only the previous week given in to the temptation to buy herself a pair of irresistibly delicious shoes, with high heels and peep toes—peep toes in winter: totally impractical—made in a deliciously soft tweed fabric. And she had even bought herself a matching bag. Not that she needed to boost her confidence in order to confront Finn...not at all. No, it had been entirely for other reasons that she had bought them. After all, she hadn't known then that she would be going to see him again. Had she?

The little designer dress she was wearing underneath her coat was equally impractical: a flimsy silk tea dress confection in fine voile printed with bees in which, the sales assistant had said, that she looked 'darling'. That comment had almost been enough to stop her from buying the dress, but in the end she hadn't been able to resist.

She had worn it to go and see her grandmother, who had exclaimed in delight that it reminded her of a dress she herself had worn in the forties. 'It was one of your grandfather's favourites...'

The little fake fur tippet that went with it somehow added to the dress's forties look, a look that was surely designed to be shown off in a sophisticated city setting, not worn in the depths of the country in the presence of a man who would only deride its impracticality—and who would no doubt lose no time in saying so.

Good, Maggie decided as she got out of the car and closed the door. She liked the idea of Finn giving her even more reason to take issue with him. Not that she had worn it to antagonise him.

Of course not.

As she left her car and walked towards the house she suddenly realised how still everything was, how silent. Not even the slightest breeze moved the air, which was winter-cold. The sky had a grey heaviness to it, and as she stared up at it a soft white flake of snow brushed her cheek.

Snow. In November. The end of November, admittedly, but it was still November. Wrapping her coat tightly around herself, she hurried up to the front door which, disconcertingly, immediately swung open.

'Finn!' she exclaimed in tones of angry resentment.

'Who else were you expecting?' Finn countered. 'After all, I do live here.'

As he spoke he stepped back so that she could walk into the hall—a much cleaner, brighter and better polished hall than she remembered from the auction, Maggie realised, as she took in the fire burning in the grate and the polished wooden floor, grateful that the need to inspect her surroundings was giving her time to prepare herself before she looked at Finn.

Not that she needed time or preparation. He was just a man, after all. Just a man who…As though he had grown tired of waiting for her to look at him, Finn moved into her line of vision, all six foot two, powerful muscle-packed maleness of him. Ridiculously, for such a cold day, he was wearing a thin white tee shirt, which hugged the contours of his chest almost as lovingly as the faded jeans he was wearing were clinging to his thighs.

Helplessly Maggie's gaze devoured him, her brown eyes smouldering passionately over every resented inch of him. How fatally easily she could picture him without that tee shirt, the soft whorls of his body hair flattened against the taut muscles of his stomach, just where she had stroked and then kissed the delicious hardness of the definition of his six-pack. Later, when he had growled and then groaned his appreciation and approval of what she was doing, she had moved lower, and then...

Dry-mouthed, she tried to wrench her gaze away from him and then realised as it clashed with his that he was studying her just as intently as she had been doing him. But it was derision and not desire she could see in his glance as it roved from the fashionably dark polish on her exposed toe nails, over her shoes, and upwards over her body, to rest momentarily on her face before dropping back to her feet.

This was better, Maggie acknowledged in relief as anticipatory antagonism filled her. Just let him say one word, make one criticism of her outfit and...

'Nice. It suits you.'

His calm words couldn't have had a more dramatic effect on Maggie. Stupefied, she stared at him, her mouth a round 'O' of bewilderment. Where were the contentious words of mockery and disapproval she had been expecting to hear?

As he watched her Finn wondered grimly if she had any idea just what the effect of seeing her was having on him, never mind seeing her wearing an outfit—a dress—which lovingly underscored every feminine centimetre of her. A dress she had no doubt bought and worn for her precious lover, Fin told himself, deliberately goading himself into jealousy and anger.

'Lucky, though, that the house's central heating system turned out to be working and efficient, otherwise I suspect you'd be rather cold. I'm using the library as my office. It's this way,' he told her, adding, 'I'm surprised you bothered to come all this way. Our solicitors could have sorted out the contract.'

Determinedly Maggie refused to move from where she was standing. 'There isn't going to be any contract,' she told him contentiously.

Finn turned and looked at her. 'No?'

His voice, like his eyes, was flat and hard, and awesomely polite in a way that sent a small shiver of electric triumph through her. He didn't like what she had said Good! Well, now he was about to hear something else he wasn't going to like.

Taking a deep breath, Maggie demanded, 'How dare you try to hold me to ransom? To tell me what I can and can't do and who with.'

'With whom,' Finn corrected her automatically.

Maggie took a deep breath, openly seething, but before she could speak, Finn continued calmly, 'Am I to take it that it's the condition that you will not be able to share a bed in the Dower House with your lover that's brought you…er…' He looked down at her shoes, before drawling tauntingly, 'Hot-foot down here.'

'My shoes, like who I share my bed with, are my concern, and only mine,' Maggie replied furiously.

'And, equally, who I choose to let the Dower House to and the conditions I choose to impose on that let are mine,' Finn countered grimly. 'Is having sex with him so much more important to you than your grandmother Maggie?'

It was like having a steel trap close round her mind. Something about him made it impossible for her to think logically and analytically, only to react emotionally, Maggie recognised as she denied furiously, 'No, it most certainly is not. My grandmother—' She stopped as her voice started to thicken with emotion. 'This has nothing to do with my feelings for my grandmother,' she insisted, almost hurling the words at Finn as she fought to avoid allowing him to verbally outwit her. 'This is about my right to live my life however I choose to live it, to share my bed with whoever I want—'

'And as we both know you are very good at doing that,' Finn intervened with a softly cruel emphasis that drove hot colour burning up over Maggie's skin. 'Very, very good,' Finn emphasised deliberately.

Maggie had started to clench her hands into small tense fists.

'I am perfectly prepared to allow you to rent the Dower House for your grandmother's occupation—

Philip explained her circumstances to me,' Finn continued.

'He had no right to discuss my private business with you—' Maggie began, but once again Finn stopped her.

'You should be grateful to him,' he told her challengingly. 'He was, in a manner of speaking, defending you, insisting that you did not want the Dower House as a pretty country toy you could retreat to with your lover, but for far more altruistic reasons.'

'You told him that I have a lover?' Maggie demanded hotly. Her grandmother was old-fashioned; if she were to live at the Dower House and hear gossip that her beloved granddaughter had a lover—and, moreover, a lover she knew nothing about—she would not just be shocked, she would be hurt that Maggie hadn't confided in her herself, Maggie knew. 'How dare you?' she continued furiously. 'How dare you lie about me like that—?'

'Lie?' Finn cut her short, tightlipped now as anger glittered dangerously in his eyes. 'Me? I heard you myself on the phone to him at the farmhouse. ''Darling…''' he whispered, savagely mimicking Maggie's softly husky voice.

Baffled, Maggie stared at him. 'The only people I telephoned from the farm were my assistant and my grandmother…' Her voice faltered, and then grew stronger as she repeated, 'My grandmother…my beloved, darling, grandmother.'

Finn went completely still. There was no mistaking the sincerity in her voice. And no mistaking her fury either. Perhaps there was more of the City trader left in him than he had thought, he admitted wryly, as he shrugged his shoulders and prepared to unashamedly blag his way out of the situation.

'So I made a mistake.'

A mistake! Maggie's chest heaved, sending the bumble bees into delicious activity—to Finn's male eyes at least. Her eyes flashed, and he could have sworn she grew two inches taller as she confronted him.

'You blacken my reputation; force me out of the bidding for the Dower House, send me the most repellent letter I have ever received, try to tell me how I should live my life, correct my grammar—and you call it a mistake.'

Fresh activity amongst the bumble bees held Finn's glance awed and enthralled, but thankfully Maggie herself was far too wrapped up in her own anger to notice his inability to drag his attention from her breasts—breasts which, as he already had good reason to know, felt and tasted every bit as deliciously feminine and honey-sweet as they looked.

Later he might admit to himself that perhaps what followed was an extremely contentious piece of verbal baiting on his part, but at the time...

'Haven't you forgotten something in that list of supposed crimes?'

The mild tone of Finn's voice caught Maggie off-guard. For some reason she couldn't fathom, and didn't dare to try to over-analyse, the sight of the muscles in his bare arms, when he folded them across his chest before leaning back against the wall, sent a soft little shiver of sensation all the way through her body, causing her to curl her toes slightly. There was something sexily awesome about Finn's arms, something about their strength, their power to hold and protect, something about their gentleness when he had wrapped them around her, something that right now was making her want...

Shakily she forced herself to concentrate on what Finn was saying—something about a crime she'd forgotten. But before she could phrase any question Finn was answering it for her, telling her succinctly and, she was sure, with a great deal of enjoyment, 'Going to bed with you.'

Going to bed with her? Was that how Finn saw what had happened between them? As a crime? Maggie didn't like the sharp pain that seared her: a pain which she was determined to ignore. Well, if it was she was just going to have to make sure he knew that, as far as she was concerned, their lovemaking—no, their *sex*, which after all was the correct word for it—had meant nothing at all to her!

Feigning uninterest, she shrugged and looked away from him. Lying to him was one thing; lying to him when he had that penetrating gaze of his fixed on her was very definitely another. 'I'm an adult. I can go to bed with whoever I like.'

'Like?' Finn pounced with lethal speed.

Hot-cheeked, Maggie tried to brave it out. 'Neither of us has ever denied that the sex between us was good.'

Finn tightened his folded arms, not trusting himself to move. If he did, if he got within range of her, she would be right there in those arms, whilst he…

'Anyway, I haven't come here to talk about sex,' Maggie told him, furiously aware of her own red face and the decidedly dangerous male gleam now lighting Finn's eyes.

'No, talking about it is a complete waste of time,' Finn agreed, straight-faced, 'especially when—'

Had she any idea how adorable she looked: all furious embarrassment, all desirable woman, the only woman he…

'I came to talk to you about your letter,' Maggie told him sharply. 'How dare you patronise me by offering me the Dower House at a peppercorn rent? I don't need your charity, Finn. I can afford to pay my own way through life. And—'

'I wasn't doing it for you. I was doing it for your grandmother,' Finn told her, completely silencing her. 'You may be able to afford to pay any amount of rent, but I suspect things may be different for your grandmother.' He held up his hand when Maggie would have interrupted him. 'Yes, I know that you'd pay the rent for her, but if she's anything like most other members of her generation—and I suspect she is—after all her granddaughter has to have got her determined independence from somewhere—she will want to pay the rent herself.'

Maggie knew that he was right. A huge lump of mixed pain and guilt was filling her throat, making it impossible for her to speak. How it was that Finn had found a flaw in her plans that had escaped her? How was it that he had somehow known exactly how her grandmother would feel when she herself had not?

Maggie wasn't sure which she resented having to acknowledge the more: his unexpected sensitivity towards the feelings of an elderly woman he didn't even know, or the fact that that sensitivity made her feel guilty because she herself had not recognised the need for it. Her grandmother was her grandmother, not his.

'I can find my grandmother another house,' she told him challengingly.

Finn gave her a hooded, unreadable look that for some reason made her heart bounce around inside her chest like a rubber ball.

'Yes, I'm sure that you can. But as I understood the situation the reason you wanted the Dower House for her was because of your grandparents' past association with it. Of course, no doubt, during the course of a long marriage they would have shared other homes together…' He paused, and Maggie looked angrily away from him.

'They began their married lives together in the Dower House,' she found herself admitting reluctantly.

As he surveyed her averted profile Finn felt a dangerous thread of unwanted tenderness for her curl itself sinuously around his heart. He itched to take hold of her and shake her for her stubbornness, and at the same time he ached to hold her, to banish from her eyes and her

voice the pain he could see and hear in them. 'You were
very close to both your grandparents?' he guessed.

Maggie couldn't deny it. 'Very,' she agreed shortly,
and then to her own consternation she heard herself telling him unsteadily, 'They gave me a home, security,
love, when my own parents—' She stopped and shook
her head, her mouth compressing, her expression betraying how much she regretted saying as much as she had.

But Finn ignored the invisible 'keep out' signs she
was posting and pressed on ruthlessly. She intrigued
him, baffled him, infuriated him, and made him ache
with the intensity of those emotions. He was determined
to find out just what it was that made her tick, what it
was that made her so antagonistic towards him. 'When
your own parents what?' he asked her.

Maggie closed her eyes. This was a conversation she
wished she had never begun. She never talked about her
parents to anyone. Not even her girlfriends knew how
frightened, how insecure, how unwanted the careless, casual attitude of her mother and her father had made her
feel.

She could still see the look of irritation on her
mother's face when she had begged her to attend her
school play.

'Oh, darling, no. James is taking me out to dinner
tonight, and anyway you wouldn't really want me to be
there, would you? You know how bored I would be…'

Oh, yes, Maggie had known how bored she would be,
how bored she so often was with Maggie herself.

'Nothing,' Maggie denied fiercely in answer to Finn's question.

As she turned away from him, because she didn't want Finn to see her expression, she wasn't prepared for the sudden movement he made as he levered his body away from the wall and strode towards her, grasping her shoulders with his hands before she could escape.

'They hurt you didn't they, Maggie?' he guessed. 'They—'

'No.' Maggie hurled the denial at him like a thunderbolt, but she could hear in her voice, as clearly as she knew he must be able to himself, the fear and anguish that made a mockery of her lie.

'Maggie…'

'I don't want to talk about it. It isn't any of your business anyway. My parents were no different from countless other people of their generation, believing that they had a right to put themselves and their own happiness first. Their mistake was in having a child like me, who wanted…'

To her own horror Maggie could feel her eyes filling with tears. Frantically she tried to wrench herself out of Finn's grasp, lifting her gaze furiously to his and then stiffening as she saw the compassion in his eyes.

Every ounce of her tensed body shrieked a silent scream of outrage that Finn could almost hear as he recognised how furiously she was rejecting his pity for the child she must have been.

'No, Maggie,' he corrected her gently. 'Their mistake was in not valuing the gift they had been given. '

Something about the dark warmth of his voice was compelling her to look at him, to relax into him, to lift her face towards his and...

As he looked down into the cloudy emotion of her brown eyes Finn knew that he was lost. His gaze skimmed her face, her mouth. Her mouth...

Maggie could feel the soft groan he gave vibrating through his body. Feel it? What on earth was she doing standing so close to him? Frantically she pulled away from him, her eyes brilliant with tiny shards of anger.

'I've had enough of this,' she told him furiously. 'I'm leaving—now.'

Quickly she spun round on her heel, heading for the front door.

'Admirable exit line though that was, I'm afraid that you aren't going to be able to go anywhere,' Finn told her dryly.

Not leave? He wasn't going to let her leave? Anger battled against fiercely sensual pleasure and excitement—and lost.

'What do you mean?' Maggie made herself challenge him. What was she going to do if he absolutely refused to let her go, if he insisted on keeping her here with him? A shocking thrill ripped through her, heating her face—and her body—with dangerously inflammatory secret thoughts and memories.

'Take a look outside,' Finn invited her, going to open the front door.

Whilst they had been arguing the afternoon had darkened into dusk, but it wasn't the darkness that made

Maggie gasp in disbelief as she stared out of the open door, her chagrin that he hadn't, after all, been speaking out of a desire to keep her with him obliterated by the sight that greeted her disbelieving gaze. Whilst they had been arguing dusk wasn't the only thing that had fallen. Everything was covered in a thick blanket of snow—snow that was still falling, driven by a strong and very cold wind, so that in the corners of the building it was already forming peaked drifts. The side of her car was a mask of white, only the double row of trees marking where the drive lay.

Maggie gulped and looked at Finn.

'It probably looks worse than it is. Once I get to the main road…'

'No way,' Finn told her, shaking his head. 'They were giving out blizzard warnings earlier, urging people not to travel. These country roads—even the A roads,' he added dryly, 'are subject to heavy drifting. I'd have second thoughts about driving in this in the Land Rover, and there's no way I'm going to let you take the risk of going out in it.'

'There were blizzard warnings?' Maggie demanded, glowering at him. 'Why on earth didn't you say something…tell me?'

That was a question Finn had been asking himself from the moment he had seen her arrive. And one he had still found no satisfactory answer to—at least not one which would satisfy any logical criteria! 'You didn't give me much chance,' he pointed out. 'You were determined to say your piece, and…'

Maggie shook her head in disbelief. 'Now what am I going to do?'

'There's only one thing you can do,' Finn told her. 'You'll have to spend the night here.'

Maggie gritted her teeth against her ire and exasperation.

'What kind of county is this?' she demanded irritably. Its extraordinarily changeable weather conditions had to be peculiar to the area; there had certainly been nothing on her car radio as she had driven west to warn her of impending blizzard conditions! Impassable fords, snow in November. 'That's twice now we've been marooned together. You'd never get anything like this happening in London,' she told Finn irritably as she surveyed the inhospitable not to say downright dangerous arctic scene in front of her.

As the wind twisted blowing an icy sheet of snow over her she stepped back into the warmth of the house. Already her face and hands were stinging from the cold.

'What about the alpaca?' she asked Finn anxiously. 'Will they be all right?'

Finn busied himself closing the door before answering her. He didn't want her to guess that he was smiling. 'The alpaca will be fine,' he assured her, keeping his face as straight as he could. 'They're used to the cold.'

'But the little ones? The babies?' Maggie protested, remembering the young animals she had seen with their mothers.

'They'll be fine,' Finn repeated.

She was looking at the closed door almost as though

she was going to rush through it and check on the animals herself, which might prove rather embarrassing, seeing as they were all tucked up safely in a specially enclosed field complete with protective bales of hay and an open barn to go into for shelter. He and Shane had moved them there only this morning, after hearing the weather forecast. The same forecast he had omitted to mention to Maggie!

'In your grandmother's time there would have been deer in the park,' he told Maggie, intending to distract her. 'I'm looking forward to meeting her. She must know quite a lot about the recent history of the house if she lived here. The two sons of the family who would have owned it at that time were both killed during the War, and the estate then passed to a second cousin who already owned a much larger estate in Scotland.'

'What do you mean, you're looking forward to meeting my grandmother?' Maggie interrupted him ominously. 'I've already told you, she won't be coming here.'

There was a long pause before Finn asked her with deliberate emphasis, 'Are you really prepared to do that, Maggie? Let me ask you something. If it were anyone else but me offering you a lease on the Dower House would you refuse it?'

Maggie bit her lip.

'I don't want to discuss the subject any longer,' she told him sharply, adding in a very formal and grand voice, 'If you would just direct me to my room?' Pointedly she lifted her eyebrows and looked at Finn.

'Your room. Mmm... Unfortunately, there's a slight problem. As yet there is only one functional bedroom...'

'One bedroom?' Maggie repeated warily.

Soft brown eyes clashed with winter-blue.

'One bedroom,' Finn agreed softly.

CHAPTER SEVEN

ONE bedroom!

And they had spent what was left of the fast-fading daylight arguing about which of them was going to occupy it—or rather which of them was going to make the noble gesture of sleeping in the drawing room on one of its two sofas.

In the end Finn had won, but only because she had allowed him to, Maggie defended her own capitulation mentally. Only because he had thrown down a trump card by declaring, 'Since this is my home, I rather think that the decision of who sleeps where lies rather more in my hands than yours, Maggie. And, as your host, I fully intend to claim the right of giving up my bed for my guest.'

Maggie had clenched her teeth together at those words 'host' and 'guest', but in the end she had had to give in. And now here she was, standing in Finn's bedroom, staring out of the window into the starlit snow-covered landscape. Turning her back on it, she faced the bed. Something she had deliberately been avoiding doing since Finn had shown her up here half an hour ago, suggesting that she 'make herself at home' whilst he cooked them a meal.

It was, as she might have expected given the size of

the room—and Finn himself—very large. Very large.
Large enough not just for two adults but potentially large
enough for a handful of children as well. Children! Now,
where had that thought come from? And, far more disconcertingly, why?

Concentrate on the room as it is, Maggie warned herself. Instead of fantasising about…about things there is
totally no point whatsoever in even thinking about—or
even wanting to think about!

Its high ceiling and decorative plasterwork were typical of the period of the house, and someone—Finn—
had washed the walls in a fresh covering of subtly tinted
bluey-green paint, picking out the plasterwork in white
and a denser colour of the tint. But, whilst Maggie would
normally have thoroughly approved of the plain white
bedding and bare stripped floorboards, somehow the
room cried out for something softer and warmer.

That floor would be so cold on those little bare feet
as their owners came rushing into their parents' room to
join them in bed, and one would have little inclination
to linger for long intimate embraces en route from bathroom to bed, surely, without the softness of a thick carpet to curl one's toes into. No, what this room needed
was the sensually rich fabrics that its original builder
must have favoured, and furniture, too: the kind of furniture owned by her grandmother, furniture one polished
with traditional beeswax and lavender polish.

Maggie gave a faint sigh and then blinked. Just for
one suffocating second, whilst she had been looking absently at the bed, she had somehow or other seen Finn

lying there, propped up against the pillows, his body bare, lean, muscular and oh, so inviting, his hair ruffled from sleep, his jaw malely rough, his mouth curling invitingly as he looked at her...

Quickly Maggie blinked again, banishing the wickedly tantalising image. In the room's *en suite* bathroom she tidied herself up, and placed the clean warm towels Finn had taken from the airing cupboard and given to her on a stool. The huge towelling robe he had given her, which was patently one of his, she determinedly placed at the bottom of the pile.

It was time she went back downstairs. If she didn't Finn might actually start thinking that she wanted him to come looking for her. As she hurried to the bedroom door she glanced towards the window, her forehead furrowing in a darkly accusing frown. It had started to snow again. It was almost as though the weather was determined to cause her problems, to keep her here with Finn.

'We'll have to eat in here,' Finn announced as Maggie walked into the kitchen. 'I suppose ultimately I'm going to have to get designers in to revamp the place, but at the moment—'

'Why didn't you tell me that you used to work in the City?'

The abruptness of her unplanned question made Maggie wish she hadn't asked. The high standards and professionalism she normally demanded of herself made her blush with embarrassment at her own unfamiliar gaucheness, but to her relief, instead of reacting with a cool put-down, Finn looked at her searchingly for a few seconds before replying quietly, 'It's a part of my life I've put behind me and which has no real relevance to the way I live now other than that the money I made then has made it possible for me to choose my own future.'

'You can't say that,' Maggie objected immediately. 'Everything that happens in a person's life has relevance.'

'You mean like your own relationship with your parents?' Finn countered.

Brown eyes met blue, the pride and pain in the brown an immediate barrier to the challenging masked compassion in blue.

'Whatever unhappiness I experienced through my parents' lack of love for me was more than outweighed by the love of my grandparents,' Maggie defended herself sharply. 'You, on the other hand, are obviously hanging on to your bad feelings about city life and city people.'

She had a very quick and incisive mind, Finn acknowledged with reluctant admiration, If there was one thing he did miss about city living in his current solitary life, it was the buzz that the exchange of conversation, opinions, news and views with other like-minded people had given him.

'Not really,' he denied, giving a small shrug as he told her, 'It's simply that I've moved on inwardly, as well as physically, and the man I am now wants a hell of a lot more out of life than material success. And besides...' He paused, opening the oven door to study its contents before adding sombrely, with just enough contempt in his voice to make Maggie's face sting with angry resentment, 'I've seen too many people damaged or destroyed by the pursuit of wealth and success— driven to abuse themselves and others by their fear of what they consider to be failure—to have any illusions left.'

'It isn't city living that causes that,' Maggie protested.

'Maybe not, but it doesn't help. The lasagne is just about ready,' he informed Maggie. 'And, since they say that arguing is not conducive to good digestion, I suggest that we find something else to talk about.'

'I've got an even better idea,' Maggie told him acerbically, adding without waiting for his response, 'Why don't we just eat in silence?'

'A silent woman! Is there such a thing?' Finn mocked her as he removed the lasagne from the oven.

Maggie threw him a murderous look, but somehow managed to restrain herself from making any verbal response.

Half an hour later, her stomach deliciously full, her earlier antagonism and with it her mental vow to herself momentarily forgotten, Maggie announced, 'That was good. I hadn't realised how hungry I was.' She stopped abruptly as she realised what she had done, but instead of taunting her for breaking her self-imposed silence, Finn simply looked at her.

When she forgot to be on her guard against him there was an endearing sweetness about her which gripped him by the throat and the heart. And wasn't his body well and truly reacting to that knowledge, and to her?

He could feel his glance sliding dangerously towards her mouth, the appetite he wanted to satisfy having nothing whatsoever to do with food, and he hastily dragged it back before Maggie could see.

If he had thought the buzz he had once got from the City traders' always-on-the-edge lifestyle possessed too much dangerous and addictive excitement, it was nothing to the charge this reckless game of advance and retreat he and Maggie were now putting one another through. But, despite what common sense and caution were telling him, he still couldn't resist the opportunity presenting itself to him.

'A city woman who likes to eat. Now you *have* surprised me. Although I suppose I shouldn't be surprised, after all...' There was a gleam in his eyes when he paused that made Maggie's muscles tense as she waited for the blow she knew was about to fall. But when it came it was not what she had been expecting, and its effect was so devastating that she suspected her reaction must have given her away completely. 'After all,' Finn continued in a softly sensual voice that felt like male fingers stroking her skin, 'They do say that a woman with a healthy appetite for sex has a healthy appetite for all the pleasures of life. Another glass of wine?' he offered, indicating the bottle of red wine he had opened when they had begun their meal.

'*No!* No, thank you,' Maggie amended in a calmer voice as she battled against her reaction to his soft words.

A healthy appetite for sex. Did he have to remind her…to torment her…?

'Perhaps it's stopped snowing. Perhaps I can leave after all.' Maggie knew that she was gabbling, giving away her panic, and her movements were flustered as she started to stand up and then sat down again very quickly as Finn moved towards her and reached out for her empty dinner plate. If she stood up now she would be standing right next to him. Just the thought of that happening was enough to make her whole body quiver as tiny rushes of nervous excitement darted through her. Agitatedly she picked up her wine glass and drank from it. She knew that Finn was watching her, and that was making her feel even more nervous.

'It hasn't,' Finn responded grimly. 'You can't. And even if you could, after three glasses of wine I doubt you'd be legally able to drive.'

Three glasses? Maggie was horrified. Had she really drunk so much? A glance at the glass in front of her was enough to have her saying with solemn dignity, 'I've only had two and a half.'

'That's still over the legal limit,' Finn told her. 'And besides,' he added, 'in those ridiculous shoes you're wearing you couldn't make it through one centimetre of snow, never mind closer to ten.'

'Ten? No, that's impossible,' Maggie gasped, adding with a glower, 'And will you please stop criticising my shoes? Just because you don't like them.'

Finn, who had been loading the dishwasher, turned round, subjecting her to the full heart-rocking force of a look of such intense sensuality that it literally made her moan softly out loud.

'I never said anything about not liking them,' he told her succinctly. 'Simply that they were impractical.'

'"Ridiculous" was the word you used. Not impractical,' Maggie reminded him. She felt as though she were clinging helplessly to a very precarious rock in the middle of an extremely dangerous body of water. Pushing back her chair, she stood up. 'I'm tired...I think I'll go to bed. Hopefully the snow will be gone by morning, and I'll be able to make an early start.'

Why on earth was the way Finn was looking at her making her stammer and walk away from him so self-consciously, all too aware of the way the height of her shoe-heels was making her body move?

As though he had read her mind, when she reached the door she heard Finn saying softly, 'I was wrong. Neither ridiculous nor impractical is the right description for them. But provocative—now, that *is*.'

Provocative! If Finn was trying to imply that that was what she was, then...

But for some reason, instead of turning round to confront him and demand a retraction of his statement—a statement that could quite definitely be described itself as both ridiculous and provocative—Maggie discovered that she was actually hurrying away from him...running away from him? From him or from what he was making her feel?

In the silence of his now Maggie-free kitchen, Finn wondered irritably what subtle ingredient her perfume possessed that made its delicate fragrance linger so long. He could swear that his bedroom at the farm had continued to carry her scent right up until the day he had moved, and now here she was occupying his bedroom yet again…his bedroom…his bed…his life…his heart…

Grimly he closed the door of the dishwasher and switched it on, glancing out into the snow-covered yard beyond the window as he did so. Snow in November? It was unseasonable, unsettling and should have been unfeasible—like his feelings for Maggie?

Maggie woke up with a start, wondering at first, in the semi-darkness of the unfamiliar bedroom, illuminated by the bedside lamp she had deliberately left on, just where she was. And then she remembered. She was in Finn's house, in Finn's bed. Finn.

Her mouth felt dry from the wine she had drunk. She was desperate for a glass of cold water. Hesitantly she sat up. It was just gone midnight. Pushing the bedclothes aside, she got out of bed. When she opened the bedroom door she saw that the landing and stairs were in darkness. A sharp nervous frisson shivered through her. Loath though she was to admit it, she was afraid of the dark.

Her fingers trembled as she reached for the light switch she had remembered seeing on the wall next to the bedroom door, relief flooding through her as the lights came on. The house felt quiet and still. She had pulled on her coat before leaving the bedroom rather than wear the folded but Finn-sized robe he had given

her. There was something about the intimacy of wearing
something that belonged to him that was far too potentially dangerous for her to risk. The brilliance of the
chandelier illuminating the stairs made her blink a little.
Quickly she padded down the stairs and into the hall.
She was less than halfway across it when the drawing
room door was suddenly flung open and Finn strode into
the hall.

Like her, he must have been asleep. But unlike her he
obviously had no hang-ups about semi-nudity—and no
modesty either, Maggie decided shakily as she frantically tried to focus on something other than his naked
torso, wondering what on earth was wrong with her re-
calcitrant gaze as it recklessly returned to his shorts-only
clad body.

'Where the hell do you think you're going?'

The harshness of his angry demand bemused her, forcing her to lift her gaze to meet his in response to his
angry challenge.

'I'm going for a drink of water,' Maggie responded.

'Dressed like that? Do you think I'm a complete
fool?' he demanded without giving her any opportunity
to answer. 'I appreciate how keen you are to leave,
Maggie—'

'Leave…?' Maggie gave him a blank look. 'I'm not
leaving.'

'Then why are you wearing your coat?' Finn asked
her grimly

Her coat! Maggie had forgotten that she was wearing
it. Pink with embarrassment, she shrugged as noncha-

lantly as she could as she told him, 'I…er…just put it on to come downstairs in…you know…as a sort of a robe. I'm not wearing my shoes,' she pointed out. 'Or…' Self-consciously she stopped.

'Or…?' Finn prompted, recovering his sang-froid with a speed she envied.

When she remained silent, he pressed her softly. 'If you don't answer me, Maggie, then I'll have to use my imagination, and right now it's telling me…' He stopped and groaned before challenging her hoarsely, as he came towards her, 'Have you any idea just what it's doing to me knowing that you're as near as dammit naked underneath that coat?'

Maggie could feel her heart beating so frantically that it literally shook her whole body. The effect the raw sensuality of Finn's voice was having on her was making it almost impossible for her to breathe. It shocked her that she should feel so wantonly excited by the knowledge that Finn found her desirable, that he wanted her. The voice of caution and common sense urged her to say nothing, to walk away from temptation whilst she still could. But when she responded it was to a far stronger and more deeply rooted instinct, a contrary reckless impulse impelling her to challenge him.

'If you're trying to tell me that you want me, then—'

'Then what?' Finn interrupted her rawly. 'Then you'd rather I showed you?'

Maggie gasped as he caught hold of her, but not out of shock or protest. No, it was her own reaction to him that caused her to tremble so violently. She could feel

the rapid tattoo of Finn's heart, even through the muf-
fling folds of her coat. But she wasn't feeling him
through her coat at all, she recognised dizzily as Finn
parted it and slid his hands inside it.

'Nothing,' she heard him whisper in a thick openly
aroused voice. 'You aren't wearing anything at all.'

'I was in bed,' Maggie responded in a voice she had
intended to be indignant but which in reality had become
soft and slurred with reactive need.

'In bed…in my bed. Have you any idea how much
I've been aching to be there with you?' Finn told her.
'Ever since…'

'Ever since I got here?' Maggie questioned, striving
to keep her balance in the midst of a passion that was
threatening to totally overwhelm her.

'No,' Finn told her starkly. 'Ever since you left it.'

It was too much. Helplessly Maggie gave in, closing
her eyes in subjugation to her own feelings.

'There hasn't been a single night since then when I
haven't wanted you,' Finn was whispering to her as he
bent his head towards hers and slowly started to kiss
her—slow, seductive kisses, strung together in an erotically dazzling chain that would tie her to him for ever,
she suspected, as her body melted into his and his fingertips stroked her neck from her jaw to her collarbone,
raising an erotic line of goosebumps that gave away her
longing for him.

'Which is it to be?' she could hear Finn whispering
as his lips found and then probed the warmth of hers.
'Your bed or mine? Mine's nearer… Or we could always

try them both... The fire's still warm in the drawing room. Have you ever made love in front of a fire, Maggie, with the firelight highlighting every delicious inch of you, and your lover's body to keep you warm...?'

Maggie shuddered in mute pleasure at the images the hypnotic seduction of his voice was conjuring up for her. 'No...' Her denial was a strangled sound that tore at her throat, making her close her eyes against the acid burn of her own tears as she wondered how many other women Finn might have shared such a pleasure with, whilst she had never...

'No...? Oh, of course, I was forgetting. Open fires and city living don't exactly go together, do they?'

There was a harshness in his voice now that physically hurt her.

'I wouldn't know,' her honesty compelled her to tell him. 'Since I don't—I haven't... There isn't...' Her voice started to tail away. She didn't want to talk, to spend time dealing with the cumbersome delay of words, and she certainly didn't want to be forced to think about the other women who might have shared Finn's life. What she wanted, *all* she wanted... Maggie gave a small shiver as she tried to ignore what she was feeling. What was it that happened to her whenever she got physically close to Finn that affected her so strongly, that made her feel that what was happening between them was the most important thing in her life?

'What are you trying to tell me, Maggie?' Finn demanded grimly, cupping her face with his hands and looking down into her eyes so that there was no way she could hide her expression from him. 'That there hasn't been anyone else?' He gave her a derisive look. 'Do you really expect me to believe that a woman as intelligent, as desirable, as downright impossible to resist as both of us know you are, lives the life of a celibate?'

It frightened Maggie to realise how much pleasure it gave her to hear him describe her in such a way—and how much more the rawly sensual message in his eyes was giving her.

'I wanted to concentrate on my career,' she told him truthfully. 'And that hasn't left me any time for...for relationships.'

The way he was looking at her made her heart slam so heavily into her chest wall that she gasped out loud.

'Oh, Maggie...Maggie...'

She gasped again at the fierce note of male passion she could hear in Finn's voice as he slid his hands into her hair and bent his head to kiss her.

'You do things to me that no other woman has ever done, do you know that?' she heard Finn whispering passionately to her several minutes later as he raised his mouth from hers.

She could feel their breath mingling as he lowered his head again, and the fine tremors running through her body echoed the much fiercer shudders galvanising his.

Wrapped in one another's arms, they made their way slowly towards the drawing room, their journey there interspersed with fiercely passionate kisses and Maggie's softly breathy little moans of pleasure as Finn's hands caressed her naked body. But it was the sight of the firelight playing on his body as he released her briefly to remove the duvet from the sofa and place it in front of the fire that sent such wild surges of arousal through her that Maggie couldn't help herself from making a small strangled cry of longing.

'What is it?'

The look of frowning anxiety he gave her as he dropped the duvet and came towards her made her blush a little at the explicitness of her thoughts. And then, as though he had guessed them, his frown gave way to a look of heavy-lidded sensuality that made her bones feel as though they were melting as it skimmed lazily over her body, and a heat that had nothing whatsoever to do with the fire burned through her.

'Finn…' she protested, so shocked by her own desires that she immediately blamed him for causing them. Prior to knowing Finn she had lusted after a pair of new shoes far more strongly than she had ever lusted after a man—but now…

'Come here,' Finn commanded softly.

Helplessly Maggie went to him, knowing that he was not so much demanding something from her as giving her the right to take whatever she wished from him.

'City lady, country man,' Finn whispered to her as he smoothed her skin with his hands, making her shudder as rivulets of hot, swift delight ran over her. 'We're poles apart, and yet there's never been anyone I've ached so much to be close to.'

Awed by the intensity of the feeling she could hear in his voice, Maggie closed her eyes against the tight ball of emotions she could feel blocking her throat. When she could finally manage to speak all she could say was a choked, 'Well, you are close to me now.'

'But not as close as I want to be,' Finn murmured as his fingertips investigated the exquisite silky sensitivity of her taut nipples. 'Skin on skin, body on body, mouth on mouth. That's how close I want to be to you, Maggie.'

She knew she must have made some reply because she heard the sudden acceleration of Finn's breathing in response to it, and then blissfully his mouth was on her throat, trailing hot kisses of sheeting fire down her arm, to the sensitive hollow of her elbow, nibbling at her fingers, licking and sucking them until she thought she might actually faint with the intensity of the desire exploding inside her.

When he kneeled in front of her and kissed her waist, the curve of her hip, her belly, Maggie moaned his name, her fingers digging into the hard muscles of his arms as she clung desperately to him, driven beyond shock by the extent of her response to him, her need for him. Through the haze of her longing she could see the long weals her nails had raked against his skin. Mindlessly she leaned into him, shuddering as his breath touched her skin.

His hands were shaping her hips, stroking down the length of her legs. Tenderly and carefully Finn lowered her to the floor. As he leaned over her Maggie watched him, her gaze drinking in the male perfection of him. She lifted her hand to his shoulder, slowly tracing the shape of his collarbone and then moving over his chest, exploring the tight hardness of his small male nipples with a wide-eyed concentration that made her soft brown eyes darken to almost black.

'How much longer are you going to torment me?'

The raw hunger in his low growl bit at her aroused emotions with the same devastating effect the erotic nibble of his teeth had had on her flesh. A thousand, no a million tiny sparks of hunger for him ignited at once, feeding a conflagration that threatened to totally overwhelm her.

Finn's fingers circled her ankle, slowly stroking its delicate bones. Maggie shivered and made a low guttural sound of shocked pleasure as he held her foot in both his hands and then slowly kissed its delicate instep. Immediately her toes curled in a rictus of female response.

'Me torment you?'

Maggie wasn't even aware of whispering the passion-husked words, nor of reaching towards him, pulling him against her, her hands trembling as they absorbed the hot velvet sleekness of his skin and the hardness of the muscles it cloaked.

They made love hungrily and fiercely, Finn holding Maggie's hips in a grip that was possessively hard as she straddled him, enjoying the power to dominate their intimacy and control the hot sleek strength of his body as it entered hers. Each stroke quickened the immediate response of her own flesh as she urged him to seek deeper, to stay longer, to move faster…harder, to give her everything that her body needed in order to satisfy the hunger for him he himself had created.

Her body was slick with sweat, arching against the taut bow of her orgasm, and Finn looked up into her face, drinking in the triumph of watching her succumb to her pleasure. The firelight gilded her damp skin, dancing in a million tiny flames as the shudders of completion convulsed her, and then it was his turn, the dying sound of his release fading into the mingled harshness of their joint breathing.

CHAPTER EIGHT

SLEEPILY Maggie turned over, savouring the warmth of Finn's bed. Finn himself was downstairs, where he had gone to make them both a cup of coffee. Maggie smiled to herself as she stretched with sensual luxury beneath the duvet. The warmth of Finn's bed wasn't all she was savouring. There was the warmth of Finn's body to be remembered as well, along with his lovemaking last night.

The tenderness he had shown her after the fierce intensity of the passion they had shared still had the power to raise a small frisson of emotional reaction from her as she mentally relived the way he had left her curled up in an exhausted tangle of limbs on the duvet, returning a few minutes later with two huge soft warm towels, gently drying her love damp body with one of them before tenderly wrapping the other around her.

Too relaxed to move, she had drifted off to sleep, waking only when he had kissed her and told her that he thought she would sleep more comfortably in his bed.

'Only if you share it with me,' she had answered.

She had woken at first light, whilst he was still asleep, lying next to him and savouring not just her memories of their lovemaking but the reality of his physical presence in bed beside her. Unable to stop herself, she had leaned across to him, studying his sleeping face, feeling the now familiar jolt run deliciously through her body as she'd given in to the temptation to stroke her fingertips exploratively along his collarbone before tangling them gently in the silky warmth of the thick whorls of dark hair the night had flattened against his skin, whilst her lips had teased wake-up-and-play kisses in the hollow of his throat.

Seconds later, when he was still asleep, she had reluctantly been about to move away from him when he had made her almost jump out of her skin by growling mock threateningly at her at the same time as he imprisoned her in his arms, adroitly rolling her beneath him.

Somehow during the play-fight that had followed he had managed to stroke and kiss every sensually vulnerable bit of her.

'That's not fair,' she had pretended to complain when he had gently pinned her arms down at her sides so that she could not touch him, whilst his mouth had had the freedom to make an explosively erotic journey from her throat to both of her naked breasts. The sensation of his tongue lapping seductively at their rapidly hardening crests had made her arch her back in wild abandon, her protests forgotten, their game forgotten as desire had engulfed them both.

Maggie closed her eyes, and then opened them again as she heard Finn demanding softly, 'You haven't gone back to sleep, have you?'

Sitting up, she smiled at him, shaking her head. 'Is the snow still there?' she asked him.

He had been leaning towards her, having put down the tray he had been carrying, and she had lifted her face to his, anticipating his kiss. A little to her chagrin it never came, and instead he straightened up, glancing towards the window, his voice suddenly almost jarringly brisk. 'It's still there,' he confirmed. 'But it is thawing…'

Thawing. That meant that she would be able to leave. Ruefully Maggie acknowledged that a part of her would have been secretly glad if he had told her that they were likely to be snowed in together for several days.

'Breakfast,' Finn was telling her, indicating the tray he had placed on the bedside table next to her. 'And don't try going all city woman on me and telling me that you don't want any.'

Maggie deliberately evaded the tenderly teasing look he was giving her. Normally she did not eat breakfast, but whenever she was with Finn she woke up with the kind of appetite—for food—that would have pleased even someone as traditional as her grandmother, who had always insisted on Maggie eating what she termed a 'proper' breakfast before leaving the house in the morning.

That she also woke up with an even greater hunger for Finn himself was something she was most certainly not going to dwell on!

Turning to pick up a glass of orange juice from the tray, Maggie wondered how he was likely to react if she were to respond with the tongue-in-cheek comment that after a night like the one they had just spent together it was no wonder that she was hungry—for food, that was. So far as sensual satisfaction went her appetite should have been more than sated.

Her face started to grow slightly pink. The lethargy filling her body was a feeling that was entirely new to her, but then the lovemaking they had shared had also been something she had never imagined experiencing. Being brought up by her grandparents had given her a certain shy modesty which, no matter how much she might deplore it as being ridiculous in a sophisticated woman of her age, did make her feel slightly inhibited about talking openly about her most private feelings— especially when they were the kind of feelings that Finn aroused in her.

Lowering her gaze, she watched from beneath her lashes as Finn bit into a piece of toast. He had pulled on a robe before going downstairs, but he hadn't fastened it, and... Unable to help herself, Maggie peeped discreetly at his bare torso. Somehow, of its own accord, her glance slid lower, whilst her breathing stilled and then quickened, matching the fluttering thrill disturbing her heartbeat.

She thought that Finn wasn't aware of what she was doing but then she heard him advising her softly, 'Don't do that. Not unless you want me to...'

'I thought you said you had to go and see how the alpaca are,' Maggie reminded him quickly.

Not because she didn't want him, she acknowledged, hot-faced, but because—shockingly—she did.

'Hmm…had enough of me?' he teased her.

'No…never…' Maggie responded fervently, unable to check her vehement response.

However, before she could feel embarrassed by her self-betrayal, Finn was putting down his coffee to cup her face in his hands whilst he told her gruffly, 'That isn't the way to encourage me to go out and check on the livestock.'

Maggie held her breath until she felt the warm brush of his lips against hers, and then she exhaled in a soft shaky rush as his kiss deepened.

Her un-drunk coffee had gone cold by the time Finn finally left the bedroom, fully dressed to go and check on his animals.

Maggie got up at a more leisurely pace, blessing the properties of modern underwear that meant that it could be rinsed through to dry overnight. If there was one thing she should have learned from her recent experiences it was that whenever she came to Shropshire she ought to bring a change of clothes with her.

She was halfway downstairs when her mobile rang. Her caller was a client urgently needing to replace a key member of staff who had unexpectedly announced her intention to relocate to Boston to be with her lover.

Maggie had her laptop with her, and within minutes of ending the call she had drawn up a shortlist of potential replacements for her client and e-mailed them to him. Less than an hour later, seated in Finn's kitchen, drinking the cup of coffee she had just made herself, she was congratulating herself on the efficiency with which she had already set up the necessary interviews.

But it wasn't the speed with which she had been able to respond to her client's request that was exciting her so much that she was pacing the kitchen floor in eager anticipation, she acknowledged giddily. No, what was filling her with so much euphoria that she just could not keep still was the sudden realisation of just how easy it was for her to work without being in London. Of course, she argued to herself, if she were, to say, for instance, relocate to Shrewsbury, she would still need to keep up to date with her contacts in London. But if she organised things properly that could be done with regular bi-weekly meetings. Meetings that would still enable her to get home in the evening, of course...

Home...

She stopped mid-turn to stare out of the kitchen window. The snow was melting rapidly now, but it wasn't the snow that was commanding her attention.

Home... The tiny hairs on the back of her neck lifted in atavistic reaction to what she was thinking.

Home and Finn. Since when had the two become synonymous? Since when had Finn become so important to her, so vital to her, that he was her home? And when had she started to allow herself to acknowledge that fact? Since last night? Because they had made love? Or was it truer to say that those feelings had been there right from the very first time they had touched?

Then she had fought against them, determined to extinguish them, to deny and destroy them. Then she had been afraid of what admitting to them would mean, of how vulnerable it might make her. But now things were different. Something had changed. She had changed. Just how or why wasn't something she could in any way analyse, Maggie acknowledged in rueful mental defeat as she tried to apply her analytical faculties to the intensity of her emotions. Brainpower alone could not unravel the complexities of her feelings, her instincts, nor explain how or why her anger and her fear had somehow been transmuted into acceptance of her love, into a feeling which had begun as a tiny trickle but had been slowly gathering force within her right from the first moment they had met.

It was only now that she was able to recognise it for what it was—and it was totally revolutionising the way she looked at things. She was experiencing a need to admit into her life a cleansing surge of desire to sweep away her old repressions, the old barriers against love which she had clung to so fearfully. She was experiencing a sense of release and relief that was lifting from her the weight of a burden she hadn't previously known that she carried, and that burden had been a responsibility, an awareness of life as a serious affair, in which the self-indulgence of falling in love was a luxury she could not permit herself.

Unlike her parents, who had lived selfishly, hedonistically intent only on indulging themselves in the experience of the moment, without giving any thought to the feelings of others or the future, Maggie had felt that it was incumbent on her to behave more responsibly, suppressing her own emotions, crushing them, if necessary, in order to do so.

Now, illuminatingly, she could see that such extremes, such self-sacrifice was not necessary, that immaturity and selfishness on the part of her parents was to blame for what they had done, not love itself. She could see, too, that love and responsibility could work together, that commitment and independence could co-exist.

The first time she had told Finn she loved him she had hated herself and resented him in the backlash of fear that had immediately swamped her. Because of that she had told herself that she had been wrong, that she did not love him. But now she knew better. She ought to have listened to her heart all along. From now on... A happy smile curved her lips and Maggie started to hum beneath her breath. Then started to blush as she recognised that she was humming the 'Wedding March'.

A small gurgle of laughter bubbled in her throat. Knowing Finn as she was now coming to know him, she suspected that, had he heard her, been privy to her thoughts, he might well have suggested, with that special irresistibly tender teasing smile of his, that Handel's *Water Music*, the 'Triumphal March' he had written so beloved by the organisers of firework displays might have been a more appropriate tune for her to hum from his point of view!

Fifteen minutes later, when Finn walked into the kitchen, she was working busily on her laptop.

'Five minutes,' she told him. 'And then I'll be finished.'

As she spoke her mobile rang and she reached for it, her voice crisp and professional. 'Don't worry,' Maggie soothed as she listened to a girl she had only recently placed with one of the newer finance houses. 'If we're talking about sexual harassment then I'm prepared to speak personally to the chairman. I should be back in London by this evening. We can set up a breakfast meeting, if you like…'

As he stood behind her, listening to her, Finn's mouth compressed. What the hell was he doing, even allowing himself to think that they could share something? For him a long-distance affair, with Maggie in the City and him here in the country, could never work. It would be the emotional equivalent of snatching at fast food when he ached for something far more satisfying—for a meal he could linger over and savour in the same way he wanted to savour Maggie herself, and all that he felt for her. Those feelings could never be fulfilled by a brief series of meetings, nor compromised by being forced into that kind of mould. The way he felt about Maggie meant that he could never be content to be part of her life on a part-time basis.

Finn looked bleakly at her downbent head as she concentrated on her laptop. She was muttering to herself beneath her breath, so wholly engrossed in what she was doing that he might just as well not have been there.

Another few seconds and she would have finished, and then… Grimly, Maggie forced herself to recite un-

der her breath what she was trying to do. If she didn't
that aching longing she had to throw herself into Finn's
arms and tell him just how she felt about him would
overwhelm her and her work would be totally forgotten.
She had her obligations, after all…

'There.' She sat back, exhaling in relief. 'All finished.
How were the alpaca?' she asked Finn, smiling up at
him as she turned round. 'Finn, what is it?' she asked
anxiously, her smile fading as she saw his grim expression.

'This can't go on, Maggie,' Finn told her tersely.

He had to turn away from her as he spoke, knowing
that if he looked directly at her he would betray what
he was really feeling. And the last thing he wanted to
do was to end up begging her to stay with him, to give
up her life in London and share his. After all, he already
knew what her answer to that would be.

The shock of his harsh words froze Maggie into numb
silence. She knew if she tried to speak she would start
to cry.

What she had expected, what she had longed to hear
Finn say to her, was how much their night together had
meant to him, how it had proved to him, as it had to
her, that what they had was far too important to take
second place in their lives. Like any woman in love she
had wanted to hear the words that confirmed her feelings
were shared, valued, reciprocated. She had wanted to
hear Finn telling her that he loved her, that he never
intended to let her go. Instead of which she could hear,

and feel, the dull aching echo of his words pounding against her heart like blows.

Desperately she tried to reach out to him, unable to accept his rejection.

'Last night…' Her throat was so dry her protest sounded blurred and raw.

'Sexually the chemistry between us is explosive,' Finn interrupted her curtly. 'Neither of us can deny that. I've never—' He stopped, his face shadowed and grim.

'You've never what?' Maggie challenged him thickly, driven to impale herself even further on the sharp spears of anguish tearing into her heart, helpless to prevent herself from causing herself more pain. 'You've never met a woman more eager to go to bed with you?' She gave him a tight proud smile that defied him to look beyond it and see her pain. 'Enjoying sex for its own sake isn't a crime, is it? Men do it all the time.'

Inwardly she felt as though she was haemorrhaging the lifeblood of her heart, as though her emotions were being ripped apart. But there was no way she was going to let Finn guess how she felt. How could she have been so wrong about what they had shared? How could she have been so stupid as to imagine it was something special, something life-changing for him as it had been for her? Just because… Just because he had looked at her, touched her, made her think and feel that he cared…

Her hands were shaking so much she could hardly pack away her laptop. 'The snow's practically gone,' she told him. 'There's no reason for me to stay here any longer now.'

'Haven't you forgotten something?' Finn challenged her as she hurried towards the door.

Just for a moment she thought he had been teasing her, testing her, not realising just how devastating she found his inadvertent cruelty, but as she turned towards him, her body going weak with longing, she saw from his expression that whatever it was he intended to say it was most definitely not a declaration of love. Gritting her teeth together, she willed herself not to break down in front of him.

'Have I?' she responded quietly.

'We still haven't resolved the situation with the lease on the Dower House,' Finn reminded her.

He could think of that at a time like this?

What kind of fool was he? Finn demanded angrily of himself. He knew for his own sanity he couldn't afford the emotional risk of any future contact with her and yet here he was, clinging to the flimsiest excuse he could find to do so, knowing that with her grandmother living so close Maggie would have to visit.

Not knowing how on earth she was managing to keep her voice level, Maggie told him, 'You wanted to make it a condition of the lease that I never stayed in the Dower House with my non-existent lover. I'll agree to more than that for you, Finn. I'll agree never to stay there myself.'

'But you'll want to see your grandmother.' Finn frowned.

Did he think she might use the excuse of visiting her

grandmother to cloak a desire to see him? Only her pride was holding her together.

'Yes, I shall,' she agreed. 'But I don't have to inflict my unwanted presence on you in order to do that, Finn. I can, after all, see her in London.'

She was opening the door as she spoke, hurrying through the hall, ignoring the cold wet bite of the remaining snow as she pulled open the front door and walked through it to her car. There was still time for him to change his mind, to stop her from leaving, to reach for her and tell her that he just couldn't let her go. As she opened her car door Maggie held her breath.

He was standing by the open front door, so close that a few steps was all it would take for her to run back to him. Tears blurred her vision. What was it he had said to her? 'This can't go on...'

He couldn't have inflicted a more savage form of rejection on her, and he certainly couldn't have made it plainer how little he wanted to see her again. Faced with that knowledge she had no other option but to walk away from him in an attempt to keep her pride intact. Her pride was, after all, all she had left. Her heart was now ripped into ribbons of screaming unendurable pain.

CHAPTER NINE

SOON it would be Christmas. Maggie had her grandmother's present all planned, providing her own and
Finn's solicitors could get the lease for the Dower House
drawn up and signed in time.

Finn.

Maggie had left Shropshire vowing that she would
have no further contact with him, but then she had gone
to visit her grandmother and had been shocked to see
how frail, how fragile and unhappy she looked.

'I miss your grandfather so much,' she had told
Maggie, adding quietly, 'This house seems so empty of
everything that he was: his vibrancy, his sense of fun,
his love of life. He was my strength, Maggie, and without him—'

She had stopped and looked away whilst Maggie's
heart had rocked heavily against her chest wall.

Filled with fierce anxiety, Maggie had started to make
plans—the foremost of them involving a letter to Finn
over which she had pored with heart-wrenching intensity, imagining him receiving it, opening. Reading it.

The receipt of an e-mail from him had caught her off
guard, but he had explained tersely at the end of it that
the amount of work he was becoming involved in with
the restoration of the house and the management of the

farmlands had made the acquisition of a computer a necessity.

Knowing that her grandmother would be expecting her to spend the Christmas holiday period with her, as she always did, and knowing too that her grandmother would want to attend church on Christmas morning, and then no doubt to visit Maggie's grandfather's grave, Maggie had decided that even if the lease was through in time it might not be possible to travel to the Dower House over Christmas itself. Instead she was trying to compose a scrapbook of relevant information about both it and the early years of her grandparents' marriage to give to her grandmother on Christmas Day.

So far she had managed to surreptitiously extract from her grandmother's albums some photographs of them outside the Dower House, and the youth of their features had brought a huge lump to Maggie's throat as she'd studied their bright expectant expressions, their eyes full of a love for one another which not even the faded black and white photographs could dim.

Via their solicitors, Maggie had enquired of Finn if it would be possible to have an up-to-date photograph of the Dower House, explaining what she needed it for, but she was still awaiting his response.

Without giving anything away she had started to ask her grandmother about the early years of her marriage, hoping to glean from her conversation information which she could use to bring those special days back to life for her, to help banish some of the unhappiness she was now feeling.

Her mention of a favourite rose of her grandfather's had sent Maggie on a mission to acquire that same rose for the garden of the Dower House. Predictably it had been Gayle who had discovered a potential source of the rose for her, tracking down a company who specialised in growing traditional varieties. Maggie had gone to visit the company herself, to explain just why it was so important to her to obtain this particular rose, and to her joy they had confirmed that they were able to supply her with it, but had gone on to add that it would be 'bare root stock', explaining that this meant it would need to be planted immediately on delivery.

Maggie would have to wait until her grandmother had moved into the Dower House and planting conditions were right before sending it to her. However, in lieu of an actual plant, they had provided Maggie with a gift voucher inscribed with the name of the rose plus a brief history of it, to give to her grandmother.

Maggie had also borrowed a photograph of her grandfather at the age he had been when her grandparents had lived at the Dower House and had it secretly copied. She had hoped to be able to have her grandfather's image superimposed on a modern-day photograph of the Dower House, but this plan had to be put on hold until she had a response from Finn to her request for some photographs.

Gayle's helpful input into her plans had confirmed Maggie's view that her assistant was well deserving of the very generous bonus that Maggie was planning to surprise her with as an extra special 'thank you' for her hard work during the year.

It had shocked her, though, following Maggie's return to work, to hear Gayle commenting thoughtfully that she felt that Maggie had changed.

'Changed…in what way?' Maggie had demanded immediately.

'I'm not sure,' Gayle had admitted. 'It's just that you seem different somehow, less…driven,' she had explained semi-apologetically.

'Driven?' Maggie had tried not to look as taken aback as she'd felt. She had certainly always prided herself on her dedication to her career, but she did not find it complimentary to be described as 'driven'. But neither did she enjoy discovering that she was spending far too much time staring unhappily into space, fighting not to allow Finn to steal into her thoughts.

She had her career, her friends, her grandmother. Her plans. Surely she wasn't going to allow herself to feel that these were no longer enough for her just because… Just because what? Just because Finn didn't want her…because Finn didn't love her?

Maggie frowned as she reached for her coat. This evening she was dining with a client who wanted to discuss a possible new venture with her.

Bella Jensen was a feisty forty-something divorcee who had built up her small and extremely successful IT personnel business following the break-up of her marriage. She had had, as she had gleefully told Maggie, the very enjoyable pleasure of being approached by her ex-husband's company, who had come to her cap in hand to beg her to work under contract for them since, without the IT skills she had learned as the company had grown, they were lost.

Her husband had sold the small business they had built up together just prior to their break-up, brokering an excellent deal for himself, plus large consultancy fees, and claiming that Bella's contribution to the business had been negligible. She had been delighted—not just to be able to prove him wrong, but to have her importance to their business recognised publicly in a professional and financial manner.

From that experience she had gone on to recognise a growing need for skilled IT staff to work on a contract basis in various mainstream industries, and she had used Maggie's skills in the past to coax highly trained people onto her books.

Maggie liked her, and normally she would have been looking forward to spending an evening in her company. But right now she seemed to have lost the ability to enjoy anything. Right now it felt as though the whole of her life, not just the present but the future as well, had been blighted—and why?

Did she really need to ask herself that?

It was hard for her to fight against seeing in Finn's rejection of her an echo of her parents' earlier failure to truly love her. But that was to think of herself as a victim, and there was no way she was ever going to let herself be that.

Predictably, Bella had chosen one of London's current

crop of 'hot' eateries for them to have dinner in—the restaurant in the kind of superb hotel that people spoke about in hushed, awed voices.

'Love the outfit,' Bella commented enthusiastically to Maggie as they exchanged warm hugs in the foyer before going through to the restaurant. 'And you've lost weight,' she added accusingly, as they were shown to their table. 'I've joined a Pilates exercise course, but so far I have only managed one class,' she admitted ruefully as they both studied their menus.

The restaurant was busy, and Maggie gave a discreet glance at the other diners, recognising several well-known faces from television and the media.

'You said you had a new venture you wanted to talk over with me?' she reminded Bella.

'Mmm... You know, of course, that with the arrival of so many American banks in the City there's been an awful lot of transatlantic movement in the executive arena?'

Maggie nodded her head and waited.

'Over half my staff now are ex-Silicon Valley, and I'm seriously thinking about relocating my business to the USA. I'd have to take on an American partner, but that's all in hand, and what I wondered, Maggie, is whether or not you would be interested in taking over those of my people who want to remain UK-based.'

Maggie frowned. 'Bella, I'm a headhunter, not...'

'Don't turn me down yet. Think about it,' Bella started to cajole determinedly. 'You've got the people skills to do it, Maggie, and I can't think of anyone who would look after my people's interests better. Financially you'd do very well out of it, too. Of course, theoretically, one should be able to work from anywhere in the world with all this modern technology, and the fact that I'm going to be based in the States should not make any difference at all, but my people are very valuable commodities, with extremely fragile egos in some cases, that require a certain amount of hands-on attention. And that's something you are very good at, Maggie. What I'd got in mind for us was a partnership whereby— Wow!'

Bella broke off the earnestness of her discussion to say breathlessly, 'Just look over there—that table for two to our right. Mmm.' She sighed appreciatively. 'There's nothing quite like a big sexy man for making a woman remember that she's a woman, and he's very definitely all man and more.'

As she glanced idly in the direction Bella was indicating Maggie froze in shocked disbelief. The man Bella was drooling over was Finn. Finn, here in London, the place he abhorred, and sharing an intimate dinner with the kind of woman he supposedly found least attractive: a stunning, elegant, city-sleek brunette who was right now leaning across their table to place her hand over his whilst she smiled up into his eyes with the kind of smile that…

'Maggie? Are you okay?'

Somehow she managed to swallow down the fiery ball of mingled fury and pain lodged in her throat; somehow she managed to drag her furious and anguished gaze away from the two people who were so patently oblivious to her presence.

'Yes, yes, I'm fine,' she lied, adding desperately, 'Look, Bella, I'm afraid I'm going to have to cut and run. I forgot when we fixed dinner that I'd got something else on.'

As she spoke Maggie was standing up, desperate to leave the restaurant before Finn saw her, desperate to escape from that intimate little tableau that would be burned across her heart for ever.

Bella was looking confused, as well she might, Maggie acknowledged, and pressing her to think about the proposal she had outlined to her.

'Yes. Yes, I will,' Maggie promised her.

Oh, please God, let her get away before Finn saw her. Please, please, please…

Finn tried not to show his impatience as his solicitor outlined some of the problems she had been having in drawing up the lease for the Dower House. Maggie's request for some photographs of the house had led to him spending a bright afternoon photographing it, both inside and out, and the prints were now carefully tucked away in his briefcase, awaiting delivery to Maggie herself—his personal delivery. He could, of course, have mailed them, but since he had had to meet with his solicitor anyway, it had seemed only sensible to pass on the photographs to Maggie at the same time.

'I can't believe I've finally got you to come to London,' Tina was teasing him ruefully, leaning across the table to tap the back of his hand in light admonition when he made no response. 'Hello, Finn? Are you there?' she asked him dryly.

'I'm sorry,' he apologised. 'You were saying…?'

'I've checked with Paul about the lease, and we think we've finally ironed out all the potential problems.'

Paul was her husband and partner, and Finn had first got to know them when he himself had worked in the City.

'Oh, by the way, you'll never guess what. We're actually thinking of relocating ourselves. Paul's dealt with so many country conveyances for our clients recently that he's got itchy feet—'

She broke off her conversation as the sound of a chair being scraped back over the immaculate wooden floor broke the hushed silence of the restaurant. Automatically both of them looked in the direction of the sound.

Maggie…here…Finn couldn't believe it. He started to get up from the table, but Maggie was already heading for the exit.

'Finn, what is it?' Tina was asking him in bemusement.

'Nothing…I don't want to rush you, Tina, but there's someone else I have to see this evening.'

Maggie… Finn could feel his heart thudding heavily. Her dinner companion had been another woman and he knew he ought to be ashamed to admit just how much that pleased him.

The ache of missing her that had become a permanent feature of his life sharpened to a raging agony of need.

If loving her was hell, then living without her was even worse. But a part-time relationship, taking second place to her career, that would never be enough for him.

He wanted her to want him, to love him with the same degree of commitment and intensity he did her.

Picking up the papers Tina had given him, he opened his briefcase to put them inside. Beneath the wallet of prints of the Dower House lay a small sheaf of estate agents' brochures—one-bedroomed city apartments, *pièd-a-terres* just in case Maggie should…

Snapping his briefcase shut, he leaned over to kiss Tina.

He hadn't alerted Maggie to the fact that he intended to call and see her just in case she refused to see him. Outside the hotel he gave the taxi driver her address and prayed grimly that she would have gone home when she left the restaurant, and not on to another venue.

Just as soon as she had put down her coat and bag and kicked off her shoes, Maggie started to rifle through the contents of her kitchen cupboard and fridge, with the panicky desperation of an addict hunting for a fix. It didn't matter that she already had a freezer full of chilli; the need to make some more gripped her in its frantic compulsion. Making chilli soothed and comforted her, and it reminded her too that she was an independent strong-minded woman who could do anything she wished.

Except stop loving Finn.

Her frenzied movements ceased, her body going still

and then stiff as her doorbell rang. It would probably be her neighbour, wanting to talk through the problems with her current relationship Maggie decided as she unlocked and opened the door.

Only it wasn't her neighbour—it was Finn...

Grimly she wondered how on earth he had got past Bill, the supposedly impenetrable barrier against unwanted and uninvited visitors in whom her grandmother placed such faith.

Finn, guessing what she might be thinking, reflected ruefully on the very imaginative 'sweetener' he had been forced to offer the doorman, along with an equally imaginative sob story, in order to gain access to the building.

'It's more than my life's worth to let you in without checking that you're expected, guv,' had been his initial reaction to Finn's arrival in the hallway.

Finn just hoped that if she ever got to know the truth Maggie's grandmother would forgive him for taking not just her name in vain, as it were, but also for the totally fictitious friendship with her which he had claimed which, even more than the money he had handed over, had swayed the Cerberus guarding the doorway in his favour.

Weakly Maggie gave in to her own need and looked hungrily at him. The city suit and crisp shirt he was wearing emphasised the country hardness of his body with its lean muscular strength.

Shakily she stepped back from the door. There was a small betraying smear of lipstick on his cheek. Unable to stop herself, she focused on it, all too easily imagining the seductive manner in which the brunette would have coaxed him to stay with her.

'I've got some photographs for you—of the Dower House,' Finn was saying as he pushed her front door shut. 'I was a bit concerned that they might get lost in the post, so I decided to deliver them myself. I had to come to London anyway, to see someone…'

'Yes, I saw you with her in the restaurant,' Maggie told him fiercely whilst her brain fought to regain control of her tongue from her wildly out of control emotions— and lost—with a vengeance. 'Obviously some city women do meet with your approval,' she heard herself saying challengingly. Then, as her brain cut in, before she could betray herself even further, 'I'd like you to leave please,' she added quickly.

'Leave?' Finn questioned. 'But…'

'Yes, leave,' Maggie confirmed. 'And right now.'

Somehow she managed to angle her way past him in the small hallway, and as she reached for the front door handle the pain driving her forced her to say acidly, 'Fortunately in the City we aren't subject to impassable fords or impenetrable blizzards, so on this occasion there won't be any need— Oh!' She gave a shocked gasp as without warning the flat was plunged into complete darkness.

Her fiercely guarded and secret fear of the dark was a hangover from her childhood which mortified her, but as the darkness blacked out every single particle of light she could feel the panic caused by the inky blackness of the windowless hallway roaring through her.

Frantically she tried to cling to her self-control. 'It must be a fuse,' she heard herself saying weakly to Finn as she stood rooted to the spot, terrified of moving.

'More like a power blackout,' she could hear him responding grimly. She could tell from his voice and the emptiness of the air close to her that he had moved away from her and into her living room. From there he called out to her. 'Everything's in darkness. I can't see a light anywhere.'

Everything. No lights. Not anywhere. Maggie could feel herself starting to tremble violently, but from somewhere she managed to find the strength of will to claim denyingly, 'This is the City; we don't have power blackouts.'

'Mmm...like fords don't flood and heavy snow doesn't fall in November,' Finn agreed sardonically. 'Well, whether you like it or not, there's no way I'm leaving you here on your own until the power returns.'

Shamingly, the first reaction Maggie had to his announcement was one of intense relief. To punish herself for it, she said grittily, 'I'm sure your dinner companion would be a much more suitable candidate for your company than me.'

'Tina?' Finn questioned. 'She's my solicitor. She and her husband Paul are old friends from my City days.'

His solicitor. Now Maggie was actually grateful for the darkness, to protect not just her hot flush of embarrassment but, more importantly, the almost intoxicatingly intense quiver of happiness that shot through her.

Even so, she still insisted, 'There really isn't any need for you to stay.'

'If you think for one minute that I'm going to leave you here on your own in a situation like this—'

Maggie's heart started to thud even more anxiously as she listened to him. If Finn were to leave now, Maggie knew that she would remain curled up right here in her small hallway until the power returned or it grew light. That was how afraid of the dark she was.

'Do you have any candles?' Finn was demanding.

'Yes… Yes, I do. They're…they're in the kitchen.' She swallowed nervously at the thought of having to make her way through the thick darkness of her flat to her kitchen. She would rather stay where she was.

She waited, dry-mouthed, for Finn to insist that she got the candles, and her legs weakened dangerously when instead he told her, 'Let's go and get them, then. You lead the way.'

And then, as he finished speaking, he reached for her hand, holding it in the warm grip of his own.

Oh, the blessed relief of that lovely warm human contact. Maggie closed her eyes and took a deep steadying breath. She could actually feel Finn's presence surrounding her, protecting her, giving her the courage and the strength to urge her shaky legs to move her towards the kitchen.

She could feel Finn standing behind her as she opened the kitchen cupboard where she kept her dinner candles. The matches were with them, and as she turned round to hand everything to Finn the discovery that he was standing so close to her that her movement had brought them body to body caused her to shake so much that she dropped the matches.

They both bent down to retrieve them at the same time and Maggie could feel the warmth of Finn's breath against her face. An aching wanton yearning for him filled her. Fiercely she fought against it.

He might be doing the correct gentlemanly thing now, in insisting on remaining with her, but she was not going to let herself fall into the delusion of thinking that it meant anything—especially the kind of 'anything' that might have her telling him about how she had had a change of heart about the absolute necessity of her living in the City, or how she could now see that it would be possible for her to live in the country and still continue to run her business. And she certainly wasn't going to tell him of the long lonely empty nights she had lived through since her return to London, nor the way that in her darkest hours she would have given anything, everything, just to be with him. Just to be held in his arms close to him. Just to be sharing the intimacy of his bed with him, wrapped in the even more precious intimacy of his arms…his love.

She tensed as she heard the rasp of a match, her eyes widening as she saw Finn's face briefly outlined in the quick flare before he protected the flame with his hand and lit the candles.

What was it about candlelight that immediately gave even the most mundane of surroundings an aura of sensuality and romance? As they both stood up, Maggie could see the way Finn looked round her kitchen.

'You're cooking chilli?' he questioned her frowningly.

'Is there any reason why I shouldn't?' Maggie responded in immediate self-defence. 'I happen to like it. Not that it's any business of yours.'

'I should hope you do,' Finn agreed, ignoring the final challenging sentence of her response. 'There's enough stuff here to feed a small army. I trust you've taught yourself how to cook mince in the last few months?'

His frown deepened, and he stared at her for so long that Maggie felt slightly nervous. 'You aren't wearing any shoes,' Finn told her, and his frown gave way to a look of wondering male amusement as he grinned. 'You're tiny.'

'I am no such thing,' Maggie denied indignantly.

'Oh, yes you are.' Finn contradicted her softly. 'Tiny and stubborn and…' Putting the newly lit candles down on the worktop, he moved purposefully towards her.

Immediately Maggie panicked, moving back from him, knocking over the candles as she did so. The small flames were instantly extinguished.

The effect of the darkness on her already sensitive nervous system caused her to cry out, a small choked sound of distress which Finn reacted to, demanding, 'Maggie, what is it? Are you all right?'

'No, I'm not all right,' Maggie burst out. 'I hate the dark. It makes me feel so afraid.'

In the silence that followed her small outburst, Maggie

cursed her reckless tongue. What on earth had she told him that for? He would think she was a complete fool. And yet despite that she still heard herself continuing, in a distinctly wobbly little voice.

'It frightens me and…'

Before she could finish Finn was saying gruffly, 'I hate spiders. They terrify me. I have nightmares about them…'

In the darkness Maggie listened to his breathing. The thought of Finn being afraid of anything—and admitting that fear to her—brought a warm rushing flood of protective love washing through her.

'At least you can do something about the darkness. Spiders are there all the time,' Finn told her.

Without thinking about what she was doing, Maggie took a step towards him.

'How about you protecting me from spiders whilst I protect you from the dark?' Finn suggested.

Finn must have moved too, because now his voice was right against her ear, and his arm was right round her waist, and his lips…

'Do you think that's really a good idea?' Maggie whispered. With Finn's lips deliberately teasing hers it was almost impossible for her to think, never mind speak.

'Mmm. And I think that this is an even better idea,' Finn muttered as his arms wrapped round her and he began to kiss her in earnest.

Maggie could feel her head starting to swim whilst

her body melted with the sweet wanton pleasure of being so close to him.

'Oh, God, Maggie, if you only knew how much I've missed you. How much I've wanted you,' she could hear Finn groaning hoarsely to her.

The only response she could make was to wrap her own arms around him and open her mouth to the hot seeking pressure of his tongue. Behind the closed velvet of her eyes the darkness beyond them didn't matter, because she could see in her mind's eye all that she wanted to see. And that was Finn. Her fingertips touched his face, tracing its bone structure, and she felt her body thrill with the unexpected sensuality of the tension in his jaw as she stroked his skin.

With an urgency that both shocked and thrilled her Finn was unfastening her clothes, his whole body shuddering sharply when he touched her bare skin.

'God, you feel so good,' he moaned against her throat. 'The scent of you in my bed has been driving me crazy, do you know that? Every time I've closed my eyes all I've seen is you, all I've wanted to touch is you. You are the air I breathe, Maggie, every thought I think…my heart…my soul.'

Maggie gasped and trembled as his hand cupped her naked breast.

'Undress me, Maggie. Take me to bed, show me that you want me. Be the wild wanton woman I know you can be, the woman who isn't afraid to put love first in her life.'

His hoarse words filled her heart with a hot vocal

torrent of fiercely moaned desire, challenging her to meet and match his need.

'Right now nothing is more important to me than you…and this,' Finn was telling her roughly. 'Kiss me, Maggie. Show me that you want me,' he begged her, but before she could move he was kissing her, taking her mouth with shockingly intense hunger.

The darkness, for so many years her dreaded, hidden and feared enemy, had suddenly become a welcome sensual cloak within which she could hide from any danger of exposure, be free to respond with every bit of the rich sensuality of her true nature to what he was demanding of her.

They made love quickly and passionately, tearing at buttons and fastenings, the raw broken sound of their frantic breathing interrupted by the sharp moan of pleasure Maggie gave when Finn lifted her onto the worktop and sank into her. Until she had felt him there even she hadn't realised how much she had longed for the fulfilment of his possession, how much her body had ached for the feel of him within it.

His own release followed hers, flooding through her as the final shimmering pulsations of her orgasm died away.

As he lifted her off the worktop Finn crooned her name between gentle kisses whilst Maggie tried to stop her body from trembling with the shocked aftermath of what had happened.

'Maggie, Maggie…' Finn was cupping her face, stroking his thumbs over her cheekbones, still damp with the release of her orgasmic tears. 'I want…'

They both blinked as the power suddenly came back on. Maggie could see scratches on Finn's bare shoulder, which she must have inflicted in the heat of their passion. The kitchen floor was strewn with discarded clothes and the air smelled of passion—and Finn. She was appalled by the ferocity of her longing to beg him to stay. To tell him that she would do anything, be anything, in order to share her life with him. The intensity of her emotions made her feel physically weak. She wanted to crawl into bed and pull the covers up over her head. No, what she really wanted was to go to bed with Finn and to curl up there against his body whilst he held her and told her how much he loved her.

But he didn't love her.

Unable to endure looking at him, she quickly pulled on her scattered clothes and told him disjointedly, 'You can't stay here. I want you to leave…'

Like her, Finn had finished dressing.

'Maggie—' he began, but Maggie couldn't bear to listen; she was so close to breaking down completely and begging him to let her into his life. Skirting past him, she walked into her sitting room.

Finn followed her, mentally cursing himself beneath his breath. No wonder she wanted him to leave after the way he had behaved. Why the hell hadn't he taken things more slowly? Did he really need to ask himself that? The sight of her, the scent of her, the reality of her had turned the final screw in the already over tightly coiled ferocity of his need and he had totally lost control. Even now, just thinking about the way she had felt when he had sunk into her, the receptive warm wetness of her, the...

She was walking across the sitting room, heading for the hallway, obviously determined to make him leave.

'Maggie...wait...I've got the draft lease here for you to look at. Tina gave it to me earlier. And those photographs I was telling you about...' As he spoke Finn was reaching for his briefcase and opening it.

Reluctantly Maggie turned round and watched him. In his desperation Finn accidentally dropped the case, spilling its contents. Maggie watched in silence as he gathered up the spilled papers and then tensed as she saw the estate agents' brochures. 'You're thinking of buying a London flat?' she demanded, unable to conceal her shock.

For a moment Finn was tempted to lie and tell her he had got them for a friend, but what was the point?

'I was,' he acknowledged, giving her a grimly wry look. 'Like I've told you before, Maggie, a part-time relationship with you isn't what I want. I thought it was better to let you go completely rather than be forced to life on the fringes of your life, fitted in between business deals, always knowing that I came a poor second best, that my love for you came second best. But the way I've been feeling these last few weeks has changed my mind, and one of the reasons I came to London was to see you and to tell you...to ask you...if it would make any difference to…to things if I were prepared to spend a couple of nights a week in London. That way—'

Maggie didn't let him finish. 'You'd do that for me?' she asked him quietly. 'You'd buy a flat in London just so that you could see me…?'

The tremor in her voice and the look in her eyes made Finn's heart ricochet against his chest wall. 'To have your love, Maggie, I'd—' He stopped and drew a deep breath before admitting huskily, 'I'd do whatever it takes. Living in the City might be one kind of hell as far as I'm concerned, but living without you is every kind of hell there is and then some, all rolled into one unbearable pain.'

'Oh, Finn.'

He gave a small grunt as he exhaled when she threw herself into his arms, but he still had the presence of mind to lock them around her and to kiss her with fiercely sweet passion before asking her hoarsely, 'Will you do it, Maggie? Will you let me into your life, share your time and yourself with me?'

'For two nights a week whilst you're in London?' Maggie questioned him, gravely looking up into his eyes.

The hope and the pain she could see there tore at her own heart. He might not have said the words 'I love you', but he didn't need to; she could see his love in that expression.

'Yes. Will you?' he repeated thickly.

Very slowly Maggie shook her head.

'No,' she told him quietly.

'No…' He had gone white with shock, anguish written—no, carved into his face, Maggie recognised on a
wave of sweetly tender love. 'Maggie…' he began, but
she stopped him, placing her finger against his lips.

'No, Finn, you've had your say,' she told him gently,
'now it's my turn. I was so jealous tonight when I saw
you in the restaurant, and so…so very unhappy when
you told me that things couldn't go on between us. Do
you remember…when we were snowed in?' she reminded him, watching his face.

'I can remember saying something, feeling…knowing
that I'd go mad if I couldn't find some way of us reaching a compromise that would allow us to be together as
lovers rather than adversaries,' Finn agreed.

'I thought you were telling me that you didn't want
me,' Maggie whispered. 'I'd been waiting for you to
come back from the animals so that I could tell you…'

She paused and played with his fingers, before running her own a little nervously up and down his arm
whilst he clenched his muscles beneath the innocent seduction of her touch and begged her though gritted teeth,
'Maggie…?'

'Sorry,' she apologised, her face suddenly pink. 'I
didn't mean… It's just that I love to touch you so much,'
she told him.

'Maggie.' This time the warning in his voice was almost a groan.

'Oh, yes,' Maggie resumed hastily. 'Well, whilst you
were out I'd been thinking that I could work quite easily
from Shropshire…' She looked up into his face again,

and then looked away quickly, telling him shakily, 'Don't do that, Finn, or I'll never be able to finish.'

'Why didn't you say something to me? Tell me?' Finn growled in despair.

'I...you seemed to be rejecting me,' was all that Maggie could say.

'Rejecting you...' Finn closed his eyes and breathed very deeply. 'After the way we'd just made love? Some rejection, Maggie. Are you really telling me that we've wasted the last four weeks living apart when we could have been together?' he demanded. 'That I've spent every single day and every single night aching for you...wanting you. God, those nights, Maggie. Have you any idea...?'

'Yes,' Maggie admitted frankly. 'Every idea!' She was still trying to come to terms with the sheer sweetness of the pleasure of knowing how much he loved her. It was making her feel giddy with its power and awesomeness.

'You'd really be prepared to work from Shropshire to be with me?' Finn was demanding gruffly in a voice that said he hardly dared believe what he was hearing.

'It makes very good economic sense,' Maggie told him demurely. 'Everyone who's anyone is downscaling these days, putting their private lives first. In my job it's important for me to be completely in tune with the needs and aspirations of my clients...'

'And so it's a business decision, is it?' Finn challenged her.

'Not entirely.' Maggie breathed in ecstatic pleasure as

he started to nibble teasing kisses along her jaw. Her eyes, which had been closed, suddenly opened as she tensed and demanded anxiously, 'I won't have to wear boots, will I, Finn? Well, I won't anyway. Not—'

'Not unless they have a designer label?' Finn supplied, tongue in cheek.

'Mmm,' Maggie sighed in soft pleasure as he started to kiss her.

'Mmm...' Finn agreed as his own voice thickened in urgent male need.

'Finn, what on earth are you doing?' Maggie demanded. They had been married just over six hours, both of them sharing a secret laughing look as they had walked down the aisle and out of the church to the victorious sound of Handel's 'Triumphal March'—Maggie having told Finn of her thoughts and feelings as she had waited for him to return to the house the morning before their fateful misunderstanding.

Now, having driven her grandmother back to the Dower House from their reception, they were supposed to be on their way to the airport to catch the flight for their tropical honeymoon destination. But instead of driving towards the airport, Finn was...Finn was...

Maggie stared in disbelief as she looked down from the window of Finn's new four-wheel drive to see that Finn was driving down towards the ford where they had first met.

When he stopped the car in the middle of its now gentle flow Maggie stared accusingly at him. She was wearing her going-away outfit, which just happened to be a raw silk white trouser suit with, of course, a pair of her favourite delicate stilettos.

'The first time we met here there was something I wanted to do that I've regretted not doing ever since,' Finn drawled.

There was a wicked glint in his eye that made Maggie's heart beat fast in female excitement.

'Oh, and what might that have been?' she teased him dulcetly, thinking that she could already guess. Perhaps if he had kissed her then it might have cut short a lot of later unhappiness, but from that they had both learned the value of loving compromise, and now they both respected one another and were equal partners in their relationship.

'This,' Finn told her promptly as he got out and went round to her door, splashing through the shallow ford as he did so. As he opened her door for her Maggie willingly allowed him to lift her out, laughing down into his eyes, but her laughter was replaced with a shocked gasp of indignation when, instead of kissing her, he smacked her firmly on her neat raw-silk-covered behind instead.

'Finn—' she began to protest indignantly, in proper female objection—although he hadn't actually hurt her, and there had been far more sensuality in his light touch than any real anger. But now he was kissing her and kissing her, with a hungry, tender loving passion that totally melted away her ire.

'And this…' he told her. 'How could you have been foolish enough to risk your pretty, wonderful, irreplaceable neck trying to cross that flood in that ridiculous city car? When I think what could have happened,' he groaned, and then checked, lifting his mouth from hers as Maggie let out a wail. 'What is it?' he demanded anxiously.

'My shoes,' she told him. 'They've fallen off...'

'Good. Now you'll never be able to escape from me,' Finn told her promptly as he lifted her back into the car. Maggie whispered something in his ear.

'Barefoot and what?' he demanded.

'You heard me.' Maggie laughed. 'And anyway,' she told him truthfully, 'I'll never want to escape, Finn. I love you too much.'

'No more than I love you,' he told her softly.

'Gran's so happy in the Dower House,' she said, smiling, when he had turned the round and they were heading for the airport.

'Mmm...and she's going to be even happier when we get back from honeymoon and tell her our good news,' Finn agreed.

Lovingly they exchanged tender private glances. The discovery that Maggie was pregnant was still too new and precious to share with anyone else. It was, as Finn had told her emotionally only that morning, the most wonderful gift of love she could possibly have given him—apart from herself.

'Like I said,' Maggie reminded him. 'You're an old-fashioned country type who wants to keep his woman barefoot and pregnant!'

'No,' Finn corrected her lovingly. 'What I want—all I want—is to keep you happy, Maggie.'

'Right,' the zephyr announced, dusting her hands together as she peered over the newest recruit's wing. 'That's those two sorted out. So who's next...?'

The Christmas Bride

PENNY JORDAN

PROLOGUE

'It's a total nightmare, it just couldn't be any worse.'

'Spending Christmas in a castle in Spain is a nightmare?'

Tilly gave a reluctant smile as she heard the wry note in her friend and flatmate's voice.

'Okay. On the face of it, it may sound good,' she agreed. 'But, Sally, the reality is that it will be a nightmare. Or rather a series of on-going nightmares,' she pronounced darkly.

'Such as?'

Tilly shook her head ruefully. 'You want a list? Fine! One, my mother is about to get married to a man she's so crazily in love with she's sends me e-mails that sound as though she's living on adrenalin and sex. Two, the man she's marrying is a multimillionaire— no, a billionaire—'

'You have a funny idea of what constitutes a nightmare,' Sally interrupted.

'I haven't finished yet,' Tilly said. 'Art—that's ma's billionaire—is American, and has very strong ideas about Family Life.'

'Meaning?'

'Patience. I *am* getting there. Ma's got this guilt thing that it's her fault that I'm anti-men and marriage, because she and Dad split up.'

'And is it?'

'Well, let's just say the fact that she's been married and divorced four times already doesn't exactly incline me to look upon marriage with optimism.'

'Four times?'

'Ma loves falling in love. And getting engaged. And getting married. This time Ma has decided she wants to be married at the stroke of midnight on New Year's Eve in a Spanish castle. So Art is transporting his entire family to spend Christmas and New Year in Spain to witness the ceremony—at his expense. We're all going to stay at the castle so that we can get to know one another properly "as a family". Because, according to Ma, Art can't think of a more Family Time than Christmas.'

'Sounds good so far.'

'Well, here's the bit that is not so good. Art's family comprises his super-perfect daughters from his first marriage, along with their husbands and their offspring.'

'And?'

'And Ma, for reasons best known to herself, has told Art that I'm engaged to be married. And of course Art has insisted that I join the happy family party at the castle, along with my fiancé.'

'But you haven't got a fiancé. You haven't even got a boyfriend.'

'Exactly. I have pointed this out to my mother, but she's pulling out all the high-drama stops. She says she's afraid Art's daughters are going to persuade him not to marry her, and that if I turn up *sans* fiancé it will add fuel to their argument that as a family we are not cut out for long-term, reliable marriages. She should really have gone on the stage.' Tilly looked at her friend. 'I know this sounds crazy, but the truth is I'm worried about her. If Art's daughters are against the marriage, then she won't stand a chance. Ma isn't a schemer. She just can't help falling in love.'

'It sounds more like you're the parent and she's the child.'

'Well, Ma does like to imply that she was little more than a child when she ran off with my father and had me. Although she was twenty-one at the time, and the reason she ran off with Dad was that she was already engaged to someone else. Who she then married after she realised she had made a mistake in marrying my dad.' Tilly was smiling as she spoke, but there was a weary resignation in her tone. 'I feel I should be there for her, but I just don't want her to blame me if things go wrong because I didn't turn up with a fiancé.'

'Well, you know what to do, don't you?'

'What?'

'Hire an escort.'

'What?'

'There's no need to look like that. I'm not talking about a "when would you like the massage" type escort. I'm talking about the genuine no-strings, no-sex, perfectly respectable and socially acceptable paid-for social escort.'

Sally could see that Tilly was looking both curious

and wary. 'Come on, pass me the telephone directory.
Let's sort it out now.'

'You could always lend me Charlie,' Tilly suggested.

'Let you take my fiancé away to some Spanish castle
for the most emotionally loaded holiday of the year for
loved-up couples?' Sally gave a vehement shake of her
head. 'No way! I'm not letting him miss the seasonal
avalanche of advertisements for happy couples with
their noses pressed up against jewellers' windows.' Sally
balanced the telephone book on her lap. 'Okay, let's try
this one first. Pass me the phone.'

'Sally, I don't…'

'Trust me. This is the perfect answer. You're doing
this for your mother, remember!'

'Will I do *what*?' Silas Stanway stared at his young
half-brother in disbelief.

'Well, I can't do it. Not in a wheelchair, with my arm
and leg in plaster,' Joe pointed out. 'And it seems mean
to let the poor girl down,' he added virtuously, before
admitting, 'I need the money I'll be paid for this, Silas,
and it's giving me some terrific contacts.'

'Working as a male escort?' Beneath the light tone
of mockery Silas felt both shock and distaste. Another
indication of the cultural gap that existed between him,
a man of thirty plus, and his barely twenty-one-year-old
sibling—the result of his father's second marriage—for
whom Silas felt a mixture of brotherly love and, since
their father's death, almost paternal concern.

'Loads of actors do it,' Joe defended himself. 'And
this agency is *respectable*. It's not one of those where

the women you escort are going to come on to you for sex. Mind you, from what I've heard they're willing to pay very well if you do, and it can be a real turn-on in a sort of Mrs Robinson way. At least that's what I've heard,' he amended hastily, when he saw the way his half-brother was looking at him. 'It's only for a few days,' he wheedled. 'Look, here's the invite. Private jet out to Spain, luxury living in a castle, and all at the expense of the bridegroom. I was really looking forward to it. Come on, be a sport.'

Silas looked uninterestedly at the invitation Joe had handed to him, and then frowned when he saw the name of the bridegroom-to-be. 'This is an invitation to Art Johnson the oil tycoon's wedding?' he demanded flatly.

'Yeah, that's right,' Joe said with exaggerated patience. 'Art Johnson the Third. The girl I'm escorting is the daughter of the woman he's going to marry.'

Silas's eyes narrowed. 'Why does she need an escort?'

'Dunno.' Joe gave a dismissive shrug. 'She probably just hasn't got a boyfriend and doesn't want to show up at the wedding looking like a loser. It's a woman thing; happens all the time,' Joe informed him airily. 'Apparently she rang the agency and told them she wanted someone young, hunky and sexy, Oh, and not gay.'

'And that doesn't tell you *anything?*' Silas asked witheringly.

'Yeah, it tells me she wants the kind of escort she can show off.'

'Have you met her?'

'No. I did e-mail her to suggest we meet up beforehand to set up some kind of background story, but she said she was too busy. She said we could discuss everything during the flight. The bridegroom is organising the private jet. All I have to do is get in a taxi, with my suitcase and passport, and collect her from her place on the way to the airport. Easy-peasy. Or at least it would have been if this hadn't happened during that rugby match.' Joe grimaced at his plaster casts.

Silas listened to his half-brother's disclosures with growing contempt for the woman who was 'hiring' him. The more he heard, the less inclined he was to believe Joe's naive assertion that his escort duties were to be strictly non-sexual. Ordinarily he would not only have given Joe a pithy definition of exactly what he thought of the woman, he would also have added a warning not to do any more agency work and a flat refusal to step into his brother's shoes.

Normally. If the bridegroom in question had not been Art Johnson. He had been trying to contact Art Johnson for the last six months for inside information about the late legendary oil tycoon Jay Byerly. Jay Byerly had, during his lifetime, straddled both the oil industry and the political scene like a colossus.

As an investigative journalist for one of the country's most prestigious broadsheets, Silas was used to interviewees being reluctant to talk to him. But this time he was investigating for a book he was writing about the sometimes slippery relationships within the oil industry. And Jay Byerly was rumoured to have once used his connections to hush up an oil-related near-ecological disaster nearly thirty years ago. Until recently Art

Johnson had been a prime mover in oil, and he had been mentored by Jay Byerly in his early days.

So far every attempt Silas had made to get anywhere near Art Johnson had been met with a complete rebuff. Supposedly semi-retired from the oil business now, having handed over the company to be run by his sons-in-law, it was widely accepted that Art still controlled the business—and its political connections—from behind the scenes.

Silas wasn't the kind of man who liked being forced to give up on anything, but he had begun to think that this time he had no choice.

Now it seemed fate had stepped in on his side.

'Okay,' he told his half-brother. 'I'll do it.'

'Wow, Silas—'

'On one condition.'

'Okay, I'll split the fee with you. And if she does turn out to be a complete dog—'

'That condition being that you don't do any more escorting.'

'Hey, Silas, come on. The money's good,' Joe protested, but then he saw Silas's expression and shook his head. 'Okay… I guess I can always go back to bar work.'

'Right. Run through the arrangements with me again.'

CHAPTER ONE

THERE was no way this was going to work. No way she was ever going to be able to persuade anyone that a hired escort was her partner for real, Tilly decided grimly. But why should she care? Given free choice, she wouldn't even be going to the wedding. Her mother hadn't picked a decent partner yet, and Tilly had no faith in her having done so this time. And as for Art's family… Tilly tried to picture her fun-loving, rule-breaking, shock-inducing mother living happily within the kind of family set-up she had described to Tilly in her e-mails, and failed.

The marriage would not last five minutes. In fact it would, in Tilly's opinion, be better if it never took place at all—even if her mother was adamant that she was finally truly in love.

She was a fool for letting herself be dragged into her mother's life to act the part of the happily engaged daughter. But, as always where anything involving her mother was concerned, it was always easier to give in than to object.

The only thing Tilly had ever been able to hold out

about against her mother was her own determination
never to fall in love or marry.

'But, darling, how can you say that?' her mother had
protested when Tilly had told her of her resolve. 'Everyone wants to meet someone and fall in love with
them. It's basic human instinct.'

'What if I find out that I'm not in love with them any
more, or they aren't in love with me?'

'Well, then you find someone else.'

'Only to marry again, and then again when that
doesn't work out? No, thanks, Ma.'

Mother and daughter they might be, and they might
even share the same physical characteristics, but sisters
under the skin they were most definitely not.

No? Who was she kidding? Wasn't it true that deep
down she longed to meet her soul mate, to find that
special someone to whom she'd feel able to give herself
completely, with whom she'd feel able to remove all
those barriers she had erected to protect herself from the
pain of loving the wrong man? A man strong enough to
believe in their love and to demolish all her own doubts,
noble enough to command not just her love but her
respect, human enough to show her his own vulnerability—oh, and of course he must be sexy, gorgeous, and
have the right kind of sense of humour. The kind of man
that came by the dozen and could be found almost
anywhere then, really, she derided herself. Just as well
she had never been foolish enough to tell anyone about
him. What would she say? *Oh, and by the way, here's
a description of my wish for Christmas...*

Get a grip, she warned herself sternly. He—her

'fiancé', and most definitely *not* soul mate—would be here any minute. Tilly frowned. She had e-mailed him last night to explain in exact detail what his role would involve, and to say that he would be required to pose convincingly as her fiancé in public. And only in public. No matter how many times Sally had assured her that she had nothing to worry about, and that hiring an escort was a perfectly reasonable and respectable thing to do, Tilly was not totally convinced.

Luckily, because she hadn't taken any time off during the summer, getting a month's leave from her job now had not been a problem. However, she could just imagine what the reaction of the young and sometimes impossibly louche male trainee bankers who worked under her would be if they knew what she was doing.

Other women in her situation might think of themselves as being let loose in a sweet shop at having so many testosterone-charged young men around. Tilly, however, tended to end up mothering her trainees more than anything else.

She tensed when she heard the doorbell ring, even though she had been waiting for it. It was too late now to wish she had taken Sally up on her offer to go into work later, so that she could vet the escort agency's choice.

The doorbell was still ringing. Stepping over her suitcase, Tilly went to open the door, tugging it inwards with what she had intended to be one smooth, I'm-the-one-in-control-here movement.

But her intention was sabotaged by the avalanche of female, hormone-driven reactions that paralysed her, causing her to grip hold of the half-open door.

The man in front of her wasn't just good-looking, she recognised with a small gulp of shock. He was... He was... She had to close her eyes and count to ten before she dared to open them again. Tiny feathery flicks of sensual heat were whipping against her nerve-endings, driving her body into a fever of what could only be lust. This man didn't just possess outstanding male good looks, he also possessed that hard-edged look of dangerous male sexuality that every woman recognised the minute she saw it. Tilly couldn't stop looking at him. He was dark-haired and tall—over six feet, she guessed—with powerfully broad shoulders and ice-blue eyes fringed with jet-black lashes. And right now he was looking at her with a kind of frowning impatience, edged with cool, male confidence, that said he certainly wasn't as awestruck by her appearance as she was by his.

'Matilda Aspinall?' he asked curtly.

'No...I mean, yes—only everyone calls me Tilly.' For heaven's sake, she sounded like a gauche teenager, not an almost thirty-year-old woman capable of running her own department in one of the most male-dominated City environments there was.

'Silas Stanway,' he introduced himself.

'*Silas?*' Tilly repeated uncertainly. 'But in your e-mails I thought—'

'I use my middle name for my e-mail correspondence,' Silas informed her coolly. It wasn't entirely untrue. He *did* use his middle name, along with his mother's maiden name as his pen-name. 'We'd better get a move on. The taxi driver wasn't too keen on stopping on double yellows. Is that your case?'

'Yes. But I can manage it myself,' Tilly told him.

Ignoring her attempts to do exactly that, he reached past her and hefted the case out of the narrow hallway as easily as though it weighed next to nothing.

'Got everything else?' he asked. 'Passport, travel documentation, keys, money…'

Tilly could feel an unfamiliar burn starting to heat her face. An equally unfamiliar sensation had invaded her body. A mixture of confusion and startlingly intense physical desire combined with disbelieving shock. Why was she not experiencing irritation that he should take charge? Why was she experiencing this unbelievably weird and alien sense of being tempted to mirror her own mother's behaviour and come over all helpless?

Was it because it was Christmas, that well-known emotional trap, baited and all ready to spring and humiliate any woman unfortunate enough to have to celebrate it without a loving partner? Christmas, according to the modern mythology of the great god of advertising, meant happy families seated around log fires in impossibly large and over-decorated drawing rooms. Or, for those who had not yet reached that stage, at the very least the loved-up coupledom of freezing cold play snow fights, interrupted by red-hot passionate kisses, the woman's hand on the man's arm revealing the icy glitter of a diamond engagement ring.

But, no matter how gaudily materialism wrapped up Christmas, the real reason people invested so much in it, both financially and emotionally, was surely because at heart, within everyone, there was still that child waking up on Christmas morning, hoping to receive the most perfect present—which the adult world surely translated as the gift of love, unquestioning, unstinting, freely given and equally freely received. A gift shared and celebrated, tinsel-wrapped in hope, with a momentary suspension of the harsh reality of the destruction that could follow.

She knew all about that, of course. So why, *why*, deep down inside was she being foolish enough to yearn to wake up on her own Christmas morning to that impossibly perfect gift? *She* was the one who was in charge, Tilly tried to remind herself firmly. Not him. And if he had really been her fiancé there was no way she would have allowed him to behave in such a high-handed manner, not even bothering to kiss her...

Kiss her?

Tilly stood in the hall and stared wildly at him, while her heart did the tango inside her chest.

'Is something wrong?'

Those ice-blue eyes didn't miss much, Tilly decided. 'No, everything's fine.' She flashed him her best "I'm the boss" professional smile and stepped through the door.

'Keys?' This woman didn't need an escort, she needed a carer, Silas decided grimly as he watched Tilly hunt feverishly through her bag for her keys and then struggle to insert them into the lock. It was just as well that Joe *wasn't* the one accompanying her. The pair of them wouldn't have got as far as Heathrow without one of them realising they had forgotten something.

What was puzzling him, though, was why on earth she had felt it necessary to hire a man. With those looks and that figure he would have expected her to be fighting men off, not paying them to escort her. Normally his own taste ran to tall, slim soignée brunettes of the French persuasion—that was to say women of intelligence who played the game of woman-to-man relationships like grand chess masters. But his hormones, lacking the discretion of his brain, were suddenly putting up a good argument for five foot six, gold and honey streaked hair, greenish-gold eyes, full soft pink lips, and a deliciously curvy hourglass figure.

He had, Silas decided, done Joe more than one favour in standing in for him. His impressionable sibling wouldn't have stood a chance of treating this as a professional exercise. Not, of course, that Silas was tempted. And even if he had been there was too much at stake from his own professional point of view for him to risk getting physically involved with Matilda. Matilda! Who on earth had been responsible for giving such a beauty the name Matilda?

What was the matter with her? Tilly wondered feverishly. She was twenty-eight years old, mature, responsible, sensible, and she just did not behave like this around men, or react to them as she did to this man. It wasn't the man who was causing her uncharacteristic behaviour, she reassured herself. It was the situation. Uncomfortably she remembered that sharp, hot, sweetly erotic surge of desire she had felt earlier. Her body still ached a little with it, and that ache intensified every time her female radar picked up the invisible forcefield of male pheromones surrounding Silas. Her body seemed to be reacting to them like metal to a magnet.

She grimaced as she looked up at the December

grey-clouded sky. It had started to rain and the pavement was wet. Wet, and treacherously slippery if you happened to be wearing new shoes with leather soles, Tilly recognised as she suddenly started to lose her balance.

Silas caught her just before she cannoned into the open taxi door. Tilly could feel the strength of his grip through the soft fabric of the sleeve of her coat and the jumper she was wearing beneath it. She could also feel its warmth...*his* warmth, she recognised, and suddenly found it hard to breathe normally. Who would have thought that such a subtle scent of cologne—so subtle, in fact, that she had to stop herself from leaning closer so she could smell it better—could make her feel this dizzy?

She looked up at Silas, intending to thank him for saving her from a fall. He was looking back down at her. Tilly blinked and felt her gaze slip helplessly down the chiselled perfection of his straight nose to his mouth. Her own, she discovered, had gone uncomfortably dry. So dry that she was tempted to run the tip of her tongue along her lips.

'I 'aven't got all day, mate...'

The impatient voice of the taxi driver brought Tilly back to reality. Thanking Silas, she clambered into the taxi while he held the door open for her before joining her.

Joe would never have been able to deal with a woman like this, Silas decided grimly as the taxi set off. Hell, after the way she had just been looking at his mouth, he was struggling with the kind of physical reaction that hadn't caught him so off-guard since he had left his teens behind. In the welcome shadowy interior of the cab he moved discreetly, to allow his suit jacket to conceal the tell-tale tightness of the fabric of his chinos.

'Why don't I take charge of the passports and travel documentation?' he suggested to Tilly. 'After all, if I'm supposed to be your escort—'

'My fiancé,' Tilly corrected him.

'Your *what*?'

'You did get my e-mail, didn't you?' she asked uncertainly. 'The one I sent you explaining the situation, and the role you would be required to play?'

For the first time Silas noticed that she was wearing a solitaire diamond ring on the third finger of her left hand.

'My understanding was that I was simply to be your escort,' he told her coolly. 'If that's changed…'

There was a look in his eyes that Tilly wasn't sure she liked. A cynical world-weary look that held neither respect nor liking for her. What exactly was a man like this doing working for an escort agency anyway? she wondered. He looked as though he ought to be running a company, or…or climbing mountains—not hiring himself out to escort women.

'You will be my escort, but you will also be my fiancé. That is the whole purpose of us going to Spain.'

'Really? I understood the purpose was for us to attend a wedding.'

She hadn't mistaken that cynicism, Tilly realised. 'We *will* be attending a wedding. My mother's. Unfortunately my mother has told her husband-to-be that I am engaged—don't ask me why; I'm not sure I know the answer myself. All I do know is that, according to her, it's imperative that I turn up with a fiancé.'

'I see.' And he did. Only too well. He had been right to suspect that there was a seedy side to this whole escort situation. His mouth compressed and, seeing it, Tilly began to wish that the agency had sent her someone else. She didn't think she was up to coping with a man like this as her fake fiancé.

'What else was in this e-mail that I ought to know about?'

Tilly's chin lifted. 'Nothing. My mother, of course, knows the truth, and naturally I've told her that we will have to have separate rooms.'

'Naturally?' Silas quirked an eyebrow. 'Surely there is nothing *natural* about an engaged couple sleeping apart?'

Tilly suspected there would certainly be no sleeping apart from a woman he was really involved with. Immediately, intimate images she hadn't known she was capable of creating filled her head, causing her to look out of the taxi's window just in case Silas saw in her eyes exactly what she was thinking.

'What we do in private is our business,' she told him quickly.

'I should hope so,' he agreed, *sotto voce*. 'Personally, I've never seen the appeal of voyeurism.'

Tilly's head turned almost of its own accord, the colour sweeping up over her throat with betraying heat.

'Which terminal do you want, gov?' the taxi driver asked.

'We're flying out in a privately owned plane. Here's where we need to go.' Tilly fumbled for the documents, almost dropping them when Silas reached out and took them from her, his fingers touching hers. She was

behaving like a complete idiot, she chided herself, as
Silas leaned forward to give the taxi driver directions—
and, what was more, behaving like an idiot who was
completely out of her depth.

Probably because she *felt* completely out of her
depth. Silas just wasn't what she had been expecting.
For a start she had assumed he would be younger, more
like the boys at work than a man quite obviously in his
thirties, and then there was his raw sexuality. She just
wasn't used to that kind of thing. It was almost a
physical presence in the cab with them.

How on earth was she going to get through nearly
four weeks of pretending that he was her fiancé? How
on earth was she going to be able to convince anyone,
and especially Art's daughters, that they were a couple
when they were sleeping in separate rooms? This just
wasn't a man who *did* separate rooms, and no woman
worthy of the name would want to sleep apart from him
if they were really lovers. Anxiously she clung to her
mother's warning that her husband-to-be was very mor-
alistic. They could say that they were occupying separate
rooms out of respect for his views, couldn't they?

'We're here,' Silas said as the taxi jerked to a halt.
'You can explain to me exactly what is going on once
we're on board.'

She could explain to him?

But there was no point arguing as he had already
turned away to speak with the taxi driver.

CHAPTER TWO

THE only other occasion when Tilly had travelled in a private jet had been in the company of half a dozen of her male colleagues, and the plane had been owned by one of bank's wealthiest clients. She hadn't dreamed then that the next time she would be driven up to the gangway of such a jet, where a steward and stewardess were waiting to relieve them of their luggage and usher them up into luxurious comfort, the jet would be owned by her stepfather-to-be.

Tilly wasn't quite sure why she found it necessary to draw attention to her large and fake solitaire "engagement ring" by playing with it when she saw the way the stewardess was smiling at Silas. It certainly seemed to focus both the other girl's and Silas's attention on her, though.

'Ms Aspinall.' The male steward's voice was as soothing as his look was flattering. 'No need to ask if you travel a lot.' He signalled to someone to take their luggage on board. 'Everyone in the know travels light and buys on arrival—especially when they're flying to somewhere like Madrid.'

Tilly hoped her answering smile didn't look as

false as it felt. The reason she was 'travelling light', as he had put it, was quite simply because she had assumed that this castle her mother's new man had hired came complete with a washing machine. The demands of her working life meant that she rarely shopped. A couple of times a year she restocked her working wardrobe with more Armani suits and plain white shirts.

But, bullied by Sally, she had allowed herself to be dragged down Knightsbridge to Harvey Nicks, in order to find a less businesslike outfit for the wedding, and a dress for Christmas day. The jeans she was wearing today were her standard weekend wear, even if they were slightly less well fitting than usual, thanks to her anxiety over her mother's decision to marry again.

Once inside the jet she settled herself in her seat, trying not to give in to her increasing urge to look at her new 'fiancé,' who seemed very much at home in the world of the super-rich for someone who needed to boost his income by hiring himself out as an escort.

Jason, the steward, offered them champagne. Tilly didn't drink very much, but she accepted the glass he was holding out to her, hoping that it might help ease the tension caused by her unwanted awareness of Silas's potent sexuality. Silas, on the other hand, shook his head.

'I prefer not to drink alcohol when I'm flying,' he told Jason. 'I'll have some water instead.'

Why did she suddenly feel that drinking one glass of champagne had turned her into a potential alcoholic who couldn't pass up on the chance to have a drink? Rebelliously she took a quick gulp of the fizzing bubbles, and then tried not to pull a face when she realised how dry the champagne was.

They were taxiing down the runway already, the jet lifting easily and smoothly into the grey sky. Tilly wasn't a keen flyer, and she could feel her stomach tensing with nervous energy as she waited for the plane to level off. Silas, on the other hand, looked coolly unmoved as he reached for a copy of the *Economist*.

'Right, you'd better tell me what's going on,' he said, flicking through the pages of the magazine. 'I was informed that you wanted an escort to accompany you to your mother's wedding.'

'Yes, that's right—I do,' Tilly agreed. 'An escort who is my fiancé—I did explain it all to you in the e-mail I sent,' she insisted defensively when she saw the way he was looking at her.

'E-mails are notoriously unreliable.' But not, perhaps, as unreliable at passing on information as his dear brother, Silas acknowledged grimly. 'You'd better explain again.'

Tilly glanced over her shoulder to make sure they were alone in the cabin. This was her mother's new man's plane, staffed by his employees. 'My mother's husband-to-be is an American. He has very strong ideas about family life and…and family relationships. He has two daughters from his first marriage, both married with children, and my mother…' She paused and took a deep breath. Why on earth should she be finding this so discomfiting? As though somehow she were on trial and had to prove herself? She was the one hiring Silas, the one in charge, not the other way around.

'My mother feels that Art's daughters aren't entirely happy about their marriage.'

Silas's eyebrows lifted. 'Why not? You've just said that they're both married with children. Surely they should be happy to see their father find happiness?'

'Well, yes… But the thing is…'

Tilly chewed anxiously on her bottom lip—a small action which automatically drew Silas's attention to her mouth. How adept the female sex was at focusing male attention on it, Silas thought cynically. Mind you, with a mouth as full and soft-looking as hers, Tilly hardly needed to employ such tired old tricks to get a man to look at it and wonder how it would feel beneath his own. His imagination had been there already, and gone further. Much further, in fact, he admitted reluctantly.

How did she put this, Tilly wondered, without being disloyal to her mother? 'My mother doesn't think that Art's daughters feel she will make him happy.'

'Why not?'

'Well, he's a widower, and Ma is a divorcee.'

Silas gave a small brusque shrug. 'So your mother made a mistake? It's hardly unusual in this day and age.'

'No…but…'

'But?'

'But Ma has made rather more than just one mistake,' Tilly informed him cautiously.

'You mean she's been married more than once?'

'Yes.'

'How much more than once?'

'Well, four times, actually. She can't help it.' Tilly defended her mother quickly when she saw Silas's expression. 'She just falls in love so easily, you see, and men fall in love with her, and then—'

'And then she divorces them, and starts over with a bigger bank balance and a richer man?'

Tilly was shocked. 'No! She's not like that. Ma would never marry just for money.'

Silas registered the 'just' and said cynically, 'But she finds it easier to love a rich man than one who is poor?'

'You're just like Art's daughters and their husbands. You're criticising my mother without knowing her. She loves Art. Or at least she believes she does. I know it sounds illogical, but Ma *is* illogical at times. She's afraid that Art's daughters will be even more antagonistic towards her if they know that I'm single. Art was boasting to her about his daughters and their marriages, and Ma lost the plot a bit and told him that I was engaged.'

It was such a ridiculous story that it had to be true, Silas decided. 'And you don't know any single available men you could have asked to help you out?'

Of course she did. She knew any number of them. But none whom she felt she could rely on to act the part convincingly enough.

'No, not really.' How easily the fib slipped from her lips. She was obviously more her mother's daughter than she had known, she admitted guiltily. But Silas knew nothing of her personal and professional circumstances—or the fact that she would have rather walked barefoot over hot coals than let the boisterous and youthful sexual predators who made up her staff know about her lack of a sexual partner. Even if it was by choice. As far as Tilly was concerned it was a small and harmless deceit—she wasn't to know that Silas, in between flying in and out of the country to complete an assignment in Brussels after his meeting with Joe, had done as much background-checking on her as he could, and thus knew exactly what her professional circumstances were.

No available men in her life? Silas was hard put to it to bite back the cynical retort he longed to make and ask why she didn't use her status as the head of her own department to provide herself with a fake fiancé from one of the ten-plus young men who worked under her.

On the other hand, for reasons he was not prepared to investigate too closely, it brought him a certain sense of relief to know that he had found her out as a liar and therefore not to be trusted. And he certainly wasn't going to be taken in by that pseudo-concern she had expressed for a mother who sounded as though she was more than a match for any number of protective daughters and their husbands.

Not, of course, that Art's daughters were exactly your run-of-the-mill average daughters. Silas had learned all about them when he had done his initial search on their father. They had learned their politics and their financial know-how at their father's knee, and while they adopted a Southern Belle manner in public, in private they were not just steel magnolias but steel magnolias with chariot spikes attached to their wheels.

More than one person had been eager to relate to him some of the urban mythology surrounding the family, about the way Art's daughters had targeted their husbands-to-be: disposing of a couple of fiancés, and at least one illegitimate child, plus a handful of quashed drink-driving and drug charges on their way to the altar.

If one thing was certain it was that they would not tolerate their father marrying a woman they themselves had not sourced and checked out.

'Okay, so your mother is afraid that her potential step-daughters might persuade their father not to go ahead with the wedding. But I still don't understand how you turning up with a fiancé can have any effect on that.'

'Neither can I, really, but my mother was getting herself in such a state it just seemed easier to give in and go along with what she wanted.'

'Easier, but surely not entirely advisable? I should have thought a calm, analytical discussion—'

'You don't know my mother. She doesn't *do* calm or analytical,' Tilly said, before adding protectively, 'I'm making her sound like a drama queen, but she isn't. She's just a person who lives in and on her emotions. My guess is that she simply got carried away with trying to compete with Art in the perfect daughter stakes. I've told her that I've managed to find someone to pose as my supposed fiancé, but I haven't told her about using the agency,' she warned. 'She'll probably assume that I already knew you.'

'Or that we're past lovers?'

Tilly was aghast. She shook her heed vehemently. 'No, she won't think that. She knows that I—'

'That you what? Took a vow of chastity?'

For some reason the drawling cynicism in his voice hurt. 'She knows that I don't have any intention of ever getting married.'

'Because you don't believe in marriage?'

Tilly gave him a level look and replied coolly, 'No, because I don't believe in divorce.'

'Interesting.'

'Not really. I daresay any number of children with divorced parents feel the same way. Why are you asking me so many questions? You sound more like a…a barrister than an actor. I thought actors liked talking about themselves, not asking questions.'

'I can assure you that I am most definitely *not* a barrister. And surely actors need to study others in order to play their roles effectively?'

Not a barrister. But she was astute enough to have recognised his instinctive need to probe and cross-question, Silas recognised.

What was it about the quality of a certain kind of silence that made a person feel so acutely uncomfortable? Tilly wondered as she hunted feverishly for a safer topic of conversation. Or in this instance was it the man himself who was making her feel so acutely conscious of things about herself and her attitude to life? Things she didn't really want to think about.

'I was a bit worried that the agency wouldn't be able to find someone suitable who was prepared to work over Christmas,' she offered, holding out a conversational olive branch as brightly as she could in an attempt to establish the proper kind of employer—her—and employee—him—relations. Not that it was true, of course. The truth was that she would have been delighted if Sally's plan to provide her with a fiancé had proved impossible to carry through.

'If that's a supposedly subtle attempt to find out if I have a partner, the answer is no, I don't. And as for working over Christmas, any number of people do it.'

Tilly had to swallow the hot ball of outrage that had lodged in her throat. She could almost visualise the small smouldering pile of charcoal that had been her olive branch.

'I was not asking if you had a partner. I was simply trying to make polite conversation,' she told him.

'More champers?'

Tilly smiled up at Jason in relief, welcoming his interruption of a conversation that was leading deeper and deeper into far too personal and dangerous territory. Far too personal and dangerous for *her*, that was.

'We'll be landing in ten minutes,' Jason warned them. 'There'll be a car and driver waiting for you, of course.'

Tilly smiled, but less warmly.

'What's wrong?' Silas asked her.

'Nothing. Well, not really.' She gave a small shrug as Jason moved out of earshot. 'I know I should be enjoying this luxury, and of course in a way I am, but it still makes me feel guilty when I think about how many people there are struggling just to feed themselves.'

'A banker who wants to save the world?' Silas mocked her.

Immediately Tilly tensed. 'How did you know that? About me being a banker?'

Silently Silas cursed himself for his small slip. 'I don't know. The agency must have told me, I suppose,' he said dismissively.

'Sometimes it's easier to change things from the

inside than from the outside,' Tilly explained after a slight pause.

'Indeed. But something tells me that it would take one hell of a lot of inner change to get the City types to think about saving the planet. Or were you thinking of some kind of inducement to help them? A new Porsche, perhaps?'

'Toys for boys goes with the territory, but they grow out of them—usually about the same time as their first child is born,' Tilly told him lightly.

The jet had started its descent, and Jason's return to the cabin brought their conversation to an end.

CHAPTER THREE

SNOW in Spain. Who knew? She supposed *she* ought to have done, Tilly admitted, as she huddled deeper into her coat, grateful for the warmth inside the large four-wheel drive that had been waiting at the airport to transport them up to the castle.

Silas had fired some rapid words in Spanish to their driver at the start of their journey, but had made no attempt to engage her in conversation, and the long, muscular arm he had stretched out across the back of the seat they were sharing was hardly likely to give anyone the impression that they were besotted with one another.

The castle was up in the mountains, beyond the ancient town of Segovia. Tilly had viewed the e-mail attachment her mother had sent, showing a perfect fairy-tale castle against a backdrop of crisp white snow, but foolishly she hadn't taken on board that the snow as well as the castle was a reality. Now, with the afternoon light fading, the landscape outside the car windows looked more hostile than beautiful.

It didn't help when Silas suddenly drawled, 'I hope you've packed your thermals.'

'No, I haven't,' she was forced to reply. 'But the castle is bound to be centrally heated.'

The now-familiar lift of dark eyebrows made her stomach lurch with anxiety.

'You think so?'

'I know so. My mother hates the cold, and she would never tolerate staying anywhere that wasn't properly heated.'

'Well, she's *your* mother, but my experience is that most owners of ancient castles hate spending money on heating them—especially when they are hiring them out to other people. Maybe on this occasion, since your mother, like us, has love to keep her warm, she won't feel the cold.'

Tilly gave him a look of smouldering antipathy. 'That wasn't funny.'

'It wasn't meant to be. Have you given any real thought as to just how intimately we'll have to interact with each other, given that we're going to be part of a very small and potentially very explosive private house party?'

'We won't have to interact intimately at all,' Tilly protested, hot-faced. 'People will accept that we're an engaged couple because we'll have told them we are. We won't be expected to indulge in public displays of physical passion to prove that we're engaged. Besides, I'm wearing a ring.'

She was totally unprepared for the sudden movement he made, reaching for her hand and taking possession of it. His fingers gripped her wrist, his thumb placed flat against her pulse so that it was impossible for her to hide the frantic way it was jumping and racing.

'What are you doing?' she demanded crossly, when he removed her fake ring with one deft movement.

'You don't really imagine that *this* is going to deceive the daughters of a billionaire, do you?' he taunted, shaking his head as he put it in his pocket. 'They'll know straight away it's a fake, and it's only a small step from knowing your ring is a fake to guessing our relationship is fake.'

Tilly couldn't conceal her dismay. His confidence had overpowered her own belief in the effectiveness of her small ploy.

'But I've *got* to wear a ring,' she told him. 'We're supposed to be engaged, and it's as her properly engaged daughter that my mother wants to parade me in front of Art and his daughters.'

'Try this.'

Tilly couldn't believe her eyes when Silas reached into his jacket pocket and removed a small shabby jeweller's box.

Uncertainly she took it from him. He couldn't possibly have *bought* a ring.

'Here, give it to me.' he told her impatiently, after he'd watched her struggle with the catch, and flicked it open so easily that she felt a complete fool. Warily she looked at the ring inside the box, her eyes widening in awe. The gold band might be slightly worn, but the rectangular emerald surrounded by perfect, glittering white diamonds was obviously very expensive and very real.

'Where—? How—?' she began.

'It was my mother's,' Silas answered laconically.

Immediately Tilly closed the box and tried to hand it back to him.

'What's wrong?'

'I can't wear your mother's ring.'

'Why not? It's certainly a hell of a lot more convincing than that piece of cheap tat you were wearing.'

'But it's your *mother's*.'

'It's a family ring, not her engagement ring. She didn't leave it to me with strict instructions to place it only on the finger of *the* woman, if that's what you're thinking. She wasn't sentimental, and I daresay she had stopped believing in Cinderella and her slipper a long time before she died.'

'Do you always carry it round with you?' Tilly asked him. Her question was uncertain, and delivered in an emotional whisper.

Silas looked at her. He couldn't remember the last time he had met a woman who was as absurdly sentimental as this one appeared to be. Silas didn't *do* sentimentality. He considered it to be a cloying, unpleasant emotion that no person of sound judgement should ever indulge in.

'Hardly,' he told her crisply. 'It just happens that I recently had it revalued for insurance purposes, and I collected it from the jewellers on my way over to you. I was on my way to the bank to put it in my safety deposit box, but the traffic was horrendous and we couldn't miss the flight. If one were to assess the odds, I should imagine it will be safer on your finger that it would be in my pocket.'

He sounded as though he was telling the truth, and he certainly did not look the sentimental type, Tilly acknowledged.

'Give me your hand again.' He took hold of it as he spoke, re-opening the box and obviously intending to slide the ring onto her finger. Immediately she tried to stop him, shaking her head.

'No, you mustn't do that,' she said. A small icy finger of presentiment touched her spine, making her shiver. She could see the mix of derision and impatience in the look he was giving her, and although inwardly she felt humiliated by his obvious contempt, she still stood her ground.

'What's wrong now? Worried that you're breaking some fearful taboo or something?' he demanded sarcastically.

'I don't like the idea of you putting the ring on. It seems wrong, somehow,' Tilly admitted.

'Oh, I see. My putting my ring on your engagement finger when we aren't engaged is wrong, but pretending that we are engaged when we aren't is perfectly all right?'

'It's the symbolism of it,' Tilly tried to explain. 'There's something about a man putting a ring on a woman's finger... It might sound illogical to you—'

'It does, and it is.' Silas stopped her impatiently, taking hold of her hand again and slipping the ring onto her finger.

Tilly had told herself that it couldn't possibly fit, but extraordinarily it did—and perfectly. So perfectly that it might have been made for her—or meant for her? What on earth had put that kind of foolish thought into her head?

'There, it's done. And nothing dramatic has happened.'

Not to him, maybe, Tilly acknowledged, but something *had* happened to her. The worn gold felt soft and heavy on her finger, and inside her chest her heart felt as constricted as though the ring had been slipped around it. When she looked down at her hand the diamonds flashed fire. Or was it the tears gathering in her own eyes that were responsible for the myriad rainbow display of colours she could see?

This wasn't how a ring like this should be given and worn, and yet somehow just by wearing it she felt as though she had committed to something. Some message, some instinctive female awareness the ring was communicating to her. A sense of pain and foreboding filled her, but it was too late now. Silas's ring was on her finger, and they were coming into Segovia, the lights from the town illuminating the interior of the car.

'What was she like?' Tilly asked softly, the question instinctive and unstoppable.

'Who?'

'Your mother.'

Silas wasn't going to answer her, but somehow he heard himself saying quietly and truthfully, 'She was a conservationist, wise and loving, and full of life. She died when I was eight. She was in a protest. Some violence broke out and my mother fell and hit her head. She died almost immediately.'

Tilly could feel the weight of the silence that followed his almost dispassionate words. Almost dispassionate, but not quite. She had sensed, even if she had not actually heard, the emotion behind them. She looked down at the ring and touched it gently, in tribute to the woman to whom it had belonged.

Silas had no idea why he had told Tilly about his mother. He rarely thought about her death these days.

He was very fond of his stepmother, who had shown him understanding and kindness, and who had always respected his relationship with his father, and he certainly loved Joe. Damn all over-emotional, sentimental women. A wise man kept them out of his life, and didn't make the mistake of getting involved with them in any way. There was only one reason he was here with Tilly now, and that was quite simply because she was providing him with the opportunity to get close to Art. And if that meant that he was using her, then he wasn't going to feel guilty about that. She, after all, was equally guilty of using him.

'I hadn't expected the castle to be quite so remote,' Tilly admitted, nearly half an hour after they had driven through Segovia, with its picturesque buildings draped in pretty Christmas decorations. 'Nor that it would be so high up in the mountains.'

They had already passed through the ski centres of Valdesqui and Navacerrada, looking as festive as a Christmas card, and although the snow-covered scenery outside the car was stunningly beautiful in the clearness of the early-evening moonlight, Tilly was surprised that her mother, who loved sunshine and heat, had chosen such a cold place for her wedding.

They turned off the main road onto a narrow track that wound up the steep mountainside, past fir trees thick with snow, towards the white-dusted, fairy-tale castle perched at its summit, lights shining welcomingly from its many tall, narrow windows. The castle was cleverly floodlit, heightening the impression that it had come straight out of a fairy story, and the surrounding snow was bathed in an almost iridescent pale pink glow

'It's beautiful,' Tilly murmured appreciatively. Silas glanced at her, about to tell her cynically that it looked like something dreamed up by a Hollywood studio. But then he saw the way the moonlight filling the car illuminated her face, dusting her skin with silvery light and betraying her quickened breathing.

Extraordinarily and unbelievably his mind switched track, and suddenly he was asking himself if he held her under him and kissed her, with a man's fierce need for a woman's body, would that pulse in her throat jump and burn the way the pulse in her wrist had done when he had held her hand? And would that pulse then run like a cord to the stiffening peak of her breast when he circled the place where the smooth pale flesh gave way to the soft pink aureole? Would that too swell in erotic response to his touch, a moan of pleasure suppressed deep in her throat causing her pulse to jump higher, while he rolled her nipple between his thumb and forefinger, savouring each further intimacy, knowing what her small restless movement meant? Knowing, too, that she would be wet and hungry for him—

Abruptly Silas blocked off his thoughts. It startled him to discover just how far and how fast they had travelled on their own erotic journey without his permission. He wasn't given to fantasising about sex with a woman he was in a relationship with, never mind one who was virtually a complete stranger to him. He didn't need to fantasise about sex, since it was always on offer to him should he want it. But, just as he was revolted by the thought of eating junk food, so, equally, he was turned off by the idea of indulging in junk sex. Which was probably why he was feeling like this now, with an erection so hard and swollen that it actually felt painful. He had been so busy working these last few months that he hadn't had time to get involved in a relationship. The ex with whom he occasionally had mutually enjoyable release sex had decided to get married, and he couldn't really remember the last time he had spent so much time in close proximity to a woman in a non-sexual way. And *that*, no doubt, was why his body was reacting like a hormone junkie who had the promise of a massive fix.

Their driver turned the four-wheel drive into the inner courtyard of the castle, coming to a stop outside the impressive iron-studded wooden doors.

Tilly smiled at the driver as he held open her door for her and helped her out. The courtyard had been cleared of snow, but she could still smell it on the early-evening air, and there was a shine on the courtyard floor that warned her the stones underfoot would be icy.

The huge double doors had been flung open, and Tilly goggled to see two fully liveried footmen stepping outside. Liveried footmen! She was so taken aback she forgot to watch where she was walking, and gasped with shock as she stepped onto a patch of ice and started to lose her balance.

Hard, sure hands gripped her arms, dragging her back against the safety of an equally hard male body.

And there she stood, her back pressed tightly into Silas's body, his arms wrapped securely around her, as her mother and the man Tilly presumed must be her

mother's new fiancé stood in the open doorway,
watching them. Her reaction was instinctive and disas-
trous. She turned her head to look at Silas, intending to
demand that he release her, but when she realised how
close she was to his mouth all she could do was look at
it instead, while the hot pulse of lust inside her became
a positive volcano of female desire. She lifted her
hand—surely not because she had actually intended to
touch him, to trace the outline of that firmly shaped
male mouth with its sensually full bottom lip? Surely
she had not actually intended to do that? No, of course
not. She simply wasn't that kind of woman. How could
she be when she had spent the better part of her young
adult life training herself not to be? All she had wanted
to do was to push her hair back off her face. And that
was what she would have done too, if Silas hadn't
caught hold of her hand.

The hand on which she was wearing his mother's
ring. A hard knot of emotions filled her chest cavity and
blocked her throat. An overwhelming sense of sadness
and love and hope.

'Silas…' Her lips framed his name and her eyes filled
with soft warm tears.

What the hell was a going on? Silas wondered in disbelief. One minute he was reacting instinctively to save
an idiotic female from falling over; the next he was
holding her in his arms and getting an emotional
message he couldn't block, feeling as if he was experiencing something of such importance that it could be the
pivot on which the whole of his future life would turn.

He watched as Tilly's lips framed his name, and felt

the aching drag of his own sexual need to bend his head to hers and to explore the shape and texture of her mouth. Not just once, but over and over again, until it was imprinted on his senses for ever. So that he could recall its memory within a heartbeat. So that he could hold it to him for always.

Silas tensed as he heard the sharp ring of an inner warning bell.

This was not a direction in which he wanted to go. This kind of emotional intensity, this kind of emotional dependency, was not for him. And certainly not with a woman like this. Tilly had lied to him once already. He did not for one moment believe the sob story of concerned and loving daughter she had used when describing her mother's marriage history. Logic told him that there had to be some darker and far more selfish reason for what she was doing. As yet he hadn't unearthed it— but then he hadn't tried very hard, had he? After all, he had his own secret agenda. He might not have discovered her hidden motive, but that didn't mean it didn't exist. For now he was content to play along with her game, and the role she had cast for him, because it suited his own purposes. But this looking at her mouth and feeling that he'd stepped into another dimension where emotion and instinct held sway rather than hard-headed logic and knowledge had to be parcelled up and locked away somewhere.

In the few seconds it had taken for him to catalogue his uncharacteristic reaction, Tilly's face had started to glow a soft pink.

'Darling…'

Abruptly Tilly wrenched her unwilling gaze from Silas's mouth to focus on her mother.

Physically, Annabelle Lucas looked very much like her daughter, although where Tilly downplayed her femininity, Annabelle cosseted and projected hers. Slightly shorter than Tilly, she had the same hourglass figure, and the same honey and butter-coloured hair. However, where Tilly rarely wore make-up, other than a hint of eyeshadow and mascara and a slick of lipgloss, Annabelle delighted in 'prettifying' herself, as she called it. Tilly favoured understated businesslike suits, and casual clothes when she wasn't working; Annabelle dressed in floaty, feminine creations.

Tilly tried to wriggle out of Silas's grip, but instead of letting her go he bent his mouth to her ear and warned, 'We're supposed to be a deliriously loved-up, newly engaged couple, remember?'

Tilly tried to ignore the effect the warmth of his breath against her ear was having on her.

'We don't have to put on an act for my mother,' she protested. But she knew her argument was as weak as her trembling knees.

The arch look her mother gave them as she hurried over to them in a cloud of her favourite perfume made Tilly want to grit her teeth, but there was nothing she could say or do—not with her mother's new fiancé within earshot.

'Art, come and say hello to my wonderful daughter, Tilly, and her gorgeous fiancé.'

Her mother was kissing Silas with rather too much enthusiasm, Tilly decided sourly.

'How sweet, Tilly, that you can't bear to let go of him.'

Tilly heard her mother laughing. Red-faced, she tried to snatch her hand back from Silas's arm, but for some reason he covered it with his own, refusing to let her go.

'Silas Stanway,' Silas introduced himself, extending his hand to Art, but still, Tilly noticed dizzily, managing to keep her tucked up against him. She could have used more force to pull away, but slipping on the ice and ending up on her bottom was hardly the best way to make a good impression in front of her stepfather-to-be, she decided.

Her mother really must have been wearing rose-tinted glosses when she had fallen in love with Art, Tilly acknowledged, relieved to have her hand shaken rather than having to submit to a kiss. Fittingly for such a fairy-tale-looking castle, he did actually look remarkably toad-like, with his square build and jowly face. Even his unblinking stare had something unnervingly toadish about it.

He was obviously a man of few words, and, perhaps because of this, her mother seemed to have gone in to verbal overdrive, behaving like an over-animated actress, clapping her hands, widening her eyes and exclaiming theatrically, 'This is all so perfect! My darling Art is like a magician, making everything so wonderful for me—and all the more wonderful now that you're here, Tilly.' Tears filled her eyes, somehow managing not to spill over and spoil her make-up. 'I'm just so very happy. I've always wanted to be part of a big happy family. Do you remember, darling, how you used to tell me that all you wanted for Christmas was a big sister? So sweet. And now here I am, getting not just the most perfect husband but two gorgeous new daughters and their adorable children.'

If only her father were here to witness this, and to share this moment of almost black humour with her, Tilly thought wryly, as she wondered how her mother had managed to mentally banish the various sets of step-families she had collected via her previous marriages.

Her mother beamed, and turned away to lead them back into the house. Silas bent his head and demanded, 'What was that look for?'

Too disconcerted to prevaricate, Tilly whispered grimly, 'Ma already has enough darling ex-steps and their offspring to fill her side of any church you could name.'

'Somehow I don't think that Art would want to know that.'

'You don't like him, do you?' Tilly said, with a shrewd guess of her own.

'Do you?'

'Hurry up, you two. You'll have plenty of time for whispering to each other later, and it's cold with the door open.'

The first thing Tilly saw as she stepped into the hallway was an enormous Christmas tree, its dark green foliage a perfect foil for the artistically hung Christmas tree decorations in shades of pale green, pink and blue, to tone with the hallway's painted panelling. Suddenly Tilly was six years old again, standing between her parents and gazing up with eyes filled with shining wonder at the Christmas tree in Harrods toy department.

That had been before she had understood that when her father complained about her mother's spending habits, and the circle of friends from which he was excluded, he wasn't 'just teasing'. And that the 'uncle' her mother had been so desperate for her to like was destined to replace her father in her mother's life. That Christmas she had been so totally, innocently happy, unaware that within a year she would know that happiness was as fragile and as easily broken as the pretty glass baubles she had gazed at with such delight.

Christmas—season of love and goodwill and more marital break-ups than any other time of year. A sensible woman would take to her heels at her first sighting of a Christmas tree and not come back until the bleakness of January had brought everyone to their senses.

'What time is dinner, Ma?' Tilly asked her mother prosaically, determined to set the tone of her enforced visit from the start. 'Only, I could do with going up to my room and getting changed first.'

Behind Art's back Annabelle made a small moue, and then said in an over-bright voice. 'Oh, I am sorry, darling, but we won't be having a formal dinner. Art doesn't like eating late, and then of course we have to consider the children. The girls are such devoted mothers, they wouldn't dream of breaking their routines. Art is quite right. It makes more sense for us to eat in our own rooms. So much more comfortable than dressing up and sitting down for a five-course dinner in the dining room.'

Tilly, who knew how much her mother adored dressing up for dinner, even when she was eating alone at home, opened her mouth to ask what was going on and then closed it again.

Her heart started to sink. She knew that she wasn't

imagining the desperation she could hear in her mother's voice.

'Isn't this the most gorgeous, magical place you have ever seen?' Annabelle was saying in an artificially bright voice, as she indicated the huge octagonal hall, decorated in its sugared almond colours, from which a delicate, intricately carved marble staircase seemed to float upwards.

'It is beautiful, Ma,' Tilly agreed. 'But rather cold.'

Immediately her mother gave small pout. 'Darling, don't be such a spoilsport. There is heating, but… With the children being used to living in a controlled-temperature environment they really do need to have the benefit of what heating there is in *their* suites, even if that means that some of the other rooms have to go without.' Annabelle was heading for the stairs. 'I've put you and Silas in the same room, just like you asked me to do.'

So he had been right, Silas decided grimly. So much for this just being an innocent, escort-duties-only commission! However, before he could say anything, Art had begun to study him, frowning.

'You look familiar… Have we met somewhere before?'

Silas felt his stomach muscles clench. 'Not so far as I know,' he responded truthfully. Art had turned down all his attempts to get an interview with him, but that didn't mean Art hadn't seen his photograph somewhere, or perhaps requested information about him. And if he had…

'So what exactly is it you do?' Art persisted.

'Silas is an actor,' Tilly answered firmly for him, preempting the criticism she sensed was coming by adding determinedly, 'And a very good one.' She gave her mother a look which she hoped she would correctly interpret as *I need to talk to you urgently about this bedroom situation*, but to her dismay her mother was refusing to make eye contact. In fact, now that she looked at her mother more closely, Tilly could see how tense and on edge she was beneath her too-bright smile, how desperate she was for everyone's approval of the castle. And of herself? Was it because of this insecurity within her mother that she had always kept the gates to her own emotions firmly padlocked? Because she was afraid of becoming like her mother?

As had happened so many times in the past when she sensed that her mother was unhappy, Tilly felt her protective instinct kick in. Leaving Silas's side, she moved over to Annabelle, linking her arm with her mother's in a gesture of daughter-to-mother solidarity.

'An actor. How exciting!' Annabelle exclaimed. 'That's probably why you think Silas's face is familiar, Artie, you must have seen him in something.'

'I doubt it. It don't waste my time watching people play at make-believe.' Art gave a snort of derision.

How could her mother be in love with a man like this? Tilly wondered despairingly. Her original misgivings about the marriage were growing by the second.

She gave her mother's arm a small squeeze. 'Why don't you take me upstairs and show me the room?' she suggested lightly, adding, 'I'm sure that Silas and Art can entertain one another while we indulge in some mother-and-daughter gossip.' She knew she was taking a risk, throwing Art and Silas together without being there herself to make sure Silas didn't say the wrong thing, but right now her need to ensure they had separate rooms took precedence over everything else. 'I haven't even seen your dress yet,' she reminded her mother.

'Oh, darling, it's so beautiful,' Annabelle enthused, the tension immediately leaving her face to be replaced by a glow of excitement. 'It's Vera Wang. You know, she does all the celebrity wedding gowns. Her people swore at first that she couldn't fit me in, but Art persuaded them to relent. It's just such a pity that I didn't think to get you to come to New York at the same time, so that we could have looked for something for you. Art's grandchildren are going to be our attendants, of course. We've agreed that they'll be wearing Southern Belles and Beaux outfits, so…sweet. And it would be lovely if your Silas would give me away…'

Suddenly Tilly wanted to cry—very badly. Here was her mother, trying desperately to put a brave face on the fact that while Art had his daughters and grandchildren to provide him with family support and fill the tradi-tional wedding roles, Annabelle had to rely on her daughter and a man who was being paid to escort her.

Swallowing hard, Tilly sniffed back the tears that were threatening to fall.

'Dad would probably have given you away if you'd asked him.'

Immediately her mother looked anxiously at Art. 'I did think of your father,' she admitted. 'But Art's daugh-ters can't see how it's possible to maintain a platonic relationship with an ex-husband, and Art feels…well, he thinks… Well, Art agrees with them.'

The retort Tilly was longing to make had to be smothered in her throat when she saw her mother's *please don't* look.

What the hell had he got himself into? Silas wondered angrily as he watched the two women walk up the stairs arm-in-arm. Whatever was going on, mother and daughter were both in on it—and deep in it too, right up to their pretty little necks. He was being used, and not just for the escort duties he was being paid for. Annabelle had let the cat out of the bag with regard to Tilly's sexual expectations. No woman asked to share a room with a man unless she expected sex to be on the agenda. Tilly had lied to him when she had claimed they would be having separate rooms, and if it wasn't for the fact that he needed information from Art he would be calling a cab right now, to take him straight back down to the airport in Madrid. Because he didn't want to have sex with a woman he had just spent the last few hours acknowledging had a mind-blowingly intense erotic effect on his body.

Who was he kidding? Okay, so he *did* want to have sex with her—but on his terms, not hers. And he certainly wasn't going to let her get away with lying to him—even if she *had* surprised him with her determination to show Art she wasn't going to let him put Silas down for being an actor. That *had* surprised him, Silas admitted. The last woman to protect him from someone's unflattering opinion had been his mother, and he had been all of five.

Tilly was gutsy; he had to give her that. But that didn't mean he was going to let her get away with manoeuvring him into her bed. There was no real danger to him in being plunged into this kind of situation. He could handle it. But what if it had been Joe she had tricked into sharing her bed? The young idiot was green enough to have had sex with her without any thought for the possible consequences: to his health, to the fate of any child that might be conceived, to anything other than giving in to a young heterosexual male's natural reaction to being in bed with a sexually attractive woman who had invited him there.

Whereas he, of course, wouldn't be facing any of those problems? Okay, he would be facing one of them, since he wasn't in the habit of travelling everywhere with a packet of condoms. Would Tilly have thought to deal with that kind of necessity? She was certainly old enough and no doubt experienced enough to be as aware of the risks as he was himself, he decided cynically as he turned to follow his uncommunicative host into the bar.

CHAPTER FOUR

'HERE is your room, darling. It's lovely, isn't it…?'

Annabelle had thrown open the door into a room on the second floor of the castle.

More because she wanted to make sure they weren't overheard than because she was genuinely interested in her accommodation, Tilly stepped past her and into the room.

It was large, certainly. Large, and cold, and very obviously an attic room, decorated in faded cabbage rose wallpaper, and scented with the unmistakable odour of damp.

'It's got its own bathroom. With the most fabbie real Edwardian bath.'

The determined brightness in her mother's voice made Tilly's spirits plummet. Annabelle looked so vulnerable, getting angry with her felt like being unkind to a child.

Very gently Tilly took hold of her mother's hands and led her across to the large double bed, pulling her down until they were both seated on it, facing one another.

'Ma, what is going on?' she asked, as calmly as she could. 'You know that Silas and I aren't really engaged. We don't even know each other. He's just someone I've hired to pretend to be my fiancé. You *know* that. We were supposed to have separate rooms. I've *told* him that we are having separate rooms. You *assured* me that we would be having separate rooms. So what's gone wrong?'

Tears filled her mother's eyes. 'Oh, Tilly darling, please don't be cross with me. It isn't my fault. I *had* planned to put you and Silas—he is gorgeous, by the way, and he would be just perfect for you—in the most heavenly pair of interconnecting rooms. More like a suite, really, both with their own bathrooms and the most divine little sitting room, but then Art's daughters arrived and everything went horribly wrong.'

Tilly waited while her mother paused to blow her nose and clear her throat. 'You see, I hadn't realised that Susan-Jane and Cissie-Rose would want to have their children sleeping on the same floor with them, or that they would expect to have connecting rooms. But of course once Susan-Jane had explained that she and Cissie-Rose need to be close by, and how it made much more sense for them to have the suite I'd earmarked for you and Silas…

'She said that the children's nannies, and the personal assistants to Dwight and Bill—that's their husbands, of course—would also have to be on the same floor, because Dwight and Bill frequently work late at night. They have to be in touch with Head Office at all times, and having to come all this way has caused them so much disruption. I felt so guilty about that—especially when Cissie-Rose told me that the children had been upset because they wouldn't be spending Christmas at home. I don't know how it happened, but somehow or other it turned out so that they practically took up the whole of the first floor, apart from the suite Art and I are sharing, and that meant the only rooms left were up here on the second floor.'

Inwardly Tilly counted to ten. Something was telling her that her relationship with her new stepsisters-to-be was not going to be one made in heaven, she thought grimly.

'Okay, but there must be more than one room up here, Ma. I mean, there's only one bed in here—'

'Darling, I know, and I am truly sorry. But I'm sure that Silas will behave like a perfect gentleman. I mean, a man like him doesn't need to go around persuading women to have sex with him, does he? Do you know what I think?' she said brightly. 'I think that he'll probably be glad of the opportunity to be with a woman who isn't coming on to him.'

'Ma, let's stick to the point. How many rooms are there on this floor?'

'Oodles,' Annabelle told her promptly. 'But there's been a problem with the roof, apparently, and most of them are damp, and the ones that aren't are already occupied by the staff. Strictly speaking we aren't supposed to be using any of the rooms up here, according to the contract the Count's legal people gave us, but when I spoke to the *major-domo* and explained the problem he was really sweet about it, and everyone has worked so hard to get this room ready for you. I'd hate for them to think that we aren't grateful.'

Tilly wrapped her arms around her cold body. 'Ma, it's freezing in here.'

'Yes. I'm sorry about that. The Count's PA did explain to us how the heating system worked, and that we weren't to turn up any of the radiators because if we did it would mean that some others wouldn't work. And I did try to explain this to Art's daughters, but I can see their point about the children needing to be kept warm.'

Tilly could hear a strange noise in her ears. It took her several seconds to realise that it was the sound of her teeth grinding in suppressed frustration.

'Ma—'

'Please don't be difficult about this, darling. I so want everything to go well, and for all of you to get on. Art's daughters have been so sweet—offering to help me once Art and I are married, explaining to me how their social circle works. They've even warned me that some of Art's late wife's friends will be hostile to me, and that some of the men might behave towards me in a flirtatious way because of the way that I look, and because I've been married before. It's kind of them, really.'

'Is it? It sounds more to me as though they're trying to undermine you,' Tilly told her mother shrewdly, and then wished that she hadn't been so blunt when she saw the hurt look on her mother's face.

'Darling, don't say that. You're going to love them, I know. Now, why don't I leave you to unpack, while I go down to the kitchen and organise evening meals for everyone?'

'Some hot water bottles might be a good idea as well,' Tilly suggested dryly.

After her mother had gone she examined the room and its adjoining bathroom. The bath was, as her mother had said, truly Edwardian. Of massive proportions, it stood in the middle of a linoleum-covered floor in a room that was so cold Tilly was shivering even though she was still wearing her coat. There was also a shower, and a separate lavatory.

She heard the outer door reopening, and hurried back into the bedroom, saying despairingly, 'Ma. I don't— Oh, it's you.' She came to an abrupt halt as she saw Silas standing just inside the door, holding it open for a young man carrying their luggage.

She had to wait for him to put it down and leave before she could speak. 'I'm really sorry about this. My mother seems to have allowed Art's daughters to bully her into letting them take the two-bedroom suite she had earmarked for us, and this appears to be the only room that's left.'

'And presumably the only bed?' Silas asked silkily.

'I don't like this any more than you do,' Tilly assured him. 'But there's nothing I can do except offer to sleep on the floor.'

'And of course you're fully prepared to do that?'

'Actually, yes, I am,' Tilly said. She didn't like the tone he was using, and she didn't like the way he was looking at her either. If she had thought the bedroom and the icy-cold bathroom were cold enough to chill her blood, they were nothing compared to the coldness of the look Silas was giving her.

'Do you make a habit of this?' It infuriated Silas that she didn't seem to think he had the intelligence to see through what she was doing.

'Do I make a habit of what?' Tilly demanded, perplexed.

'Hiring men to have sex with you.'

Tilly was glad she had the bed behind her to sink down onto. His accusation hadn't just shocked her, it had also blocked her chest with a huge lump of indigestible and unwanted emotional vulnerability—and pain. *Pain?* Because a man she didn't know was misjudging her? Why should that cause her to feel like this? She had only just met Silas. He meant nothing whatsoever to her, and yet here she was reacting to his unpleasant remarks with the kind of hurt feelings and sense of betrayal that were more appropriate for a long-standing and far more intimate relationship. Was that it? Did she secretly *want* to have sex with him? Had he somehow sensed that, even though she hadn't been aware of it herself? Was *that* the reason for his accusation, and her own emotional reaction to it?

This time when Tilly shivered it wasn't just because she was cold. She didn't like what was happening. She had never wanted to do any of this in the first place—not coming here, not hiring herself an escort, and most certainly not sharing a bed with Silas. She took a deep breath.

'I do not hire men to have sex with me. I don't need to.' Well, it was true, wasn't it? 'I've already made it perfectly clear to you why I need an escort, and if you thought I was lying or had some ulterior motive then surely it was up to you to refuse the commission. You don't strike me as the kind of man who would allow himself to be put in a situation you don't want,' she told him shrewdly.

Her reaction wasn't what Silas had been expecting. He had assumed that she would use his accusation as an excuse to lay her cards on the table. At which point he had intended to make it plain that, while he was prepared to act as her fiancé in public, making use of the intimacy provided by their shared accommodation was most definitely not on the agenda.

The nature of his profession meant that Silas was immediately and instinctively suspicious of everyone's motives. As far as he was concerned, everyone had something to hide, something they were prepared to sell, and something they were prepared to buy. He himself wanted to hide the fact that he was using his position as a fake fiancé to get closer to Art, but he was only prepared to sell his time, not his body. He was also a man who hated being wrong-footed and forced to accept that he had made an error of judgement—especially by a woman he had no reason whatsoever to respect.

'I thought your explanation owed more to imagination than truth,' he told her uncompromisingly. 'As far as I am concerned, and in view of what has transpired, I was right to question the validity of what you were telling me. Not, I must say, that I admire your taste in sexual boltholes,' he added disparagingly. 'Apart from anything else, it's freezing. Are those radiators on?' He walked over to one of them and put his hand against it.

'Apparently Art's daughters have messed up the delicate balance of radiator temperature and fair heating for all,' Tilly told him tiredly. 'Or at least I think that's what my mother was trying to tell me.'

Somehow Tilly managed to answer his mundane question with an equally mundane answer, even though her heart was pumping so much blood through her veins she could actually feel the adrenaline surge. There was no way she was going to let his insults go unchallenged.

'You don't have to stay here, you know,' she told him. 'There's nothing to stop you leaving if you want. I certainly won't be trying.' She tried to put as much withering scorn into her words as she could.

Silas gave her a derisory look. 'We've only just arrived, and we're supposed to be engaged. I can hardly walk out now.'

'Why not?' Tilly demanded, in a brittle voice that betrayed her tension. 'Engaged couples do quarrel and break up. It happens all the time. In fact, I think it's a very good idea.'

She could feel the comfort of her own relief at the thought of him leaving. He was having an effect on her she really did not like or want. It—*he*—had made her feel uncomfortable and on edge even before he had accused her of lying to him. There was no way she wanted to spend a week sharing a room with a man who thought she was gagging for sex with him and about to pounce on him at any minute. She might be being a tad old-fashioned, but the truth was that she much preferred the traditional scenario in which *she* was the one imagining that he might pounce on *her*. Not that she wanted him to do so, of course. Not for one minute.

'In fact,' she continued fiercely, 'I think it would be an excellent idea if I went down right now to find my mother and tell her that the engagement is off.'

'Wouldn't that be somewhat counter-productive? I thought the whole idea of this was to help your mother.' The conversation and Tilly's behaviour were taking a direction Silas hadn't expected, and one he did not want. Tilly was quite obviously working herself up into a mood of moral outrage and, worse, she was throwing out the kind of challenges he had no intention of taking up.

It wasn't like him to misjudge a situation, and it irked him that he might have here. But Tilly was behaving in a way he considered out of character for the slot he had mentally fitted her into. He despised women who insisted on playing games, and normally he wouldn't have tolerated an assumed 'injured innocent' act, but right now he had too much at stake to risk her carrying out her threat. Much as he disliked having to admit it, he recognised that it night have been wiser for him to have played along with her pretence for a bit longer before letting her know that he had guessed what she was planning. He couldn't allow this new situation to accelerate.

He might not mind walking out on Tilly, but if he did he would also be walking out on his chance to talk to Art. He had already sown the seeds for what he hoped would become more informative confidences once Art had let down his guard a bit more.

He walked over to the bed and eyed it assessingly. At least it was large enough for him to ensure that Tilly kept her distance from him.

He was standing next to her when they both heard Annabelle calling out from the other side of the door. 'It's only us, darlings!'

'That's my mother now,' Tilly told him unnecessarily. 'I've made up my mind. There's no way I want to continue with this charade now, after the accusations you've just made. I'm going to tell her that we've had a row, that our engagement is over and that you're leaving.'

She was making to remove the ring he had given her as she spoke, and Silas could tell that she meant what she was saying. The door was already opening. He thought quickly, and then acted with even greater speed.

It shocked Tilly how silently and lethally fast Silas moved, dropping down onto the bed next to her and imprisoning her in his arms as he rolled her torso down under his own and then covered her mouth with his.

Tilly tried to push him away, but he was holding her too tightly, one muscular leg thrown over her in what was surely one of the most intimate embraces a fully clad couple could perform—even if he was only adopting it to keep her pinned beneath the weight of his body. Pinned in such a way that she was shockingly aware of the physical differences between them—his hardness pressed to her softness, his body dominating and unyielding, while, to her outraged horror, her own was soft and accommodating, as though her flesh welcomed the possessive maleness of his.

While she tried to grapple with her own confused reactions he started to kiss her. Not gently, but fiercely and possessively, and with an added edge of almost dangerous urgency, as though there was nothing he wanted more than to have her mouth under his, as though at any moment now he would strip the clothes from their bodies so that her only covering would be him, and then… Somehow or other his free hand was cupping her breast, the hard pad of his thumb resting against her hard nipple.

This couldn't be happening. It certainly *should* not be happening. Incredulously she struggled to resist him, distantly aware of her mother's amused, 'Whoops! Sorree...' and then the immediate closing of the bedroom door.

He could let Tilly go now. Silas knew that. The danger was over. No way could she tell her mother now that they had quarrelled and that he was leaving after what she had just witnessed. But the bedroom was bitingly cold, and the rounded warmth of Tilly's breast fitted into his hand as though it had been made for him. It surprised him to discover just how much he wanted to go on cupping it, and just how strong his urge was to caress the hard thrust of her nipple slowly and thoroughly, until she responded to his touch with her own urgency, arching up into his hands, wanting him to peel back the layers of her clothing until they could both see her arousal. He could certainly feel his own. He slid his other hand up into Tilly's hair, lifting his mouth briefly from hers, watching as her eyes opened, her gaze soft and clouded. He traced the shape of her mouth with small, teasingly light kisses that mirrored the delicate touch of his fingertips on her breast.

Tilly was hazily aware that what she was doing was very dangerous—that *Silas* was very dangerous. But the room was so cold that it seemed to be numbing her ability to respond and react in a normal way. And Silas felt so warm, lying on top of her, even if he *was* tormenting her with those tiny kisses that were compelling her to arch up to him, wanting something much more intimate. She shuddered with pleasure when he spread his fingers against her scalp and held her head while he plundered her mouth with the intimate thrust of his tongue, over and over again, until she was shuddering in the grip of the most intense physical longing she had ever experienced.

The shock of her own sexual arousal was enough to bring her to her senses and make her push Silas away. She was trembling from head to foot and felt foolishly close to tears. What she was feeling made her feel both vulnerable and confused. She didn't even know how it had happened—or why.

'You had no right to do that,' she told him, almost tearfully.

'I thought it was what you wanted.'

'*What?* How could you think that? I'd just told you that I wanted you to leave.'

Silas looked into her flushed, mutinous face and a sensation, an emotion he couldn't recognise, speared through the armour-plating of his cynicism. He lifted his hand to his chest, as though he could actually feel the sharp, unfamiliar pain as a physical reality, and then let it drop to his side as he pushed the feeling back out of the way.

'And I've just shown you that I don't want to,' he responded softly. 'In fact…right now I don't even think I want to leave this room.' A corrosive inner voice, no doubt prompted by his conscience, was demanding if not a retraction then at least an explanation of this outright lie. But he had a job to do, a truth to find, and he needed real, hard facts. As far as Silas was concerned it was his ethical duty to get those facts, and that came before any duty he might have to maintaining the same degree of truth within this current aspect of his personal life.

As ugly and unpleasant as it sounded, Tilly was using him—and he was using her. Both of them could claim that they were being forced into doing so in order to benefit others, of course. And that made it acceptable? Maybe not, but it certainly made it necessary, Silas told himself harshly.

Tilly's mouth had gone dry. She couldn't bring herself to look at him. Her heart was pounding so heavily she wanted to press her hand against her chest to calm it.

'If you're trying to imply that you...' She picked her words as carefully as she could, but they still literally stuck it her throat. 'That you want me, then I don't believe you,' she finally managed to say. 'It's less than ten minutes since you were warning me off and accusing me of hiring you for sex,' she reminded him.

'Ten minutes ago I hadn't kissed you or touched you,' Silas told her meaningfully. 'Ten minutes ago I hadn't been so turned on by the way your body was responding to my touch that right now I can't think beyond taking that response to its natural conclusion— to our mutual benefit.'

To Silas's chagrin his own words were conjuring up the most erotic images inside his head, and his body was responding powerfully to them. So powerfully that it was making it clear to him that, no matter what his brain might have to say, his body was more than willing to have sex with Tilly.

The room might still be icy cold, but suddenly Tilly

felt far too hot. He had to be lying to her, and she had better remember that. Instead of… Instead of what? Wanting him to be telling the truth? Wanting him to mean what he was saying? Wanting him to want her? Was she crazy? This kind of thing was her mother's emotional territory, not hers. She knew better. Didn't she? She started to shiver. She didn't want to stay here in this room with Silas any longer—a room that she could have sworn now smelled subtly of their mutual arousal, and his deceit, and her own foolish longing. She wanted to go back downstairs, where she would be safer—and warmer.

'It's your own fault that I kissed you, you know,' Silas told her.

Tilly had had enough. 'Look, I've already told you, I did *not* hire you to have sex with me,' she insisted fiercely.

'I didn't mean that.' Silas was smiling so tenderly at her that her insides twisted with need. 'I meant that it's your fault because when you offered me the chance to leave I knew that I couldn't, and that in turn told me how much I want you.'

Tilly stared at him. It really wasn't fair of fate to inflict this on her. It was almost Christmas, for heaven's sake, and she was very vulnerable. Silas had touched a note, a chord deep within her, that she badly wanted to ignore. It would be far too dangerous to let herself believe that he meant what he had said, and even more dangerous to admit how much she *wanted* him to have meant it.

'We've only just met,' she reminded him. 'We hardly know each other…' She was almost stuttering, she realised, as she squirmed inwardly at the sound of her own ridiculous words.

'So? Isn't fate giving us an opportunity to remedy that?' He smiled at her again, and Tilly felt her heart literally flip over inside her chest as though it were a pancake. 'She's even ensured that we'll be sharing a room, and a bed, and she's provided the added incentive of the need to share our body heat just to keep warm.'

Tilly could feel not just her face but her whole body suddenly growing hot as she curled her toes into her shoes and looked helplessly down at the bed. Things like this just did not happen to her. She wasn't that sort of person. She was too sensible, too cautious, too wary...too damn dull! She looked at Silas.

'We are engaged, after all. Who knows what might happen, or where fate might lead us?' As he spoke he reached out, sliding his fingers between her own so that they were intimately held together. 'Why don't we just let her take us where she wishes?' he suggested sexily.

'No, no, *no*! I don't want to hear any more.' Tilly put her hands over her ears in despair. 'I'm going downstairs.'

'Then I'm coming with you,' Silas said promptly. He wasn't going to give her the opportunity to end their 'engagement' in his absence.

CHAPTER FIVE

'OH, THERE you are, darlings. Oh, Tilly, you haven't even changed for dinner.' There was a reproachful note in her mother's voice that made Tilly's stomach muscles clench defensively, but she stood her ground.

'But you said it had been arranged that we'd all be eating in our rooms,' she reminded her mother, as calmly as she could.

'Oh, well, yes, I did say that. But I must have misunderstood the girls, because they've both come down dressed for dinner. Tilly, why don't you pop back up to your room and get changed into something pretty and formal? You'll have time, because the chef says that it will be another half-hour before everything will be ready.'

It was becoming increasingly plain to Tilly that Art's daughters were determined to behave as selfishly and make life as difficult for her mother as they could.

'I haven't unpacked yet, Ma,' she reminded her mother. 'And it's freezing in our room.'

'Oh, darling, please don't be such a crosspatch. What on earth will Art's girls think?'

'I daresay I might be sweeter if I had a warm bedroom,' Tilly couldn't help responding. 'And what exactly do you mean—something pretty and formal?'

'Well, the girls are both wearing the most gorgeous vintage Halston gowns. I've told them how good-looking you are, Silas, and I think they want to have a look at you,' Annabelle confided, adding blithely, 'It's dinner jackets for the men, of course—and wait until you see the drawing room and the dining room, Tilly. They are gorgeous—pure Versailles.'

Tilly had finally had enough, and she was sure that her sudden flash of temper didn't have anything to do with the thought of other women appreciating Silas's sexy masculinity. 'I don't care how gorgeous they are,' she snapped at her mother. 'I am not going back upstairs to that icebox of a room to get changed. Not, of course, that I'm not dying to show off my own vintage Oxfam.' She relented almost immediately when she saw her mother's chastened expression, going over to her to hug her tenderly, and apologising. 'I'm sorry, Ma.' How could she explain to her mother that it wasn't the cold bedroom she was dreading so much as her own desire to succumb to Silas's sexual overtures once they were in it?

'No, it's my fault, darling. I am really sorry about that dreadful room. What must Silas think of me?'

'What Silas thinks is that you've given him the perfect excuse for sharing his body warmth with his fiancée,' Silas answered promptly.

As her mother turned away Tilly shook her head at Silas and mouthed silently, *Ma knows our engagement is* fake, *remember?*

'Tilly, why don't you come to my room with me and let me find you something to borrow,' Annabelle offered.

'Yes, you go with your mother, Tee, and I'll nip up and change into my DJ,' Silas suggested.

Tee. No one had ever called her Tee before, and Tilly discovered it made her feel slightly giddy, dizzy with a dangerous sort of fizzing delight, that Silas should be the one to do so. Just as though they were really a couple, and Tee was his special pet name for her.

'You and Art have separate rooms?' Tilly queried several minutes later, as she surveyed the feminine fabric-festooned bedroom her mother was occupying.

'Art didn't think it was right that we should share, especially not with his girls and their children being here. We aren't like you modern young ones, you know, Tilly. Here, put this on. It's a bit big for me, but I think it will fit you perfectly.'

Tilly took the sliver of amber silk chiffon her mother had just removed from the wall of mirror-fronted closets and surveyed it doubtfully.

She looked at the label and then shook her head. 'Isn't this the designer who designs those outrageously sexy things that film stars' wives wear?' she asked her mother accusingly.

'Darling, it was summer when I bought it in Saint-Tropez—everyone was wearing his stuff, and I just fell in love with it. In fact, I nearly wore it the night I met Art. But then I changed my mind.'

Tilly held the dress up in front of herself and looked at her reflection in the mirror. 'This isn't a dress,' she protested. 'It's half a dozen strips of material *pretending* to be a dress.'

'Sweetheart, that's the whole secret of his style—it's all in the cut. You wait and see when you put it on. You can use my bathroom.' She was already bustling Tilly towards the opulent marble and gold-ornamented chamber that masqueraded as a bathroom. 'Oh, and why don't you put a bit more make-up on? And perhaps smooth on some of this wonderful body cream I use?'

Very determinedly, Tilly closed the door between them.

She showered first, very quickly, and then used some of the cream her mother had mentioned because her skin felt dry. It was scented, as well as gold-coloured, and she couldn't help sniffing it appreciatively as she stroked it onto her bare skin.

Now for the dress…

'Tilly? What are you doing…? Aren't you ready yet?' Annabelle knocked anxiously on the bathroom door, and when there was no response she turned the handle, relieved to discover that the door wasn't locked.

Tilly was standing in the middle of the bathroom, wearing the designer dress and staring at her reflection in the mirror.

'Oh, my!' Annabelle breathed.

'Oh, my God, don't you mean?' Tilly corrected her grimly. 'Ma, I can't possibly wear this.'

'Why not? You look gorgeous.'

'Just look at me. I'm spilling out of it everywhere. I look like a…a hooker,' Tilly said through gritted teeth.

'Sorry to interrupt you both, but Art sent me up to

find out where you are. He said to tell you that his stomach thinks his throat's been cut.

'Silas.' Annabelle beamed. 'You're just the person we need. Come and tell Tilly to stop being so silly. She looks gorgeous in this dress, but she says it makes her look like a hooker.'

Tilly's face burned as Silas stepped into view and stood studying her in silence. He had changed into a dinner suit, and her heart did its pancake trick again. How unfair it was that men should look so wonderful in their evening clothes.

'Tilly's quite right,' he announced uncompromisingly, adding softly, as her face burned with chagrin, 'and yet totally wrong. She looks like a classy, very expensive kept woman—or an equally classy and very expensive rich man's wife.' He crooked his arm. 'May I have the pleasure of escorting you both down to dinner? Because if I don't I'd better warn you that Art is going to be on his way up here, and his mood isn't good.'

Silas was smiling, but it shocked Tilly to see how apprehensive her mother suddenly looked. If they'd been on their own she would have asked her outright if she was as afraid of Art as she looked—as well as insisting that her mother loan her something else to wear. Right now, though, her concern for her mother disturbed her far more than her own self-conscious discomfort at wearing a dress that was way too revealing for her own personal taste.

Her disquiet was still with her five minutes later, when she watched Annabelle hurry over to where Art was waiting impatiently for them by the drawing room door, apologise prettily to her fiancé and reach up to kiss his cheek—or rather his jowl, Tilly thought grimly, as she tried to control her own growing unease about her mother's marriage plans.

Tilly tried to look discreetly at her watch, heaving a small sigh of relief when she saw that it was almost midnight. Tonight had to have been the worst evening of her life. How could her mother even *think* about joining a family so appallingly dysfunctional and so arrogantly oblivious to it?

Art's daughters, Susan-Jane and Cissie-Rose, were stick-thin and must, Tilly imagined, take after their mother. There was nothing of their father's heavy squareness about them. Their husbands, though, were both unpleasantly overweight. Art's daughters were, according to Tilly's mother, 'Southern Belles.' If so, they were certainly Southern Belles who had been left out in the sun so long that all humanity had been burned out of them, Tilly decided, as she listened to them deliberately and cruelly trying to destroy her mother with their innuendos and subtle put-downs.

At one point during the evening, when she had been obliged to listen politely yet again to Cissie-Rose praising herself to the skies for the high quality of her hands-on mothering, and complaining about the children's nanny daring to ask for time off over Christmas so that she could visit her own family, Tilly had longed to turn round and tell her what she thought of her. But of course she hadn't, knowing how horrified her mother would have been.

For such an apparently clean-living family, they seemed to consume an incredible amount of alcohol. Although very little food had passed what Tilly suspected were the artificially inflated and certainly perfectly glossed lips of Art's 'girls', as he referred to them. Predictably, they had expressed horror and then sympathy when Tilly had tucked into her own meal with gusto, shuddering with distaste at her appetite.

'Dwight would probably take a stick to me if I put on so much as an ounce—wouldn't you honey?' Cissie-Rose had observed.

'No guy likes an overweight gal. Ain't that the truth, Silas?' Dwight had drunkenly roped Silas into the conversation.

'Oh, you mustn't tease Silas, Dwighty,' Cissie-Rose had told her husband in her soft baby whisper of a voice. 'He and Tilly are newly engaged, and of course right now he thinks she's wonderful. I can remember how romantic it was when *we* first got engaged. Although I must say, Tilly, I was shocked when Daddy told us about the way you and Silas were carryin' on earlier.'

'T'ain't right, doing that kind of thing in a house where there's young 'uns around,' Dwight had put in.

'Which begs the point that presumably young 'un number one was sent away somewhere when young 'un number two was conceived?' Silas had murmured indiscreetly to Tilly, on the pretext of filling her wine glass.

She had desperately wanted to laugh, only too glad of the light relief his dry comment had provided, but she hadn't allowed herself. He had no business linking the two of them together in private intimate conversation of the kind only good friends or lovers exchanged.

Tilly didn't think she'd ever seen two men drink as much as Art and Dwight. Art's other son-in-law— Susan-Jane's husband, Bill, a quiet man with a warm smile, hadn't drunk as much as the other two—although Tilly suspected from the amount of attention he was paying her that either he and Susan-Jane had had a quarrel before coming down for dinner, or he was a serial flirt who didn't care how much he humiliated his wife by paying attention to another woman.

Tilly tried not to show what she was feeling when she watched Art down yet another whiskey sour, but she was relieved to see that Silas wasn't joining the other men in what seemed to be some sort of contest to see who could mix the strongest drink.

In truth, the only good thing about being downstairs was the warmth—and the excellent food. Had her room been more comfortable, and had she had it to herself, she would have escaped to it long ago, Tilly admitted as she tried and failed to smother a yawn.

'Darling, you look worn out,' Annabelle exclaimed with maternal concern. 'Art, I think we should call it a night…'

'You can call it what the hell you like, honey, but me and the boys are callin' for another jug of liquor—ain't that right, boys?'

Tilly's heart ached for her mother when she saw her anguished look.

'The staff must have had a long day, with everyone arriving. It would be considerate, perhaps, to let them clear away and get to bed?' Silas spoke quietly, but with such firm authority that everyone turned to look at him.

'Who the hell needs to be considerate to the staff? They're paid to look after us.' Dwight's face was red with resentment as he glared at Silas.

Tilly discovered that she was holding her breath, and her stomach muscles were cramped with tension. But Silas had the advantage, since he had already stood up and was moving to her chair to pull it out for her.

'You're right. I apologise if I overstepped the mark.' Silas ignored Dwight to address his apology direct to Art. 'It was only a thought.'

'And a good one Silas,' Tilly heard her mother saying heroically. 'I'm tired myself, Artie, do let's all go to bed.'

Tilly wasn't at all sure that Art would have complied if a flustered young girl hadn't come hurrying in to the room to tell Cissie-Rose that one of her children had been sick and was asking for her.

'Oh, my poor baby!' Cissie-Rose exclaimed theatrically. 'I knew coming here was gonna make her sick. I told you—you know that I did.'

'Come on. Let's make our escape now, whilst we can,' Silas muttered to Tilly.

She was tired enough to give in, going over to her mother first to give her a quick kiss, and then saying a general goodnight, while Art's daughters were still protesting in high-pitched whiny voices about the disruption to their children's routine.

'Does your mother know what she's letting herself in for?' Silas demanded as they headed for the stairs.

'I don't know,' Tilly was forced to admit. Her own

concern betrayed her into adding, 'She says she's in love with Art, but I don't see how she can be.'

By the time they reached the second floor her skin had broken out in goosebumps, and she was so cold that her longing to crawl into bed to try and get warm was overwhelming her apprehension about sharing it with Silas.

'Do you suppose there'll be any hot water up here?' she asked Silas as he opened the bedroom door for her.

'Potentially,' Silas answered her dryly. 'There's an electrically heated shower in the bathroom, although my experience of it so far suggests that it isn't totally efficient.'

'Meaning what?' Tilly asked him suspiciously.

'Meaning lukewarm is probably as good as it's going to get,' he replied. 'At least the bed should be warm, though. I went down to the kitchen earlier and borrowed a kettle and a couple of hot water bottles.'

Tilly's eyes widened, and then blurred with tired tears. Somehow he wasn't the type she had imagined doing something so domestic and so thoughtful.

He would be a fool to start feeling sorry for Tilly, Silas warned himself, hardening his heart against her obvious misery. His only purpose in being here was to get his story. And that was exactly what he intended to do, no matter what methods he had to use to do so.

'I don't think I can bear a week of this.' Tilly was too tired to care about how vulnerable her admission might make her seem. 'I hate the cold, and I hate even more the thought of not being able to have a decent hot shower whenever I want.'

Silas looked at her. 'If that's a hint that you're expecting me to be a gentleman and offer to let you use the shower first, I've got a better idea.'

'You mean I should use my mother's bathroom?' Tilly asked absently, as she stepped into the lamp-lit bedroom that looked cosier and felt slightly warmer than she had expected.

'No, I was going to say that it would make sense for us to share the shower, to make the best use of what hot water it provides.'

Was he serious? He couldn't be, could he? She looked at him, and then wished she hadn't as her body reacted to the intimacy of discovering that he was looking right back at her.

'It's warmer in here than I was expecting.' She gave him a too-bright smile to match the light tone of her voice. Anything—just as long as she didn't have to respond to the suggestion that they share a shower. Already her senses were working overtime, bombarding her with erotic messages and images.

'That's because I bribed one of the maids to find us a plug-in electric radiator.' He had closed the door and was looking at her in a way that made her heart bounce about inside her chest like a tennis ball hit by a pro. 'Now, about that shower…'

Tilly shook her head, trying to cling on to her normal, firm common sense, and to react to what he was saying as though it had been said by one of her young subordinates. The kindly but firm maternal voice of authority she used on them would surely make it plain to Silas that she wasn't expecting what he thought, as well as controlling her own dangerous longing.

'Silas, I've already told you, you've got it all wrong. You don't have to have sex with me.'

The effect of her words wasn't what she had hoped for. Instead of obediently backing off, Silas stopped leaning casually against the wall and straightened up to his full height. Such a small movement, barely more than a single step, but in terms of meaningful body language it sent her a message that had her muscles cramping with sexual tension.

'Well, that certainly isn't what my body is telling me,' he announced silkily. 'It's telling me that right now there is nothing I need or want more than to take you to bed and make love to you slowly and thoroughly and completely.'

Tilly was beyond words. She could only shake her head.

He smiled at her, and her resistance melted under the heat of the look in his eyes.

'This is crazy.' Was that quavering, somehow betraying, yearning voice really hers? 'I mean, we've only just met. We don't know one another. We're *strangers*.'

'Is there a law that says strangers can't become lovers?' He was walking very purposefully towards her now, and she felt positively light-headed with shocked excitement.

The only reason he was doing this was as a form of insurance against her threatening to break off their engagement and forcing him to leave, Silas told himself. If he could keep her happy in bed she would get what she wanted, whether she knew it or not, and he, with any luck, would get his information. The fact that he was so strongly physically attracted to Tilly wasn't what was motivating him at all. This was simply something that it was necessary for him to do.

Very necessary.

If only she was the sort of person who could just live for the moment and enjoy what that moment was offering, Tilly acknowledged giddily. If only she didn't have these crazy hang-ups about love and sex working together. If only she was able to separate them as others could. If only she didn't have even more inhibiting hang-ups about permanency and commitment, and a fear that they simply did not exist. She closed her eyes. What was wrong with her? She wanted Silas sexually so much. So why not indulge in that wanting? Why not simply offer herself up to him now? Why not slide her arms around his neck, press her body eagerly against his and lift her face for his kiss…?

Why not? Because she could not. She simply couldn't cold-bloodedly have sex with a man just because physically he turned her on. Cold-bloodedly? She was so hot for him that it hurt!

Silas was used to playing a waiting game. So why the hell did he feel so impatient now that he was tempted to cross the distance that separated them and show Tilly what they would have instead of waiting for her to agree to it?

'I'm sorry. I can't do it.' The words burst out from Tilly in a flurried tremble, causing Silas to check in mid-step and stare at Tilly in disbelief. 'It's true that I do… That is…you… Physically I *am* attracted to you,' she managed to say primly, whilst her stomach went hollow with the intensity of her body's disappointment. 'But I don't want to have sex with you.'

It surprised Silas that she was prepared to go to such lengths to show him that he had originally misjudged the situation, but what surprised him even more was how gut-wrenchingly savagely deprived he felt. The intensity of his disappointment was a measure of just how much he wanted her—and that was far too much, he decided grimly.

'If that's your decision then that's your decision,' he told her flatly. If she expected him to coax and plead she had the wrong man. Because he had no intention of doing so.

CHAPTER SIX

TILLY blinked in the darkness, luxuriating in the bed's delicious warmth. She had no idea what had woken her, unless somehow the sound of Silas's breathing had penetrated her sleep.

She was, she realised, thirsty. She remembered there was a bottle of water on the small table in front of the window. Sliding out of bed as carefully as she could so that she wouldn't disturb Silas, she made her way towards the window. Enough light was coming in through the thin curtain to guide her. She held her breath and watched Silas apprehensively, in case the sound of her uncapping the bottle woke him.

Silas was already awake, and had been awake from the second Tilly had moved and murmured in her sleep. The bed was large enough for them to sleep apart, but at some stage while she slept Tilly had moved closer to him, so that she had been sleeping almost curled into him.

As she drank her water, Tilly pulled back the curtain slightly to look out through the window, her eyes rounding with delight when she realised that it was snowing: huge, fat flakes whirling down from the moonlit sky. A childhood sense of excitement and joy she had forgotten it was possible to feel filled her, and she leaned closer to the window to watch the snow. How could something so delicate and so beautiful to watch from the safety and warmth inside also be so deadly? She was already beginning to shiver in her thin and flimsy vest, but somehow she couldn't drag herself away from the magic of watching the snow fall.

Silas studied Tilly's unguarded expression as she watched the snow. She looked as joyful and excited as a child might have done. Something that felt like a heavy stone trap door being shifted by a long-unused mechanism seemed to be happening inside his chest. Both the movement and the sensation of something touching what was raw and unprotected within him physically hurt. He badly wanted to turn over and ignore Tilly, to push back the heavy door he had locked against his own emotions. But for some reason he couldn't.

She really was cold now, Tilly admitted as she left the window to make her way carefully back to her side of the bed. The far side—which meant that she had to skirt very quietly past the end of the bed so that she didn't wake Silas.

The bed felt welcomingly warm as she slid back into it, but her feet were freezing, and as she snuggled down beneath the duvet the delicious heat coming off Silas's sleeping body acted like a magnet to her cold toes. The dip in the bed made her feel as though she was trying to go to sleep on a slope—a cold, snow-covered slope that was all the more inhospitable because of the warmth that she knew lay waiting for her if she just let her body roll a little bit closer to Silas.

She relaxed and let herself roll, luxuriating for several blissful seconds in an almost purring enjoyment of the solid wall of warm male flesh she was now lying against. Her feet seemed of their own accord to find the perfect toasty resting place on Silas's lovely warm bare calves. *Bare?* She had already been in bed when Silas had emerged from the bathroom, and of course she hadn't looked to see what he was or wasn't wearing, and she certainly wasn't going to start doing a hands-on body-check now.

Snow falling from a midnight sky, and the pleasure of exploring Silas's body with every single one of her senses divided into every individual delight they could bring. What could possibly be more perfect? She would start by looking at him, enjoying the security of the moonlit semi-darkness as she allowed her eager gaze to move over the hundreds of subtle variations of light and shadow. She would lie here doing that until it slowly got light enough to see the contours clearly.

That was if she could wait that long before she touched him. It would be a special sort of sensual heaven and hell to touch him in the darkness without previously knowing his body, to use her fingertips to guide her and to relay every nuance of his flesh, its texture firm and taut where it padded his muscles, sleek and cool over the length and strength of his bones, deliciously male-scented and erotic in the vulnerable hollows of his throat, the inside of his elbows, behind his knees.

Her own flesh seemed to be vibrating in a hymn of sensuality that was beyond her own hearing. She could feel it growing and expanding within her, deepening and tightening, filling her senses until it spilled over and flooded every bit of her.

Silas, who had been lying wide awake, gritting his teeth against his own aching desire, heard her soft moan and the accompanying acceleration of her breathing. It was too much for his self-control. He turned over, reaching for her, covering her mouth with his own before she could object and kissing her with so much skilled sensuality that she didn't even want to.

She reached up and wrapped her arms around him, trembling under the forceful pressure of her need for him as he gathered her up against himself. He *was* naked, she recognised, submitting to the starburst of heated pleasure that the knowledge brought.

When and how had she learned to open her legs just enough to be able to feel the delight of the space she had created accommodating the hard strength of his erection as he slid her down against it? His hands were sliding beneath the waist of her thin cut-offs so that he could cup her buttocks and press her more deeply against it, moving her rhythmically as he did so. Up and then down the thickness of his flesh, just a little, just enough to make her want to cry out in fierce recognition of her own aching frustration every time the movement sensitised her growing ache for a deeper intimacy.

She tried to focus away from the clamouring demands of her clitoris and to concentrate instead on the slow, explorative thrust of his tongue against her own. Only it wasn't slow any more, and she didn't know if the urgent movements galvanising her body were the result of what he was doing to her or the cause of it. She could feel the hot, tight, piercingly erotic ache of her nipples as her movements brought them into contact with his naked chest. She wanted him to touch them, to caress them, to soothe their hard need with the comfort of his kiss and then to inflame it again with the hotter, harder lash of his tongue and the rake of his teeth. She wanted him to slide her body free of her sleepwear and then explore each and every part of it while she gave herself up to the pleasure of that intimacy.

'You're going to have to provide the condom; I didn't think to bring any with me.'

Tilly stared up into Silas's face and gulped. 'Neither did I,' she told him. 'I'm a woman. They aren't the kind of thing I usually carry around with me.'

'But presumably, like me, you don't have unprotected sex?'

It was a question rather than a statement.

'I don't have sex, full stop,' Tilly admitted honestly.

She sounded so self-conscious that Silas knew immediately that she was telling the truth. He reached out and switched on the bedside lamp, keeping a firm grip on her arm when she would have squirmed away.

'It isn't that I have any problem with having sex,' Tilly assured him. 'The problem has been meeting the right kind of partner.'

Silas arched one dark eyebrow in disbelief.

'You work in the City. You're in charge of a department of testosterone-fuelled young males.'

'Exactly,' Tilly agreed vehemently, adding in exasperation when he continued to look slightly aloof and disinclined to believe her, 'Don't you see? If I started dating one of them, then it would be bound to be discussed by the others, and then they'd all…'

'Want to take you to bed?' Silas suggested, and then wished he hadn't when he was suddenly savaged by the most unexpected raw male jealousy.

'Hardly. But in order to maintain my authority over them I have to ensure that they respect me. They wouldn't do that if they thought they could have sex with me.' She gave a small shrug. 'It sounds brutal I know, but it's the truth. The City has a very macho image, and the young men working there are keen to uphold that image. They're pushing the boundaries all the time. They're like pack animals—if you show a weakness they'll sense blood and go in for the kill. If I want to date a man it has to be someone outside the City, and the hours I work make that almost impossible.'

Silas knew what she was saying was true. 'Hence your decision to include some recreational sex in the deal you set up when you hired an escort?' he suggested.

Tilly stiffened in angry outrage. 'How many times do I have to tell you that there was no such decision—either by me or for me?'

'You haven't had sex in a very long time, to judge from the way you were responding to me. It makes sense that you should think of getting a double deal for the price of one.'

Tilly's face had started to burn with the heat of her emotions. 'I *do* not and *would* not pay for sex. I've already told you that. And if that had been my intention you can be sure that I would have taken steps to ensure that I was properly protected. I don't use *any* kind of contraception,' she told him fiercely. 'Never mind carry condoms with me just in case.'

Silas could hear the emotional tears thickening her voice. If she was telling the truth then his accusations weren't just in bad taste and unfair, they were also cruel. Her need must have been very great indeed to make her respond to him as intensely as she had.

'Okay, I was out of order. You'll have to put my lack of subtlety down to the fact that I'm frustrated and disappointed as hell that we can't take this to its natural conclusion.'

Tilly gave a muffled sound and let him draw her back against his body and hold her there, with her head tucked into his shoulder.

'It's been a long time for me as well,' he told her quietly. He felt her sudden shocked movement. 'No, I'm not lying. It's the truth. Contrary to the impression I'm probably giving right now, I don't go in for impulsive spur-of-the-moment sex. My own work means that finding the right kind of partner isn't easy.'

Tilly assumed he meant that because he was an actor the opportunities were many, but so were the risks. As Sally had once graphically said to her, every time she slept with a new man she felt totally put off by the thought that she was also in part sleeping with all his previous partners—and their partners too.

'Perhaps I'm not thinking laterally enough,' Silas murmured.

'About finding a sexual partner?'

'No, about having the satisfaction of giving you the

pleasure and fulfilment I want to give you. After all, we don't need a condom to achieve that.'

Tilly's heart somersaulted, and then slammed into her chest wall. She didn't know now whether to feel shocked or excited, and ended up feeling a mix of both, tinged with wary resoluteness.

'If you're saying that because you *still* think I hired you with the ulterior motive of having sex with you—' she began.

But Silas didn't let her finish her objection, putting his fingers to her lips instead to silence her, and then bending his head to her ear to tell her meaningfully, 'Right now I ache like hell with frustration, and, like I said, it's the best way I can think of to go at least part-way towards getting rid of that.'

'By satisfying *me*?'

Silas could hear the disbelief in her voice. 'I don't know what kind of men you've known, but I can't believe they haven't shown you how much pleasure a man can get from bringing his partner to fulfilment. From seeing it in her eyes, feeling it in her kiss, from witnessing that he's satisfied her.'

'There haven't been *men*,' Tilly felt obliged to admit. 'Just one man. It was when we were at university, and I felt I should…'.

She'd only had *one* previous lover? Silas was caught off-guard by the wave of unexpected tenderness that surged through him. And even more startled by the ease with which he could accept the truth of what she had said.

He started to pull her down against him, his hands shaping her body, but Tilly resisted.

'What's wrong?' he asked. 'Don't you want me to?'

'Yes,' Tilly told him honestly, pausing before she said, even more honestly, in a small breathless rush of words, 'But I want our first time together to *be* together.'

It seemed a long time during which she had to bear his silent scrutiny before Silas reacted to what she had said, but when he did it wasn't with words. Instead he cupped her face, brushing the soft quiver of her lips over and over again with the pad of his thumb before bending his head to kiss her so intimately that she was afraid that she might actually orgasm after all.

When he finally lifted his mouth from hers it made her shiver in delicious awareness of his arousal to hear the thick roughness in his voice when he said, 'I wonder if you know how much I was tempted to break all my own rules on health and irresponsibility? But, while I might have broken them for myself, I don't have the right to expect you to break your own rules for me. Another time we'll have to organise things better.'

Not the most romantic words in the world, perhaps, but to Tilly they had a meaning and depth to them that went beyond the lightweight glitter of mere romance. 'What are the plans for today?' Silas asked.

'I'm not sure,' Tilly admitted. 'But if it's possible I wouldn't mind going back into that town we came through on the way here. I feel I ought to get the children a small Christmas present each.'

Silas hesitated for a second. From his own point of view it made sense for him to spend as much time as he could with Art, and yet he felt strangely reluctant to pass up on the opportunity to have Tilly to himself and get to know her better.

'I'll see if I can find out the best way for us to get into town, if you like,' he offered. After all, they were here for a week. Plenty of time for him to get close to Art later.

CHAPTER SEVEN

'DARLING. I hope you won't be offended, but I'm afraid you and Silas are going to have to entertain yourselves today, because the florist is coming out from Madrid to see me this morning, and then this afternoon I need to finalise the menu with the chef.'

'Don't worry about us, Annabelle,' Silas answered, before Tilly could say anything. 'Art, I hope you don't mind,' he continued. 'Before we joined you for breakfast I took the liberty of having a word with the chap who is in charge of your fleet of vehicles here to ask if there was any possibility of us borrowing a car and driving down into Segovia. We had to leave London in a bit of a rush and we both still have some essential Christmas shopping to do. Martin said it was okay with him if I borrowed one of the four-wheel drives so long as you had no objections.'

'Of course he doesn't—do you, sweetheart?' Annabelle smiled, looking relieved. 'You are so lucky, Tilly, to have such a thoughtful fiancé. Art hates going shopping.'

'Maybe Silas doesn't mind because *he* isn't a billionaire.'

Tilly felt a rush of anger on her mother's behalf as Art's younger daughter dropped the venom-tipped words onto the now-silent air of the room where they had eaten breakfast. It was no wonder her husband was looking embarrassed and shame-faced, Tilly decided, feeling sorry for him.

However, it was Silas who took up the gauntlet on her mother's behalf, saying coolly, 'I daresay the experience of bringing up two daughters has made Art wise enough to see through predatory females.'

The insult was delivered so lightly and easily that it was almost like a fine needle plunged into the heart, Tilly decided. You knew you'd received a mortal wound, but you couldn't see how or where. That it *had* been delivered, though, was obvious in the sudden red flush on Susan-Jane's face.

When Tilly had woken up alone in the attic bedroom that morning, she had been torn between hurrying to get showered, dressed and out of the room before Silas returned, because she felt so embarrassed about the previous night, and an equally strong impulse to remain hidden under the bedclothes, because she wasn't sure she could face Silas at all. In the event he had behaved so naturally towards her that it had been unexpectedly easy to return his good-morning kiss when he had come into the dining room several seconds behind her, smelling of cold air and explaining that he had been outside.

Now, of course, she knew why. Just as she knew what the nature of the essential shopping he had referred to was.

For a man who was perilously close to being an out-of-work actor, he possessed a rare degree of self-confidence. In fact the lack of flamboyance in his manner, allied with the cool purposefulness he displayed, seemed to Tilly to be closer to the behaviour of the top handful of her clients—wealthy, self-assured men, some of whom had inherited their wealth and some of whom had made it from scratch, but all of whom were the kind of men who didn't need to prove anything to anyone, and to whom other men seemed to automatically defer.

'I've told Martin that we should be ready to leave at about eleven,' Silas told Tilly. He glanced at his watch, which looked simple and robust but, as Tilly well knew from the boys on her team, was an expensive and highly covetable Rolex. 'That gives us just over half an hour to get ready. Is that enough time? Or shall I—?'

'Half an hour is fine,' Tilly assured him.

She was just about to push back her chair and go up to the bedroom to get her coat when Cissie-Rose suddenly announced, 'I was planning to take the kids into Segovia myself today. They're so bored, cooped up here. Since you're driving in, Silas, we may as well come with you, so that Daddy will still have the other SUV here if he needs to go out.'

'You could be spoiling Silas and Tilly's fun if you do that,' her husband chuckled.

'Oh, don't be silly. Silas won't mind. After all, it's not as if he's still courtin' Tilly. I mean, Tilly and Silas are practically living together—even though they aren't legally married yet.'

For bitchiness, Art's daughters would take some beating, Tilly decided, as Silas stood up to pull her chair out for her. She tried to imagine how she might be feeling right now if she and Silas *were* newly engaged and passionately in love, desperate for some time alone. Oddly enough it wasn't hard at all for her to conjure up exactly what she would feel. In fact it wasn't very much different from what she *was* feeling, she admitted. Which meant *what*, exactly? Because she and Silas *weren't* engaged, and they *weren't* in love. But something was happening between them, and she couldn't pretend that it wasn't. Last night, for instance... The ache last night's interrupted lovemaking had left behind, like a tamped-down fire, smouldering beneath the surface, suddenly burst into fresh life.

All the way up the stairs, too conscious of Silas, walking alongside her, Tilly struggled to smother her aching desire. It overwhelmed her that she should feel like this for a man she barely knew. Inside herself a monumental tug of war seemed to be taking place, between her head and her heart. She knew as surely as she knew her own name that she was someone who could only touch the heights of her own sensuality when her physical desire was equalled by her emotional commitment. Loveless sex had no appeal at all for her, which was why she had always held back from allowing herself to get involved with anyone. Up until now.

So what had happened to make things so different? Silas had happened, that was what! Silas, an out-of-work actor, who hired himself out as an escort. She, with all she knew about the vulnerability of love, was actually admitting that she was close to committing the insanity of falling in love with a man engaged in just about the most relationship-unfriendly career there was. She was kidding, right? She was simply testing herself—seeing how far she could stretch her self-imposed boundaries; she wasn't seriously falling in love with a man she had only just met. She couldn't be.

They had reached their bedroom door. Silas opened it for her.

'Thanks for saying what you did to Cissie-Rose. I wanted to say something myself, but I know if I had it wouldn't have been anything like such a masterly put-down.'

Silas gave a dismissive shrug. 'It was obvious when she tried to make a dig about your mother being motivated by money that that is *exactly* what motivates her. There's something profoundly ugly and depressing about the pathetic need the sons and daughters of the very wealthy often seem to have, to ring-fence their parents' assets and stick a "mine all mine" label on them.' He gave another shrug. 'Mind you, I suppose if you've been brought up to think that everything can be bought, including your own love, the thought of anyone else getting their hands on your parents' money is threatening. Makes me glad my own father was just comfortably off.'

Yes, she could see him in the social background described by the brief sketch he had just drawn. Good school, and a good university too, she judged shrewdly. The kind of background she would normally have expected to lead to a career in the City, or the law. 'Is there a tradition of acting in your family?' she asked curiously.

'Like the Redgraves, you mean?' He shook his head. 'No.'

His half-brother's desire to act had surprised them all, and it had been Silas who had had to act as a bridge between Joe and their father in Joe's early teenage years, when he had first decided he wanted to act.

'Disappointed that I'm not connected to theatre aristocracy?' he asked dryly.

It was Tilly's turn to shake her head. 'No, not at all. It's just that I find it hard to imagine you as an actor, somehow. You don't seem the type.'

'No? So what type do I seem, then?' This was dangerous territory, but he couldn't resist asking her—even as he was inwardly deriding himself for his predictable male vanity.

'Something big in the City—not a City-boy type. Something else, perhaps in one of the controlling bodies, a sort of overlooking and critical role.'

Her perspicacity reminded him that he was not dealing with a woman of Art's daughters' ilk. Tilly didn't only have far more humanity than them, she also had far more intelligence. Intelligence in a lover when you were keeping something hidden from them was not exactly an asset, he warned himself. But it was too late for him to backtrack now. Last night he had made Tilly the kind of promises—verbally as well as non-verbally—that were likely to cause him an awful lot of problems.

'Is it my imagination, or is this room actually slightly warmer?' Tilly asked.

She was glad of an excuse to change the subject and get away from the personal. Not that she didn't want to find out as much about Silas's background and his way of life as she could—she did. In fact she craved details about him. But that in itself was enough to make her want to take to her heels and put as much distance between them as she could. She was involved in a tug of war, with her head pulling in one direction and her heart in another.

'I had a word with the Count's PA,' Silas said. 'Apparently the Count won't be too pleased if he finds out his instructions with regard to the necessity of keeping all the rooms equally heated have been ignored. Even the insurance on this place is dependent on certain conditions—one of which is keeping all the rooms equally heated. I doubt that even Art, with all his billions, would be too happy if he were landed with a bill for the renovation work on one damaged castle.'

'Art's daughters aren't going to be very pleased.'

'Probably not, but they are free to take up their argument with the PA if they wish to.' He paused, and then asked dryly, 'I know it's none of my business, but does your mother have *any* idea of what she's taking on?'

'My mother prefers to only see what she wants to see, and right now what she wants to see is that Art is a wonderful man and his daughters are going to be loving stepdaughters to her. She's so unworldly. I can't help worrying about her,' Tilly admitted.

'So who does the worrying about you?'

'No one,' Tilly answered promptly. 'No one needs to worry about me. I'm not like my mother. The way she falls in love and then falls out of it again would leave me too disillusioned to keep on looking for Mr Right, but she seems to be able to pick herself up and start all over again.'

Silas could hear the underlying troubled note in Tilly's voice. It was his opinion that her mother was rather shallow, but the more he saw of Annabelle the less inclined he was to think of her as being avaricious or manipulative. 'How old were you when your mother fell out of love with your father?'

The unexpectedness of his own abrupt question startled Silas as much as it did Tilly.

'I was six when they divorced, and from what they've both told me the marriage had been in trouble for some time. I think Dad tried to stay the course because of me, but Ma had had enough.' Tilly opened the wardrobe and removed her coat and boots.

'You're going to need something a bit sturdier than those,' Silas warned her. 'Martin told me that they're expecting a fresh fall of snow later today.'

'I don't have anything else,' Tilly admitted ruefully. 'I shall have to see what I can buy while we're out. It didn't register properly with me that the weather was going to be like this.'

'If we had really come here as a newly engaged couple I daresay we'd have been only too happy to use the snow as an excuse to stay up here in bed. And no doubt we would have come prepared,' Silas said.

Tilly could feel her face turning pink, and the surge of longing that gripped her body was so intense that it made her give a small, low gasp of protest. She placed her hand flat to her lower body, in an attempt to quell the pulse of raw need that had kicked into life.

She could see from Silas's expression that he knew exactly what she was feeling. When he stepped towards her, she protested shakily, 'No.' But she didn't make any attempt to step back or to avoid him when he cupped her shoulder with one hand and slid the other into the small hollow of lower back, determinedly propelling her towards him.

'That look says you ache for me in the same way I do for you.' Even the warmth of his breath as he murmured the words against her ear was a form of caress and arousal, making her quiver with pleasure and exhale on a small, shuddering breath, desperate to turn her face to his so that his mouth would be closer to her own.

What was it about this particular woman that made him behave in ways that ran counter to all his plans? Silas wondered grimly. This agonisingly sharp and re-lentlessly demanding stab of need burning through him wasn't what he had intended at all. It had to be some-thing in the small quiver within her body that alerted him to her physical susceptibility to him that was re-sponsible for this fierce, male, *driven* urge within him, pushing him to cover her mouth with his own, rather than any independent desire of his own. It had to be. Otherwise… Otherwise, what? Otherwise he would be getting himself into a situation that he couldn't control?

'We'd better go downstairs before Martin thinks we've changed our minds and we don't want the car any more.'

She was glad that he wasn't taking things any further, Tilly told herself firmly, when Silas released her and started to step back.

'Don't do that!' Silas groaned, almost dragging her back into his arms.

'Don't do what?' Tilly protested.

'Don't look at me as though all you want is the feel of my mouth on yours,' Silas told her harshly.

'I wasn't—' Tilly began to object, but it was too late. Silas had imprisoned her face between his hands and he was bending towards her, his kiss silencing her.

Long after she should have been asleep the night before she had lain awake, desperately trying to tell herself that Silas's kisses couldn't possibly have been as wonderful as she was now thinking. She had derided herself for being bewitched by a potent combination of her own physical desire, the moonlight outside on the snow and the proximity of Christmas. She had told herself sternly that if Silas had kissed her, say, in her own flat in London, she probably wouldn't have been affected by him at all. But here she was, being swept up under last night's magical spell all over again—and if anything this time his effect on her was even more intense. If he chose to pick her up and carry her over to the waiting bed now, she knew that she wouldn't want to stop him.

An intense ache pulsed deep in the core of her sexuality. She wanted him so badly she felt shocked, almost drugged, by the overwhelming strength of her need. Panic flared inside her, causing her to push Silas away. She didn't want to feel like this about any man, and especially *his* kind of man.

The minute he released her she headed for the door. When he reached it ahead of her she held her breath, half fearful and half hopeful that he would lean against it, barring her exit, but instead he opened it for her, simply saying, 'Don't forget your coat.'

* * *

'Right, kids, you get in the back with Matilda. You won't mind if I sit in front with you, Silas, will you? Only I get so carsick if I sit in the back.'

Not a word of apology to *her*, Tilly seethed, as Cissie-Rose appropriated the passenger seat of the large four-wheel drive. Unlike her, Cissie-Rose seemed to have arrived in Spain well equipped for the snow, Tilly realised, as she looked a little enviously at her expensive winter sports-style outfit.

'I want a window seat.'

'So do I.' Cissie-Rose's children were already clambering into the back seat.

'You'll have to sit in the middle, Tilly,' Cissie-Rose instructed—for all the world as though she were some kind of servant, Tilly thought crossly.

'One of the children will have to sit in the middle. Not Tilly,' Silas intervened, in the kind of voice that said there would be no argument. 'They can take turns to have the window seat—one when we drive out and the other when we drive back.'

'*Maria* always sits in the middle,' the elder of Cissie-Rose's sons piped up.

'Maybe she does. But Tilly is not Maria.'

'Goodness, what a fuss you're making, Tilly,' Cissie-Rose said spitefully, and so blatantly untruthfully that Tilly was too taken aback to retaliate.

'Call this an SUV?' the older boy commented derogatively. 'You should see our SUVs back home.'

'Fix my seat belt for me,' the other commanded Tilly in a disagreeable voice.

She was just leaning forward to help him when Silas stopped her. *'Please will you help me with my seat belt, Tilly?* That's what I think you meant to say, isn't it?'

Tilly couldn't help feeling a bit sorry for the two boys. They were only young, and it was obvious their mother was the type of woman who treated her sons as useful bargaining tools—to be fussed over when it suited her, and then be dismissed and kept out of her way when it didn't.

For the entire length of the time it took them to drive into Segovia Cissie-Rose focused her attention on Silas—to such a degree that she and the children might just as well not have been there, Tilly decided, more upset on behalf of the children than for herself. After all, Silas had already shown her that he had no interest in Cissie-Rose, and without knowing quite how it had happened Tilly discovered that she was actually allowing herself to trust him. That would make her dangerously vulnerable, an inner voice warned her, but Tilly chose to ignore it. In fact she was choosing to ignore a lot of warnings from her inner protective voice since she had met Silas.

The boys, once they realised Tilly wasn't the kind of person who could be cowed or spoken to in the way they were used to speaking to Maria, the young girl Cissie-Rose hired to look after them, began to respect her calm firmness and even responded to it. Tilly liked children, and she enjoyed enlivening the journey for the boys, teaching them some simple travel games and talking to them about their sports and hobbies.

To Silas, forced to endure the unwanted intimacy of Cissie-Rose's deliberate and unsubtle touches to his arm and occasionally his thigh, as she underlined various points of an unutterably boring monologue, the snatches of giggles reaching him from the back seat felt like longed-for sips of clean, cold water after the cloying taste of cheap corked wine. He could only marvel at the miraculous way in which Tilly was drawing out Cissie-Rose's two young sons. Something about her calm, matter-of-fact way of talking to them touched a chord in his own memory. Inside his head he could almost hear the echo of his own mother's voice, and with it his own responding laughter.

No child should have to grow up without a mother. He had been lucky in his stepmother, he knew that, and he genuinely loved her, but listening to Tilly had brought to life an old pain. He flicked the switch on the steering column that controlled the radio, increasing the volume so that it blotted out the laughter and chatter from the back seat. Immediately Cissie-Rose gave him an approving smile, and wetted her already over-glossed lips with the tip of her tongue. When he failed to respond she leaned towards him, very deliberately placing one manicured hand high up on his thigh.

'I am so glad you did that,' she told him huskily. 'Tilly's voice is quite shrill, isn't it? I suppose it must be her English accent. It was beginning to make my head ache. How long have you known one another, did you say?'

'I didn't,' Silas answered her coolly.

'She's a very lucky young woman to have landed a man like you in her bed.'

'The luck's all mine,' Silas responded.

Cissie-Rose was coming on to him strongly, and he

recognised that if he encouraged her she might provide him with a shortcut to the information he needed. But his immediate rejection of the idea was so intense it was almost as if he was recoiling physically and emotionally from the thought of sharing the kind of intimacy he had begun with Tilly with anyone else. A physical and an *emotional* recoil? Just what exactly did that mean? If he carried on like this he would soon be telling himself he felt guilty about what he was doing, and he couldn't afford that kind of self-indulgent luxury.

Even when they had reached town and parked the car, Cissie-Rose was still trying to claim Silas's attention, leaving Tilly to help her two sons out of the car, checking that they were well wrapped up against the icy cold wind whipping down Segovia's narrow streets.

The ground underfoot was covered in snow and ice, and—predictably—Cissie-Rose clutched at Silas's arm. The two boys positioned themselves either side of Tilly, clinging to her so trustingly that she didn't have the heart to say anything.

Silas looked grimly at Tilly's bent head and wondered why she had this ability to make him feel emotions he didn't want to feel, and how she managed to activate a protective, almost possessive male instinct in him that no other woman had ever touched. It certainly wasn't what he wanted to feel. Yet, watching her now with the two boys, he was conscious of a sharp sense of irritation that they were there, fuelling his need to have her to himself.

'Tilly and I have rather a lot to do, so we might as well split up, Cissie-Rose, and let you and the boys get on with your shopping. How long do you think you'll need?' he asked, lifting his arm to check his watch so that Cissie-Rose was forced to remove her hand from it.

'Oh! I thought we could all shop together,' she protested. 'It would be so much more fun that way. Tilly and I could do some girly stuff, and you guys could go have a soda or something, and then we could all meet up for lunch.'

This was Cissie-Rose in smiling 'good mom' mode, Tilly recognised, as the boys looked uncertainly at their mother.

'You're okay with that, aren't you, you guys?' Cissie-Rose appealed to her sons. 'Or would you prefer to stay with Tilly.'

Witch! Tilly thought with uncharacteristic venom. Tails you win, heads I lose.

'We want to stay with Tilly,' the two boys chanted together.

Immediately Silas shook his head. 'Sorry, boys, but I'm afraid you can't.'

The vehemence in his voice made Tilly curl her toes in excited reaction to the intimacy his determination to have her to himself suggested. 'Tilly and I have some Christmas shopping to do. And she *is* my fiancé.' The look he was giving her made her face burn, and Cissie-Rose's expression changed to one of acid venom as she glared at Silas.

She would make a bad enemy, Tilly realised when she saw the look in her eyes.

Silas didn't seem too concerned, though. Ignoring Cissie-Rose's obvious hostility to his suggestion, he continued calmly. 'I don't want to linger in town, Cissie-Rose. The weather forecast they gave out on the way over didn't sound very good.'

'Oh. I see. Well, okay, then.'

It was obvious that Cissie-Rose did not think it was anything like okay at all, Tilly realised, feeling uncomfortable as she saw the furious look the other woman was giving her.

'Look, why don't we meet back here in, say, a couple of hours?' Silas suggested. 'Here's a spare key for the car in case you get back before us. That way you won't have to stand around waiting in the cold. And I'll give you my mobile number just in case you need it. Ready, Tee?'

Tilly disengaged herself from the boys and hurried towards him, hating herself for being so grateful both for the supporting arm he slid round her and the warmth of the smile he gave her.

'It's okay. You can let go of me,' she told him slightly breathlessly five minutes later. 'Cissie-Rose can't see us now.'

'You are my fiancé; we're passionately in love. We're hardly going to walk feet apart from one another, are we? And you never know—we could bump into Cissie-Rose anywhere. It is only a small town. Besides,' Silas told her softly, 'I don't want to let go of you.'

Was it necessary for him to go to these lengths? He had established himself now as Tilly's fiancé. And after last night... After last night, what? It was because of last night that he had been left with this ache that had somehow taken on a life force of its own. This ache that right now...

What was Silas thinking? Tilly wondered. What was

making him look so distant and yet at the same time, now that he had turned his head to look at her, so hungry for her?

When he reached for her Tilly didn't even try to resist. He turned her around to face him in the shelter of an overhanging building, where no one could see them, and then pressed her back against the wall, covering her body with the warmth of his own.

He whispered into the softness of her parting lips, 'I know there are any number of reasons why I shouldn't be doing this, but right now I don't want to know about them. Right now, right here, what I want, *all* I want, is you, Tilly.'

Why was he doing this when he didn't have to? Why ask himself questions that he couldn't answer? Silas answered himself as he gave in to the need that had been aching through him since last night and bent his head to kiss Tilly.

This wasn't a sensible thing for her to be doing, Tilly warned herself. But suddenly being sensible wasn't what she wanted. What she wanted was… What she wanted was Silas, she admitted. And she stopped thinking and worrying and judging, and simply gave herself over to feeling, as they clung together, kissing like two desire-drugged teenagers, oblivious to everything and everyone else.

What followed should have been an anticlimax. Instead it was the start of the most wonderful few hours Tilly had ever had.

The small town was picture-perfect, with its honey-coloured stone houses covered in pristine snow—which, thankfully, had been swept off the streets. Silas insisted on keeping her arm tucked through his. And when at one point he simply stopped walking and looked at her, she could feel her cheeks turning pink in response to the look in his eyes.

'Don't do that,' she protested.

'Don't do what?'

'Look at me like that.'

'You mean like I want to kiss you again?'

'This is crazy,' Tilly said, shaking her head.

'Isn't that what people are supposed to say when they start to fall in love?'

Silas could see the shock in her eyes. He could feel that same shock running through his own body. What the hell was he doing, dragging love into the situation? He felt as though he had suddenly become two people whose behaviour was totally alien to each other—one of whom was saying that he never played emotional games with women, that he despised men who did, so why the hell was he using a word like "love", while the other demanded to know who had said anything about playing games? It was as though he was at war with himself. He tried to shake off the feeling that they had somehow strayed into a maze and come up against a blank wall.

'There's a coffee shop over there. Shall we go in and have a drink?' Anything to try and get himself back to normal.

Tilly nodded her head in relief. Now that she was free of the spell the intimacy of Silas's sexuality seemed to cast over her, she was shakily aware of how vulnerable she was. Things were moving far too fast for her. She wasn't used to this kind of situation. And somehow she couldn't quite get her head round accepting that Silas could actually *mean* what he was saying. It was too much too soon. But she wanted him. She couldn't deny that.

She drank the coffee Silas ordered for them both, and tried to focus on the people hurrying up and down the street outside the window rather than on Silas, as she secretly wanted to do. In fact right now what she wanted more than anything else was just to be able to look at him, to absorb every tiny physical detail while she tried to come to terms with what was happening.

Silas watched her. He felt as though he could almost read her thoughts. She didn't know whether to believe he was being honest with her. He could sense it in every small action she made. She wanted him; he knew that. But he could see that she was dubious about accepting the immediacy of the situation.

They had both finished their coffee. Silas stood up. 'I'll be back in a minute,' he said, nodding his head in the direction of a pharmacy on the other side of the street.

Tilly didn't catch on immediately, but when she saw the green cross over the building her face burned, and she made an incoherent sound of assent, using Silas's absence to go to the ladies' room to comb her hair and replace the lipstick he had kissed off earlier. By the time she emerged, Silas had returned and was waiting for her.

'I think I'd better buy your mother a small Christmas

gift, but I'm going to need you to advise me,' he said, steering her in the direction of a small gift shop with a mouthwatering window display. To Tilly's relief he didn't say a word about his visit to the pharmacy.

The gift shop proved to be a treasure trove of the unusual and the enticing, and Tilly found presents for each of the children. It was only when the small ornamental jewellery box Silas had bought for her mother was being giftwrapped that Tilly looked at her watch and realised that it was almost two hours since they had left the car park.

'We ought to be heading back,' she warned Silas.

'Yes, I know. Not that I'm particularly looking forward to the return trip with Cissie-Rose. She can sit in the back this time—car sickness or not,' he told Tilly, before adding in a warmer tone, 'I thought you handled the boys very well, by the way. You obviously like children.'

'Yes. And it's just as well, really. My father remarried and has a second younger family, and all my mother's exes have children—most of whom also have children of their own now.'

'The ramifications of the modern extended family can be quite complicated,' Silas observed as he took the package from the shop assistant.

As they stepped out in the street, Tilly gave a small gasp of delight. 'It's snowing!' she exclaimed.

'Martin warned me that heavy snow had been forecast.'

This time it was Tilly who automatically slipped her arm through his as they headed for the car park.

A clock was just striking the hour when they reached it, making their way through the parked vehicles to where Silas had left the four-wheel drive.

But when they got to where it should have been there was only an empty space that the snow was just beginning to cover.

CHAPTER EIGHT

'SILAS, someone must have stolen the car,' Tilly exclaimed, shocked.

'I doubt that.' There was a grimness in his voice that made Tilly look uncertainly at him. His mobile had started to ring and he removed it from his pocket, flicking it on, while Tilly moved discreetly out of earshot so as not to seem as though she were listening in.

'That was Cissie-Rose,' Silas announced, coming over to her. 'Apparently she'd had enough of Segovia, and the boys were cold and tired, so she decided to take the car and drive back without us.'

Tilly's face revealed her shocked disbelief.

'You mean she's left us here with no way of getting back to the castle?'

'I mean exactly that,' Silas agreed curtly.

'But why on earth would she do that?'

Silas suspected that he knew the answer. Cissie-Rose had made it plain that she was offended because he hadn't responded to her sexual overtures on the drive to Segovia, and this, he suspected, was her way of paying him back for his refusal to play along. This development

was a complication he hadn't allowed for, he admitted.
From the point of view of achieving his purpose in
coming to Spain, it made sense to cool things down
with Tilly. He could continue to play the role of her
fiancé while at the same time discreetly making use of
Cissie-Rose's none-too-subtle hint that she was open to
a flirtation with him, since Cissie-Rose would undoubtedly provide him with a more direct route to Art's confidences than Tilly. With his research at stake he wasn't
in a position to allow himself the luxury of moral
scruples. He had a duty to reveal the truth.

But no duty to live it?

If he had to choose between vindicating those who
had worked to reveal the truth about Jay Byerly and sacrificing Tilly's good opinion of him, he had to choose
the greater need. And what about Tilly herself. What
about her need and her feelings?

Silas could feel anger with himself boiling up inside
him. He was dragging issues into the equation that did
not need to be there. He and Tilly were sexually attracted to one another. There was no logical or moral
reason why, as two consenting adults, they shouldn't be
free to explore that mutual sexual attraction, and no
reason either why they should not enjoy a shared relationship. It didn't need to affect his original purpose in
coming here.

And it could be over as quickly as it had started. Was
that what he hoped for and wanted? Because he didn't
want to have to see the look in Tilly's eyes if she discovered the truth?

There was no point in telling her. His original

decision had been made before he had met her, and had nothing whatsoever to do with her. Semantics, Silas warned himself. And they weren't enough to take away the acid sour taste of growing dislike of his dishonesty.

Tilly looked up at the sky, from which snow was falling increasingly heavily and fast. Icy prickles of anxiety skidded down her spine. She was pretty sure that Cissie-Rose had acted out of spite and selfishness, but she didn't want to run her down in front of Silas and end up sounding catty and judgemental. Besides, she had more important things to worry about than complaining about what Cissie-Rose had done. Like worrying about how on earth they were now going to get back to the castle.

'Perhaps we should ring the castle and ask if someone could come and collect us?' she suggested to Silas.

He shook his head. 'It will be much simpler if we try and organise a car from this end. I noticed a car-hire place earlier.'

Half an hour later, there was a grim look on Silas's face as he was told that the earliest anyone could provide them with a car would be the following day.

The snow was now falling thick and fast.

'There's nothing else for it, I'm afraid,' he told Tilly. 'We're going to have to spend the night here in town. I noticed a couple of hotels when we were walking round.'

What Silas said made good sense, but Tilly's heart had sunk further with every word. She too had noticed the hotels as they'd walked past them. Both of them had looked very exclusive, and would therefore be expensive. Knowing she was on a limited budget, she had deliberately left her credit card at the castle, in case she was tempted to use it, and all she had in her bag was a small amount of currency that would be nowhere near enough to pay for even one hotel room, never mind two and the cost of a hire car.

'It does make sense to stay here,' she agreed. 'But I'm afraid we're going to have to find somewhere inexpensive, Silas. You see, I didn't bring my credit card with me...'

Silas could see how uncomfortable and worried she was. 'It's my fault we've been stranded here,' he told her calmly. 'I suppose I should have guessed that Cissie-Rose might play this kind of trick on us. Don't worry about the cost of the hotel and the car hire. I'll pay for them.'

'You can't do that,' Tilly objected. 'Both those hotels looked dreadfully expensive. It wouldn't be fair. They could cost you more than I've paid the agency...'

'It's okay. Calm down. The agency always give us emergency cover money. I daresay they'll reclaim it from you once we get back home,' he fibbed, adding briskly, 'Look, we either book in somewhere or we hang around for hours in the hope that Martin can be called in from his half-day off to come and collect us.'

His reference to Martin being on his half-day off had the effect on Tilly's conscience he had known it would. Immediately she shook her head and protested, 'Oh, no, we can't do that. It wouldn't be fair.'

'And it won't be fair to us either, if we stand here and freeze to death—will it?' he said, taking hold of her arm and firmly turning her round in the direction of the town.

'It's going to look very odd if we book in without any luggage,' Tilly warned him.

'Not in these weather conditions. They're probably used to travellers getting stranded.'

Ten minutes later they were standing in the snow outside one of the hotels Tilly had noticed. It looked even more exclusive close up than she had thought when she'd seen it earlier.

'We can't book in here,' she protested to Silas.

'Of course we can,' he said, ignoring her inclination to hang back and nodding his head in acknowledgement of the uniformed doorman holding open the door for them.

Although he had a relatively well-paid job, Silas wasn't dependent on it financially. His maternal grandparents had been wealthy, and Silas, as their only grandchild, had inherited the bulk of it. Ordinarily he chose to live on what he earned, but he was perfectly comfortable in the kind of moneyed surroundings they were now entering—as Tilly noted when she stood back while he approached the reception desk.

Within five minutes he had returned to her side, explaining, 'They're pretty fully booked, because of the time of year, but they can give us a suite and they'll sort out a hire car for us for the morning.'

'A suite? But that will cost the earth!' Tilly protested.

'It's all they had left,' Silas told her grimly. 'We'd better go up and make sure it's okay. Then, since we won't be returning to the castle until tomorrow morning, I think that we might as well find somewhere to have a late lunch and explore the rest of the town.'

He didn't want to admit even in his most private thoughts how torn he was between the sheer urgency of his physical desire for Tilly and the cautionary voice inside him that was warning him that if he had any sense he would keep Tilly at arm's length, instead of increasing the intimacy between them—for her sake as well as his. *Her* sake? When exactly had he started to care about wanting to protect her?

Tilly nodded her head in approval of Silas's plan. The lift had arrived, and Silas stood back to allow her to precede him into it, his hand resting against her waist in the kind of discreet but very proprietorial gesture powerful men tended to use towards their partners. She could feel an almost sensual warmth spreading out from where he was touching her to envelop virtually the whole of her body. It made her want to move closer to him, so that she could absorb even more of it. In fact it made her want to do things she would normally have a run a mile rather than do…such as lifting her face for his kiss the second the lift doors closed.

How could it have happened that she had become so desperate for his touch that she felt like this? She had grown used to thinking of herself as the kind of woman who scorned such things as passionate embraces in lifts. But now she felt achingly disappointed because Silas was not making any move towards her at all.

Getting into the lift with Tilly instead of using the stairs had been a serious misjudgement, Silas admitted. The small enclosed space meant he was standing close enough to Tilly to be surrounded by the woman-scent of her skin and hair. They drew him to her with the irresistible pull nature had expressly designed them to have. Standing this close to her made him want to stand even closer still, and to do far more than just stand with her. He wanted to take her and lay her down beneath him, so that he could explore and savour every delicious inch of her, starting with the toes he had watched her curl up in sexual reaction to him, and moving all the way up to her mouth.

The lift jolted to a halt, its doors opening. Tilly stepped out into an elegant corridor and waited for Silas to join her.

'We're in here,' he told her, indicating a door to their right and going to open it.

Silas had said he'd booked them a suite, and she had assumed this meant they would have two bedrooms and their own bathroom, Tilly thought as she stood in the middle of the smart sitting room of the suite. She said uncertainly, 'There's only one bedroom.'

'I know, but, as I said, this suite was all they had left. And, after all, it isn't as though we aren't already sharing a bed.' Something about the words 'already sharing a bed' had an effect on her emotions Tilly wasn't sure she was ready for. They made them sound so intimate, so partnered—almost as though they were not just having a relationship but were already a couple.

'If you aren't happy with this we could always try the other hotel,' Silas offered.

Tilly shook her head. 'That would be silly. We might not get in.'

Ordinarily she would have been thrilled to be staying somewhere so upmarket and elegant. The building in which the hotel was housed was centuries old, but somehow the designers had managed to complement the age of the building by teaming it with the very best in modern design, rather than create a discordant mismatch.

Their suite comprised a sitting room, a bedroom, a state-of-the-art limestone bathroom, and a separate dressing room. While the bedroom overlooked the street, the sitting room overlooked a private courtyard garden to the rear of the hotel, which Tilly guessed would be used as an outdoor dining area in summer but which right now was covered in inches of snow.

'I just wish I had the clothes with me to do this place justice,' Tilly admitted ruefully.

At least she was wearing her good winter coat and her equally good leather boots. She'd become a fan of careful investment dressing with her first job in the City, even though her mother frequently complained that her choice of immaculately tailored suits was dull and unsexy. The black coat she was wearing today was cut simply, and her leather boots were neat-fitting and smart, just like the knee-length skirt she had on underneath the coat, and the plain cashmere sweater she was wearing with it. Thank heavens she had decided at the last minute this morning, after mentally reviewing the impression she had gained of the town the day before, not to wear jeans.

'I really ought to ring my mother and explain what's happened,' she told Silas.

'Why don't I ring Art instead?' he suggested.

Tilly looked at him. She had a good idea that he wanted to speak to Art and make his feelings about Cissie-Rose's behaviour very clear.

'There's no point in making a fuss about what's

happened. Cissie-Rose will have calmed down by the time she gets back to the castle, and I don't want Ma to get herself upset.'

'You mean you think we should let Cissie-Rose get away with it?' Silas shook his head. 'No. When we tolerate that kind of behaviour in others, we allow them to continue with it. She needs to know that what she did is not acceptable.'

'I know what you're saying, but it's obvious that Art adores his daughters.' And equally obvious—to her at least—that her mother was living in mortal fear that they might somehow persuade their father not to marry her. So, no matter how much she might agree with Silas, her concern for her mother made her want to protect her. 'I do agree in principle,' she acknowledged. 'But since we're all going to be spending the next week together at the castle, I think on this occasion it makes sense to turn the other cheek, so to speak.'

'Giving in to Cissie-Rose won't prevent her from trying to oust your mother from her father's life, you know.'

Tilly wasn't quite quick enough to conceal from him how much his awareness of her private thoughts had caught her off-guard.

'Did you really think I wouldn't guess why you wanted Cissie-Rose spared the repercussions of her nastiness? It wasn't hard to work out what you were thinking. After all, Cissie-Rose hasn't given you any valid reason to want to protect *her*.'

'I feel so sorry for her sons. She uses them like…'

'Bargaining counters?' Silas supplied astutely.

'Well, I wouldn't have put it as directly as that. I

meant more that she uses them to highlight and under-line her own role as a good mother.'

'Oh, yes, she does that all right. But you can bet your City bonus that should the need arise she would have no compunction whatsoever about reminding Art where the future lies and who it lies with—and that won't be your mother.'

'You don't think that Art will marry Ma, do you?' Tilly said.

'He'd be doing her a favour if he didn't,' Silas re-sponded harshly. 'I assumed at first that your mother was marrying him for the financial status and privileges marriage to him would give her, but it's obvious that she doesn't have the—'

'Careful,' Tilly warned him. 'Especially if you were thinking of using words such as *intelligence*, *nous* or *as-tuteness*.'

'You're right. It wouldn't be fair to use any of them in connection with your mother,' Silas responded, with such a straight face that it took Tilly several seconds to recognise that he was deliberately teasing her.

'Oh, you,' she protested, picking up one of the cushions from the sofa and throwing it at him.

He caught it easily, but when he threw it back down on the sofa he said menacingly, 'Right...' and began to walk purposefully towards her.

Tilly did what came naturally, and took to her heels.

Silas, as she had known he would, caught her in seconds and with ease, turning her round in his arms to face him as she laughed and pretended to protest.

This wasn't what he had allowed for at all, Silas acknowledged as he felt the heavy slam of his heart in his chest wall and the flood of awareness it brought with it. 'This is completely crazy—you know that, don't you?' he heard himself saying thickly.

'What's crazy?' Tilly asked.

'Us. What's happening between us. *This*,' Silas answered.

Tilly knew that he was going to kiss her, and she knew too how much she wanted him to. So much that she was already standing on tiptoe so that she could wrap her arms around his neck to speed up the process.

Beneath his mouth she gave a soft sound of pleasure when he slid his hands inside her coat and then pulled her top free of her skirt, so that he was touching her bare skin. His hands were warm, their strength somehow underlining her own female weakness. She wanted to give herself over completely to his touch and his hold, and to know that he would keep her safe within that hold for ever. His hands moved further up her back, slowly caressing her skin, his thumbs probing the line of her bra, making her shudder in recognition of just how much she wanted to feel his hands cupping her breasts, stimulating her already tightening nipples with the urgent tugging demand of his fingers. In fact her desire was so great she had to stop herself from reaching out and guiding his hand to her breast.

Silas, though, had no such inhibitions, and openly moved against her so that she could feel his arousal. He wanted her as much as she did him.

Or did he? Was he just pretending to want her because he thought it was what she wanted? Was the kindness and the intimacy he was showing her nothing more than a cynical act? He had accused her of hiring him for sex. She had vehemently denied it. But what if he hadn't believed her?

Frantically, Tilly started to push him away.

Silas's immediate and very male reaction was to keep her where she was. He was already strongly aroused, and his body and his experience were both telling him that she wanted him just as much as he did her. But he could also see the agitation and panic in her eyes, and he knew it was *that* he had to respond to, not his own desire. Unwillingly, he let her go.

It was her old fear of getting out of her emotional depth as much as the current situation that had led to her blind, panicky decision to put an end to the growing intimacy of Silas's caresses, Tilly admitted. She shivered slightly, already missing the physical warmth of Silas's body. The trouble was that she simply wasn't used to this kind of sexual intimacy and intensity. And it scared her. Or rather her increasing hunger for Silas scared her. She had fought so hard against the danger of falling in love and giving herself to someone, of allowing herself to be vulnerable to them emotionally. And yet now here she was, virtually ready to throw away all that effort, ready to ignore everything she had warned herself about, to break down all the protective barriers she had set in place to guard herself simply because of Silas. A man she had only known a matter of days. Known? She didn't know him, did she?

'Are you going to tell me what's wrong, or do I have to guess?'

The formidable determination in Silas's voice made her whirl round to look at him.

'There isn't anything—' she began.

But he cut ruthlessly through the platitudes she would have mouthed, shaking his head and stating curtly, 'Of course there's something. You're no Cissie-Rose, Tilly. You aren't the game-playing type. You want me.'

'Yes,' she agreed, as lightly as she could. 'But, since I'm already heavily in debt to you for the cost of this suite, I didn't think it was a good idea to put even more pressure on my bank account by letting you think— Silas!' she protested shakily.

He had crossed the distance separating them so quickly that she had barely seen him move, never mind had time to take evasive action. And now he was holding her arms in an almost painful grip, looking at her as though he wanted to physically shake her, and with such a blaze of passion in his eyes…

'If you are actually daring to suggest what I think you are…'

She had never seen such anger in a man's eyes— and yet oddly, instead of frightening her, it actually empowered her.

'You were the one who accused me of wanting to hire a man for sex,' she reminded him fiercely.

'You're making excuses,' Silas said dismissively. 'I consider myself to be a pretty good judge of character, and I've spent enough time with you now to know that my first assumption was incorrect. You didn't push me away because you thought I'd be demanding payment from you, Tilly. We both know that.' Abruptly his eyes narrowed, and he continued softly, 'Or was it perhaps that you were afraid that the payment I might demand would be something other than money?'

What was he doing? Silas asked himself. Why hadn't he let Tilly just walk away from him? Because he wanted her so badly that he couldn't? And what exactly did *that* mean?

First he had been forced to deal with questions that came perilously close to admitting to a feeling of guilt, and now this. This feeling that he wanted to protect both Tilly and their burgeoning relationship from being damaged by the truth about why he was here.

Silas was getting far too close to the truth. Tilly wriggled uncomfortably in his grip, torn between a longing to lay her vulnerabilities bare to him and tell him how she felt and her deeply rooted habit of protecting her feelings from others.

'The situation we're in is promoting intimacy between us faster than I'm used to, so I suppose that I *do* feel a bit wary about it—and about you,' Tilly told him, covering her real feelings with careful half-truths, and hoping that he'd challenge her again.

Why was he doing this? Silas asked himself irritably. His behaviour was totally unfamiliar and irrational. He had agreed to stand in for Joe simply because acting as Tilly's fictional fiancé would give him the chance to get closer to Art Johnson, but now he was behaving as though the person he was most interested in getting closer to was Tilly herself. This kind of behaviour just wasn't him.

It wasn't that he was against committed relationships. It was simply that he hadn't as yet come up with any logical reason why he should want to be involved in one. He had always known that if the time ever came when he really believed he loved a woman he would want their commitment to one another to be exclusive and lead to marriage, but he had also decided that he didn't really believe that kind of love existed. So far he had been perfectly happy to substitute good-quality sexual relationships for the muddled emotional mess-ups that others called 'love', and he had never had any reason to want to push those relationships onto his sexual partners. In fact if anything he had always held off a little, and allowed them to be the ones to invite him to pursue them.

So what the hell was happening to him now? Because Tilly most certainly was not inviting him to do any such thing, and yet all he could think about was not just getting her into his bed and keeping her there but… But what? Getting her into his *life* and keeping her there?

Silas reminded himself again that his first duty was to his writing. He was too intelligent not to recognise that his determination to reveal the hidden scandal of the environmental damage caused by Jay Byerly's oil company had its roots in his childhood, his desire to support the cause his mother had espoused and in supporting had lost her life.

Millions of children suffered far worse childhood traumas than his own. He had been wanted. He had been loved. By both his parents. Those parents had been committed to one another and to him. And his father had done everything he could to ensure that the tragedy of his mother's death strengthened his own commitment to Silas rather than weakened it. When his father had re-married, nearly ten years after his mother's death, his introduction to his stepmother had been handled wisely and compassionately. Silas admired and liked his step-mother, and he genuinely loved his half-brother. He had no reason to feel hard done by in life.

But the loss of his mother had hurt. So how must Tilly feel, watching her mother enter into one bad rela-tionship after another? Tilly! How had she crept into his chain of thought? What the hell was happening to him?

'There is only one reason I would ever take a woman to bed,' he told Tilly harshly, as he pushed aside his inner thoughts and feelings. 'And that is my desire for her and hers for me.'

If only she was the kind of woman who had the courage to go up to him now and suggest boldly and openly that taking her to bed was exactly what he should do—and sooner rather than later. But she wasn't. And she was afraid to trust the over-excited eager need inside her that was trying to push her out of her relationship comfort zone. She had got so used to protecting her emotions that her sense of self and self-judgement no longer seemed to be working properly.

But she couldn't just walk away from a situation she had helped to create and pretend it wasn't happening. That was rank dishonesty, and if there was one thing she prided herself on and looked for in others it was total and complete honesty.

She took a deep breath, and then said to Silas, 'I know I gave you the impression that…that sex between us was something that could be on the agenda if it was what we both wanted. But…'

'But?'

'What happened last night wasn't…isn't… I just don't *do* casual sex,' she told him truthfully. 'Last night I got a bit carried away by the heat of the moment, so to speak, but now that we've both had time to reflect…'

'You've changed your mind?' Silas finished for her.

'I haven't changed my mind about finding you sexually attractive,' Tilly felt obliged to admit. 'But I have changed my mind about how sensible it would be to go ahead.'

She wanted him so badly, and yet at the same time she was afraid of taking the step that would take her from her emotionally secure present into a future that couldn't be guaranteed. Perhaps it was old-fashioned, but for her giving her body couldn't happen without giving something of herself emotionally. Modern men didn't always want that. She certainly didn't want to burden Silas with something he didn't want, and she didn't want to burden herself with an emotional commitment to a man who couldn't return it. It might be illogical, but she felt that by holding back sexually she was protecting herself emotionally.

Tilly was handing him the perfect get-out from his own unwanted temptation, and he would be a fool not to take it. So why was Silas even thinking about hesitating? Guilt wasn't a condition he liked experiencing. Neither were the feelings gripping him right now. Silas told himself that it wasn't too late for him to draw back and tell himself that he didn't really feel what he was feeling.

'My thoughts exactly,' he told her tersely. 'After all, one should never mix business with pleasure.'

Tilly felt his words like a physical blow, but she told herself that it was a good, clean blow she herself had invited, and that what didn't kill a person made them stronger. And she wanted to be strong to fight the very dangerous and intoxicating mix of emotions and desires Silas aroused in her.

'I'll give Art a ring to explain what's happened, and then I suggest we go and eat and explore the rest of the town.'

Why was she looking at him like that? Making him want to go to her and hold her and tell her… Tell her what? That he had lied to her?

His guilt lay so heavily on his conscience that it felt like a physical weight.

Tilly nodded her head. She was willing to agree to anything that meant she would be safe from the intimacy of being alone with him and the effect both it and he had on her.

It was his frustration at not being able to get on with his research that was fuelling his mood now, Silas tried to tell himself. Not Tilly, or how he felt about her.

CHAPTER NINE

TILLY looked uncertainly at her reflection in the shop mirror. Not because she was in any doubt about the dress she was trying on—she had known the moment she had seen it in the window that it would be perfect for her, and it was. No, her doubts were coming from the guilty conscience that made her remember that even though her mother might have apologised to her over the phone for what Cissie-Rose had done, and urged her to treat herself to 'something pretty' for which she would pay, Tilly knew that on her return to London she would have to find the money to pay back their hotel bill.

And if that wasn't enough to put her off the admittedly very reasonable cost of the little black dress that was clinging so lovingly to her curves, then she only had to point out to herself that she did not live the kind of lifestyle that actually required the wearing of little black dresses. But perhaps if she had one, another inner voice persuaded, she might accept more invitations where she could wear it.

She had seen the dress in the window of a small shop close to the hotel when she and Silas had walked past it earlier, on their way to find somewhere to have a late lunch. Afterwards she had made an excuse to slip away from Silas to have a closer look at it, telling him that she needed to buy a few personal items because of their overnight stay.

'It is perfect on you,' the sales assistant told her with a small smile. 'It's a dress that requires a woman to have curves. Its designer is Spanish, and it is a new range we have only just started to carry.'

It was just as well the other woman's English was better than her own Spanish, Tilly acknowledged, as she smoothed the fine-knit black jersey over the curve of her hip. The dress might be fitted, but it was also elegant, without any hint of tartiness or flamboyance. It was, in fact, the kind of dress one might spend a lifetime looking for and not find.

'With the right jewellery or a scarf it could be so versatile. See…' the shop assistant coaxed, bringing a chunky-looking costume jewellery necklace of black beads, glass drops and cream pearls tied with black silk ribbon and slipping it around Tilly's neck to show her what she meant. Then, putting the necklace on one side, she tied a brightly coloured silk scarf around Tilly's waist in the same way Tilly had noticed the elegant assistants in Sloane Street's Hermès shop wearing their scarves.

She needed something to wear for dinner at the hotel tonight, Tilly told herself, weakening.

Silas, who had been standing on the other side of the road watching her, reached into his pocket for his wallet. He had spent enough time on shopping missions with both his stepmother and his lovers to be able to recognise when a woman and an outfit were made for one another. If Tilly didn't go ahead and buy herself that dress in which she looked so intoxicatingly desirable then he would buy it for her. Even if he had to do so surreptitiously. He was, after all, her fiancé.

But why did he want her to have it? Because of the look of dazed disbelief he could see so plainly in her reflection as she stared at herself in the mirror, or because of what he was doing? Angrily he pushed aside his inner questioning of his motives. He had no option other than to use Tilly as the key to the locked door of Art Johnson's confidence.

'I'll take it,' Tilly told the waiting shop assistant.

'And the shoes?' the girl asked with a smile, indicating the pretty black satin evening shoes she had persuaded Tilly to try on with the dress.

Tilly looked down and then nodded her head, trying to control the almost dizzying sense of euphoria that was speeding through her. She had never thought of herself as the kind of woman who got excited about buying new clothes—but then she had never thought of herself as the kind of woman who got excited about the thought of having sex with a man she barely knew either, before Silas had come into her life.

Silas! He would be wondering where on earth she was. They had agreed to meet back at the restaurant where they had had lunch, and she still had another purchase to make. She gestured towards the pretty underwear set on display—a matching bra and boy-cut shorts in soft black and pale baby pink.

'It's another new range,' the saleswoman told her approvingly. 'It's been one of our most popular sellers.'

* * *

'Got everything you wanted?' Silas asked calmly when she met him outside the restaurant, as if she hadn't been half an hour longer than she'd said she'd be.

Silas had obviously been shopping himself, she noted, because he was carrying a very masculine-looking carrier bag.

'I didn't think the *maître d'* would be too pleased with me if I turned up for dinner tonight in chinos and a polo shirt,' he informed Tilly easily.

'I thought the same thing. Not about you. I meant about me,' Tilly said hurriedly. 'Well, I mean, I thought I'd better buy myself something to wear for dinner.' She was gabbling like a person on speed. Why? Surely not because just for a second, when she had watched the sales assistant packing up the rather more sexily cut bra than she would normally have chosen to wear and its accompanying briefs, she had had a sudden mental image of Silas removing her new dress to reveal them? And that, of course, was *not* the reason she had changed her mind about buying a pair of tights and had opted for hold-ups instead, was it?

It had stopped snowing while she had been in the shop, but now it had started again, falling so quickly and so thickly that she knew Silas was right when he told her to hold on to him. She still refused. 'I'll be perfectly all right.' What she really meant was that she would rather risk losing her balance in the snow than lose her heart in the intimacy of being physically close to him.

'Okay. Are you ready to go back to the hotel?' he asked. 'Or…?'

'I think we'd better, otherwise we're going to end up looking like walking snowmen.' She gave a small shiver, and then gasped as a crowd of young people came hurrying round the corner. One of them accidentally bumped into her, and Silas reacted immediately, grabbing her with both hands to keep her upright while she regained her balance.

Each time she was close to him the feelings she remembered from the time before came back—and more strongly, so that now her heart was racing, thudding clumsily into her chest wall and then bouncing off it, as though his body was a magnet to which it was helplessly drawn.

She lifted her head to thank him, but her gaze got as far as his mouth and then refused to go any further. It also refused to allow any of her other senses to override it. She was, Tilly recognised distantly, totally unable to do anything other than focus helplessly on Silas's mouth and long for the feel of it possessing her own. She had made her decision back in the suite. Had she? Was she sure about that? Given a second chance, would she make the same decision? Wasn't she already regretting the opportunity she had let slip from her through a fear that no longer seemed important compared with her desire? How had it come to this? That she should be so bewitched by the shape and cut of a pair of male lips to the extent that she yearned with everything in herself to reach out and touch them with her fingertip, to trace the shape of them and store it inside her memory.

The way Tilly was looking at him was making Silas aware of himself as a man in ways and with nuances he hadn't known were possible, he acknowledged. If she reached out and touched his mouth now, as she looked as though she was about to do, he knew that the touch of her fingertips against his lips would end up with the intimate caress of his mouth against the lips of her sex, by way of a hundred different kisses and touches, until his tongue probed for the hard bead of her clitoris so that he could bring her to orgasm and watch her pleasure filling her. He also knew that he couldn't let that happen. Not now that he had begun to see her as the woman she really was. How had it come to this? How had *he* come to this? How had it happened that he wanted her so badly and so completely?

'If we stay here much longer we'll freeze.' The harsh rejection in Silas's voice as he released her and turned away hurt far more than the icy sting of the blizzard-like snowfall, Tilly admitted, as he waited for her.

This time when he took a firm hold of her arm she didn't protest, but she did make sure that she kept as much space between them as she could—unlike the young couple she could see up ahead, with the girl tucked intimately into the boy's side, her head resting against his shoulder. Something inside her turned over painfully when they stopped walking, oblivious to everyone else, and the girl lifted her face to the boy's. Tilly heard her laugh softly as he brushed the snow from her face, and then stop laughing when he bent his head to kiss her. There was no need to guess or to question their feelings; they were enclosed in their own personal halo of delirious happiness and love.

CHAPTER TEN

'SO WHAT you're saying is that your responsibility
within the bank is to find ethical investment opportunities for your client base?'

They were in the elegant restaurant attached to the
hotel, having dinner. Tilly had told herself she was glad
when Silas had suggested that he get ready first and then
go down to the bar and wait for her there, so that she
would have the suite to herself to get changed in privacy.
It made so much more sense for them to do that. That
way there would be no awkwardness or embarrassment,
and no risk of any unwanted intimacy. And no risk either
of her making a fool of herself, as she had done earlier
in the street. She couldn't really blame Silas for taking
the steps he had. Not after the way she had stared at his
mouth as though…as though… Hurriedly she tried to
redirect her thoughts and answer Silas's question.

'Yes. My department is responsible for finding
ethical and ecologically safe investments for those
clients who specify them. We don't earn the huge
bonuses other sections of the City do, but I enjoy what
I do, and I enjoy teaching the young bankers in my

charge to think of ways in which to link profit to things that may benefit others.'

'Somehow I don't think you'd get someone like Art interested in your kind of portfolio,' Silas said cynically.

The waiter was refilling her wine glass and Tilly thanked him. She had been shocked when she had seen the prices on the menu, but Silas had told her not to worry because he had secured a deal for their room which had included dinner.

So far their meal had been delicious. After a seafood starter she had been tempted by the lamb for which the area was famous, and she had not been disappointed. She was beginning to feel slightly light-headed, though. The wine—her second glass—was obviously stronger than she had realised. Or was it Silas who was having such a dramatic effect on her? It was far too dangerous to take that line of thought any further. It would be safer to focus instead on the conversation Silas had insti- gated, even if right now recklessly she would much rather have been... What? In bed, with Silas making love to her? She shuddered so intensely that she had to put down her glass of wine.

'Cold?' Silas asked, frowning.

Hot was more like the truth, Tilly thought giddily. Hot for him, for his touch, his kiss, his body...

'If Art ever asks for my financial advice or input I'll be delighted to help him,' she told Silas, as lightly as she could. The truth was she suspected that Art, to judge from the interaction between the members of his family, probably had the kind of business ethics she most deplored. But her mother loved him, or at least believed that she did, and for her mother's sake she knew she would keep her own private opinions as exactly that.

'But you don't think that he will?' Silas knew that he was probing and pushing too hard—so hard, in fact, that it was almost as though he wanted to provoke an argument with Tilly. To offset the effect of seeing her in that dress that somehow managed to be both prim and incredibly sexy at the same time. He tried to ease his lower body into a more comfortable position. The table might be doing a good job of hiding the unwanted erection that was aching through him, but that didn't make its presence any easier for him to endure.

'You seem an unlikely candidate for ethical conservation,' he told Tilly abruptly, deciding to stop pushing her for a response to his earlier question.

Was there something in the air that was causing Silas to behave towards her so antagonistically? Tilly wondered miserably. Or was this simply his way of warning her that he wanted her to keep her distance from him?

'If that's some kind of dig at my mother,' she said, giving up on her earlier attempts to pretend that she wasn't aware that he was trying to needle her, 'just because she's fallen in love with Art it doesn't mean that she agrees with his opinions. As a matter of fact, my mother met my father at a fundraising event for Save the Children.' She wasn't going to tell him that her mother had attended the event thinking it was a charity ball. 'My father is a very committed conservationist; he and my stepmother run a small organic farm in Dorset.'

He could see her against that kind of background, Silas recognised. Free-range hens, a quartet of unruly children, and probably a couple of even more unruly goats. What locked his heart muscle, though, was that he could see those children with a mixture of their shared colouring and features. Him? With four children? He frowned at his wine glass. He was skating on very thin ice now, and what lay beneath it was deep and dark and had the potential to change his whole world. Was that what he wanted? Because if it wasn't he needed to banish those kind of thoughts right now, and put something in their place that would remind him of all the reasons why he needed to keep Tilly out of his life. Like how guilty he was going to feel when he saw the look in her eyes if she learned the truth. He couldn't afford that kind of emotional involvement with Tilly.

'Finished?'

Tilly nodded her head. She had been toying with the last dregs of the coffee they had been served half an hour ago for so long that she was not really surprised by Silas's question. But she was unnerved by it. By it and by him, she admitted as she got to her feet on legs that suddenly seemed unfamiliar and shaky.

With every step she took out of the restaurant and along the corridor to the lift, the shakiness and the mixture of longing and apprehension that accompanied it grew. In a few minutes she would be alone with Silas in their suite. And then she would be alone with him in its bed… And then…

Tilly had to have one of the smallest waists he had ever seen, Silas decided as he tried to distract his thoughts from what was really on his mind by mentally measuring it with his hands. And then, far more erotically, mentally allowing those hands to slide slowly down to the curve of her hips and up over her back, so that he could tug down the zip of her dress and encourage the fullness of her breasts to spill into his hands.

She and Silas were inside the lift. Tilly could hardly breathe she felt so on edge.

'I have to say that I find it hard to understand how someone who purports to be so keen on environmental ethics doesn't feel more inclined to take issue with the mindset of a man like Art Johnson—especially when her mother is going to marry him. Or does the fact that he is a billionaire excuse him?'

The lift had stopped, and Silas was getting out. Tilly was in shock from the unexpectedness and savagery of his verbal attack on her. She could feel the hot burn of tears at the backs of her eyes.

'No, it doesn't,' she told him fiercely as he opened the suite door for her. Walking past him, she went over to the window, unable to trust herself to look at him in case he saw how much his words had hurt her. 'I may not agree with his business ethics, but I have to think of my mother.' She spoke with her back to Silas, biting hard on the inside of her bottom lip as she felt the betraying tears escape and fill her eyes.

It had been hard for her the previous evening, not to speak out against some of the things that Art and his family had said, but she had warned herself that arguing with them would not change the way they thought, and could potentially make things even more difficult for her mother. She could end up being hurt.

But now *she* was the one being hurt, and the shock of discovering just how easily and lethally Silas's critical comments could hurt her was making it very difficult for her to find her normal calm resistance to the negative opinions of others. The problem was that Silas wasn't 'others'. Somehow he had managed to stride over the subtle defences she'd thought she had so securely in place and put himself in a position where she was vulnerable to him. Far too vulnerable. As her reaction now was proving.

Silas could see Tilly's reflection in the window. The sight of the tears she was battling to suppress caused him a physical pain that felt like a giant fist hammering into his heart. His reaction to her tears rocked his belief system on its axis, throwing up a whole new and unfamiliar emotional landscape within himself. He inspected it cautiously, whilst his heart hammered against his ribs. He scarcely recognised himself in what he had become. And he certainly didn't recognise the intensity of the emotions battling it out inside him. His guilt, his pain for Tilly's own pain, were raw open wounds into which he had poured acid. How could he have changed so dramatically and swiftly? He felt as though something beyond his own control had blasted a pathway within him, along which were travelling emotions and truths that only days ago had been wholly alien to the way he felt and thought.

He strode over to where Tilly was standing, driven there by him. She was so engrossed in trying to control her unwanted emotions that she didn't even realise he was there until she felt Silas's hand on her arm.

She stiffened immediately, in proud rejection of what she felt must be his pitying contempt for her vulnerability, and tried to turn away from him. But it was too late. He was turning her towards him. She'd thought she had herself under control, but a single tear betrayed her, rolling down her set face. She heard the muffled explosive sound Silas made, but she was battling too desperately to control her emotions to interpret it.

When he reached out and touched her face with his fingertips, catching the tear, she flinched and started to push him away, telling him fiercely, 'Don't patronise me. Just leave me alone.'

'Patronise you?' Silas groaned.

'Don't pity me, then, or feel sorry for me.'

'If I feel sorry for you it's because I'm burdening you with the weight of my need for you, Tilly.'

Tilly could hear his voice thicken with a mixture of pain and angry self-contempt that was so raw it made her throat ache. She looked up at him and saw the tension in his face. She could feel it too in the pressure of his hands on her arms, drawing her towards him.

'I want you with a compulsion I don't understand. You make me feel emotions I don't recognise. Being with you feels like walking through a landscape that is so alien to me I have no way of negotiating it, no inbuilt compass—nothing other than the need itself. You've made me a stranger to myself, Tilly. You've found something within me I didn't know was there.'

'I haven't done anything—' Tilly started to protest, but Silas stopped her, stealing the denial from her lips, tasting the *oh, please, yes* concealed within the *no* along with the salt of her tears as he kissed her and went on kissing her, until she was clinging to him, tears spilling from her open eyes, leaving them clear for him to read the emotions that were filling them.

'You know what's happening to us, don't you?' Silas demanded against her mouth as he kissed away the final tear.

What? Tilly wanted to beg him, but she was afraid to ask the question in case it spoiled the magic that had transported her to this new world, and broke the spell that was binding them together. So instead she whispered passionately to him. 'Show me! Don't tell me about it, Silas. Show it to me.'

CHAPTER ELEVEN

A HEARTBEAT later—or was it a lifetime?—Silas was undressing her in between fiercely possessive and demanding kisses, and she was undressing him. The room was full of the sound of rustling clothes, soft sighs and hungry kisses, as fabric slithered and slipped to the floor, and eager hands moved over even more eager flesh.

Somehow Silas had managed to remove all of his own clothes, as well as most of hers. Now, as he held her against him and slid his hands from her waist down over her hips, past her bottom and then up again under the fluted legs of her pretty new briefs, to cup her warm flesh and press her into his body, her own hand was free to give in to the unfamiliarly wanton demands of her emotions and explore the shape and texture of his rigid erection.

'Don't—' Tilly heard him protest thickly. But it was too late for him to deny the effect her touch was having on him. She had felt it in the savagely intense shudder of pleasure that had gripped and convulsed him.

His reaction gave her the courage to explore more intimately and to give way to the erotic urgings of her own senses. It both excited and aroused her to see and feel him responding so helplessly to her, so possessed by desire and need that he couldn't control the visibly physical pleasure she was giving him.

She could feel the heavy slam of his heart against her own body, its arousal mirrored by the uneven sound of his breathing in her ear as he held her and caressed her with growing passion. But when he stroked a shockingly erotic caressing fingertip down her back, beyond the base of her spine, it was her turn to moan in fevered arousal and melt into him.

Immediately she curled her hand around him, wanting to reciprocate the pleasure he was giving her, but Silas stopped her, telling her hotly, 'I can't let you do that. If I do…' She felt him shudder, and then shuddered herself when he told her, 'I want you so damn much that I can't trust myself not to come too soon if you touch me.'

'That works both ways,' Tilly protested breathlessly, squirming with heated pleasure under his exploratory touch, shocked by her own verbal boldness and yet at the same time acknowledging how much it meant to her to be able to be so open and natural with him about her sexual responsiveness.

How tame her imaginings in the shop as she had bought the new underwear seemed now, compared to the reality of what Silas's touch was actually doing to her. And as for her not touching him. How could she not when her need to do so was growing by the heartbeat? When she ached so badly to stroke her fingertips along the full length of his erection? She wanted to know every single nuance of the texture of its flesh. She wanted to

explore the inviting slick suppleness of its pulse-racing
male rhythm beneath her caress. She wanted…

She shuddered wildly under the erotic influence of her
own thoughts, and then more wildly still when Silas
stroked slowly all the way up her spine. His tongue-tip
prised her lips apart and she admitted it eagerly, giving
herself over completely to the thrusting passion of his
kiss. His hand cupped her breast, and the heat inside her
exploded in a firework display of shimmering pleasure.
She caught his hand and pressed it fiercely against her
breast as she moved rhythmically against him, every single
part of her gripped by and focused on her longing for him.

Somehow, at some deep level, he had known it would
be like this between them, Silas admitted as he lost the
battle to control his response to Tilly's arousal. What she
was doing to him was causing what felt like a huge unstoppable wave of aching intensity and need to power
through him. He knew that he was helplessly unable to
stop himself from succumbing to it and to her. He knew
that he didn't even want to stop himself. And he knew
that both of them were going to be overwhelmed by it,
swept along together with only each other to cling to as
the full power of what was happening to them possessed
them. It was too late to stop it now, even if he wanted
to. The openly urgent rhythmic movement of Tilly's
body against his own was driving him over the edge of
his self control.

'I want you,' he cried out in a raw voice. 'I want you
more than I have ever wanted any other woman or will
ever want any other woman ever again.' He heard the
words, thick and half-crazed with emotion, being

dragged from his throat, and he knew that they were true. He could see shock, delight and yearning in Tilly's eyes. He took her mouth in a kiss of fierce, consuming possession, picking her up and carrying her over to the bed.

Tilly moaned when Silas put her down, unable to bear even for a handful of seconds not to have him touching her or to be touching him.

She could see him kneeling over her, and she watched as he bent his head and traced a line of kisses down her body. His hands cupped and held her hips, and she shuddered when he anointed her hipbones in turn with slow, tender kisses and then moved lower. She could feel his fingers sliding through her ready wetness as he deliberately parted the outer lips of her sex. She could see him looking at her as he touched her.

Her flesh was flushed and swollen with arousal, making Silas ache to taste her, to feel the sharp shudders of her orgasm against his mouth. He wanted to slide his fingers through the wetness of her sex, between the fullness of the labia, and then part them so that he could stroke his tongue along the path made by his fingertip. He wanted to take the small responsive bead of her clitoris and caress it until he had brought her to the edge he had already reached, and then he wanted to slide slowly and deeply the full length of her, so that he was filling her, and she was holding him, and her flesh was taking him and using him for its pleasure, making that pleasure his own.

What he wanted, he recognised, was a degree of intimacy with her, a connection with her, a *completeness* with her that was outside any sexual experience he had ever had previously, or imagined he could want. Because what was happening for him wasn't something he only wanted to experience on a sexual level. What he wanted from her went way beyond that into a realm he had always thought more akin to make-believe and fiction than reality.

Tilly gave a small aching moan. Silas bent his head and parted her labia, stroking his tongue-tip the full length of her sex.

It was more than Tilly could stand. She cried out and dug her nails into his shoulders, clinging desperately to the edge of her own self-control.

'No,' she told him fiercely. 'Not yet. Not until you're inside me. That's how I want it to be, Silas.' Determined tears sprang into her eyes as she looked at him. 'It has to be both of us. I want *you*, Silas,' she insisted. 'I want you *inside* me. I want that so much.'

She felt him move, heard the brief rustle of a wrapper being opened and then discarded, and then blissfully he was holding her, kissing her, sliding his hands down to her hips and lifting her. Hungrily Tilly wrapped her legs around him, arching up eagerly to meet his first slow, sweet thrust into her.

Silas shuddered as he felt her muscles grip and hold him. Even this was a new kind of pleasure. Where he had previously known experience, with Tilly there was freshness, an untutored naturalness that was so much more erotic. Her body welcomed him joyfully and eagerly, offering all its pleasures to him, wanting him to take them, wanting him to thrust deeper and harder until he fitted her so well that they might almost have been one flesh.

Was *this* what love was? Silas wondered. Was *this* why he had always refused to believe in it before? Because he had been waiting for Tilly?

She cried out his name, her flesh gripping him, pulsing fiercely.

Through the fierce contractions of her orgasm Tilly felt Silas's final deep thrust as he joined her in the soaring ecstasy that was binding them both together and taking them to infinity.

Silas moved away from the window and looked towards the bed. It was nearly two o'clock in the morning, but he hadn't been able to sleep. He hadn't been able to do anything since they had made love except go over and over inside his head the now familiar journey that had led from his first meeting with Tilly to this. He felt as though his whole life had suddenly veered off course and gone out of his control. How was it possible for him to have changed so much so quickly? How was it possible for him to feel so differently?

He made his way back to the bed. Not being within touching distance of Tilly made him feel as though a part of him was missing, that he was somehow incomplete.

As he slid back the duvet he realised that she was awake.

'You know what's going on, don't you?'

'I think so, and it isn't something I wanted to happen,' Tilly answered, trying to make her voice sound light and careless but hearing it crack as easily as he'd cracked apart the protective casing she had put around her heart.

'Falling in love wasn't exactly on my agenda either,' Silas told her dryly.

'Perhaps if we try really hard we can stop it.'

There was enough light from the moon for her to see the cynically amused look Silas was giving her. 'Like we've already tried once tonight, you mean?' he derided, causing Tilly to give a small shiver.

'Silas, I don't want to love you. I don't want to love anyone. Loving someone means being hurt when they stop loving you.'

'I won't stop loving you, Tilly. I couldn't.' It was, Silas recognised, the truth.

'This is crazy,' Tilly whispered, but she knew that her protests meant nothing and that her own emotions were overwhelming her.

'Love is crazy. It's well known that it's a form of madness.'

'Maybe it's just the sex?' she suggested. 'I mean…'

Silas shook his head.

'No, it isn't just the sex,' he assured her. 'You can trust me on that.'

'There can't be love without trust. And honesty,' Tilly whispered solemnly.

This was all so new to her, and so very precious and vulnerable. Acknowledging her feelings felt like holding a new baby. Her heart did a slow high-dive. A baby. Silas's baby.

Trust and honesty. Silas reached for Tilly. He was going to have to tell her the truth about himself, and his reason for taking Joe's place.

But not tonight. Not now, when all he wanted to do

was hold her and kiss her and feel the responsive silky heat of her body, taking him and holding him, while he showed her his love.

Tilly glanced anxiously at Silas. He had hardly spoken to her as he drove them back to the castle, and whatever he was thinking his thoughts didn't look as though they were happy ones.

'Second thoughts?' she asked him lightly.

'About the wisdom of returning to the castle? Yes. About us? No,' Silas answered her truthfully. 'What about you?'

'I rather think I've made it obvious how I feel.' They had made love again before breakfast, and now her body ached heavily and pleasurably with an unfamiliar, satisfied lassitude. She touched the comfortable weight of the ring on her left hand and then coloured self-consciously when she saw the gleam in Silas's eyes.

'I wish we could go back to London and get to know one another properly, instead of having to go back to the castle,' Tilly admitted. 'And I can't help worrying about my mother. It's obvious that Art's family doesn't want him to marry her.'

'My guess is that if they don't manage to break them up before they marry, they'll make her life hell afterwards. To be honest, I'm surprised she can't see that for herself.'

'Ma only sees what she wants to see,' Tilly told him. 'She can be very naive like that. I just don't want her to be hurt. When her last marriage broke up she was desperately unhappy. It was the first time she hadn't been the one to end things. If Art decides not to go

ahead with the wedding, I don't know what it will do
to her. Ma's one of those women who doesn't feel she's
a viable human being unless she's got a man in her
life.' Tilly smiled ruefully. 'That's probably more than
you want to know. I'm sorry. But this is the first time
I've felt close enough to someone to be able to be talk
honestly about how I feel without thinking I'm being
disloyal.'

'What about your father?'

'Oh, I love Dad, of course. But he disapproves of Ma,
and they don't see eye to eye. I'd feel I was letting her
down if I told him how much I worry about her, and
why. They were so unsuited—but that's the trouble
about falling in love, isn't it? You don't always know
until it's too late that you aren't compatible. And sometimes even when you are it isn't enough.'

'Sometimes a couple meet and are fortunate enough
to recognise that what they share goes far beyond mere
compatibility,' Silas told her. 'Like soul mates.'

Tilly felt a fine thrill of the most intense emotion she
had ever experienced run through her as he turned to
look at her.

It moved her beyond words that Silas should say
such a thing to her, almost as though he already knew
how vitally important it was to her that the love growing
between them should be perfect in every way.

And yet the closer they got to the castle the more she
sensed that Silas seemed to be distancing himself from her,
retreating to a place where he didn't want her to follow
him. His answers to her efforts to make conversation
became terse and unencouraging, giving her the message

that he preferred the privacy of his own silence to any attempt to create a more intimate mood between them.

She told herself that she was being over-sensitive, and that what to her felt like a distancing tactic was probably nothing more than a desire to concentrate on his driving.

The closer they got to the castle the more Silas recognised the dual agenda he would now be operating under. From the outset he had been totally clear to himself about his purpose in stepping into Joe's shoes. He had told himself that deceiving a young woman he didn't know, while regrettable, would be justified by the exposure that would be the end result of his research. But he hadn't anticipated then that the impossible would happen and he would fall in love with Tilly.

Now that he had, his deceit had taken on a much more personal turn. He was now in effect lying by default to the woman he loved. He was lying to her about his real identity, the real nature of his work, the fact that he was using her as a cover to screen his own agenda.

For each and every one of those lies he had an explanation he believed she would understand and accept— after all, he had not set out with the deliberate intention of deceiving *her*. But the highly emotionally charged atmosphere of the castle, where they would be surrounded by Art and his family, was not, in Silas's opinion, the best place for him to admit totally what he had done, or his reasons—even though normally his first priority would have been to tell her the truth. For that he felt he— they—needed real privacy, and the security of being able to discuss the issue without any onlookers.

Knowing Tilly as he believed he did know her now, he couldn't ignore the instinct that told him that if his suspicions about Art's involvement in Jay Byerly's underhand dealings were confirmed, Tilly would at the very least want to warn her mother about the true nature of the man she was planning to marry. And if she did that, Silas thought it entirely likely that Annabelle would go straight to Art and beg him to deny the accusations being levelled against him.

Silas knew the last thing his publishers would want was to be threatened with a lawsuit by some expensive lawyer before his book was even written. And he certainly had no intention of putting himself in a position where the truths he had already worked so long to make public were silenced before they had been heard.

Tilly would, of course, be hurt, and no doubt angry when he told her the truth on their return to London, but he felt sure that once he had explained the reasons he had not been able to confide in her she would understand and forgive him. But while logically it made sense not to say anything to Tilly yet, loving her as he did meant that he wanted to share his every thought and feeling with her. It was for her own sake that he could not do it, he reminded himself. She was already doing enough worrying about her mother, a woman who in Silas's opinion ought to recognise how truly fortunate she was to have such a wonderful daughter.

Something was on Silas's mind, Tilly decided. In another few minutes they would be reaching the castle and the opportunity to ask him would be gone. She took a deep breath and said quietly, 'You look rather preoccupied. Is something wrong?'

Her awareness of his concern caused Silas to turn his head and look at her, and to go on looking at her. 'Yes,' he told her truthfully, adding, not quite so truthfully, 'The closer we get to the castle the more I wish I could snatch you up and take you somewhere we could really be on our own. There's so much I want to learn about you, Tilly. So much I want to know about you and so much I want you to know about me. And, selfishly, I want you all to myself so that we can do that. I've never thought of myself as a possessive man, but now I'm beginning to realise how little I really know myself—because where you are concerned I feel very unwilling to share you with anyone else.'

'Don't say any more,' Tilly begged. 'Otherwise I'll be pleading with you to turn around and drive back to the hotel.'

'The first thing I intend to do when we reach the castle is take you upstairs to our room and make love to you,' Silas told her thickly.

'I rather think that we'll be called upon to explain ourselves to Cissie-Rose first, and apologise for putting her to the trouble of having to drive back alone,' Tilly warned him wryly. 'She won't be happy to see us together, Silas.' That was the closest Tilly felt she wanted to go in telling Silas that she was aware that Cissie-Rose's interest in him was sexual and predatory.

'We don't owe her any explanations. She chose to leave in a strop and abandon us because I'd shown her that I wasn't interested in what she was offering.'

Tilly heard the hardness in his voice and winced a little.

Silas saw her small movement and shook his head. 'Don't waste your sympathy on her, Tilly. She doesn't deserve it.'

'I can't blame her for wanting you when I want you so much myself,' Tilly told him honestly.

Silas drove in to the courtyard, turning to look at her as he stopped the four-wheel drive to say softly, 'Promise me something, Tilly?'

Something? Her heart was so filled with love and happiness she wanted to promise him *everything*. 'What?' she asked instead.

'Promise me that you'll always be as honest and open with me as you are now. I love it when you tell me that you want me. And, just as soon as we get the chance, I intend to show you just how much.'

'Yes, poor Tilly needs to go and lie down. She started with a headache on the way back—didn't you, darling?'

Tilly shot Silas a reproving look, but he was too busy convincing her mother that she wasn't going to be well enough to emerge from their bedroom for at least a couple of hours.

'Well, I'm sure that Art and the boys won't mind keeping you company in the bar, Silas,' Annabelle told him, before turning to Tilly to say reproachfully, 'I wanted to show you my dress and the sketches Lucy has done for the flowers. Perhaps if you just took a couple of aspirin you wouldn't need to lie down...?'

Tilly wavered. She was so used to answering her mother's needs when she was with her, and Annabelle was looking at her like a disappointed child deprived of a special treat, making her feel wretchedly guilty. But Silas had reached for her hand and was very discreetly, but very sensually, caressing the pulse-point on the inside of her wrist. Her desire for him was turning her bones and her conscience to jelly.

She looked at her mother and lifted her free hand to her forehead. 'Silas is right, Ma.' she told her. 'I really do need to lie down.'

Five minutes later, when Silas locked the door to their room and leaned on it for good measure, taking her in his arms and drawing her very deliberately into the cradle of his hips so that she could feel his arousal, Tilly shook her head at him.

'I don't believe I've just done that. I've never lied to my mother before...'

'When there's a conflict of interests I'm delighted that you opted to choose me,' Silas teased her.

Tilly didn't respond to his smile as readily as he had expected. 'Loving someone shouldn't mean abandoning your own moral code. Telling my mother I had a headache when I haven't...'

'What would you have preferred to do? Tell her that we wanted to make love?'

Tilly exhaled in defeat. 'No,' she admitted. 'But it still doesn't make me feel good.'

'Maybe this will, though.'

Silas was teasing her with small, unsatisfying kisses that made her reach up for him and pull his head down to hers...

* * *

'You remember that TV show *Dallas*? Well, I'm telling you that was nothing compared with the reality of how the oil business was in my father's time. I started working in the family business straight out of school. My father said that was the best way to learn.' Art reached for his drink and emptied his glass, demanding, 'Come on Dwight, I thought you were playing bartender. Set them up again, will you?'

It was almost dinnertime, and to judge from his slurred voice and red face Silas suspected that Art had been drinking for the best part of the afternoon. He had greeted them affably enough when they had finally come downstairs dressed for dinner, and had then begun reminiscing about the early days of his family's oil business. Silas, sensing that this might be the breakthrough he needed, had encouraged him to keep talking by asking him judicially timed questions. He suspected from the bored expressions on the faces of Art's sons-in-law that they had heard all Art's stories before.

'I imagine you must have known all the big players in the old oil world?' Silas suggested casually.

'Sure did,' Art agreed boastfully. 'I knew 'em all.'

'Even Jay Byerly?'

'Yep. He was some guy, was Jay. He had a handle on just about everything that was goin' on.'

'I know that the shareholders voted him off the board of his own company in the end, but no one ever said why.' While they had been talking Silas had filled up Art's glass, making sure that he didn't fill up his own.

'For goodness' sake, no one wants to hear all those

old stories all over again. Poor Annabelle will be so bored she'll change her mind about wanting to marry you if you don't change the subject,' Cissie-Rose exclaimed with acid sweetness, sweeping into the room in a dress that was more suitable for a full-scale diplomatic reception rather than what was supposed to be a quiet family dinner. 'You really mustn't encourage him, Silas,' she added, giving Silas and Tilly the kind of posed and patently artificial smile that showed off her excellent teeth and the cold enmity in her eyes. 'Are you really sure you're over your headache, Tilly?' she asked. 'Only, if you don't mind my saying so, you really don't look well. There's nothing like a headache for making a person look run-down.'

'Annabelle, why don't you girls go and talk wedding talk in one of the other rooms?' Art suggested.

Tilly suspected that he had been enjoying basking in the attention of Silas's good-mannered social questions, and that he wasn't very pleased about Cissie-Rose's interruption. Although he wasn't exactly slurring his words, he had had what to Tilly seemed to be rather a lot to drink. Her doubts about the wisdom of her mother marrying him were growing by the hour.

'Silas is just being polite, Dad. Why on earth should he be interested in what happened over thirty years ago? Unless, of course, someone's thinking of making a film of Jay's life and you're hoping to be invited to try for the lead part, Silas.'

Cissie-Rose's claws were definitely unsheathed now, Tilly recognised. The other woman's cattiness made her want to place herself physically in front of Silas to protect him. Although the thought of Silas needing anyone defending him, least of all her, made her smile to herself.

'Ignore her, Silas,' Art instructed, giving his daughter a baleful look. 'You're right. There was a scandal Jay was involved in that threatened to blow him and the business sky-high. Luckily a few of the big old boys called in some of their debts and managed to get it all quietened down. Jay had been buying up oil leases and then—'

'Daddy, I don't think you should say any more,' Cissie-Rose interrupted her father sharply. 'It's all in the past now, anyway. Annabelle, I have to say that those sketches you were showing me for the flowers are just so pretty.'

It wasn't worth pushing Art any further, Silas decided. There would still be plenty of opportunity for him to pick up their conversation between now and the wedding on New Year's Eve. All he had to do was to make sure he mixed Art a jugful of extra-strong whiskey sour.

CHAPTER TWELVE

'CHRISTMAS EVE and I've already had the best present I could ever have,' Tilly told Silas emotionally.

They were in their bedroom getting ready for dinner, having spent the afternoon outside in the snowy garden playing with the children. Or rather Tilly had played with them while Silas had watched.

'It's kind of you to be so patient with Art, Silas. His face positively lights up when you walk in and let him tell his stories. He must be exaggerating some of them, though.' Tilly gave a small shiver. 'It seems wrong that men like Art should have had that kind of power and abused it the way they did.'

'Things are different now,' Silas agreed. 'But as for Art exaggerating what happened in the past...' He paused, all too aware of what he knew that Tilly did not. 'If anything,' he told her heavily, 'I suspect that Art is using rather a lot of whitewash to conceal some of what went on. Of course most of those who perpetrated the worst of the crimes are no longer around, but that doesn't mean the world doesn't need to know about them.'

'I'm so lucky to have met you,' Tilly said spontaneously. As he looked at her Silas felt his heart turn over inside his chest slowly and achingly as his love for her overwhelmed him. He reached for her hand, entwining his fingers with hers. He still found it hard at times to come to terms with the speed with which his life had changed so dramatically. And all because of one person.

'You're a saint for putting up with everything the way you have.'

'A saint! That's the last thing I am. In fact...' He had to tell her the truth, Silas decided, even though he knew that in doing so he would be subjecting her to divided loyalties. He was finding the deceit that he knew lay between them increasingly burdensome, plus he wanted to share his work with her now that he recognised that she was the most vital and important part of his life. Not involving her in what he was thinking and planning somehow felt like being deprived of the ability to work the way he wanted to do. He wanted her input and her support. He wanted her to know, to understand, and to accept what he was doing and why. He wanted, Silas recognised, to lay not just his heart but his very soul at her feet, so that she could know his every strength and vulnerability.

'Tilly, there's something—' he began, and then had to stop when there was a brief knock on their bedroom door and they both heard Tilly's mother calling out anxiously.

'Are you ready yet?'

'Almost,' Tilly answered, giving Silas a rueful look as she slipped from his arms and went reluctantly to open the door.

'Oh, you must hurry, then—because Cissie-Rose has

just rung through to our room to say she wants us all downstairs now, because she's got something important to say. Do you think she could possibly be expecting another baby, Tilly? Wouldn't that be lovely? Oh, you both look fine. Come on, we may as well go down together. Art's already down…'

'You said we'd have the buffet at seven,' Tilly reminded her. 'It's not even six yet.' She had been looking forward to having some private time with Silas before they had to join the others, but it was obvious that her mother wasn't going to leave without them.

He would tell Tilly later, when they came back up to their room, Silas promised himself. Preferably in bed, when he was holding her in his arms.

The familiar ache of his body for hers began to speed through him.

As they descended the stairs Tilly could hear the sound of familiar Christmas carols filling the hallway.

'I remembered to bring a CD of carols with me,' Annabelle told Tilly proudly. 'You used to love them so much when you were a little girl.'

The children were all in one of the smaller salons, watching television and trying to guess what Santa would be bringing them.

'There you are, Silas.' Art's voice boomed out. 'You're already a couple of drinks down on us.'

Tilly shook her head when Dwight offered to make her a drink, knowing from previous experience how strong it would be.

'So what's this news Cissie-Rose has for us, Dwight?' Annabelle asked excitedly. 'And where is she?'

'She's upstairs, taking a call.'

'If I know Cissie she's probably checking up on Hal to make sure he's got the wording of our pre-nup right,' Art joked.

Tilly looked anxiously at her mother, worrying about how she might be taking this less than romantic comment from her husband-to-be.

'Sorry to have to keep you all waiting, but I just wanted to make sure I had all my facts right before I came down.' Cissie-Rose paused dramatically in the doorway, and then slowly made her way over to Tilly. 'That's a mighty pretty engagement ring you're wearing, Tilly. Pity that neither it nor your engagement is real, though. In fact there isn't much that *is* real about you—is there, Silas? You see, Silas here isn't Tilly's fiancé at all. Are you, Silas?'

White-faced, Tilly reached for Silas's hand and drew on the warm comfort of its reassuring grip. This was awful—dreadful. And she could hardly bear to look at her mother. There was no doubt in Tilly's mind that this was Cissie-Rose's revenge on them for Silas's rejection. But Tilly still had no idea how on earth she had found out about them.

'Tilly thinks that Silas is an out-of-work actor she hired to come here and pretend to be her fiancé, so that we'd think she was a clean-living girl who was about to get married. Poor Tilly,' Cissie mocked, giving her a malicious smile. 'I really do feel sorry for you. Look at you, clinging on to him. How sweet. But I'm afraid there's worse to come. Isn't there, *Silas*? You see, Silas has been deceiving us all about the true purpose of his being here.'

'You don't understand,' Tilly protested fiercely. 'Yes, I admit that I originally hired Silas as an escort to accompany me here. But since we've been here…' She turned to Silas and gave him an anxious, pleading look that twisted his heart with pain.

'Since you've been here *what*?' Cissie-Rose taunted her triumphantly. 'He's taken you to bed and told you he wants you? Poor Tilly. I'm afraid it is *you* who don't understand. Because if that is the case then he's been lying to you as well as to us, and he's made a complete fool of you. There's only one thing he wants—only one reason he's come here—and it's got nothing to do with wanting you, has it, Silas? Or should I call you James? You see, everyone, this is *James* Silas Connaught.'

Tilly, who was battling to take in what Cissie-Rose was saying, saw the swift look of recognition Art and Dwight were exchanging, and something as cold as death started to creep through her veins like poison.

'Yes,' Cissie-Rose confirmed. 'The journalist who has been trying to get an interview with Dad for the best part of a year. That's right, isn't it, Silas? He must have thought it was his lucky day when you gave him the opportunity to use you, Tilly. *Of course* he took you to bed. He's known for being a journalist who always gets his story—aren't you, Silas?'

'No, that's not true. It can't be! There's been some mistake,' Tilly protested, white-faced. 'Please tell me this isn't true,' Tilly begged, turning to face Silas.

'Yes, there has been a *very* big mistake.' Cissie-Rose laughed unkindly. 'And you're the one who's made it, Tilly. Of course I saw right through you in a minute,

Silas,' she said. 'Which is why I've had Dad's lawyers doing some digging on you.'

'Silas?' Tilly begged. Why wasn't he denying what Cissie-Rose had said?

'Tilly, I can explain everything,' Silas told her fiercely.

Tilly stared at him. Where was the denial she had expected to hear? She couldn't bear to see what she was seeing in Silas's eyes. She wanted to run and hide herself away from the pain of it. She could feel herself starting to tremble violently inside. Nausea gripped her stomach, and a pain like none she had ever previously known tore at her.

'How could you? *How could you?*' She was still holding onto Silas's hand, but now she released it, not caring what anyone else might think as she ran towards the door and headed for the stairs.

She had to escape from their mockery and contempt. She had to escape from her own pain and humiliation. But most of all she had to escape from Silas. She wanted to lock herself away somewhere private and dark while she tried to come to terms with what she had just learned. She would have defended Silas against all accusations Cissie-Rose had made against him, just as she would have given him her trust and her belief unquestioningly if he had denied what Cissie-Rose had said. But instead he had shown her with his plea, and more tellingly with the look in his eyes, that everything Cissie-Rose had accused him of was true.

She could hardly think or reason logically for the pain that was swamping her. What a fool she had been— to believe his lies about falling in love with her. And no wonder he had been so keen to talk with Art. A mirth-less smile twisted her mouth. How ironic it was that she had been stupid enough, dense enough, besotted enough to praise him for his kindness. The pain tightened its grip, raking her emotions raw.

Silas caught up with her outside their bedroom door, refusing to let go of her when she tried to drag her wrist free of his imprisoning grip, bundling her inside the room and closing the door, enclosing them in what was for Tilly its tainted and treacherous intimacy.

'Let go of me,' she demanded.

'Not yet. Not until you've listened to me. I know you're upset, and I understand how you must feel—'

'How dare you say that to me? You know nothing. If you did you would never… You used me. You lied to me. You pretended to care about me when all the time—'

'Tilly, no!'

'So it's not true? You're not this James Connaught?'

Silas's mouth compressed. Why the hell hadn't he followed his own instinct and his heart and told Tilly the truth earlier? 'I *do* write as James Connaught, yes.'

'And you also moonlight as an out-of-work-actor, hiring yourself out as an escort?'

The bitterness in Tilly's voice made him want to hold her as tightly as he could, until he had absorbed her pain into himself.

'No,' he told her quietly. 'It was my half-brother Joe who was supposed to come here with you. He asked me to stand in for him because he'd had an accident. At first I refused, but then when he mentioned Art—'

'You changed your mind.'

It wasn't in Silas's nature to lie, especially not to someone who was as important to him as Tilly. 'Yes.'

'And when you accused me of hiring you for sex you were just testing the water, were you? Seeing how far you'd have to go to get what you wanted?'

'That had nothing to do with my hope that I could get closer to Art. I was concerned for Joe. He's young and impressionable, and I wasn't convinced that the outfit he was working for was as above board as he claimed.'

Silas took a deep breath. What he had to say to her now was going to be the hardest thing he had ever had to say. He knew his honesty was going to hurt her, but the truth had to be told, so that they could move on from today.

'That first night here, when you threatened to end our "engagement", I did think in terms of establishing a relationship with you to ensure that I stayed.'

'You used me,' Tilly accused him, her voice flat and devoid of the emotion she was desperately afraid might overwhelm her. 'You deliberately lied to me, pretended that you were falling in love with me, when all the time I meant nothing to you.'

'No, that's not true.'

'You're right,' Tilly agreed. 'The fact that I was falling in love with you *was* quite important to you. After all, it made everything so much easier for you, didn't it?'

'That's not what I meant and you know it. You can't really believe that I would lie to you about loving you?'

'Why not? You've lied to me about everything else, haven't you? If you'd really cared about me, Silas, you would have told me the truth.'

'I intended to.'

Tilly laughed mirthlessly. 'When? After you'd got your story?'

'I should have told you. I admit that. But I felt... I didn't want to risk spoiling what was happening between us.'

Tilly could hardly bear to listen to him. The rawness in his voice made her eyes sting with fierce tears. He sounded so genuine, but of course he wasn't.

'As a matter of fact, I was about to tell you earlier—just before your mother interrupted us.'

Tilly frowned, her heart missing a heavy beat as it clung desperately to the fragile hope of his words. She remembered that he had been on the verge of saying something to her. She ached with longing to be able to believe him, but she wasn't going to let herself give in to that weakness. Not a second time. Her was using her, manipulating her vulnerable emotions, just as he had done all along.

'If you had really loved me you would have been honest with me right from the start.'

'Life is not like that, Tilly. I didn't know I was going to fall in love with you. I didn't even realise at first that was what I was doing. By the time I did, it was too late. You'd already accepted me as what you believed I was. And, rightly or wrongly, I felt that our love was still too new and too fragile to bear the weight of the kind of revelations I would have had to make. But that doesn't mean that I didn't plan to tell you everything. I did. I love you, Tilly, and you love me. Surely that love—our love—deserves a chance?'

Tilly gave him a cynical look. 'You really think you can go on lying to me, don't you? I may have been stupid enough to fall for your lies the first time round, Silas, but I'm not stupid enough to fall for them again now. You don't love me. And as for me loving you—the man I thought I loved doesn't exist, does he? You've still got the hire car here. I think the best thing you can do now is pack your things and leave. There's nothing here for you now.'

Silas felt the shock of her rejection slicing through him, snapping the chain with which he had been leashing his own emotions. 'Nothing? Then what exactly is *this*, then?' he demanded.

He was still holding her wrist, and so he was able to catch her off balance enough to drag her into his arms and then cover the furious protest she made with the fierce heat of his mouth.

She wanted to resist him. She fought to do so. But something stronger than pride or pain was wrenching control of her responses from her, so that instead of closing into a tight, hard line against him her lips were opening under his, to return the full fury of his anguished passion. Somehow it was as though this was the only way she could show him the damage he had done—by violating the memory of what he had told her was love but what she now who knew was a lie.

This was all they had shared. Not love, not tenderness, and most certainly not the kind of almost spiritual emotional bond she had so stupidly deluded herself into thinking they had. Just this ferally savage physical need, poisoned with bitterness and deceit. Let it have its way, then; let it take her. Let it take them both and destroy itself as it did so, Tilly decided furiously.

Somehow he would break down Tilly's anger and re-sistance. Somehow he would find the right way to show her that their love was strong enough to survive the damage he had inflicted on it and on her. He had to find it. Because he couldn't endure the thought of losing her, Silas acknowledged as he tried to gentle the fierceness of his need and bring tenderness back into their intimacy.

He wanted to take Tilly and show her everything he felt—his remorse and regret, his pain and despair, his sorrow that he had hurt her and his reasons for having done so. He wanted to hold her in his arms, body to body, skin to skin, and to kiss the tears from her eyes. He wanted to beg for her forgiveness and to heal the wounds he had inflicted with the salve of his true love. He wanted to wipe away everything that had gone wrong and give them a fresh start. But most of all he wanted her to know that his love for her was hers for ever.

And this wasn't the way to show her that, Silas warned himself as he fought against succumbing to the drug of his own need. If he took her now, like this, when she was acting out of anger and bitterness, he would be damaging them both. He knew that, and yet at the same time he ached to take the chance that somehow he could mend things between them by showing her physically how much she meant to him.

The fire was dying out of her anger now, leaving behind a void that was filling with pain. Tilly shivered in Silas's hold.

'Tilly…'

'Just go, Silas. Please, just go.'

CHAPTER THIRTEEN

'SILAS rang again this morning.'

Tilly heard her father's words but she didn't give any sign. It was over two months since she had last seen Silas. Two months during which he had attempted with relentless determination to make contact with her, and she had refused to let him with equal determination.

He had even tracked her down here, to her father's farm in Dorset, where she had come for a much-needed break not so much from her job as from Silas himself, and the ghost of their love.

'He's sent you this,' her father continued, holding out to her a large A4-sized parcel. 'It's the typescript for his book. He asked me to tell you that he wants you to be the first to read it.'

Tilly's mouth compressed. Somehow or other Silas seemed to have managed to persuade her father to act as his supporter, even though she had told her father what he had done.

'Tilly, I know what he did was very wrong, but why don't you give him a chance to explain and make amends?'

'Why should I?'

'Do you really need me to tell you that?' Her father asked dryly. 'You still love him, no matter how much you might try to convince yourself that you don't, and from what he's said to me he certainly loves you.'

'It's because of what he did that Art broke off his engagement to Ma,' Tilly pointed out.

Her father raised his eyebrows. 'If you ask me, your mother had a lucky escape. *She* certainly seems to think so. And she hasn't lost much time in finding someone to replace Art, has she?'

Tilly gave a small uncomfortable wriggle. It was true that her mother was now blissfully in love with a new man—and, although Tilly wasn't about to say so to her father, Annabelle too had been doing her utmost to persuade Tilly to give Silas a second chance.

'We're going out now,' her father said. 'See you later.'

Tilly was trying very hard not to look at the manuscript on the table in front of her. She didn't even know why she had removed the packaging. But she had, and now, like Pandora with the lid of the box lifted, she was unable to control her own curiosity to see what lay inside.

Pinned to the first page of the manuscript was a letter addressed to her. She wasn't going to read it. She was going to tear it up, as she had all the other letters Silas had sent her. But somehow her fingers weren't obeying her brain, because the letter was open and unfolded, and Silas's firm, masculine handwriting was dancing on the page in front of her through the sudden surge of tears filming her eyes.

How could she still love a man who had already

shown her so devastatingly that his career would always come first and that in order for it to do so he was prepared to lie to her? What kind of future would they have if she gave in and let Silas back into her life? Did she really need to ask herself that? It would be a future in which she and their children could never completely trust in Silas's love and honesty; a future in which they could never totally rely on him to be there for them. The future, in fact, that she had always feared.

Her fingers trembled as she held the letter. Why bother to add to her own pain by reading it? But it was too late.

I won't write to you yet again of my love for you. Love is, or should be, two halves of one whole, Tilly. I know my own half for what it is, but only you know yours. I had thought—mistakenly, perhaps—that your half matched mine in its absoluteness and constancy. Perhaps the message you want to send me via your silence is not that you refuse to forgive me or accept my explanations for my errors, but rather that you yourself have had second thoughts and have welcomed the chance to act on them.

As she read what he had written Tilly could hear him speaking the words as clearly as though he were standing next to her. She closed her eyes and let the pain take her. *Silas.*

She still loved him. She knew that. Just as she knew that she always would. She opened her eyes and continued to read.

If that is so, then that is your right, and I cannot persuade you otherwise, but so far as my own feelings are concerned my love for you exists as truly as it always has done and always will. Meeting you has had a profound effect on me in more ways than one. If you read this manuscript then I hope you will see and understand.

Tilly turned over the first page. On the second there was a brief dedication which read *For my mother*.

She read for so long that her body felt stiff and cramped, but she was so engrossed in what she was reading that she hadn't been able to drag herself away, Tilly admitted.

She had expected Silas's book to be about the oil industry—which in some respects it was. But only some. What it told was the story of his mother, and those like her, who had crusaded against the tyranny of materialism over human life and the environment. What she'd read compelled her to go on reading, and moved her immensely. Now she had almost reached the end, and as she turned the final page of the penultimate chapter she found an envelope pinned to the manuscript.

It was addressed to her.

Inside she found a brief note, and another envelope.

If you have read this far then you will know by now that I decided against writing about Jay Byerly and have written instead about my mother's life and work. I made that decision because of you,

Tilly. I was wrong not to tell you right from the first who I was and why I took Joe's place. I love you, and I'd like the chance to prove my love to you if you will give it to me. In the envelope is a ticket. If you choose to give me a chance then please use it. If you choose not to—if you don't, after all, love me enough to accept me with my faults and flaws—then I won't bother you again.

Did Silas really dare to question her love for him? Angrily, Tilly opened the second envelope. It contained an air ticket to Madrid.

Very carefully she put it to one side, and went back to the manuscript. When she read Silas's spare description of his mother's death in an accident that should never have happened, and *would* never have happened if it hadn't been for the actions of Jay Byerly, Tilly had to stop reading because her tears had blurred the print so badly.

At the end of the chapter Silas had written:

The very best gift my mother gave me was her love for me; the legacy she left me was to learn to grow enough to understand that love achieves more than bitterness or resentment. It was her love for her fellow man that prompted her to give so much to others, and it is my love for one very special person that has led me to write about the love that motivated my mother rather than my own bitterness at the manner of her death.

And then, underneath:

You are that woman, Tilly. Just as my mother's
ring fitted you perfectly, I would like to think that
in one way she was responsible for bringing you,
the woman who fits me so perfectly, into my life
and my heart. Both of them are empty without you.

She was a fool for doing this. It was crazy. No, Tilly
corrected herself as she walked through the Arrivals
hall and blinked in the sharp Spanish spring sunshine.
She was crazy. What was the point of doing this? It was
over between her and Silas. So over that there hadn't
been a single night since they had been apart when she
had not fallen asleep thinking about him, nor a single
day that hadn't been shadowed by her bitterness and
pain? Just how over was that, exactly? Tilly derided
herself.

She could see a small plump Spaniard, holding up a
placard bearing her name.

'I am José,' he informed her cheerfully. 'I am your
driver. You have just the one bag?'

'Just the one,' Tilly agreed. She had no idea what
Silas was planning, and even less why she should be
travelling like this—on trust and hope and something
that came perilously close to the love she had spent the
last few weeks furiously denying existed.

There was no snow in Madrid, but as they began to
climb Tilly could see where it still lay across the mountains, and she could see too where their route was taking

them. Her heart thudded into her chest wall, and she gave in to the ache inside her that contained longing as well as pain.

It was no real surprise when they finally reached Segovia, and José brought the car to a halt outside the hotel where she had stayed with Silas.

A smiling receptionist welcomed her, and in no time at all she was being shown up to the familiar suite.

The only thing that did surprise her was that it was empty and there was no sign of Silas. Surprised her or disappointed her?

She looked out of the window and down into the street below. On some impulse she didn't want to answer to she had brought with her the black dress she had bought here. She heard the outer door to the suite open and she turned round.

Silas! The bones in his face were surely more prominent, and he wore something in the aura he carried with him that looked like shadowed pain.

'All this is a bit dramatic, isn't it?' she asked, striving to sound cool and self-possessed.

'It wasn't intended to be.'

'No? Then what *was* it intended to be?' she challenged him.

'A hope that although it isn't possible to physically turn back time, I can at least show you how much I wish that I could do so.'

It had been here that they had finally made love, and she had given herself to him in love and in hope and with trust and belief. And now, with him standing here in front of her, her body and her emotions were filled with the memory of all that they had shared before reality had destroyed her dreams.

'When would you turn back time to? The moment you rejected Cissie-Rose's advances? After all, she could have helped you so much more than I did.'

'She could have. But by that stage you had become far more important to me than my book—even though I didn't have the wit to admit that to myself. No. I'd turn it back to the time before we made love, when I held you in my arms, knowing that we would do so. To when I should have told you the truth but was too afraid of spoiling things between us. Perhaps I sensed then more strongly than you did yourself that you already had doubts about your own feelings.'

Tilly couldn't answer him. While his challenge to her in his letter had shocked and angered her, she was honest enough to know that there was an element of truth in it.

'I'd spent so long planning to reveal Jay Byerly and his coterie of associates for what they were because of my mother that I felt honour-bound to stick to my plan—even though I knew I would have to deceive you. I couldn't see then that I would honour my mother's memory far more positively by writing about what she believed in rather than denouncing those who had stood against those beliefs. I hope I have done her justice.'

'You have,' Tilly told him softly. 'No one could read your book and not be moved by it, Silas. If you had told me from the first…'

'I'd planned to tell you once we were back in London, when you wouldn't be under so much pressure from conflicting interests.'

'What about your own conflict of interests?' Tilly asked him quietly. 'How can you expect me ever to feel that the emotional security of our relationship and our children will be safe in your hands, Silas, when I've already witnessed you lying to me for the sake of your ambitions?'

'It wasn't like that. I had committed to that ambition before I met you and fell in love with you, and I had already abandoned my commitment to it because of my love for you—even though I didn't get the opportunity to tell you that. You and our four children will always come first with me, Tilly.'

'Our *what*?'

Tilly watched, fascinated, to see a faint tide of colour creeping along Silas's jawline.

'That was when I knew how much you meant to me. When you told me about your father's farm and out of nowhere I started visualising you living in the country with four children—our children.'

'I've always thought that four children would be the ideal family,' Tilly told him shakily.

'You'll have to marry me to get them. And you'll have to love me and let me love you—and them—for always.'

Just being with him and listening to him was melting away all her stubborn resistance. Reading Silas's book had already filled her with a tide of emotion that had swept away everything that had dammed up her love and turned it sour and bitter with anger and resentment. And now…

'Silas…' she began unsteadily.

'Don't look at me like that,' he warned her. 'Because if you do, then I will have to do this…'

How could she ever have convinced herself that she could live without him, when here in his arms was the only place she really wanted to be?

'Silas,' she said again, but this time she was whispering his name eagerly and happily against his lips, and letting him take the aching sigh of her breath from her as he kissed her.

An hour later, lying curled up next to Silas in the warmth of the bed where he had just shown her how much he missed her, and promised her that their future together would be everything she wanted it to be, Silas lifted Tilly's left hand to his lips, kissing the finger on which he had replaced his mother's ring.

'Just promise me one thing?' he said.

'What?' Tilly asked.

'That you won't tell me that you want to get married on New Year's Eve in a castle in Spain. Because there is no way I can bear to wait that long.'

'Neither can I,' Tilly admitted, laughing. And then she stopped laughing as Silas bent his head to kiss her.

millsandboon.co.uk Community

Join Us!

The Community is the perfect place to meet and chat to kindred spirits who love books and reading as much as you do, but it's also the place to:

- **Get the inside scoop from authors about their latest books**
- **Learn how to write a romance book with advice from our editors**
- **Help us to continue publishing the best in women's fiction**
- **Share your thoughts on the books we publish**
- **Befriend other users**

Forums: Interact with each other as well as authors, editors and a whole host of other users worldwide.

Blogs: Every registered community member has their own blog to tell the world what they're up to and what's on their mind.

Book Challenge: We're aiming to read 5,000 books and have joined forces with The Reading Agency in our inaugural Book Challenge.

Profile Page: Showcase yourself and keep a record of your recent community activity.

Social Networking: We've added buttons at the end of every post to share via digg, Facebook, Google, Yahoo, technorati and de.licio.us.

www.millsandboon.co.uk